Also by Heather Dune Macadam
Rena's Promise: A Story of Sisters in Auschwitz
by Rena Kornreich Gelissen and Heather Dune Macadam

the weeping buddha

A MYSTERY BY HEATHER DUNE MACADAM

AKASHIC BOOKS
NEW YORK

Published by Akashic Books
©2002 Heather Dune Macadam

Cover design by Jason Farrell
Inside design and layout by Sohrab Habibion
Cover graphic by Zen master Hakuin Ekaku (1686-1769)
For permission to use copyrighted or protected material, we thank the following literary executors and publishers for some of the chapter headings and koans used in this text: *The Zen Koan* by Isshu Miura and Ruth Fuller Sasaki (Harcourt Brace, 1965), *The Little Zen Companion* by David Schiller (Workman Publishing, 1994).
Author photo by Karen Abato

ISBN: 1-888451-39-4
Library of Congress Control Number: 2002106362
First printing
Printed in Canada

Akashic Books
PO Box 1456
New York, NY 10009
Akashic7@aol.com
www.akashicbooks.com

ACKNOWLEDGMENTS

I would like to express my unbinding gratitude, appreciation, and multitudinous other forms of thanks to: Karen Abato, for her unwavering faith in me; Kaylie Jones, whose critical eye, constant encouragement, confidence, and devotion to this project made it possible; Rena Gelissen, for giving me my first book; Det. Laurel Tobias, for giving me my character, and Det. Gary Ferrucci, for *being* a character!; the detectives and officers in both the Nassau and Suffolk County police departments, for being available for questions and tours, and for being so willing to share stories and information with me; the Telbergs, for a home and extended family in Sag Harbor; Peter Matthiessen, for reminding me that fiction means making things up; everyone at the zendo; Jules Feiffer, for teaching me to write humor and truth; Joy Harris and Stephanie Abou, for believing in this story before anyone else would; The Basher; Joanne Pankow, for reading more drafts than anyone should have to; Goddess Green, for being a goddess; Southampton College Writing Program and, of course, the loftmates: Jane, Rebecca, Eric, Seth, Kwame, and all the others who lived with us, crashed on our floors, or came to our parties. For those who had to die in this fictive, but live on in real life—Suzi, Eileen, Godwyn, Katiti—I'm sorry, but I hope you understand that writing demands we "murder our darlings." For those who have already gone beyond and were reincarnated in these pages—Sam Todd (wherever you are, I hope you are jumping over parking meters and laughing at mortality), Hans, Edilio, and Boo—I miss you and cherish your memories.

For Karen, my Laughing Buddha

AUTHOR'S NOTE

I was twenty-three the night Sam Todd disappeared from our New Year's Eve party in Chinatown, and I have been writing endings to the mystery of his disappearance ever since. I suppose this story is an attempt to put that past to rest. I got the idea during *Soka Gokkai*—an all-night meditation for Buddha's birthday—and was so enthralled with it that I left the zendo hours before dawn to begin writing.

The question of Sam Todd had been haunting me for years; it finally seemed that the only way to exorcise the past was to make it fiction. As a part of my research I went into the *New York Times* archives at the NYU Library and pulled up the old articles about Sam, the loft, our party. I copied them, made notes on them, remembered things about that time in my life. On my way out of the library I headed along West Fourth Street toward the East Village and the now-trendy area called NoHo. A bitter wind blasted off the East River and darkness descended as it does around those old factory buildings—quick and dense. I looked up and down Lafayette Street, still able to hear Sam's name echoing down the alleyways, our voices forever calling him home.

Until that moment I thought I had left New York City because I was burned out, my career as a professional dancer over. Standing there on Lafayette, a few blocks from my old loft—a few doors down from the homeless shelter where we had scouted for Sam, night after ruthless night—I realized that I left New York because Sam Todd left me on the dance floor to get a breath of fresh air and never returned. Ever.

The Weeping Buddha is my worst nightmare made manifest in fiction. It is the result of imagination being left alone too long with an unanswerable riddle—a Zen koan, if you will: *What really happened to Sam Todd?*

PROLOGUE

Sound rudely pierced the air. It was one of the two beepers lying side by side on the nightstand interrupting them. Detective Lochwood Brennen stopped what he was doing and rolled over on his side. "It's yours," he said. "Mine's on quiver."

"So am I." Detective Devon Halsey sighed. "What is it about making love and beepers?" She reached for the contraption, checked the number, and turned it off. "It's Beka."

"Can't she leave us be just once on New Year's Eve?" Drawing his finger along the soft area of her waist up to her shoulders, he tried to coax her back into his arms.

"Sorry." She looked at the clock—they only had an hour before their shift. Her thick hair fell across the pillows of their hotel bed as she melted into his hands, seriously considering not returning the call for the first time in her life. "I've decided to make up with her."

Devon stretched her head down toward the pillow, shutting her eyes so he could better massage the tension from the right side of her neck. Her mind was far away. Once more she and Beka Imamura were in sync and had come to the same realization on the same day: Life was too short to hold a grudge. Beka's New Year's Eve phone call had been a part of Devon's festivities for years. Calling Devon was the closest Beka got to a champagne toast, because she had refused to celebrate New Year's Eve since 1984.

Loch dug his thumbs deeper into the knots between her shoulder blades. "Think she'll ever celebrate New Year's like the rest of us?"

"By working overtime?" The irony of his question had not escaped her.

His mouth was busy massaging her shoulders now. "I thought working would be fun." He bit her neck, first teasingly then more earnestly.

"This is fun." She stifled a moan. He was dangerously close to her most erogenous zone. "But you don't really enjoy yourself unless we're arresting somebody, do you?"

"I've got my cuffs." He kissed her ear, allowing his breath to linger so

it sent shivers along her neck, down her spine, and under the covers. He tugged on her earlobe with his teeth.

That was it.

He pushed her back down to the bed as she grabbed her beeper, changed the setting to vibrate, and tossed it next to his. An hour later their beepers went off simultaneously—this time it was Headquarters.

CHAPTER ONE

*If you take up one koan and investigate it unceasingly, your
mind will die and you will will be destroyed. It is as though a
vast, empty abyss lay before you, with no place to set your hands
and feet . . .*

— MASTER HAKUIN EKAKU

The crime scene had already been roped off with *DO NOT CROSS
POLICE LINE* tape flapping in the bitter New Year's wind as lead
Homicide Detective Lochwood Brennen and his partner, Detective
Gary DeBritzi, watched the Crime Scene van pull part of the way up
the drive and stop. Lochwood could see her through the window of
the van talking with her partner. She didn't look too upset, but then
Devon knew how to hide her feelings.

"I'm going to go talk to Halsey," Brennen told his partner, and
started across the whitening lawn. His feet crunched through the
thin layer of ice now hidden beneath the new fallen snow. The sleet
had begun before midnight, about the time he and Devon clocked
in—late—but now the big flakes floating to the ground were forming deeper drifts.

Usually he felt an electric charge when they arrived on a crime
scene; the challenge of deciphering the unknown fed his craving for
excitement and problem-solving. Tonight he felt only the dismal
reality of knowing how the friend of a victim—victims—feels. There
was no one to soften the blow, no one to assure him that they hadn't
suffered needlessly—that was his job. And one look at the scene told
him just how much they had endured. He kicked the turf under his
shoe. He'd done it again, thought of the victims as *they*. Hell, he
didn't even know if *they* both were victims.

It was part of his job to make it easier for civilians who had lost
a loved one. He knew what to say in those cases, but Devon Halsey
was a cop and his girlfriend. He always called her Halsey on the job,

but that did not seem appropriate now. He wasn't sure what befit the situation in which they suddenly found themselves. He stopped halfway to the Crime Scene van to watch Devon and her partner, Frank Landal, begin to unload their equipment. Frank looked older than usual. Maybe it was the way the snow blended with his silver hair; maybe it was the time of night. Frank hated working third shift. Devon caught Loch's eye, then dropped her gaze to the ground.

He wished there were some way to help her. Codependent. That was the term people liked to toss around nowadays—it used to mean compassion. Somehow, her hair was shimmering in the dark; he wanted to touch it—bury his nose into it—and hold her as close as he had two hours ago. His chest ached as she wrapped a hair cap around her head and slipped into her white Tyvek suit. The jaunty self-assurance she normally brought to a crime scene was gone—she looked pale and stern, as if the simple act of zipping up was taking severe concentration. He wanted to wrap his hands around her waist and tell her it was going to be all right. Such a useless and meaningless phrase, yet that's what he wanted to say because he didn't know how to change the fact that Beka Imamura and her husband were both dead. He opened his mouth but she shook her head, looking beyond him and up at the house where her best friend had lived until a few hours ago.

* * *

Devon felt her stomach drop and a sudden wave of nausea wash over her as she looked at Beka's house—a house she had helped Beka decorate the year Beka moved into her husband's Hamptons estate.

A group of police officers and detectives milled around the perimeter of the house as she and Frank made their way up the drive. It was always like this outside a murder scene; everyone showed up but no one could do a thing until Homicide did a walkthrough and Crime Scene finished recording the vicinity—everyone was waiting for them. As they walked past the local cops, she scanned the crowd for any brass.

"The lieutenant isn't here yet," Frank whispered to her. "That means we may still have a scene."

She felt a small smile crease its way along her lips; Frank always had a way of getting her to lighten up.

Dressed in disposable paper Tyvek suits and their Suffolk County Crime Scene winter coats, she and Frank signed the roster and ducked under the yellow tape.

"Landal, how you doing?" Lochwood stepped over to them. Frank nodded his answer. "Halsey, are you sure you're up for this?"

"I have to call my dog-sitter." Devon punched in the numbers of Aileen's cellphone. It was late to be calling, but Devon wanted her to know that Boo would need a walk in the morning. She ignored Lochwood's protective eyes as she left a message on the voice-mail. "I won't be home until tomorrow afternoon—something's come up." Devon did not say anything more about where she was, or why. It was not the sort of thing one left on a message: Our friend is dead and so is her husband. She hung up the phone wishing suddenly that she had a nice cushy job in a boring office where the only backstabbing was figurative, not literal.

"If you run into trouble . . ." Lochwood looked like he was going to try and comfort her in front of everyone.

"I'll tell you, Brennen." She knew she sounded irritable, but couldn't help herself.

"What she can't handle, I can," Frank told him.

"Okay, then. I'm our lead on this one. You know the drill. We've got two bodies, one in the house and one up the hill." Devon looked up the hill, straining to see who had died outside but unable to ask.

Sergeant Houck came up from behind them. "Detective Landal. Halsey." He shook hands with the two Crime Scene detectives. "Brennen tells me you knew both of the victims. You have my condolences."

"Thank you, sir."

"And I don't mean to be unfeeling," he continued, "but I need to know before you start, can you finish the job?"

"Yes sir."

"We could always call in another team."

"Frank's my partner and this is our job." Her voice sounded grave. She'd meant to sound less troubled; she didn't want the sergeant to think she was weak. She shifted the yellow clapboards and a stack of six-inch-high orange traffic cones in her right hand while cradling the Nikon in her left.

"All right, I'm going to call Headquarters to see if I can get some of our lab guys on overtime. It's a holiday though, so don't count on it. If you flag something we need a rush on, let Brennen know ASAP. The more reason I have for overtime the better chance we have of getting it." He pulled his cellphone out and started to walk away, then stopped. "Oh, and your lieutenant is tied up for the night." He winked at them and turned away.

They started back toward the house. "I still have her number on my beeper," she whispered to Loch.

"I tried to call you, but you were already on your way here." He paused. "I wish I'd been the one to tell you."

She inhaled so sharply the air hurt her lungs. Her eyes teared in the wind. "Did you find her phone?"

"No."

"Has anybody tried calling her?" He shook his head. She pulled her cellphone out of her pocket and dialed Beka's number. The night was silent of any ringing.

"Good try."

"I want to be here," she said, more to convince herself than Lochwood. "Make sure Houck knows that. If there is something out of place, I'll know it quicker than any of you."

"That's what I was thinking."

Devon cast her gaze up at the house. "The last time we were here was last August."

"Last time you spoke to her, too."

She knew he wanted to take her hand, but couldn't. "It was a stupid fight. Stupid."

"Can I do anything?" He meant it sincerely, however it sounded.

She shook her head. She didn't want his assurances, just his silent support, and to be left alone while she did her part of the job. If he gave her any more than that, she'd lose it.

Detective DeBritzi met them on the front steps leading into the house. "He's inside. She's up there," he said. They all looked up a small incline where police tape flickered in the wind. She could just make out the outline of Beka's body and shuddered as an arctic blast of wind sank its teeth into the flesh of her neck.

Frank hoisted his video camera up onto his shoulders. "Let's go, then. If it gets rough in there you take a break, Devon. I'll work the area around her. You don't have to go up there, okay?"

She nodded, reminding herself that she had spent two months working Ground Zero. This was not—nothing could be—worse than that. She knew how to detach from a scene and observe everything without any emotion. She just wanted to do her job, and do it well. She knew if she could keep her mind focused on her job, she'd be fine.

She followed Frank into the house to begin their assessment. He would record the physical pattern of events while she reconstructed each incident the physical evidence revealed: prints, bloodstains, trace evidence. Deciphering all the road maps of the crime— that's what the Crime Scene Unit did. She swallowed and reminded herself that it didn't matter how well she knew the house; her job was to follow the trail. If she slipped up and thought about whose blood she was following, she would never be able to finish processing the scene, and that was more important than grieving her loss— she could do that later. She turned her feelings off like a faucet and thought only about the evidence around her.

"It looks as if it started in the living room," Loch said, "but shoot it how you see it. He's back in their bedroom."

Devon noticed the slip of his tongue. Normally, they would have referred to the bodies as the victims or corpses, but not this time. Loch had bequeathed them the gift of gender-specific pronouns, although no one had uttered their names, yet.

Involuntarily, Devon checked the neatly placed shoes on the rice mat in the mudroom. Beka's shoes were there, but Beka was outside, dead. She must have fled in a hurry.

Devon's mouth creased as she fought the urge to remove her shoes as she had done so often before upon entering the house. Instead, keeping partway with Japanese tradition, she slipped Tyvek booties over her shoes. Next she pulled latex gloves over her hands and raised the camera to her eye to take the first of many scene-establishing shots.

* * *

Beka Imamura had been Gabriel Montebello's model since the early '80s—long before they had finally married—and appeared in almost every *objet d'art* in the house. Gabe had said he would make her a star through his art, and he probably had. Whether it was a sculpture, an abstract, or a portrait, Beka reigned supreme even in death, and Devon had the feeling that her friend's eyes were following her every move through the living room. Twenty-foot ceilings arched above her, and the picture windows reflected the light of the room rather than the moon on the pond outside. Furniture was an afterthought, as if the necessity of sitting down were a curse upon the space.

A path of dark red spatter marks lapped the inside wall almost to the ceiling. It was a stabbing. She saw the Buddha and, raising one hand in line with her forehead, gave an imperceptible bow. There were even spatter marks on his enlightened face. A six-foot-high halogen lamp lay across the floor, and on a rough-cut, marble-slab coffee table sat a bottle of Jack Daniel's. The house smelled of bourbon and blood.

Devon and Frank walked through the house examining each room, from the front door to the bedroom and back again. Once the sequence of events was clear, she placed the first yellow number-card, numbered one, under Gabriel's nine-by-six painting over the fireplace. Lochwood was right; this was where the violence began, under the painting that Gabe had given to Beka for a wedding gift. *Her Red Shoes* was an oil with a lot of red in it already. Beka had always said that dance was in her blood. The painting had now become more than a metaphor for her statement—Devon could barely tell the difference between the killer's spatter marks and the painter's.

She lifted the camera up to her eye and began photographing the room, moving from the painting outward in a spiral. Residue from the blade's point left an arc of red splotches, indicating that the knife had been raised high in the air and thrust into Gabe several times, but the light color of the spatters suggested that the assault had hit muscle tissue, not arteries or vital organs.

She photographed the bottle where it lay, focusing first on position and then moving in to cover a latent print coagulating on the glass. It was probably too thick to be accurate, but Devon would try to pull the whorls and ridges later in the lab. She scraped the residue of nude color-stick—Beka's color—creased along the lip of the bottle. With a white number-card by the bottle she photographed the finger and lip prints, then shot the black label—the *Jack* portion had been torn off and carefully pushed down to the glass. The adhesive had bunched into small ridges where a fingernail had plowed through the paper. The last time Beka drank Jack Daniel's was in 1984—of that Devon was certain.

Acts of violence have a story line, and Devon knew how to read them. It was her job to paint the pictures that would help Homicide tell the story to the DA, who would later tell the story to the jury. Like a complicated version of the child's game of Telephone, they passed on the information from one to the other and hoped it didn't get withheld, suppressed, or ruled inadmissible, because leaving out one part of the story could change the entire ending. Devon rarely felt bothered by the stories she read—it was simply her duty to help the victims speak so justice could prevail.

"I'm done here." Frank balanced the video camera casually on his right shoulder as he walked back down the hallway. "You need more clapboards?" Devon shook her head, but couldn't find her tongue. "You okay?"

"Fine," her voice squeaked.

"It gets kind of rough back there."

She swallowed. "I'm okay."

"Just go slow."

She started to inhale deeply but stopped herself. It wasn't the sickening sweet stench of blood invading her nose that was making her queasy, but whose blood it was. Frank squeezed her elbow and headed out the door.

* * *

The medical examiner's Ford Taurus station wagon pulled up to the crime scene just as Lochwood and his partner were coming back outside. It was always best to let the Crime Scene Unit shoot the house with as little activity as was feasible, and Lochwood always tried to keep a scene as free of people as possible.

Dr. Pankow was already dressed in the departmental issue paper suit. She hated the things, but lawyers had found so many problems with evidence collection in recent years that police departments across the nation now treated crime scenes very differently. She stamped her feet in the snow and looked at Lochwood coming down the drive. "Brennen, you just get handsomer and handsomer with every gray hair. Why is it men always age so well?"

"Jo, if you weren't a married woman, I'd tell you."

She slapped his arm. "I'm going to tell Ken you were flirting with me again!" Dr. Pankow leaned her heftiness back into her car to pull out an equally rotund purple leather medical bag, and Lochwood smiled for the first time since the news that Gabriel Montebello and his wife Beka were dead had reached the Fourth Precinct.

Dr. Pankow sighed as she stood upright. "How come you folks can't put a moratorium on holiday violence?" Her North Carolina twang strummed words like a bluegrass banjo player made music.

"I was just asking myself the same thing."

"You just had to call me up outta bed for the first one of the year, didn't you?" Despite all her years above the Mason-Dixon Line, Jo kept true to her roots. She had once told Brennen that it took too much energy "to talk Yankee."

"This one's hitting a little too close to home tonight, Jo." Brennen quietly told her who the victims were.

"Poor Halsey." It was the shortest response he'd ever heard her give.

"Don't say that to her."

"Course not."

He held out his arm. "We're up here." The big-bodied woman squeezed his elbow tightly in her hand and let him lead her up the hill to where the corpse of Devon's best friend lay, face up.

* * *

There were footwear impressions throughout the house that Devon captured on film; some of them were left by the local authorities who had arrived first on the scene. She was always cautious on this point because it was hard to tell at first glance which footwear impressions pertained to a case. More than one Crime Scene detective had photographed the perfect footprint only to find out it belonged to a paramedic or cop. There had been no need for paramedics tonight.

She took close-ups of the footwear impressions in the living room in hopes that they might later be able to distinguish which bloodstains belonged to the perpetrator. The living room carpet had soaked up too much, though, and Devon knew the tracks she wanted would be farther away from the scene, on the wood floor perhaps, or outside on the pavement now being covered by snow. Blood tended to stick up inside of shoe treads and drip down yards away from a crime scene, leaving nice latents in unsuspecting places. Even when the soles looked clean on the outside there could be blood up in the treads . . . unless the someone was barefoot, Devon reasoned, like Beka. She placed a small orange cone and turned her mind like a camera lens. Focus. She clicked the frame, then stopped to change rolls and mark the outside of the cartridge with a black Sharpie. When the living room was done, she had shot two rolls.

She turned her focus to the hallway where something, a blow perhaps, had brought him to his knees. Handprints on the floor verified her quickly forming theory. The scene played out in her mind; she could see how he crawled away on all fours down the hall toward the bedrooms. Like feet, palms were just as unique as fingerprints; she photographed the palm imprints on the maplewood floor. Next to his struggling crawl were the curved ridges of someone's bare foot, about the size of Beka's. Devon clicked the shutter twice, then a third time. She would be able to compare Beka's feet with the photograph later, when she got back to the morgue.

The hall revealed how the violence had escalated. The floor beneath the samurai sword that had once belonged to Beka's grandfather had smear tracks on it. He had probably been dragged the rest of the way to the master bedroom. Smears on the wood-paneled walls indicated that the victim had started to struggle for freedom halfway down the hall but had found nothing firm to grasp until the master bedroom doorjamb. His fingers must have gripped the molding, leaving little fingernail crescents in the wood. Devon focused on these elements as if she were adding detail to an oil painting that was anything but abstract—these were the ambient factors of the story she had to tell. Whoever had dragged him had been exceptionally strong. She left a cone by the fingernail marks in the doorjamb so they wouldn't miss them when it came time to collect evidence.

The master bedroom still had a night-light by the door casting an eerie green glow. Surveying the room in one sweep Halsey snapped the first of several wide shots, then entered. His corpse was wedged upright against the closet door. The stomach wound gaped like an open mouth trying to tell her something she would never hear. Whoever killed him had wanted him dead—very, very dead.

There were no more arcs of spray, just the simple gush of life spewing from the body of a dying man. The face had been disfigured by long slashes across the eyes. In cases where an attack was perpetrated upon an acquaintance or loved one, the eyes were often assaulted, as if this one feat could stop the dead from identifying the murderer.

She leaned down to get a closer look at the marks strangely crisscrossing his chest. The blood had clotted in the wounds, meaning he was not alive when they had been carved. They seemed oddly familiar, but she could not figure out why. She clicked off six photographs and twisted her lip around in puzzlement. Why had this one act occurred after death?

Her camera flashed. She blinked, then angled the light away and to the left of the body before drawing the lens of her Nikon even closer. The light bulb flashed involuntarily.

Focus, she reminded herself. Her eyes felt dry. Stay in control. It wasn't the gore that was distracting her concentration. She had been on the scene in the TWA Flight 800 crash, been brought in to assist at the Long Island Railroad massacre. She focused the camera once more and clicked the shutter. It was the light flashing that made her think about the party. There had been a camera then, too.

"Shit." Devon stood up and changed rolls of film while surveying the scene around her. "I should have returned her call," she told the corpse sadly. "Maybe it wasn't about Todd. Maybe she was in danger."

She had said the name—Todd.

Focus. She reminded herself and wound the film. Take your time. She stooped down, looked right at Gabe through the lens of her camera, and reeled off three strobes. One, two, three. Devon's eyes ached.

CHAPTER TWO

There's death in that damp, clammy grasp. Oh God! . . .
There must be life yet in that heart—he could not thus me.
— LORD BYRON, *The Two Foscari*

The camera illuminated the crowd of New Year's revelers with three blinding strobes of light, right in their faces. David Bowie was hypnotically chanting the mantra of their age—"1984"—above their heads.

1984. The year they had all been waiting for. Ever since the book had become required reading in high school. A majority of the party-goers had ranted, no, *raved* about the advent of this year, touting its promise as if 1984 were guaranteed to be a wonder etched on memory's calendar. In 1983 everyone was hoping that on the stroke of midnight some miracle of society would change the world forever. It was the first important New Year's for them—the brat pack—the kids who, missing the '60s, had gotten lost to the '70s and swallowed up by the '80s. It wasn't that they had forgotten that Orwell's novel portrayed a futuristic science fiction nightmare—subconsciously, they were all too aware of the possibilities technology was already providing their culture—but they were young, full of hopeful delusions. They were immortal.

1984. Devon made her way through the crowd and down the hall. Some guy was leaning on the wall chatting up Aileen, her childhood friend. Devon came to the rescue. "Leenie, can you help me open the front window? It's so stuffy in here."

Aileen darted under the confused man's arm and followed Devon down the hall. They climbed out on the fire escape and watched the sparks of gold and pink and white lights spew across Canal Street. It was as if dragons had entered Chinatown and were setting the night ablaze with scarlet streamers.

Aileen stood against the railing on the fire escape. "Why I come into the city for these parties is beyond me."

"I thought you were going to find your soul mate this year," Devon replied.

"If my soul mate's at this party, his soul is in serious jeopardy!"

"So is yours!" They knocked their beer cans together in a toast.

Every year, between the Gregorian and Chinese New Years, the air on Canal Street crackled like sizzling rice soup. Firecracker vendors hawked their wares long after midnight, and red tissue paper spurted from rooftops like blood across the snow-white streets and alleyways. The night air was helping Devon regroup. For some reason the incessant popping of Zebras, Blooming Flowers, and the occasional boom of a Cherry Bomb echoing deep within the borders of Chinatown seemed to ground her more than the driving beat of the dance music behind them.

"This is not our crowd," Aileen reminded her. They were both born and raised in rural Sag Harbor—the un-Hampton—where fishermen and artists comingled in semicontentment and mutual resentment of the encroaching rich who were taking over the land. Aileen's parents had owned the local fish store where both girls learned to bait hooks, gut fish, and flirt with the local boys.

"It wouldn't be any different in Sag Harbor. We'd be doing the same thing at Bay Street's Disco."

"But I could walk home."

"I like New York. I like this crowd."

Aileen shook her head at her friend. "They're a bunch of wannabe artists who don't know how to make a living in the real world. What are you doing here?"

"Research." Devon laughed suddenly, realizing that what she had said was true.

"Researching what? Sex, drugs, and rock 'n' roll?" Gabe stuck his head through the window.

"Going nowhere fast." Devon swigged the last of her beer.

"I'm tired of going nowhere," Aileen said. "I want to make my mark, you know?"

"The hardest part is figuring out what mark to make." Devon looked up to the roof where someone was dangling their feet over the ledge.

"It doesn't matter what mark you make, as long as you make one!" Gabe advised them. "Like Beka—she'll be a star. My sculptures, my paintings of her will help make her star—we have a symbiotic relationship."

"Symbi-what?" Aileen looked at him like he was full of it.

"Two life forms living off one another, providing each with what the other needs to survive. Like the shark and its pilot fish."

"Whose the shark?" Devon asked him.

"Beka, of course. She's a man-eater."

Aileen started laughing. "On that note, I need a drink!"

Gabe shook his head earnestly. "This year is going to be it! I can feel it in my bones."

"Do you really think things will change because the clock changes from 12:00 to 12:01? That's stupid." Aileen headed back through the window.

"Happy New Year anyway," Devon called after her. She and Gabe stared at each other.

"Does she really think I'm a wannabe artist?" He was incredulous. "I own two homes."

Aileen was right that most of these people were not their crowd—they belonged in the Hamptons at summer parties, but they would never make it through the isolation of winter on the East End. Only fishermen, farmers, and real artists could do that. Gabe could do that.

* * *

Time hung like the parachute on the ceiling, draping over the loft and ensnaring them in its folds. Devon had no idea what time it was, or how long she had been standing in the crowd sipping her drink and flirting with strangers. Beka was starting to transform herself from one of the dancing mob into the performer that she was—a Japanese version of a Chinese firecracker, an inferno of flashing legs and spiraling hair. Her high heels dug gouges into the loft's unfinished floor and small chunks of wood sprayed out from under her feet until it looked as if she were making tinder to feed the fire in her soul. There were no low sparks or high-heeled boys—Beka was the only diva in the loft.

Beka began preparing herself for a career as a soloist back in high school, when boys fled the dance floor before the demon erupted and they were suddenly the center of attention. Devon remembered those days, before anyone knew Beka's name or recognized her face, before she had finally, in one grand *tour jété*, reached Carnegie Hall and "made it."

At the Mud Club some guy had once tried to stop Beka from dancing. Hanging onto her wrist he had demanded, "What are you on?"

"Life!" she had answered.

"Where do I get some?"

She had wrapped her arms around his neck and pulled him onto the floor—in much the same way she was now wrapping herself around Todd. "Me!" she had shouted over the music.

The same energy was pulsing off of her now, but where Beka had been high on *life* then, now she seemed desperate to capture it. Devon was not sure what had changed or why.

Awkward on his feet and clumsy, Todd Daniels stumbled alongside Beka's grace and power. He looked drunk and was obviously smitten with the ebony-haired temptress as her arms wove the air over his head and her legs seemed to float up to her ears. When she twirled, it was as if he were the sun she revolved around. She could make anyone look good, and Todd was no exception. He leapt in the air like a young colt kicking up its heels, and gave a war whoop.

Gabriel Montebello grabbed Devon and shouted over the din. "She's radiant!" It was a statement of fact. Watching Beka dance was like soaring without moving a muscle, and the party's energy seemed to swirl into a maelstrom of her making. "Why is she wasting her energy on Mr. Klutz though?"

"If you can't beat them, dance with them!" Devon grabbed Gabe's hand and dragged him as close to the eye of the storm as was physically possible.

Todd looked as if he were laughing but no sound emanated from his open mouth. Beka smiled at them, grabbed Gabe's hand, and twirled first around him, then Todd. The room spun. Above their heads the lights that had been draped across the ceiling seemed to create a vortex, and Devon felt as if they were outside dancing under the stars. Beka leapt off the ground, twisting in midair as her leg swung over Todd's head. The camera flashed in their faces.

Todd's face flushed pink and Devon had the impression that he was falling toward Beka, whirling into her like water down a drain. "I can't keep up with you!" he yelled over the music.

One, two, three. Spots blinded Devon's eyes and Todd stumbled off the floor away from the tempest, unable to see. Beka, far more familiar with the indiscretions of cameras, kept moving.

Devon blinked. The flashes had been rude, uncalled-for. She followed Todd, leaving Gabe and Beka to tear up the dance floor together. Everything was out of focus—the old yellow *Toy Factory* sign with Chinese symbols on either side, the neon sign flashing over the stairwell, the faces of the people around her. It took a moment for the yellow and black spots to clear from her eyes, and when they did she could see Todd Daniels leaning against the loft's black banister as if it were the deck of a foundering ship. His face was faintly green, but it was hard to tell if it was him or the neon *Kosher Meat* sign that was tinting his flesh a ghostly ill color.

Devon looked across the room. Godwyn was winding his film. He winked at her and shrugged his shoulders; she pointed to her eyes and flipped him the bird. He kissed the air and shot her picture again. More spots. And when she looked back he was gone, his blue-black skin covered by true black clothes making him one with the dark of the room.

He knew how Beka felt about picture-taking when she was dancing, but he also enjoyed messing with her, ever since she had dumped him for somebody else. Who that someone was, Devon couldn't remember—just one in a long line of tossed-off lovers that Beka went through like toe shoes: wear them once to break them in, twice and they're broken.

"Sorry, love. Didn't mean to blind you, but you know, a pic's a pic." Godwyn's lips brushed Devon's ear as he apologized in his sexy English accent. She was about to tell him to stop when he planted his mouth on hers and nearly sucked the breath from her lungs. It was the most erotic kiss of her young life. "Happy New Year, Devon Halsey." Her mouth was tingling and numb, and by the time she could form words again, he had disappeared, swallowed up by the crowd.

She headed toward where Todd was still tottering, half-clinging to the banister. "Are you all right?" she yelled over the noise. He looked as if he was trying to nod his head, but instead it swayed from side to side. He started down the stairs.

His older brother came over to them. "Where you goin', buddy?" Sam's voice cut through the clamor.

"Gotta clear my head." He tripped on his shoe, righted himself, and continued downward with Sam and Devon following.

"Don't go Mount St. Helens on us!" Sam warned.

Todd tried to laugh, then raised his hand to his mouth and quickly ran down the remaining flights of stairs to the street, with Sam and Devon close behind.

"You okay, sport?"

Todd answered by puking into the gutter. Sam watched his brother but didn't try to help. Slowly, Todd stood up, leaned against the subway entrance railings, and wiped his mouth. "Beka makes me dizzy." His boyish smile was disarming and still remarkably innocent.

"She has that effect on people." Sam slapped him on the back and for a moment their eyes locked in merriment. "Just don't get hung up on her." Devon couldn't have agreed more, but kept her mouth shut.

"She's great." Todd staggered a little.

"Sit down, man."

"Don't tell me what to do!" He tried to punch his big brother, but his feet were too unsteady. "I'm not a kid!"

"You're wasted." Sam held him at arm's length until Todd stopped flailing at the air and laughed again.

"Yes, I am." Their guffaws caught between the buildings and bounced back and forth like pinballs between the gently falling flakes of snow.

"Sit down."

"No. And you can't change my mind." He swayed to and fro, steadied only by Sam's hand on his elbow.

"I'm your big brother; I'm supposed to tell you what to do. It's in my contract."

Todd seemed to snap awake suddenly. "I love you, man." Todd hugged him heartily with one arm tossed around Sam's neck.

"Don't puke on me, asshole." They laughed again, and Devon thought she should go inside.

"I'm goin' for a run." His words slurred.

"You sure?" his brother asked.

"Sure I'm sure." Todd brushed him away. They feigned a few more punches, then hugged drunkenly, pounding each other on the back as if they were stamping out fires.

"You know your way?" Sam ruffled his curly chestnut hair.

"Goin' around the block." Someone came out the door behind them and rounded the corner onto Lafayette Street. Todd waved, then started to jog down Canal Street. He stumbled once, righted himself, and kept going. Firecracker red dye from shredded pieces of tissue paper oozed into the freshly fallen snow of Canal Street as if a battle, not a celebration, had just taken place.

Sam watched him waver and started to yell some kind of warning, but kept quiet. Devon could see it in his face as she held the door open for him. His mouth hung open with the words still on his tongue, stuck as if they wouldn't come off until he'd committed them verbally to the night. She blocked his entrance. "Just say it, Sam."

He turned around fully prepared to shout, "*Be careful.*" Todd was nowhere to be seen.

* * *

Focus, Devon thought, while dabbing the corner of her left eye with her gloved hand. She felt removed from the circumstances glaring in her face and yet in the same instant all too present. Focus. She let the camera hang from her neck and searched the corpse as if Gabriel Montebello were still alive and simply hiding behind vacant eyes.

CHAPTER THREE

We must remove the body.
Touch it not, dungeon miscreants . . .
Leave his remains to those who know to honor them.
— LORD BYRON, *The Two Foscari*

It had always fascinated Lochwood how Dr. Pankow could walk through a scene oblivious to everything but corpses. He, on the other hand, was fascinated by all the complexities of information left behind. They had finished with Beka rather quickly—Jo did not like to be cold—and now he and Gary led her up the front stairs and to the left of the foyer. As usual, Jo walked straight into the house without paying any attention to the trail of blood that the Crime Scene Unit was chronicling. When it came to a body though, she didn't miss a mark.

"What's that?" The question surprised both him and his partner. She was pointing at the closet door. "*Just Do It.*" She raised a curious eyebrow at the bumper sticker of a once-popular slogan on the door over the corpse's head. "Not exactly the action the advertisers were hoping for, but to the point."

"According to Halsey, it was a joke in the house," Loch explained. "His wife used to change her clothes five and six times a day until the bed was piled high with costume changes." Halfway through his explanation he realized he was using the past tense; the words slapped him like spitting snow.

"How theatrical." Jo yawned. She held out her thermometer in the air and checked her watch. It was two in the morning. "Devon knowing them should make your job easier."

"Halsey's good." He paused.

Jo pressed her tape recorder and spoke into it. "Second body: male, Caucasian. Age: between forty-five and fifty; looks to be about five foot eleven inches. Room temperature: sixty-eight degrees." She pressed her finger into his flesh and pulled it back. A white spot appeared, then faded. "No fixed lividity."

She pulled out her ear thermometer and pressed a button. "I love modern technology. You know where I used to have to stick this?" She placed the cone-shaped instrument into the corpse's ear and waited for a beep. "95.8." She picked up the right arm and let it drop with a thud to the floor. "Rigor not set. And in this stable atmosphere, with the body losing approximately 1.5 degrees per hour, I'd say he's been dead two hours. It could be less if there was much of a struggle. Loss of ATP could speed up rigor. If rigor has set in by the time we get him back to the morgue, I'm right. If it's later than that we could be looking at a half-hour adjustment to that time."

"Midnight, then."

"More or less."

"Love you, Jo." Brennen had always found Jo's accuracy with time of death impeccable.

"Honey, you say that to all the girls who cut up cadavers for a living." The words sounded like syrup dripping off her tongue.

"What about the wounds, Jo?" Gary DeBritzi asked.

"Well, it's pretty obvious that the fatal wound was this hole in the stomach. From what I can see right here, the initial stab wounds were bleeders, but nothing vital was hit. I count eighteen stab wounds including the stomach. Then we have these marks. She pointed to the chest where crisscrossing lines had been carved into the flesh. "These were an afterthought. See the coagulation? He was already dead."

Gary peered at the marks. "Looks like chicken scratch or san-skirt."

"That's San*skrit*, DeBritzi," Jo corrected him, then continued her summation without pause. "The instruments used to stab the victim and inflict the stomach wound were different."

Loch jotted down her findings. "What about wounds versus these lines?"

She pulled out a ruler. "Insertion width is consistent. It could be the same knife."

"And the stab wounds?" Gary asked.

"Most of them are downward strokes, while this one," she pointed at the stomach, "was a thrust in and up. I'll know more once we get him up on the slab." Her mouth ticked off facts like the New York Stock Exchange. "The eighteen other wounds were most likely made with a blade about four to five inches long with a hilt about one and a half inches wide."

"The exact length of the one Beka was holding."

"I just tell you what happened, Brennen, you figure out how." Jo checked the fatal wound, going deeper this time. "This was a thrust with a wicked turn."

"Like a samurai warrior's *hara-kiri* stroke?" Gary tapped his pen on his notepad to get the ink flowing.

"Well, I haven't had the chance to look at many of those wounds in my practice, but from what I've heard this could be similar. Samurais knew what they were doing." Jo and the detectives moved out of the bedroom and down the hall where Devon was waiting. "Devon." Jo stopped to greet her friend and colleague. "We're done in there. If you're finished they can take him out. You coming for the autopsy?"

"I don't know yet, Jo." Devon clenched and unclenched her teeth.

"It might help to follow through like you usually do. You wouldn't miss an autopsy, under normal circumstances." Jo took the younger woman's hand. "Two o'clock tomorrow, in case you change your mind. I got you covered in my prayers."

* * *

Detectives Brennen and DeBritzi walked Jo the rest of the way out of the scene and watched as she reversed down the drive. "I'm going back up the hill to see how Landal's doing and oversee the morgue guys," Lochwood told his partner.

"I'll make sure they get the other body out okay," Gary said.

"Good. Then meet me up at the artist's studio."

"You think we need Crime Scene up there?"

"Let's take a look and decide."

Gary returned to the house as Loch tramped back up the hill.

The morgue attendants waited patiently in the doorway of the bedroom where Gabriel Montebello still lay. Devon looked up from her work. "DeBritzi." She acknowledged Lochwood's partner, but put no effort into small talk.

"If you're done." Gary shifted from one foot to the other.

"He's ready to go." She stood up too quickly and felt the blood rush from her head. Gary stepped toward her, but she waved him away and moved out the door.

"Just need some air." She headed outside. Cold snow pricked her skin but her cheeks burned hot and the dizziness didn't stop. There was something else she needed out of the van, but she couldn't recall what. This was not like her—she had to get a grip. Leaning on the outside of the vehicle she peered into its dark interior and tried to steady her breathing; when that didn't work she turned around to face the outer dark.

Frank was talking with Lochwood up the hill, next to the body—Beka's body. They were speaking about Beka, her best friend, in the past tense, and trying to figure out what had made her past tense. Flakes scurried through the spotlight beam from Frank's video camera and cut a bright path through the dark.

It had been snowing then, too; in the '80s it was always snowing inside and out. It had fallen through the hole in the ceiling and into the New Year's Eve party with lacy elegance, melting into rain before it had drifted halfway into the room.

* * *

Devon watched Alexandra Parnel capture the flakes through the zoom lens of her video camera and then pan out to include the whole room. Whatever the camera's eye saw was displayed simultaneously on a sextet of TV screens against the far wall. Godwyn and a punk rocker with safety-pinned earlobes and dragon tattoos were contemplating the party via the camera's point of view, as if the party existed only on the screens, not around them.

"Nice!" Godwyn approved of the snowflake shot. "Now do the reverse, and pan in to a close-up of the sky-hole." Alexandra did what he suggested, but a foot coming down from the roof ruined the shot.

Watching Alex work made Devon think maybe she should get into video, too. She had to do something with her life. Everyone else seemed to have made it, or had at least decided how they were going to make it; Devon only knew that she didn't want to be a commercial illustrator and didn't have the temperament, like Gabriel Montebello, to be a fine artist.

Alex combed her fingers through her buzzed-off hair. She had lines along the side of her head where the hair had been cut down to the flesh with a razor blade—it was a weird do, but not as weird as when Alex had shaved her head entirely so she could look like a Buddhist monk.

Alex, one of Beka's three roommates, had been videotaping their parties for posterity ever since they'd first started throwing them in 1981. The loftmates often kidded each other about the footage she had recorded and how someday she could blackmail them and retire on the money (if they ever made any money). After sweeping the room, her camera seemed to gravitate toward the center of the throng where Beka was still dancing—always dancing.

Josh, one of the other loftmates, was dancing with a creamy-skinned black woman. Katiti—Devon thought that was her name—had come on strong to Josh as soon as she found out he was pre-med. It was one of his favorite lines to pick up girls; Devon knew because he had practiced on her earlier that evening. "Which works better, Devon?" he had asked. "If I say I'm OB-GYN or Ear, Nose, and Throat?"

"I don't know, Josh." Devon laughed. "I'm not in the market for a doctor."

"Well," he told her, "you wouldn't believe how quick you get laid when you're looking at a six-figure income in three years."

Back on the dance floor, Katiti tousled the curls on his head with her manicured fingernails, then grabbed Josh around the hips and sidled up to him. She could dance, too; her extensions weren't as high as Beka's, but she could spin like a top, and between the two dancers a kind of silent competition erupted as each tried to one-up the other's technique. Katiti bumped into Beka, and Devon was pretty sure it was not a mistake. Beka pretended not to notice, but Devon knew what would happen next, and Alex must have, too, because she had already moved from the snow falling to Beka's silent fury. It was a safe assumption; one could be relatively certain that if there was an audience, Beka Imamura would make a stage.

"Focus," Alex hissed as she pressed the automatic lens adjustment. Beka's movements were becoming grander, as if she knew that she was on camera. She moved in wider and wider concentric circles and any second, Devon knew, Beka's energy would start to push people, especially Katiti, away from her until she was the sole dancer in the room. It was a phenomenon that existed among performing artists and something only they understood—bystanders could watch but they could never partake.

Devon wished that Alex had an image-resonance camera to document the energy field—the vortex Beka created around herself. To capture the actual presence of what some called charisma, now that would be something worth recording. The music changed from Sheila Chandra's exotic East Indian rhythms to Bryan Ferry's throaty voice singing "Avalon." A solo siren swaying in the falling snow, Beka's spirit encompassed the room. She kept moving even after Sam came upstairs and abruptly turned the music off. Looking puzzled, she kept swaying as the rest of the room grew still. Beka had never understood that regular people didn't have symphonies and bands playing backup in their heads. Devon looked at her watch. It was four a.m. and Sam had obviously decided the party was over.

Sam's statement broadsided them like an avalanche. Beka stopped dancing to the music in her head, but the snow kept falling into the room.

"My b . . . brother," Sam stammered. "Todd is missing."

* * *

It was four in the morning. Devon checked her watch just to make sure—it seemed as if present time were matching her reminiscence as the anniversary of Todd Daniel's disappearance drew to a close. Or was the anniversary just beginning?

Leaning against the van and looking up at Gabe and Beka's house, Devon was pelted by tiny beads of ice as she wondered if it would turn to rain or snow again—it was as if the world itself couldn't decide whether to be warm or cold. She clipped her marsupial pouch, full of all the little extras she might need, around her waist and was about to grab her field kit and head back to the house when the gurney, with Gabriel bagged and securely strapped to it, came down the steps. It was definitely getting colder.

She could see her partner Frank using the black light up on the hill, trying to pick up any trace particles that normally would have disappeared in the dark.

* * *

Patches of fresh snow glowed as the purple light passed over them, and Lochwood waited until the detective was finished sweeping the scene before he said anything. Beka Imamura lay in the snow like an origami bird whose wings had been clipped. Her legs were folded awkwardly to one side as if she'd been frozen in mid-run like a deer on the highway, and both arms reached up over her head and lay twisted around the wrists and folded as if in prayer. Her skin had already begun to turn waxy, paler than usual, and for a moment Lochwood thought that she looked like a geisha doll. Her eyes stared up at him, slanted and accusing, as they had always looked at him. Beka had never liked him, he knew that, but he never knew why.

Frank stood up and looked at him expectantly. "I told them to wait a minute before they put her in the Wagon and Basket," Lochwood informed him.

"I've been up and down this area twice now and I don't see any fucking footprints. What'd she do, fly? And the damn weather is wiping everything up as it goes." Frank pointed to the area around the body. "There are pockets which could have been footprints two hours ago, but they're so smooth now I can't tell for sure. This area's pretty rough."

"Can we tell if there was a scuffle?"

"I don't see any signs of a struggle. She either walked here or was carried, but I don't see evidence of either."

"Carried—interesting idea."

"She's so light that her bare feet wouldn't have left much of an imprint if she had come out here to die. Carrying would have left a deeper impression." Frank thwarted his own theory. "It was an hour or more before we got here, which probably allowed the snow and sleet to erase her tracks."

"What about trace?"

"Some hair that looks like it's hers, and the knife has her prints on it."

"It's pretty clear what happened." Lochwood looked at his notes, then at the body. "But why'd she kill herself here? It doesn't look like her kind of spot."

"See, that's the thing." Frank liked to think out loud. "A woman like that doesn't want to die in the mud. She likes to lay herself out in silk, pour a Brandy with just the right amount of Seconal in it, put on something sentimental, like opera, a nice aria, and slip away. And then there's her old man. Why'd she kill him like that?"

"Got me. I mean, if she'd just hit him over the head with a frying pan that'd be one thing, but this, this was no fooling around. She butchered him."

"It's like a death scene," Frank said.

"Exactly."

They looked at the knee prints in the path where she must have knelt down to perform her final act. "How many murder/suicides use two weapons?"

"It's usually one, and the murder weapon is turned against the murderer."

"Exactly. Still, it looks like a murder/suicide to me."

"Devon's not going to like it," Frank mumbled.

"It's not her job to like or dislike," Loch said, more to himself than to Frank, her partner. "It's her job to report the facts, no matter what they are." He tapped his pen against his hand until it hurt.

"You don't have to tell me, Brennen."

"Sorry. You heading back to the house?" Frank nodded again, but both men stood for a moment in silence. "I never saw her dance, but Devon says she was amazing," Loch said quietly, then promptly realized he'd used Devon's first name. He coughed, hoping to cover his slip.

"I know about you two."

"Any problems with it?"

"None of my business."

"You ever fool around on your wife?"

"Me? Nah, she'd kill me and no one would be able to prove it. She pays attention to what I do for a living." Lochwood coughed again, uncomfortable with the implication. "It's a different situation, Loch."

"Yeah, but it never made sense before I met Halsey."

"Just remember, you hurt her and something might happen to you . . ." Frank stopped midsentence and pointed down the hill.

Devon stood there staring, not at them but at Beka. Her mouth fell open and snowflakes seemed to hover in and out with her breath.

"What's wrong?" Loch started to move toward her, but she waved him away.

"Where's her hair? My god, what happened to her hair?"

CHAPTER FOUR

Jade is tested by fire, a sword is tested by a hair.

—Zen phrase

Women do cut their hair, even though Devon swore Beka would never have cut hers. It was strange, Loch would give it that, but inconclusive. There were a few other things that were strange, too. He and Gary stood in the doorway of the art studio Montebello and his staff called the Art Barn. "Did her position strike you as odd?" he asked.

"She was a dancer. I figured it was normal for her."

"I wonder what Devon thought."

"Maybe when she gets over the hair you can ask her." Gary stepped into the space and looked up at the hayloft.

The barn was full of all kinds of equipment, none of which had anything to do with farming. There were paint-blowers, welding torches, two kilns—one upright and one square—rolls of canvas stacked in the northwest corner next to a vertical pile of wood moldings to stretch canvas on, and a miter saw; there were buckets, and bags of plaster and alginate. There was a corner that looked almost like a clothing rack in a department store that was full of painter's pants and jackets and paper Tyvek suits, most of which were spattered with paint and plaster and clay. There was even a small foundry for lighter metal castings and a pouring bin.

"Quite a studio," Gary marveled.

"You don't become as well-known as Gabriel Montebello without being well-versed in a number of mediums."

"You sound like Halsey," Gary scoffed at his partner. He opened a large metal locker at the side of the room. Clean paper jumpsuits were hanging in a row, seemingly new and untouched. "Hey, what's this look like?"

Lochwood peered at it and paused. "A Crime Scene locker."

"Where the hell did he get Tyvek suits, from Halsey?"

"You can buy those at Canal Street Jeans a few blocks from his Soho studio."

"He has a studio in Soho?"

"He has a building in Soho," Loch replied. "Four floors. Each one a separate loft of about two thousand square feet. It's bigger than this place."

"Man, can you believe some guy who plays around with paint and clay for a living lives like this?" Gary picked up a pair of booties and a paper cap like the ones the Crime Scene Unit usually wore. "What about these? You can't tell me he got these at Canal Street Jeans."

"Maybe he buys them from the distributor." Lochwood picked up a drop cloth and looked at the sculpture hiding underneath, then dragged his forefinger under the tarp and across the floor. "It's too clean. Let's get Halsey up here. She's been here before; she can tell us if this is normal."

* * *

Devon's field kit was reassuring in its order and familiarity: the test tubes with their blank labels waiting for samples; the sterile swabs wrapped in foil packages of two—one for a control sample, one for the sample itself; the small bottle of distilled water she would sprinkle onto the sterile Q-tip swab in order to take a control and then a blood sample; the Amido Black to make blood appear on white objects; the Luminol to make blood appear on black; the sterile scalpel for scrapings. Everything was relatively untouched by human hands until the moment she opened the ordinary-looking toolbox and the equipment inside became property of the Imamura-Montebello Crime Scene.

The house was almost as quiet as a zendo full of deeply concentrating people. Devon watched the Crime Scene detectives-in-training pull out their own plastic bags—they looked like aliens moving through a world they did not yet understand. She walked to the fireplace mantel and took her first swab off the painting, sealed it into vial 1-a, then took a swab of blood and sealed it into vial 1-b. Then, because she was both cautious and thorough, she took a control sample off the painted wall and another swab of blood. "2-*a*, 2-*b*," she wrote on the outside of the test tubes, then slipped them into her pocket before continuing to track the scene she had just documented on film. She didn't think they were looking for more than a single blood type, but one could never be sure when there was so much of it around. She recalled the case where Homicide had proved a murder had been committed by the amount of blood at the scene alone, even though the body was never found. The DA had argued that no one could lose so much blood and still be alive.

She loved the careful rituals of evidence collection. It took a creative mind to walk through a crime scene and read it correctly, and she felt her mental arm stretch and flex as she walked contemplatively, breathing deeply and slowly, through the living room.

The coffee table was made of copper tubing, with two slabs of broken marble set in the middle that fit together like the jagged edges of a jigsaw puzzle. But it was the bottle of bourbon on the table that caught and held her attention.

Kneeling down on the floor, Devon picked up the fragments of peeled paper from the Jack Daniel's label and placed them in a bag. There might be a partial print that she could pull later. Then, following her intuition, she checked under the couch; there was a prescription bottle of Norflex. Beka used muscle relaxers for back pain, and that's what Norflex provided.

Lochwood had come back inside. She caught his eye. "Did Beka overdose?"

The profiles for male and female suicide victims were very different, and a drug overdose was definitely more Beka's style—women were generally more concerned with appearances and how they looked after death, while men opted for a more violent, certain death. In the case of murder/suicide, however, the weapon used on the murder victim was almost always the one used in the suicide as well. Devon had to know the answer to her own question.

Loch's voice broke through her reverie. "Jo says her eyes were dilated, which could indicate cardiac arrest, but for now it looks like loss of blood."

"Really?" Devon looked at the prescription bottle she had just bagged. It had been filled three days ago for twenty pills and was now empty. "Have Toxicology check for Norflex in her system." She handed him the bag.

He held it up and raised an eyebrow. "We're going to need you up at the studio when you're done in here."

"Okay." She looked at the bottle of Jack Daniel's again. "Who made the 911 call?"

"It wasn't Gabe."

"So why make it?"

"Maybe she wanted them to be found quickly." He didn't want to tell her what he really thought, that Beka had wanted Devon to find them.

"She?" She looked at him questioningly.

He wanted to give her more time, but she saw the same things he saw—she had to have reached the same conclusion. "It looks like a murder/suicide."

She snorted. "Don't jump the gun, Brennen."

"We aren't jumping anything, Halsey. We're evaluating each piece of evidence we find and reading the signs as they've been left for us."

Her voice was calm but she could feel her muscles quaking. "Beka was temperamental and self-destructive, but she was not homicidal. And Gabe, whatever his faults, didn't deserve this."

Their voices were hoarse from traveling between the cold air outside and the warm air in the house, and they tried to argue in hushed tones so as not to disturb the other workers.

"We've both seen it happen before," he reminded her. "Maybe she just snapped."

"There's no way she had the strength to drag him down the hallway."

He paused. "Clytemnestra," was all he said.

Devon's eyes reflected a brief trace of doubt, then she nodded in agreement. Beka had dragged Orestes, also known as her dance partner, Edilio Ferraro—all six feet, one hundred and seventy-five pounds of him—around stage during every night and matinee performance of the fall season five years earlier.

* * *

"The Bourbon in the bottom needs to be analyzed, it looks like it's been rinsed." A detective-in-training opened a bag as Devon placed the bottle inside. Just a year ago, she'd been the one in training and on her way to becoming a full-fledged Crime Scene detective. Now, with her probationary period over and her promotion official, Devon Halsey, the first female Crime Scene detective in Suffolk County, was training others.

She continued through the room dusting objects that were in unusual places and pulling latents. It was the first time she had ever worked a house she already knew, and she found that her preknowledge both helped and hindered her. For one thing, she was aware of what was new in the house and what was old. She even recognized her wedding present, a raku vase, in the corner of the room. On the other hand, these details carried emotional attachments for her, and she felt she was tripping over memories instead of crime-scene cones and tape.

From the doorway to the master bedroom, Devon retraced the impressions of footwear and the bare footprints on the wood floor in the hall. Halfway down the hallway she stopped and took a closer look at the samurai sword hanging off-kilter on the wall. The sword had been passed down in the Imamura family for centuries and brought over by Beka's grandfather from Kyoto when he first settled in Hawaii. To Beka, who considered herself one-hundred-percent American, it was just a family heirloom. To Devon, it was the sword of Damocles. It looked clean—too clean.

Pulling a small bottle of Amido Black out of her kit, she paused. The weight of what she might find pressed down on her as she raised the spray bottle—the pressure to complete her job, the consequence of what her work might reveal. A light spray of Amido Black grabbed hold of the protein residue of blood as she rinsed it off with acetic glacial acid. It shifted and collected like beads of mercury around what was invisible to the naked eye.

"What is it?" Loch asked.

"Blood . . ." She stepped back. "Lots of it." She pointed to the coagulation up and down the hilt of the sword. "What the hell happened here, Brennen?" She was beginning to feel lightheaded.

"Come over here and sit down. You look faint." He tried to push her head between her legs but she refused. That would just provide more grist for the rumor mill: Women shouldn't work in Crime Scene or Homicide. She pulled a stick of gum out of her pouch and used the methodic rhythm of her jaws to calm her nerves.

"I can't believe she did this," she whispered. "I'm sorry. I'm trying to keep an open mind but I can't buy it."

He knelt down by her side to discuss their differing opinions more quietly. "We can't be sure about anything this early," he conceded.

She searched his eyes for reassurance, but they were glazed over with that faraway glint he got whenever they passed the scene of some crisis. He was like a bloodhound when it came to trouble, always sniffing it out when it didn't come looking for him. She watched him walk over to the stereo where it was recessed into the wall. The light was on and the digital display indicated disc two was in repeat mode. He pulled out his handkerchief and turned up the volume.

The CD changer immediately went into its recall mode, and in seconds Kiri Te Kanawa's voice engulfed the room in Madame Butterfly's tragic wail. Frank stopped what he was doing and looked over at his partner. She shut her eyes.

Devon felt as if she were hanging in the air as *Un Bel Di Verdremo* stung her heart with the voice of betrayal and lost love. When she opened her eyes again, Lochwood and Frank were still staring at her, as if she held the answer. Her voice was flat against the graceful lyricism of the soprano when she said, "She's about to commit suicide."

CHAPTER FIVE

A skillful craftsman leaves no traces

The monk stamped his feet as he walked through the snow and ducked beneath the privet hedge. Though it was still dark he could make out the gray shape of the garden Buddha and bowed in respect toward the shadowy corner of the yard. As he raised his eyes from the ground though, he stopped mid-bow. Despite the darkness of the grove, he could just make out something in the Buddha's hands. Someone had left an offering of long black hair, and even Buddha's supreme serenity seemed puzzled by the presence of the locks. Hans didn't remove the offering; he was merely mindful of its presence. He was used to finding little gifts to the Buddha, and more than one member of the Northwest Woods Zendo came to meditate at night. That last night was New Year's Eve did not disturb him in the least. He turned, felt his robes catch on the wet ground, gathered the hem up, and headed toward the tiny barn where the morning sit would begin in thirty minutes.

The door to the zendo swung open in the wind as Hans stooped through the doorway. He lit the small oil heater in the main sitting room and began to sweep the floor as he did everyday before the early-morning meditation. The planks of wood in the old barn were wide and hid dirt well, but he muscled the broom in between the cracks and swept the dirt out the door. Warmth slowly sucked the damp smell of mildew out of the air, and through the windows of the barn he could see the sky slowly changing from dark to light gray as he prepared incense and fresh candles for the shrine.

He bowed as he approached the altar but found his morning ritual disturbed by the presence of more strands of hair and a pair of scissors on the platform. He grumbled under his breath. Members of the *Sangha* knew better than to leave their garbage behind. He would have to talk to them at the next meeting. He inhaled and exhaled, focusing his thoughts back on the task at hand. Be mindful of each movement, he recollected his *Roshi* saying, be mindful whether you are walking, working, or drinking tea—it is all meditation.

He heard the door to the zendo open. Two of the members were in the foyer removing their shoes as he came out of the sitting room. They bowed to him, then went inside, and by the time he had returned from dumping the dustpan full of hair they were quietly sitting *zazen*, facing the walls of the old barn. Normally, he sat at the front of the room to the right of the altar, and that was where he belonged, but today Hans was *Jikido*. When the room had filled— only six people today, precisely at seven a.m.—he bowed and slowly hit the singing bowl three times. Its bass timbre rang through the room and promised peace and stillness. Hans shut his eyes partway.

Thirty seconds later his eyes popped open. Someone was missing. She was always at the morning sit, albeit today was a holiday; still, she had made a point of telling him she would be here. She had wanted to speak to him about something.

The clock by his right knee clicked by the seconds. He breathed deeply and tried to reach *samadhi* by contemplating his koan, but instead began pondering the koan he had given Beka Imamura:

A monk takes a vow of silence to remain in a tree at the fork in a road until he reaches enlightenment. However, a traveler does not know which direction to take, and asks the monk for directions. In order to fulfill his *dharma* the monk must tell the man which direction to take, but to tell the man which way to go means instantaneous death.

"What if the traveler is someone I know?" Beka had asked. "I might die for someone I know, but not for a stranger."

"Meditate," he told her. "Don't think."

Despite his seniority, he fidgeted beneath his robes. Minutes dragged on for what seemed hours, and his mind wandered as much as a novice's as the dawn ticked away. Where was Beka?

CHAPTER SIX

What is the Blown Hair Sword?
The tip of each branch of coral supports the moon.

—Haryo Osho

The dark clung like residue to her skin—night didn't seem to be anywhere close to ending. Every time she checked the horizon it seemed darker than before; even the peach-colored glow over the Sag Harbor dump had disappeared as the fog rolled in. Fog always followed snow out on the East End and it was going to ruin any further outside searches—for instance, if Beka had called 911 and then killed herself, where was the phone? They had looked in the area closest to the body—nothing.

It was the longest night of her life. Reporters lingered along the outskirts of the taped-off area like vampires unable to pass the sign of the cross, as if the yellow police line could hold them at bay. They paced back and forth along the perimeter hungry for the blood of a story and headlines.

Frank and Devon made their last trip to the van. She unhooked her waist-pack and dumped it in the front seat.

"Devon Halsey, fifth-grade long-jump champion." The voice was familiar and taunting, like that of a boy pulling her pigtails in elementary school, and that's exactly who he was.

"Tom Hurley." They'd seen each other off and on for years. Sag Harbor was a difficult town to get lost in even if one worked hard at remaining anonymous.

"Your first-grade boyfriend." He was obviously enjoying catching her off guard.

"One kiss under the monkey bars does not make you my first boyfriend," she retorted. "And since I wiped it off and called 'cooties,' it doesn't count."

Her eyes casually scanned his body for credentials.

He scanned her body less professionally, then flicked his press badge toward her inquisitive eyes. "So, you're a cop?"

"Detective."

"My how things develop." His eyes had rested where most men's did.

"We're not in the school yard, Tom. What do you want?"

He snapped his fingers—a gesture she felt was in poor taste. "To congratulate you. The *Long Island Times*—first female Crime Scene detective in Suffolk County. About time Suffolk joined the twentieth century . . . No, wait! It's the twenty-first! How come you decided to come back home after all that private schooling and 'New Yorking'?"

"Best pay in the country after Beverly Hills."

"No shit."

"And I have a house here."

"That's right, I heard your grandmother died. Sorry."

"Thanks for your concern. It was eight years ago."

She spied the memo pad hiding in his hand. "You working for the *Press* or the *Star*, now?"

"*Newsday.*"

He'd been promoted, too. She winced at her faux pas.

"Didn't I used to see you and Beka at art openings together, back when I worked for Aunt Mona at the *Star?*"

Devon didn't blink. "You have your statement from Detective Brennen and Sergeant Houck." She reached into the van in order to look busy.

"I'd much rather have a statement from you. Come on, just a little tidbit for old time's sake?"

"Detective Halsey has work to do and I wouldn't want you to report that the taxpayers pay her to reminisce." Loch's voice disrupted Hurley's queries.

He shoved his notepad into his pocket. "I was just interested in the Halseys of Southampton angle. You know, why would the department allow a close personal friend of a suspect onto the scene of a crime? Unless you didn't know that Detective Halsey knew the suspect? She did tell you, didn't she?"

"Detective Halsey, we need you and Landal up at the barn."

"You'll excuse us, Tom," she addressed the reporter sternly.

"What's happened in the barn? Is it a crime scene? I thought she killed him in the house!" Hurley was jotting something down in his pad as she began to walk away. "Are you going to try and prove your best friend's innocence?"

"I can't prove innocence if we don't know who's guilty!" Devon replied angrily. Loch's eyes flashed a warning at her.

"I believe you have our statement on record and know that we haven't named any suspects at this point," Loch stated calmly. "Now we have about twenty-four more hours of work to do. Why don't you report that?"

"Jesus, Devon, how's that make you feel?" Hurley yelled after her. "Your best friend murdering her husband and then offing herself? If you don't give me more than that, you know what I'll print!"

As soon as they were out of hearing distance, Devon turned on Loch, fuming. "Why didn't you tell him you knew Beka was my friend!"

"You know as well as I do there was nothing we could say that he wasn't going to turn into a soundbite. If I so much as used her name he could have quoted me, probably out of context, and who knows where that would have ended."

She sucked the air under her tongue. Her eyelids seemed to have gained weight in the last few minutes and she had to blink a few times to make sure the sky was actually beginning to grow pale and it wasn't her imagination. "Do you think there's going to be a problem with me working the scene?"

"There'd be more trouble if you didn't. Sergeant Houck's behind you and so am I. We're counting on you and Frank to put it together like you always do."

"I have a bad feeling about this. If the press decides to make something of my presence at the scene I'm going to get fried."

"Why? Because you're a woman?"

"Possibly." Devon tried to keep her voice noncommittal on the emotional issue of gender bias, which no man, not even Loch, seemed to comprehend entirely.

"Give it a rest, Dev. Everything that happens in the department does not come down to sexism." He stopped and looked at her merrily. "It comes down to having sex." She did not argue.

Dawn finally broke through the overcast horizon—it was not a splendid sunrise. The clouds merely went from black to dark gray to light gray. There was a purplish tint around the puffy edges, but that only made it seem darker as another flurry of flakes began to drift down upon their heads.

"Which way is the ocean?" Loch asked.

She shook her head, disbelieving. "You grew up on Long Island and you still don't your way around? Pitiful."

"I'm from Brooklyn; technically that's a separate universe."

She pointed toward an anvil-shaped bank of clouds just beginning to blush with morning light. "Right over that hill and a few dunes." The brisk salt air scrubbed at her lungs and she had to blink back the water as the wind brought tears to her eyes.

They heard Frank breathing heavily as he made his way up the hill toward them. "I tell you what, this body is too old for these hours."

"We just need your professional eye to glance over the art studio. Then you can go home."

Frank looked at his partner. "Don't you love how he refers to the office as home? Be afraid, be very afraid of a man who thinks his desk is a pillow."

"Since Brennen never sleeps," Devon reminded her partner, "that's not a problem."

The barn looked different with the faint light of morning coming through the picture windows. "Gabe loved to paint in here around this time," Devon recalled. "Beka would go to the zendo to meditate while he painted, then they'd meet up around eight-thirty for breakfast."

"Almost sounds romantic, in a pseudo, kind of intellectual way," Gary said, stomping his feet in an effort to warm them.

She walked through the studio she had visited a number of times over the years and made one blanket statement. "Looks clean."

"Too clean?" Loch dragged his foot along the cement floor for her to see that nothing came up on his shoes.

"Someone comes in. Once a month, I think."

Gary opened the locker with the Tyvek suits in it. "What about these?"

She touched them with her gloved hand. "He used them to keep his clothes clean, like we do."

"Do you know where he got them?"

"No, but he got the idea from me." She looked inside one of them and wrinkled her nose. "He must not change them as often as we have to." She held onto the suit, trying to remember something that was nagging at her brain, but she couldn't place the fragment of thought.

"You have something?" Gary asked.

"Yeah, short-term memory loss." She walked to the end of the studio and back. "It doesn't look like a crime scene to me. Frank, what's your read?"

"No signs of struggle. A little too organized for an artist's studio, but maybe he was your anal-retentive-type artist."

"Definitely," Devon affirmed. "Have you called Jenny O'Doherty yet?"

Lochwood looked at his notes. "The secretary?"

"Yeah, she could tell you when the maid came last and whether she did the studio or not."

"We're heading over to see her in a few minutes."

"Something was swept up recently." Frank pointed to the stripes along the cement floor.

Devon peered into the trashcan. "It looks like something broke. They've dumped the trash, though. Gabe does a lot of plaster casts before he pours the final bronze. Sometimes he breaks—broke—them for fun. He liked smashing imperfection." She tried to smile fondly over the memory etched in her mind—how she had watched Gabe mold plaster directly onto Beka's body—but the attempt to smile failed. Beka had hated the feel of plaster on her skin, and questioned whether his use of molds detracted from true art. There had been too much active creation in the studio for such destruction to now echo between its walls.

The four detectives walked back out the barn door and down the hill in the ashen dawn. "Houck says he tried but the labs are going to remain closed today," Loch told his team.

Gary snorted. "That just blows."

"Well, at least we've been approved for overtime."

Devon knew Loch was trying to lighten their mood, but there was nothing worse than being stalled in an investigation.

"Money, that's what's really important," Frank replied mockingly .

"Since it doesn't look like we have a murderer running around loose, we won't have any help until after the holiday," Lochwood reminded them.

Frank tapped his partner on the shoulder. "Come on, Dev. I'll drive back."

Loch wanted to drive her back, but it would look out of the ordinary. "See you around two at Jo's Place?" he asked. That was what they called the morgue—it gave an endearing diner quality to the cold reality of corpses on ice. Devon's nod was imperceptible.

They had just pulled onto Sunrise Highway when Devon's beeper began to vibrate on her belt. She quickly unsnapped it and looked at the number. 999-999-9999—it was Loch's way of telling her what he so often had trouble saying out loud. Warmth seeped through her chest as she craned her head to look in the side-view mirror at his car. I love you, too, she thought.

CHAPTER SEVEN

Now the party's over, I'm so tired . . .
—Bryan Ferry, "Avalon"

The bleak January roads, gray as the sky above them, ran beneath the tires, and little swirls of dry snow dusted the roadside along the pine barrens. Frank shifted the van into the left lane as Devon's thoughts sifted through the events of the night. Her toes were beginning to thaw as the van's stale heat blasted across them. Her hair was damp and heavy on her neck, and she tried fluffing it by the vent before giving up and tuning into one of the few local stations. As the crackling static stilled, she heard Bryan Ferry's hypnotic voice.

> *Now the party's over,*
> *I'm so tired,*
> *Then I see you coming out of nowhere . . .*

Beka seemed to be dancing through the snow snakes winding up the roadway, her waist-length dark hair sweeping across her face just a hundred yards ahead. She was dancing in Avalon, now, Devon thought to herself. Beka had finally made it.

> *Much communication in a motion,*
> *Without conversation or a notion,*
> *Avalon . . .*

* * *

The last vibrations of music still hung in the air as Sam Daniels faced them. "It's really cold out there. I've been looking for an hour and can't find him anywhere. He didn't even have his coat on." His voice cracked as Devon watched the frantic grip of hysteria tighten around his throat.

"Come on, gang, let's go find Todd," Josh declared. He poured Sam a shot of Jack Daniel's and then shoved the bottle into Sam's pocket. "We'll need this."

"Bring the brandy!" Beka had quipped, tossing on her vintage fur coat and heading for the door. Moments later, the last stragglers of the loft's Chinatown bash were heading down the stairs of 255 Canal Street.

When the samba takes you
Out of nowhere,
And the background's fading
Out of focus . . .

Snow swept down the streets. Beka slipped her arm around Devon's elbow and peered concernedly into her friend's eyes as if to make sure that Todd was okay, then looked abruptly around at the faces in the group. "Where's Gabe?"

"He went out for cigars and a nightcap at *La Gamelle*," Maddie informed her.

"He's such a snob." Beka grabbed Godwyn so she was sand-wiched between them. She was like a butterfly aflutter with every whim and change of breeze, still only when she was anchored by the presence of friends.

On the serene streets of Soho, a light new snow had begun to fall over the neighborhood. The search party headed toward Broadway, hoping they might be able to retrace Todd's trek around the block and perhaps find him passed out in one of the many alley-ways. Ahead of them, Maddie—the most vertically challenged of the party—was laughing and taking a swig from the bottle. Beka let go of her anchors and ran ahead. She was careful not to wipe the lip and downed the Jack Daniel's, then asked, "Where's the brandy?"

Maddie Fong, the other Asian-American in the group, was more a stew than a melting pot. She had just enough Chinese in her to give her hair a wicked gleam and her eyes a slight almond shape, but the rest of her heritage was a mystery.

"Yes the picture's changing, every moment . . . And your destination, you don't know it . . . Would you have me dancing out of nowhere? Avalon," Beka sang under her breath, *"Avalon."* Making sweeping movements with her arms as if conducting the snowflakes, and every so often adding a few quick steps with her feet, she kicked bits of red paper and ashes into the air.

Alexandra and Godwyn were talking animatedly, making gestures in the air that looked like camera lenses and tilting their heads to one side or the other as if exploring all the angles.

Josh and Katiti had moved from flirting to heavy-petting, and their trek through the street was slowed by constant groping. Matching black curls of hair, tousled by the wind and laced with large white flakes of snow, made them look more like siblings than lovers. Devon, the quiet watcher of the scene, thought how Sam looked like the head of their dragon. And if Sam was the head, Devon mused, she must be the tail, while the rest of them appeared to make up the torso, undulating through Chinatown, trying to chase away the evil spirits with their laughter. The soiree had simply adjourned to the street—they passed the flasks of bourbon and brandy among themselves and yelled, "Todd Daniels! All ye, all ye, all come free!"

It was all part of a game. Their voices rang out his name like good cheer until it echoed between the dark and empty buildings.

"Happy New Year!" Broadway Bob blew a noisemaker and greeted the group with a familiar wave of his hand and head. He knew the loft gang well. They had, after all, provided him with blankets on cold nights as well as booze for the three years they'd lived on his block.

Bob lived in the entrance of the Canal Street subway station. His tweed coat was worn and faded by time and rough living, and his face was scruffy with the gray-brown stubble of God's unshaven. He wore three pairs of fluorescent fuzzy balls on his head to improve his reception with the outer limits of the Big Apple, or perhaps he really was receiving messages from outer space. One thing was certain, he was the eyes, ears, and antenna of the neighborhood.

"Happy New Year, Bob." Beka handed him the bottle of Jack Daniel's.

"Bourbon and smoke. Gonna be a good year." His florescent headgear bobbed at them as he puffed on his cigar.

"Have you seen my brother run past here?" Sam knelt down to speak to the man. It was a technique he had learned when working with children—always go to their level to maintain eye contact.

Bob looked as if he was trying hard to think. "Seen some aliens." He took a swig as his brain skipped a groove. "Seen a few of them. They're all over this fuckin' city."

"We invited a few to our party," Alex encouraged him.

"Damn nice, earthlings. You damn nice." He mumbled into the mouth of the bottle so that it hummed. "I seen one with curly hair."

"What was that, Bob?" Sam tried to get him to focus on something besides the bottle in his hand.

"Curly red hair."

"Did he stop here?"

"Happy New Year!" He blew his party favor at them again.

Devon leaned down and looked at the noisemaker. "That's the same kind you guys gave out at the party."

"A quarter apiece at Chung's," Maddie affirmed.

"Todd would give his away. He's like that," Sam said hopefully. "Which way did he go, Bob?"

Bob pointed toward the sky.

Sam, despite having a masters degree in psychology, forgot all he had learned in school about dealing with mental illness and retorted angrily, "Bob, this is serious!"

Devon touched Sam's elbow and shook her head. "Bob?" Her voice was calm and soothing. "What did he do before he went up?"

"Flapped his arms." His antennae nodded affirmatively in the January wind, but his moment of clarity had dissipated like a puff of cigar smoke into the air.

Sam patted the old man on the shoulder. "Thanks anyway, Bob."

They continued scouring everything from the Bowery west, covering the areas between Houston and Canal, Soho and Little Italy. It was almost five-thirty in the morning but they were still laughing. They had been laughing all night.

Beka found an open door swinging in the wind. "Todd?" She

leaned inside and shouted. She screamed. Her voice dug into their ears as her body seemed to hang over an abyss of blackness.

Sam lunged for her arm. She still had one hand on the doorknob but Sam only had hold of the edge of the building. "Help me!" he yelled.

Devon raced forward and reached over the precipice for Beka's belt, as Josh grabbed Sam's waist. A gust of wind pushed at the door and it swayed away, tugging Beka inside. Only Devon and Sam anchored her between empty space and solid ground. Teetering like a rock on a precipice, they held their breath. The wind shifted back, and they quickly hauled Beka away from the edge of the elevator shaft and to the safety of the street.

It was a hoax no longer. In utter silence they stood and stared into the building. Vapors rose from their mouths. Beka laughed nervously. "Good thing I have such good balance."

"Oh my god, Beka!" Maddie sniveled. "You could've died!"

Sam hugged Devon tightly. Josh squeezed Beka; Alex leaned against Godwyn. Katiti watched them all. No one could stop shaking. It wasn't just the cold that was creeping under their skin—there were so many things that could happen on the streets of New York. So many places where someone could slip and fall—disappear.

Beka reached for the bottle in Josh's hands and slugged it down, then handed it to Devon. Devon had never needed a drink so badly.

"Todd! Where are you?" Beka shouted against gusts from the Hudson River that seemed to rip the words from her throat. "This isn't funny anymore!"

Their good cheer faded as the once-friendly streets grew ominous without his answering mirth. Nonchalance dissolved with the predawn drop in temperature as their quest for the lost Yale divinity student became desperate.

CHAPTER EIGHT

Tis their duty to trample on all human feelings . . .
The fiends, who will one day requite them in
Variety of torturing!

— LORD BYRON, *The Two Foscari*

The LIE was almost empty of traffic so Devon and Frank soon arrived at headquarters. They unloaded the van into two temporary evidence lockers until they could reassign their collection to the appropriate labs—whenever the labs actually opened. Back in the break room, Frank turned on the TV and popped a bagel into the toaster oven. "You want half?"

"Not really," Devon answered.

"You've got to eat." He handed her a cup of coffee.

"*Internationally renowned artist Gabriel Montebello was stabbed to death last night and his wife, dancer Beka Imamura, has been found dead on the scene,*" the morning news anchor announced. "*Detectives at the scene are calling it a possible murder/suicide. Beka Imamura danced with the International Contemporary Dance . . .*" A clip of Beka dancing one of her more famous roles as the knife-wielding Clytemnestra was shared with the viewing public and had been artistically edited so that scenes of Beka dragging her dance partner across the stage were intercut with those of Gabriel's body being carted away.

"*Well that certainly sounds like a Greek tragedy. Any idea why she would allegedly kill her husband, Pat?*" the coanchor asked.

"*Not yet, but the case is under investigation by Suffolk County Homicide. Stay tuned to this station for further developments on the first murder of this year.*"

Devon watched the news with a growing sense of foreboding. Hurley's article would be out in the morning with far more depth and detail than the TV news had yet dug up, and she knew how it would play out. At least they had missed the holiday edition of the paper—that gave them one more day to give something to the press that wouldn't reek of the PR department. But would the evidence they analyzed today prove Beka's innocence? Or had she, like Loch suggested, snapped?

* * *

Lochwood and Gary met Jenny O'Doherty at her home in Bridgehampton. Dark circles ringed her eyes. She didn't look as if she'd slept at all. Her face was wrought with concern and she frowned at the detectives when they flipped their badges in the morning light.

She was still in her bathrobe and Lochwood could hear a fresh pot of coffee gurgling through its filter as they stepped inside. Gary cast a surprised look at Loch. She certainly hadn't been on her way to bed. This was a community where people rarely locked doors and a stranger was generally regarded as safe first, never dangerous. What was strange, though, was that Jenny O'Doherty seemed to be expecting them.

"We're with Suffolk County." Loch left out the word *Homicide* on purpose.

"Of course you are. Would you like some coffee?" She turned her back on the men and walked into the kitchen as if expecting them to follow her. "What did George do this time?" She reached for the phone.

"We're not here about George . . ." Gary couldn't finish his sentence because she had pressed an auto-dial button and begun speaking into the handset.

"Barbara, is Harry up? George has got himself in trouble again. I expect he's going to need bail." She looked at the men in her kitchen. "Cream? Sugar?" They shook their heads.

"I don't know, let me ask." She turned back to the detectives. "Is it a DUI?" (She pronounced it *dewee*.) "I suppose you took the car this time? Barbara, what am I going to do without the car?"

"We're not in Traffic," Gary explained, "we're Homicide."

Her mouth dropped open. "Lord, Barbara, he's killed someone. I knew it was only a matter of time. I swear this time I'm going to divorce him! I've had it! I spent all night waiting up for that ungrateful son of a . . ."

Lochwood walked over and took the phone from Mrs. O'Doherty. "Excuse us, Barbara, but this is not about George." He looked at Gabriel Montebello's secretary. "You can call her back later. We're here about someone else." He hung up the phone. "Would you like to sit down?"

She handed him his coffee and remained standing.

"Mrs. O'Doherty, I'm sorry to inform you that your employers, both of them, are dead." This was not how Loch had wanted to tell her, but it was the best he could do under the circumstances.

"Jesus, Mary, and Joseph!" She sat down with a thud on a hard gray vinyl chair next to a matching gray-and-white plaid table—the kitchen was retro, very chic in a 1950s sort of way. "Take a moment to collect yourself, Mrs. O'Doherty. I know this has come as a blow to you, but my partner and I need to ask you a few questions and get a list of employees and their phone numbers from you."

Jenny O'Doherty drank her coffee like it was a shot of scotch, then poured herself another cup. She was nodding at him as if she understood every word he said, but he knew she was merely agreeing with her own shock. In a few minutes he'd have to tell her they were dead again, and then they'd be able to get some information from her. He and Gary waited.

Lochwood took it as a good sign that she didn't start playing hostess again. It meant the impact of what had happened was sinking in, but even he didn't expect the question that came out of her mouth next.

"Well, if you're here about Gabe and Beka, where the hell is George?"

* * *

As soon as the morning sit was over Hans changed out of his monk's robes, put on his overalls, and headed for Beka's house in his old mail truck. Maybe he had misunderstood. He thought Beka had asked if they could meet after the morning *zazen*, but maybe she'd meant he was supposed to come to her house. They'd done that sometimes, when she couldn't get away.

After Beka had retired from the world of dance, she'd been on the fringe of things. She had tried to become a businesswoman of sorts and started a Pilates studio, but it didn't seem to fit her nature. Hans had sensed an even deeper unrest in the past six months, a fidgeting of her spirit accompanied by a sadness in her eyes, as if she knew the answer to something unanswerable, but not the question. He could feel the anxiety radiating from her body when they meditated together, and couldn't help but be concerned.

Hans's best friend was Devon's father, and he could remember the first time Devon came to the zendo with Beka. They had been reading Lao Tze in high school, and Evan Halsey had thought they should experience a real meditation service. They sat *zazen* for half an hour without a giggle, so Hans invited them back. They had started coming whenever they were out visiting Devon's parents, and had even found a place to sit in the city. Devon's visits eventually tapered off, but in the past three years Beka had become a more serious Zen practitioner.

His mail truck pulled up the driveway and almost directly into a bright perimeter of yellow police tape, sputtered, then coughed to a stop as a uniformed officer came down the drive.

"You got mail?" the officer asked, despite the holiday.

Hans shook his balding head. "I'm a friend. What's happened?"

"There's been a murder."

Hans's hands began to shake. "Is Beka okay?"

"What's your name, sir?"

"Hans. Where is Ms. Imamura?"

The officer made a note. "And how do you know the deceased?"

"She's dead?"

"They're both dead, sir."

The Buddhist monk began to cross himself, an involuntary action that his arm muscles had learned years ago when he was a young boy. He stopped in sudden confusion. "I have to see Devon Halsey."

"She's left the scene, sir."

"Devon was here?" He was speaking more to himself, rolling the thought through his mind and over his tongue.

"Can I see some ID, sir?"

"Thank you, but I know where she lives." Hans turned the truck's steering wheel almost a full hundred and eighty degrees and sped down the road toward Sag Harbor.

* * *

Loch and Gary finally quieted Jenny O'Doherty enough to get a few questions answered, but between the deaths of her employers and her errant husband, it was difficult to tell who she was sniffing and sobbing over.

"I haven't seen them since Christmas Eve. Gabe gave everyone the week off."

"Was there anything out of the ordinary going on in the household or at work?"

"Beka seemed depressed, but she was like that, and they were bickering more than usual." She sipped her coffee and then added, "She broke a bust up in the studio—aimed it at Gabe's head. He ducked."

Lochwood looked at Gary and raised his eyebrows. "She must have been fairly strong to throw a plaster bust."

"We called her mighty-mite." She looked at them confidingly. "She has outbursts. Gabe calls them rage attacks. I call them temper tantrums."

Loch noticed that she had gone back to referring to them in the present tense and did not bother to correct her.

"Had Beka cut her hair recently?"

"Rapunzel? You've got to be kidding! It bothered her to see it come out in the hairbrush. She was like Samson about her hair. She'd die first!"

So the hair was a mystery—Loch made a note about it while his partner asked if she thought Beka could have killed her husband.

"Right now, I think any woman could kill her husband." She laughed, looking at the clock and clicking her nails on the ceramic side of her coffee mug. "Do you boys leave your wives alone all night without so much as a howdy-do?"

Loch was certainly not going to volunteer any information.

"Aside from your personal feelings for husbands at this moment, do you think Beka Imamura was capable of murder?"

She sighed. "Given the right circumstances, anyone is capable of murder."

"What about other employees? Is there anyone else we should know about?" Gary asked.

"Gabe had two apprentices from Pratt working as interns in his studio. They went home for Christmas break and aren't due back until next semester. End of January, I believe."

"Are they local?"

"Aaron lives in Woodstock. Lucas in Delaware."

"We'll need their phone numbers." She nodded absently but didn't move.

"How was Mr. Montebello to work for?" Lochwood asked.

"Temperamental, particular, but once you know his idiosyncrasies and figure out how to work around them, he's fine. Some of the interns have trouble dealing with his ego, but they're young and have egos of their own. He's the only artist I know who has a cleaning lady come in to scrub the floors and walls twice a year. She dusts every other week."

"When was the last time she came in?"

"Just before Christmas." She began to cry, softly. "I can't believe they're dead. Why? Who would do such a thing?"

"Is there someone you can think of who would want to kill them?"

"No one. I mean, Beka had a fight with Edilio last week but I don't think it was cause for murder."

"Who's Edilio?" Gary asked.

"Her old dance partner. They started a Pilates studio out here a few years back."

"Do you know what the fight was about?"

"It had nothing to do with Beka's business, but as I was leaving Christmas Eve I heard him saying, 'You're not going to screw me!' And she said, 'I already have.'" Jenny blew her nose and looked at the clock on the kitchen wall. "Do you mind if I get dressed?"

"Just one more thing, ma'am. Where were you last night between eleven and one?"

"Waiting for George. We were going to Gurney's in Montauk for dinner and their New Year's Eve celebration. It cost five hundred dollars for those reservations, but did he show up? Like we can afford to throw around money like that! We're part of the Hamptons working poor, you know. There are poor people who live out here. We were here way before the rest of 'em!" She tossed back her third cup of coffee and snorted. "I was all dressed up with nowhere to go, gentlemen. And if Gabe left Beka in the same cir-cumstance, I think that would be called justifiable homicide."

CHAPTER NINE

Alas, how should you?
She knows not herself,
In all her mystery.

—LORD BYRON, *The Two Foscari*

Except for the occasional bigwig popping his head in to see how they were doing and checking to make sure they'd been approved for overtime, Frank and Devon had been able to work uninterrupted all morning and finished logging all of the evidence by ten a.m.

"You feel like pulling some of the latents now?" Frank asked.

"I sure don't feel like going to sleep," Devon answered, pouring them both another cup of coffee.

"I thought I'd get started on that sword."

"I'll take the bottle." She pulled the bag with the Jack Daniel's bottle in it and wrote "*10:05, 14B, latents*" on the evidence sheet and signed her name.

Frank did the same with the sword, then looked around the room for a container that was large enough to hold it. He held up a garbage bag and compared its size with the sword. "This should work."

"I'll get a hanger." She walked into the coed changing room and pulled a wire hanger off the coat rack. When she came back, Frank was standing on a chair and removing the philodendron from over the Crime Scene secretary's desk. They constructed a makeshift tent for the sword and secured it to the plant hanger with wire. Then, just before securing the opening at the top of the tent, Frank put a few drops of superglue on the hanger and tied it shut.

Devon placed the watered-down contents from the Jack Daniel's bottle into a petri dish, then viewed it through a magnifying glass. Little white dustlike particles clung to the sides of the vial. "Frank? What do you make of this?"

He peered into the plastic cylinder from over her shoulder. "Looks like something was added."

"And somebody tried to wash it out?"

"Let the lab analyze it, but that's what it looks like to me."

She had already swabbed the interior at the scene, but now she carefully poured the rest of the liquid into a container—more was always better when it came to chemical analysis. She covered the dish and labeled it. "Beka hated bourbon. Why'd she drink it?"

"Maybe she didn't."

"She drugged him so he was easier to kill, then took an overdose herself?"

"Seems likely."

She didn't say anything. On the other side of the lab was a worn-out aluminum box with ghostly white specks covering the inside. She placed the bottle inside the tank, covered the top, and poured a small amount of superglue from its industrial container into an opening at the bottom of the tank. It would only take a few minutes for the adhesive to attach to the oily residue from any fingerprints.

Frank sat down to wait the procedures out. He was a good partner, fair and loyal. He had been the first one on the unit to shake her hand and had never acted demeaning toward her. Frank—the most senior detective in the Crime Scene squad—treated her like an equal. It was an enormous change from what she was used to, and what she had gone through before her promotion.

Lochwood had seemed different than the rest of the squad, always asking her what her career goals were, not what she was doing later that night. Despite her better judgment that he was just another cop who wanted to get laid, she had finally gone out for coffee with him one night. They began to meet after their shifts to share stories, drink coffee—that was all. She knew he had a wife. But everyone had a wife.

He liked to run license plates on the police computer anchored to the dashboard of his car. One night the car ahead of them came up stolen, and Loch winked at her as he put on the flashing lights. He took the driver while she sprinted after the passenger and tackled him to the ground. Instead of getting dinner that night they got a collar—that was their first real date.

She had fifteen years on the force when a new sergeant was transferred to her unit who took an immediate dislike to her. He treated her like a rookie, made "dumb blonde" jokes, and refused to acknowledge work that should have been written up for merit. He'd put her on the desk for weeks on end and for no reason at all, or show up at her car in the middle of the night to harass her. She did not tell Lochwood what was going on; she figured she could handle it herself.

She dealt with the new sergeant, but when Loch started noticing that she was not getting the accommodations she should have been, and was spending a lot of time at the desk, he began to ask questions. Finally, she told him how her sergeant was destroying her morale. "I thought this was my niche. You know? Like, I had finally found my place in the world. Now I just feel like resigning." She dabbed her eyes with a dirty napkin.

He reached into his pocket and pulled out not a handkerchief—Loch was not a hanky kind of guy—but a microcassette tape recorder. "It has a clip-on microphone. He'll never know. Take the tape to your PBA rep. Don't play it. Just show it to her. They'll make him go away."

She did what he told her. Her sergeant was transferred a few weeks later. One year, two accommodations, and an exam later, she was finally promoted to detective. It was Loch's quiet response to her situation that made her trust him as much as she now trusted Frank. She had never known a man who could be so strong and courageous, tough and funny, caring and compassionate at the same time. A good partner was hard to find.

Frank was watching her, a trace of concern quickly slipping from his eyes as she looked up at him. He walked over to the sword and peered through the plastic bag to see how the superglue was adhering to any latents. "I wonder how many blood types are on this sword."

"Well, we know one of them is Gabriel's."

"Maybe there's some ancient samurai's blood on it, too." He sounded twelve years old.

"Cool," she mocked him gently. "We don't get much call for samurai blood analysis, do we?"

Frank looked more closely at the sword hilt. "How long did you say your friend had this sword?"

"Her parents died in 1974. She inherited it then. Beka was so un-Japanese, she hung it over the doorway of the loft. Then Uncle Bismarck comes to visit and has a fit! It's bad luck to hang a sword over someone's door. It means death to the house." Devon stopped. "Beka told him it was just a superstition and she was American so it didn't count. Then Todd disappeared."

Devon opened up the glue tank and pulled the bottle out with a pair of metal tongs. "Look at that." A nearly perfect print hung, as if suspended, on the inside of the bottle's neck.

"It's a beaut," Frank agreed. "Strange place, though."

She placed it on her desk, photographed the print, and studied the rest of the area. There wasn't one bump or smudge on the rest of the glass. It didn't make sense. The print was wide, like a man's finger, rather than Beka's long, tapered digits. Devon put it back in its bag.

"Too bad there aren't any prints on this." Frank interrupted her ruminations with the removal of the sword from its plastic entombment. The two of them surveyed the sword scrupulously, but quickly. Prints were so obvious with the glue method of exposure that they didn't need to search too hard. The sword, aside from the blood, was clean.

* * *

Loch speared a pepperonchini with his fork and pushed a calamata olive around his plate with his knife. The three interviews he and Gary had conducted in the aftermath of New Year's Eve had found nothing even slightly helpful regarding the fates of Gabe and Beka. Secretly, he had hoped that something would appear in their questioning of the employees at the Art Barn that would prove that Beka had not murdered her husband, but everything everyone had told them pointed to the obvious. It sounded to Loch as if Beka was emotionally unstable, and that would fit the profile he was building on her character. All three employees had verified that Beka and Gabe fought a lot, and that often the fights turned physical, with Beka leading the violence. She broke things—doors, windows, bottles, molds—but would those kinds of outbursts have led to the violent aftermath they had discovered?

Lochwood had met Gabriel and Beka a number of times. Of course, he was always with Devon and their encounters were at social events, usually one of the parties the couple threw, but on a rare occasion they had all gone out to dinner together. He'd never been able to peg Gabe and Beka as a unit, though—it was as if they lived two separate lives—but then, who didn't? Even Devon seemed to be keeping Loch separate from her other life in the Hamptons, and he was no different. He thought about Jenny O'Doherty's errant husband and popped a chunk of feta into his mouth. He should call his own wife.

* * *

Devon wasn't sure she was ready to hear what Jo had to say. Autopsies were almost like the ritual of Sky Burial in the Tibetan Buddhist tradition. Hans had once told her that Sky Burial was the most intimate experience one could have with another person. In the ceremony, a monk feeds sacred vultures the body of the dead, then the bones are crushed to powder and thrown to the wind. What was an autopsy other than an American version of Sky Burial? And she and Loch, Gary, and Jo were the vultures looking for tidbits of information. Devon was not Tibetan, though.

Maybe looking at the autopsy as a ritual would help her detach from her emotions, but she wasn't sure thinking about Sky Burial would help. She just wanted to find the truth, even if it hurt. Devon looked down at the print she was working on and squinted to make sure she was seeing the ridges accurately, then absentmindedly pulled her dark blond hair back and tied it into a knot behind her head without the help of any clip or other hair accoutrements.

"I'll never figure out how you do that." She heard Loch's voice behind her. His own hair was short and graying at the temples, almost exactly matching the gray sky outside the lab window. She wanted him to hold her, right there in front of the rest of the damn department, but providing their peers with something more than circumstantial evidence of their affair was not high on her list of New Year's resolutions.

"So, are you going to tell me what you think about this case or keep it to yourself?" she asked.

"You tell me." Loch faltered at the brusqueness in her voice.

Her eyes felt damp so she blinked, hard. "It's not her. I know that."

"Knowing is different than feeling." His voice was soft and soothing, and she recognized it immediately as the tone he used whenever someone seemed emotionally distraught. She did not appreciate his civilian procedures being applied to her. That was the problem with cops, they always knew too much.

"You're a therapist now?"

"Let's just say I've done this for a few more years than you."

She was about to tell him what he could do with all his years, but stopped herself.

He tried again. "If you need anything you'd tell me, right? I don't know what to do to help, but if you tell me what you need, I can give it to you."

She smiled. "That's better, Brennen." She could see the tension in his neck and shoulders release; he'd finally found the right thing to say.

* * *

The morgue was air-conditioned even in the winter, and Lochwood hoped his woolen socks and coat would suffice. Jo, who had been working in the coroner's office for twenty years, wore a turtleneck. She probably had more turtlenecks at home than the L.L. Bean and Eddie Bauer catalogs combined. Coming from the South had not prepared her for cold weather or morgue life, and the woman seemed to be in a perpetual state of refrigeration—not unlike her corpses. That Jo was a rambunctious, warm individual was probably, in Lochwood's professional opinion, a subconscious attempt to raise her body temperature

He peeked through the viewing window and knocked on the examining room door before they entered. "How you doing, Jo?"

Her pink turtleneck peeked out from under her lab coat. "Lower than a snake's belly. How're you two?" Jo slurped a Jolt soda, specially shipped from North Carolina, through a silly straw and tapped her Bart Simpson eraser-head pencil as if sending a Morse code message to her assistant on the other side of the room. "Where's DeBritzi? It's a holiday, you know. I'm only here out of the goodness of my heart, even if I am getting paid double." She winked at Devon. "Can I start or do I have to wait for that lamebrain partner of yours?"

Gary popped into the examining room. "Sorry I'm late, Jo. Thanks for waiting for me."

She tapped her watch with Bart Simpson's head. "I wasn't waiting for you. We just finished up." She looked over at Devon and winked again, then nodded as if she'd decided Devon looked steady enough to begin. "Okay, let's do it. It's like I said at the scene, the stomach wound killed him. There are precisely eighteen stab wounds, and except for the scribbles, nothing else unusual." Loch had to smile, only Jo would say that about such a scene.

"What you see is almost exactly what you get," Jo continued. Loch and Gary made few notes. They hadn't expected any surprises, but the unexpected was always possible, even in Suffolk County, where there were fewer homicides in a year than occurred in Manhattan in a month. "The depth of the wounds is fairly consistent if one takes into account that there was a struggle. There's bruising and a few scratch marks to verify a scuffle. Your murderer might have skin under the fingernails." Lochwood cleared his throat. "Yes, we took scrapings from under both of their nails, and as soon as the lab opens," Jo looked pointedly at Loch, "we'll test for DNA."

"Of course, they could have each other's skin under the fingers for a number of reasons other than murder. They were married." Devon pointed out the obvious.

Jo never speculated on the events that might have led up to a death. She simply stated what consequence the wounds, and other telling marks, had on the victim. She continued her recitation of the facts. She could tell the detectives from what direction a foreign instrument (bullet or knife blade) had entered the body, which hand had been used, and what impact the instrument had had on a victim's vital organs, but she never told them what she thought had happened outside of the physical evidence. "There is something other than skin under his fingernails."

Gary and Loch looked up at her expectantly. They were used to her springing a dramatic moment on them whenever she had the privilege of finding something unusual.

"Powder?" Devon piped up. She knew she had ruined Jo's riddle but couldn't help herself. Jo tapped Bart Simpson's head on the aluminum examining table.

"What kind of powder?" Lochwood asked.

"We found Norflex at the scene," Devon said.

"You can't know anything for sure till we have the lab results though, can you?" Jo gave Devon the stink eye.

"I'm depending on you, Jo." Loch cast a glance at Devon in the hope that she would let him run the rest of the investigation; she paused long enough for him to ask, "How long?"

"You love to rush me, don't you, Brennen? You think just cause I'm Southern, I'm slow?" He didn't answer. "Well, then don't get all twisted up over nothing. When they get back from *their* holiday, they'll run it. Don't blame my people when it takes all day to get what you want."

"I hate holidays," Loch mumbled under his breath.

Jo ignored him. "He hadn't eaten much of a supper: Brie, French bread, olives, and what looked like roasted peppers. He'd had a bit to drink, and time of death was right around midnight, give or take a few minutes."

"Any fingerprints in the bloodstains on the body?" Gary asked. Jo shook her head.

"Could the stab wounds have been made by a woman who's five foot seven inches, Jo?" That was Beka's height. Devon knew she should have let Loch ask the question, but she wasn't about to let it slide. She had to know the answer.

Jo wiggled Bart's head in the air, held the pencil at a tilt, and squinted her eyes together. "Did the woman have on heels?"

"There were significant foot impressions made by bare feet." Devon looked directly at Loch, daring him to stop her. "People had to remove their shoes before entering the house. The chance of any-one, even a murderer, wearing shoes in the house is very small."

"There are seven wounds on the shoulders and chest that come down at this angle." She demonstrated with her Bart pencil. "He was five foot eleven inches, so, I would say the assailant had to be his height or taller. But if he had been bent over, or on his hands and knees, or even sitting, a shorter person could have inflicted them."

Gabe had crawled down the hallway, Devon recollected, so five foot seven was not a problem. She could tell by Loch's face he was thinking along the same lines.

"In fact, the murderer could have been taller or shorter, depending on his position when he received the wounds. Isn't that right, Jo?" Jo nodded in answer to Lochwood's question. "Can you tell which wounds were made first? That might help us figure height better, since we know where he ended up on all fours."

Jo looked at the wounds on the corpse with the help of her assis-tant and mumbled a few things under her breath that Devon couldn't hear, then stood up and cussed. "This was done good. Looky here, he was stabbed in the stomach prior to the sword! It's hard to see, but there's a smaller entrance wound just to the right here." She showed Loch and Gary what she was talking about.

"From the scene it looked as if the attack began in the living room by the fireplace. If he was stabbed in the stomach first that might have caused him to double over," Devon suggested. "Then we get the shoulder wounds." Jo was nodding as Devon pointed to the wounds she thought came next in the attack. "There were long spatter marks that would not have been initially debilitating, so he tried to escape."

"The spurting you're describing probably came from these wounds by the bicep tendon." Jo pointed to four wounds near the shoulder artery. "But everything happened so fast, there's very little time differential here." Jo maneuvered the flesh around with a meas-uring instrument. "The angle is downward and into the shoulder, consistent with someone who was taller than the victim. Unless, as Devon suggests, he was doubled over when he received those four wounds."

"The other stab wounds could have been delivered in the hall where we have proof that he was on his hands and knees."

"You've just proved the murderer could have been Beka," Loch informed her.

Jo continued reciting a litany of facts. "The stomach wound was circular. It entered under the right rib, came up to the lungs under the left rib, and then into the stomach."

"Left-handed?" Loch returned to his questioning.

"Possibly. A right-handed thrust would most likely have been in the reverse."

"Is Beka left-handed?" Loch asked Devon.

"Gabriel was also."

"Gabriel did not commit *hara-kiri* and then go hang up the sword after he wiped it down," Loch said.

Jo countered, "If it is a Norflex overdose, the drug would have caused a coma and convulsions an hour after the drug was in her system. But y'all have to wait until I can tell you for sure if that's what she took."

"She took something, though?" Devon urged Jo.

"It's a possibility."

"And if she was drugged," Devon continued, "she certainly couldn't have killed him in a stupor, walked up that hill, and killed herself." She gave Loch an I-told-you-so look. "The media is all ready to fry her and serve her up to the public. Let's not assume she's guilty just because she's dead, Brennen."

"I'm not assuming anything," Brennen replied. "But I expect you to find the facts and find the murderer no matter who it is."

"And I will!" she almost yelled at him.

"I know you will!" His eyes blazed back at her, an equal opponent on a level playing field.

"Are you two through? Ken and I want to have our black-eyed peas and collards before the year 2003! And we do have another body." Jo started washing her hands as Devon pulled out the print tray.

"You really think what you eat New Year's day brings you luck?" Lochwood asked.

"What are you going to do for luck, celebrate the New Year by arresting someone?"

Gary and Jo chuckled. He gave them a small smile, but Devon

had to wonder when she and Loch were going to start building traditions outside of the department. On their second date they had busted a serial convenience-store robber, on their third they had stopped an attempted murder. Loch's idea of a date was multiple arrests first, multiple orgasms later.

Devon wanted something more than working cases together, clandestine coffee clutches, and making love on the sly. But what was that something? Sometimes she wanted him to leave his wife, so they could at least have a chance to see if they worked as a couple. Sometimes she was afraid he would leave his wife, and then they'd have to face each other completely, with no way out. She liked her independence and didn't want to have to answer to anyone. Then again, the thought of life without Loch seemed bleak and dull.

She still wasn't sure why she had dropped the dating scene and become exclusive with Loch. Maybe it was because she knew that even though he was married he wasn't seeing anyone else, including his poor wife. Devon was touched that Loch couldn't leave Marty, and, while it got in the way of their relationship, she couldn't help but respect him for not abandoning his schizophrenic wife. It wasn't as though Devon wanted to settle down and have a family, was it? That was not on her list of priorities. She had played around with the idea of adopting and raising a kid, but didn't see how anyone could do that and have her career. She certainly didn't know how the other female cops did it, and didn't see them enough to ask.

Jo and Loch took off their lab coats in preparation to go to the next autopsy room and left Devon to print the victim alone. She didn't think about Gabriel Montebello the artist and friend as she pressed the ink roller across his palm. Instead she thought about the crime that had been committed against him. It was the act of malevolence that she was concerned with, not her own sense of loss. With the palm prints secured, she rolled each finger, pulling the body's own uncopyable Social Security identification form.

Finished with the first body, Devon hesitated outside the door of Beka's autopsy room. Loch and Gary were standing in front of her and blocking the upper portion of the body. She waited and watched Jo move around the room with her scalpel, speaking into her microphone about the cause of death. Devon inhaled deeply, then shut the door behind her with barely a click of the latch, staying inconspicuous along the perimeter of the room.

"We have a dilemma here, guys," Jo was saying to Loch and Gary. "She slit her wrists, and I'd hazard to say loss of blood was the cause of death. But look at her eyes."

Devon looked, then turned her head.

"What was time of death, Jo?" Gary asked.

"Twenty to thirty minutes after Gabriel Montebello's. I can't tell you what her blood-alcohol level was yet." She smiled at Loch as if she'd beat him to the question. "But I can tell you the stomach contents." She noticed Devon at that moment, then spoke to her assistant. "We'll run a chem test for Norflex; that seems most likely considering the prescription found at the scene. The dilation in the pupil indicates cardiac arrest—possibly from drugs. I've seen it before. People who really want to die have a back-up plan. And if she really wanted to die, she might have OD'd to help stem the pain of slitting her wrists. The answer will be in the heart, but I'm not sure we're ready for a Y incision yet." She looked at Devon.

Devon wasn't sure she was ever going to be ready for that. Her eyes burned. "Maybe I should print her first, then you can finish," she suggested.

Jo stepped back from the body and pulled her gloves off. "Why don't we leave you alone for a few moments. Come on, boys."

Devon tried to nod her appreciation and say thank you, but could not find her voice. She felt Loch's hand on her shoulder as they left the room, and the tears she had held at bay for thirteen hours finally soothed the heat in her eyes. She didn't hear the door shut, but she could tell the room was empty by the absence of anyone else's breathing. "I'm sorry," she whispered, as she reached out to hold her best friend's hand for the last time.

CHAPTER TEN

For I knew that I would pay dearly
In prison, in the grave, in the madhouse,
Wherever someone like me must awaken.

—J. BRODSKY, About the 1910's

Immediately after Beka's autopsy Devon and Loch headed out of the M.E. building. He could tell she was upset by the furrowed line between her eyebrows, but he didn't want to push her to confide in him. "See you later?"

She shook her head. "I need some time alone. I've got something on the Jack Daniel's bottle that doesn't fit."

"What's that?"

"The label, for one thing."

"I just figured she was bonding with the bottle, remembering Todd Daniels, and feeling sorry for herself."

"I found a print inside the neck of it." She pressed her car's remote and automatically unlocked the driver's door from across the lot.

"Whose?"

"I don't know yet. There's another set of prints on the knife."

"What?"

"Yep, and they don't match the print in the bottle. There's also a waxy residue on the knife, very strange."

"Is it possible the print inside the bottle was left there by someone doing that whole ritual of rinsing then drying recyclables?"

"Oh come on! If Beka was feeling so sentimental why would she wipe her prints off the outside of the bottle after she ripped part of the label off?"

"Dev, I know where you're going with this, but just because she didn't shoot him like most spouses do nowadays doesn't mean she didn't kill him. She was Japanese. Different."

Devon looked stunned. "She was American! I know more about Japanese culture than she does! *Did*."

He knew he'd slipped up, but he couldn't bring himself to admit it. "You're so close to this case you can't trust your own nose. You're a damn good detective, but take Frank's lead. Face it, you are connected to this. Finding out that your best friend is capable of murder is a horrifying thought. I can't even imagine what you're feeling right now."

She was finally listening to him, and as he spoke he saw the defensive line along her forehead drop from her face.

"You've lost two friends." He took her hand and squeezed it. "It looks like she took an overdose with complete foreknowledge that she was going to kill her husband and then kill herself—if that's true, then she staged a death scene and the whole house is a theater set, right down to where she left his body. We're talking about an actress here. She wasn't just a dancer and you know it. Beka was always staging scenes, in public and in private, and the bottle was one of her props, just like the sword."

"And if it isn't how it looks?" she asked coolly.

"Then somebody else staged the scene. But we have to figure out what is real first," he reminded her. "Put yourself in my position, Devon. If this was all an act, I need you to be aware of what that means." He let his words sink in. "She knew you were working last night. She knew you would be at the scene. Isn't it possible that she left that Jack Daniel's bottle for you?"

"She didn't cut her own hair, Loch. I know that."

"How? Intuition?" He softened his voice but spoke plainly and clearly. "You didn't even know she was leaving her husband."

She kicked the snow into the pavement. He knew that she was kicking herself and pondering the same question that had occurred to him but he would never voice—what kind of best friend was she? They hadn't spoken in almost six months. What did that make Beka, an ex–best friend? A dead ex–best friend.

"If there's a message from her on your machine when you get home, I want you to remember what I said. What if, and this is a big if, Devon, but it's one I have to examine . . ." He looked her straight in the eyes. "What if Beka wanted to fuck with you? Isn't it possible that she left you personal clues because of the fight you two had?"

He saw her wince but could not regret his words. He was a tough investigator; that's what made him a good detective, not mincing around the obvious or ignoring the less apparent.

"It's not possible," she said sadly, "but maybe that's what happened."

She left him standing in the precinct parking lot feeling as if he had kicked her guts out. He could feel the chasm inside her and wanted to fill it so the pain and loss would go away. He hadn't felt like that in a long time—the desire to cherish someone so badly it hurt. He couldn't stand to see her leave him behind, but as he watched she got in her car and drove off without looking back.

He had two choices: He could continue working or he could swing by the house and check on his daughter and his wife. Normally he would have kept working the case, but he felt he owed at least an appearance to his daughter—Marty wouldn't notice one way or the other. He followed the faint trace of Devon's green tea perfume still lingering in the air to his car and got in.

He patted the head of the toy dalmatian Devon had given him which had taken up permanent residence on his dashboard. She had found it in the Staten Island dumps while sorting through the rubble and debris of 9/11. It was the kind that belonged on a fireman's dashboard. It looked like her dog Boo with a patch of soot around the eye. She had slipped it into her pocket, unwilling to leave it behind in the remains and ruins of so many lives. Covered with dirt and smelling like tragedy, the head now bobbed at him happily innocent.

The drive home took less than ten minutes, and for fun he ran license plates on his computer as he followed unknowing holiday travelers down the LIE Usually, Devon would be right in there with him, running tags, speculating on the passengers in the cars they passed. He felt alone, and as much as he hated to admit it to himself, it didn't feel right.

The Brennen house was as nondescript as the neighborhood within which it was nestled. Everything was typical of a suburban neighborhood, with about as much care and forethought as the plastic houses in a Monopoly game. It was inside his house that the scene changed.

He walked in the back door and through the kitchen where his daughter Brea, unsurprisingly, was on the phone. She waved, then turned her back on him in order to preserve her privacy. He squeezed her shoulder and headed upstairs to Marty's room.

He knocked twice. Waited. Then announced, "Marty, it's me," as he opened the door.

"They were here again." Her voice was so tiny and high-pitched she sounded like a cartoon character.

He kissed her forehead and sat down next to her. "That wasn't real, honey."

"But I heard them."

"I know." He couldn't go into it tonight. The doctor had told him to be specific with her every time she spoke about her delusions, but he knew she would argue for her hallucinations and he didn't have the energy tonight to fight her insanity.

"I told them you were a cop and would arrest them if they didn't leave." She was sitting, as she always was, in the center of the room with all the curtains drawn.

"Did that work?"

"They always come when you're gone. Why can't you be here more?"

"I'm staking out the house, honey. You know, I'm right outside."

"They're so sneaky. How do they get past you?"

They had had eight fairly happy years before she had a psychotic break. Two years later she was an agoraphobic with occasional delusions, and then she had had another episode.

He could deal with the fear of going outside. He was a cop after all and knew better than anyone all that was out there to be afraid of, but then she began to deteriorate into full-blown delusions. Brea had been nine when her mother was finally diagnosed with late-onset paranoid schizophrenia. Her weight had escalated from a hundred and twenty-five pounds to two hundred and fifty—the larger she became, the safer she felt. They had to monitor her food intake or she would still be growing.

She hadn't been dangerous. That was not the type of delusion her mind inflicted on them. For a couple of years she had even been able to cook dinner and get Brea off to school; she just couldn't go out of the house. Then, in Brea's freshmen year of middle school, Marty stopped taking her medication and had an even worse episode. She spent six months in a residential-care facility before coming home, and when she finally returned, she wouldn't leave her bedroom. His mother-in-law came to their house during the day to care for her daughter and her granddaughter while Lochwood worked to pay for the mortgage and a part-time nurse, and save the world. He had met Devon a year before Marty's last and most devastating episode. Lochwood had thought his life was over. Devon made him see that it wasn't over yet.

He looked at the woman he had once loved so much, a woman he still loved but hadn't really seen in years. She barely resembled the girl in the wedding photographs on her dressing table.

She patted his hand as if she were the one comforting him. "You won't let them hurt us?"

"They can't hurt us, honey." *They* were part of her delusion, and while Lochwood wasn't sure who *they* included, he had a feeling anybody outside of the immediate household was eligible.

"They'll try. You know that."

"How's your mom today?"

"She's crazy."

He chuckled; secretly he agreed with her assessment of his mother-in-law, but her mother was not the one taking anti-psychotic drugs. "Did you take your meds?" His voice was patient and calm, the same voice he used when speaking to children.

"I don't like them," she whined.

"I know. Where's the bottle?"

She pointed to the table where the nurse had left a tray of food, a glass of juice. "How can you know who I am if I'm always taking something to make me different?"

"Honey, you get more scared if you don't take your meds. Remember?" She shook her head. "Come on, we'll take them together."

"I like when we do that." She looked up at him adoringly.

He brought the tray over to her side and handed her the glass of juice and four pills. "Ready? One, two, three, upsy daisy!" He tilted his head back as if he were swallowing the pills with her. Her eyes watched him as she mimicked his movements. "Now they'll stay away all night."

"You always say that."

"Am I right?"

"Always right." Her voice had the singsong lilt, like a teeter-totter going up and down. Loch hated the way it made his skin crawl—worse, though, he hated feeling that way. Her illness betrayed more than her mind; it had betrayed her family.

"I have to go back to my watch."

"You'll be outside?"

"Always am."

"I just can't see you."

"That's right."

She nodded absently; a shadow of sadness crossed her face as tears began to seep into her eyes.

He kissed her forehead again. It was all he could do to keep from running out of her room and the house altogether. He could handle serial killers, acts of terrorism, murder, fire, car accidents; he could handle the mentally ill in crisis situations. He had thought he could handle anything—he'd been wrong. The routine, the drain of her illness, was a never-ending limbo he had no way of escaping.

Then there was the hope Devon gave him. When he'd found her, he'd found an equal partner, both physically and intellectually. But how long would she wait for him to make up his mind?

His daughter was off the phone by the time he reached the kitchen. "Happy New Year, honey." He kissed her forehead, too.

"Happy New Year, Daddy. Grandma went out to the store, but she wants to talk to you."

"I don't want to talk to Grandma."

"About Mom."

"Especially about Mom. Tell her I've got a murder investigation I have to get back to." He did not want to talk to his mother-in-law.

"Dad?"

"What, sweetheart?"

"I'm gonna move out. Me and Sabrina found a place to share."

He felt as if he'd just been socked in the stomach. "Not now, Brea. Please don't leave now."

"I'm eighteen."

"It's not that."

"I can't stay here." Her eyes silently pleaded with him.

"I know."

"I'm going to finish the year at Stonybrook, but then I want to go to the University of Colorado, in Boulder."

"So far?" She nodded. "We'll talk."

"When?"

"Soon as this investigation is clear, in a few days. I have to go." He kissed her again and walked back outside. How could he stop her from running away when he couldn't stop himself?

* * *

Devon pushed the hair scrunchies she had wrapped around the gear-shift up to the steering wheel and watched them pop back. She picked up the beanbag head on her dashboard and plopped it down hard. *"I'm not that kind of girl!"* Mean Harriet scolded. Even that did not make her smile.

Her jeep was a collection of work and play. In the side pocket of the door she had a pair of handcuffs, mace, rouge, and lip gloss. Between the passenger and driver's seats, beneath the coffee cup holders, was a spare gun, a torch light, a lint roller (to remove dog hair), the Toons' Tasmanian Devil, two flares, an all-in-one tool, some foundation and face powder, a Slinky, two more pairs of handcuffs, mouthwash, a Lady Schick razor, antiperspirant, a traffic-ticket book, a Bart Simpson eraser-head pencil (a gift from Jo), and tampons. There was a roll of crime-scene tape circling the coffee cup, a tool kit under one seat, a crime-scene kit under the other, and a makeup kit in the glove compartment. On the visor on the driver's side of the car she had a mirror with a picture of Charlie's Angels in bikinis next to it, and on the passenger-side visor there was a strobe light for pulling idiots off the road. Devon was ready for anything, anything but her best friend's murder or possible suicide. She plopped Mean Harriet down on the dash-board again—the head did not respond. Even Devon's toys weren't working right.

She let the highway abscond with her thoughts until time and space merged into one and she was suddenly, a half-hour later, on the crosscut heading to Sag Harbor and just seven miles from home. The light was beginning to slant from the west as she drove past Whalebone Landing and Trout Pond, the haunts of her youth. She took Long Beach to North Haven because it was the prettier route home. The water was so still it looked like a slice of mica, and the sun, dipping toward the horizon despite the fact that it was four in the afternoon, cast a rosy glow over the surface. Other cops and detectives who lived closer in to work never understood the reason the drive was worth her time, but crossing the Sag Harbor bridge and the stormy blue of the bay, Devon was reminded once again why she had made the decision to live so far out on the East End.

On Bay Street she slowed down to the maximum 20-mph speed limit and slowly coasted toward her grandmother's old house. Its Victorian roof and the graceful bend of the porch appeared even older amid the renovated homes of the nouveau riche. Devon's family fought to maintain the original qualities that once made Sag Harbor unique in the world, and that meant they hadn't painted the house since 1968—or was it 1958?

Directly across the street from her house an ugly battleship-gray monstrosity some jerk had built simply because "he could" loomed. She and Aileen called it the Mausoleum. Now, if someone had murdered him or his architect she would have understood, but Gabe and Beka? It didn't make sense.

The Imamura-Montebello family had lived typical East End artist lives—they had opened their home to up-and-coming talent, fostered and mentored many new names in the art and dance worlds, and were generally acknowledged, if not liked, by everyone. True, she and Beka hadn't talked as much as they once had in their youth, when every decision they made depended on the other's opinion. But they still got together for lunch or talked on the phone every few weeks, and they always spoke every New Year's Eve, until this one. This was after they'd had that stupid argument last summer at the annual Sag Pond clam-bake.

"Ten years is too long to be waiting in the wings, Dev," Beka had concluded after fifteen minutes of disagreement over Devon's love life. "You're a principal dancer, not *corps de ballet*."

Devon was tired of being judged and ridiculed, and angry with Beka for continually picking on her relationship with Lochwood. "You don't understand," she snapped. "Loch and I aren't like one of your affairs!" She felt evil as she said the words but couldn't stop herself.

"My affairs ended when I married Gabe, they didn't begin!"

"Loch loves me. His wife is ill, and I *can* understand why he stays with her."

"You believe that load of crap? You're a cop, how gullible can you be?"

"I must be pretty gullible to think you weren't doing coke back in the '80s."

"Everyone did it. And don't go acting all high and mighty with me. You could party just as much as the next person."

"At least I didn't let partying get in the way of my life."

"No, you let life get in the way of your art!"

"That's always what it comes back to, isn't it? I stopped being an artist. Did it ever occur to you that I am doing *my* art?" She could see Beka fighting back the word "*No*." What either of them said next would make or break the relationship, and they both seemed to know it.

"You don't let anyone into your world," Beka said finally.

If Devon had just kept her mouth shut their friendship might not have ended in stalemate. She had been mad, though. "And you can't imagine giving up your art for anything or anyone. You can't even imagine giving your life to someone you love—Loch can."

"What if he came to you right now and said *let's get married*? Could you take forever?" Beka challenged. "When was the last time you had a relationship that wasn't an affair? You're terrified of intimacy."

"Oh, and you're the intimacy queen?" Devon never should have said it like that.

Why had she quit painting? Part of what Beka had said to her in their fight was true—Devon liked to think that she wasn't selfish enough to be an artist, but the fact was she had been afraid. What if she failed? When she was brutally honest with herself, Devon Halsey knew she lacked the genius of a deKoonig, Pollack, or Montebello. However, she was meticulous when it came to observation and detail, and while those qualities might have made her artwork too planned and controlled, they were assets in a Crime Scene detective.

Beka's hand flashed in the air like a fish rising out of the water and hung there, her eyes narrowing spitefully. "He's never going to leave her."

Devon bristled. "You forget, Beka, that I know why Todd ran off that night and so do you! Because you wanted to fuck someone else!"

"I'll tell you something, Devon, I'm the only friend you have anymore. You've ignored your friends for so long we've all given up on you. I keep waiting for the real Devon to come back, but she's gone."

"And where's the real Beka? At some party, posing for the society sheets?"

"You used to be an artist!"

"You used to be nice!"

"You're wasting your life on a married man."

Beka's words still stung. Devon had not stayed to hear the rest.

Her car pulled up into her driveway where a welcoming committee of spots wiggled and barked excitedly, and Devon felt a concrete certainty that she had made the right decision. She loved what she had: her job, her home, her dog, Loch, Aileen, her folks four miles down the road.

"Hey, Boo!" she greeted her seventy-five pound dalmatian. He was the Boo in the "Just Me and You and a Dog Named Boo," the first present Lochwood had ever given her.

"Since I can't be with you all the time I want someone who is," he'd told her. The puppy's pirate-patched eye had winked at her, then he had burst out of the box and into her arms. "They're one-man dogs. That means he'll always love only you." It was the closest Loch had ever come to saying he loved her.

Beka had never understood that Loch was just like the dalmatian—even if he was married to the wrong woman, he loved Devon, and he always would.

CHAPTER ELEVEN

What is Tao? A bright-eyed man falls into a well.

—Haryo Osho

Devon had been lucky to inherit her grandmother's house in the new "hot spot of the Hamptons." She had tried renting the place in the summers, but stopped after the tenants called to complain about the mosquitoes.

"In the house?" she had asked, genuinely concerned that there might be holes in the screens.

"No, outside!"

Her next tenant—another high-strung New Yorker—had been terrorized by wildlife. "There's a raccoon in the yard!"

"You're in the country," Devon reminded her.

"I can't sleep knowing there are wild animals out there!"

Devon gave up dealing with city people and moved home.

It had been hard to commute and take care of Boo. Then her childhood friend, Aileen, who was now a pet-sitter by trade and had lived in Sag Harbor all of her life, was ousted from her apartment. She had lived in the same place for fifteen years and had never worried about a place to live before. But her landlord's son inherited the property. Desperate or greedy, no one was sure which, he threw Aileen and three others out of their year-round housing to make room for summer people who could pay summer prices. Devon figured he deserved what he got and promptly called her previous tenants to tell them of this brand-new rental offering.

That May—the beginning of the "season"—Aileen needed to move. It was a yearly ritual for locals all over the Hamptons who, upon vacating their winter rentals, scrambled to find anything—a hovel, a tent, a couch to sleep on—so they could keep their jobs until fall when the towns were vacated once more. For Devon, Aileen's homelessness was a godsend. They had learned how to swim, ride ponies, and shoplift together. They had smoked their first cigarette and swigged their first bitter taste of bourbon together. It had happened on the same night, and to cover up the odor they had eaten a gallon of ice cream immediately afterward. They had always been friends—it only made sense to offer Aileen a place to live in Grandma Haile's house.

Aileen moved into the upstairs bedroom and paid rent by feeding and walking a dog that needed attention and exercise during Devon's ten-hour, and often longer, days. It was a fair trade. Devon had someone who could take care of Boo, and Aileen, who had lost her own dog Quincy earlier that spring, had a home to live in while continuing her business, walking other people's dogs, and saving money to buy her own house.

Devon pulled her bag out of the car, waved to Aileen, and then wondered if she'd heard about Beka and Gabe yet.

"Happy New Year, roomie!" Aileen waved.

Devon patted Boo on the head one more time. Beka was wrong; she did have friends. Her dog and Aileen were her friends. Hell, she'd known Aileen longer than she'd known Beka.

"He's been here since noon," Aileen said—she had a way of starting conversations in the middle as if Devon had just stepped out of the room rather than having been gone for twenty hours—"just sitting out in the yard and staring at the bay."

"Who, Boo?" Devon had no idea what Aileen was talking about.

Aileen chuckled. "Hans. He wouldn't even come in for a cup of tea."

"He must have heard about Beka." Devon stood up slowly. She didn't want to deal with other people's feelings regarding Beka's death; she still had to deal with her own.

"Oh, she called."

"Who?"

"Beka. Left a message last night for you."

Loch had been right.

Devon walked toward the house with her spotted shadow close at her heels. "Beka and Gabe are dead."

"Oh my gawd! You're joking." Aileen's Long Island twang made her O's sound like Au's.

"I'm surprised you didn't hear about it at 7-Eleven."

"It's closed for the holiday; besides, I got too many dogs to walk. I work on holidays, know what I mean?"

Devon knew exactly what she meant. "Hurley was at the scene. It'll be in *Newsday* tomorrow." She pressed the playback button on the answering machine and waited for the messages to rewind.

"*Hi, Devon. Hi, Aileen. It's Alex. I'm out here for the holidays. Dev, I hope you're coming to Number One Chinese Restaurant for dim sum tomorrow. Beka arranged a loft reunion, so I'm sure you know about it.*" Devon made a black swiggle on the notepad in front of her. No, she had not known about the reunion and couldn't help feeling resentful that Beka hadn't called to tell her. "*Everyone's coming: Maddie and Godwyn, Josh and Katiti, and I just got hold of Sam! Bring that cop you've been dating. What's his name? Can't wait to see you. Call me. I'm listed if you don't have my number. Maybe we can all drive in together. If you talk to Beka tell her to call me. Ciao bella!*"

"Ciao bella! She is so full of herself." Aileen shook her head.

Devon made a note to call Alex and then, as if invoked from the past, Beka's voice crackled through the room.

"*Where are you? I really need to talk. I'm sorry about what I said. I need my friend back.*" Beka sniffed loudly as if she had been crying. "*Come over when you can, okay? Please? It's about Todd.*" There was static, typical of her cellphone, and a click. Aileen and Devon stared at each other but neither moved.

"That's so creepy." Aileen shivered.

"I'm going to see Hans." Devon held the door open for Boo and together they headed across the first dune and toward Havens Beach.

The sun was truly setting by the time Devon found Hans sitting on a rock facing Sag Harbor Bay. The monk's back was broad and dark as a carved Buddha, and the stillness surrounding him made her hesitate before speaking.

"Hans?"

He kept staring at the remnants of scarlet and lavender along the horizon. "Devon Halsey, how are you this day?" His Swedish accent was thick, but Devon was fairly used to trying to interpret Hans's words and listened carefully.

"Not so good, Hans. Beka is dead."

"It is a terrible thing. Not at all like our Beka."

"What's not like her?"

He put his large carpenter's hand on hers and squeezed. He sighed heavily. "I'm afraid to have wrecked things for you, but . . ." Devon strained to grasp the meaning behind his words, ". . . to see for yourself."

"See what?" She felt as small as a child next to him.

He stood up. "I think I have her hair at the zendo."

* * *

Lochwood sat at his desk and opened the Imamura-Montebello casebook. How could he make Devon see that Beka—probably because of an innate instability—had murdered Gabe and killed herself? He reread his notes and concluded once more that he couldn't. He had to let the evidence talk and thus prove it to her. He knew how important it was to keep an open mind, but so did Devon. He had to trust her to follow this through in her own way, just as he was going to. Still, from all he and Gary had heard it seemed to fit— Beka Imamura had killed Gabriel Montebello. The real mystery was why. He looked at a few of the Polaroids Devon and Frank had shot of the bodies and knew if he forced Devon to see Beka's guilt, he'd lose her.

Could he bear to lose Devon and Brea at the same time?

All of his life the only thing he had longed for was a family, people to protect and depend on him. Well, he had gotten his wish. Marty was completely dependent. Devon was not, and she didn't even need his protection. All she needed, all she asked for, was to be with him, and that seemed harder to give than anything.

He picked up the phone and left a message at the photo lab to rush the crime-scene photographs, then called hematology and toxicology for a rush on the blood. They'd love coming back from vacation a day early and hearing his voice first thing. He flipped his calendar from December 31 to January 1—the years just kept on coming.

He and Devon had planned to work New Year's Eve because they thought there might be some strange case involving the new age—mass suicide or mass murder from one of those weird "spiritual" groups on the North Fork. The far-out stuff only happened in California though. New Yorkers just killed each other—with samurai swords from the look of it. He glanced at his watch. It was only six o'clock. He had another six hours before he was on duty and he wasn't tired in the least. He reached for the casebook one more time as the phone rang.

"Brennen," he said as noncommittally as possible. He could tell by the hollowness of the voice that she was speaking into her car phone. "I was just thinking about you," he lied. He wished he'd just been thinking about her. He wondered what she was up to, without him.

"There's a new development out here." She told him about Hans.

"Is this some weird Buddhist thing?"

"Maybe? I'm on my way now. I'm treating it like a crime scene."

"Treat it like a Crime Scene."

"That's what I said," she replied with a lighthearted chuckle.

"F-you!" He suddenly felt optimistic. It was the first time he'd heard levity in her voice in twenty-four hours. "Sorry about earlier."

"Yeah, well. There was a message from her." She knew he was grinning. "Wipe that condescending smile off your damn face. It doesn't mean she killed Gabe, just that you were right."

"She call about Todd?"

"What do you think?" She hung up the phone and kept her left hand on the steering wheel as she followed Hans off of Highway 114 and into the Northwest Woods. They veered down Swamp Road; the lights from residences disappeared in the depths of trees and rather suddenly it became a dark, cold night.

They parked in his driveway and walked through the picket fence and under an overgrown hedge. Tufts of snow floated to the ground as the privet, with its heavily laden branches, bowed to the wind. The scene had changed in the years since she had been here; it felt foreign and strange in the gloaming, and in the absence of Beka. Hans bowed to the Buddha in the garden and Devon followed suit, stooping awkwardly, suddenly afraid that she was bowing incorrectly.

"I left the offering over there," he whispered, and pointed to Buddha's hands. "There is more inside, where she cut it, but this is the offering."

Barney, the zendo watch dog, trotted up to them and eyed her warily.

"Hey, Barney!" Devon knelt to the ground and held out her hand in a submissive gesture. He grumbled and turned his back on her, only to lick the back of Hans's hand before lumbering through the old picket gate. Her absence had just been commented upon by the zendo's most senior member.

They walked across the yard to the garden Buddha. "Was Beka sitting regularly?"

"Almost every morning; she wanted to take *Jukai* and was studying hard."

"Studying what?" Devon stooped to the ground and brushed away the snow to see if any footprints might have been left near the Buddha. There were no tracks near or around the sculpture, even though the Buddha itself was almost completely uncovered, sheltered as it was by a low-hanging bow weighed down with snow.

"The texts."

"I don't remember cutting one's hair as part of *Jukai*." She stood up and looked at the scene, disappointed. There was nothing that stood out to her, nothing unusual.

"No, that's *Tokudo*."

"But Beka was not becoming a monk."

"Beka would never cut her hair." He smiled at Devon.

Devon made a small bow, took the hair out of Buddha's hands, and placed it in a bag.

"In Japan, a woman whose husband dies will cut off her hair in grief," Hans said from behind her.

A chill traced its fingers down her spine. That was not what she had wanted to hear. "Did Beka know that?"

"She had started to study Japanese and read *Kanji*."

That did not sound like the party-girl Devon had spent high school getting in trouble with.

They moved back across the courtyard toward the small barn that housed the zendo. Devon had spent her early childhood in such ports as Honolulu, Taiwan, and Singapore, following her father's naval career. It made sense that she should find solace here, even if she was not looking for it. Her father and mother had taken her to many temples as a child, and when they returned to the States her father had begun meditating in the barn with his friend Hans. That was how the Northwest Woods zendo started, in an old barn that now served as a spiritual haven to a burgeoning Buddhist community in the Hamptons. By the time she was sixteen, she and Beka were referring to themselves as Buddhists, and while back then it had mostly been for shock value and a desire to be cool at school, it had stuck. Well, almost stuck; Devon considered herself a part-time Buddhist.

Hans held the door open for her, but she reached out to touch the wood. It was well-worn, soft as cotton under her flesh and oiled by the loving touch of hands that pushed it open in search of enlightenment . . . Devon was only looking for answers though—enlightenment would have to wait. She stepped inside trying to remember, should she bow or shouldn't she? When around Buddhists one could always count on bowing. She bowed as she entered the foyer. Hans did not.

The cloakroom was neat as usual—black robes belonging to the *Sangha's* monks and novices hung in a perfect row on their proper pegs with a place for their black bib-like *ruksas* folded neatly over-head. Devon sighed at the sense of order and home that she felt just stepping inside.

"Can you show me what you moved?"

"Scissors, and I swept. I did not know it was important. I thought someone was being unmindful."

"It's okay, Hans. Just retrace your steps and tell me what you did. We'll go from there."

He went to the supply alcove, pulled back a small black curtain, and pointed to the scissors. She put on her plastic gloves, pulled out her print kit, and dusted them carefully; there was not a complete print anywhere on the handle or the blades. "Is anything missing?"

"A knife."

She waited. Hans could be sparing with words, but she knew if she listened long enough he would give her the information she was seeking.

"The knife we use to clean the wax out of the candleholders."

"Was it sharp?"

"Sharp enough."

"I'm going to need to get your prints, Hans." She took out her printless pad and pressed his fingers into their appropriate section. He looked at his hands, puzzled. "Inkless," she explained. Then she pulled the gum sheet out from under the plate and looked at his prints. She was almost positive Hans's were the same prints on the knife back at the station. She sighed. "I think we have your knife in evidence."

"It was used as a weapon?" His voice betrayed his innocence.

"I'm afraid so." She was always surprised when people did not believe that violence existed in the world. Maybe that was why she had stopped coming to the zendo—it seemed too removed from reality. She stood up, put her print pad back in her pack, and went into the main room to see if there was anything else missing.

They entered the main meditation chamber where the Buddha of Compassion smiled serenely down on them. The mystery of the room was diminished by the brightness of the lights, but the Buddha at the front of the room remained a commanding presence. She bowed and approached the Buddha as she had seen Hans do back when she had frequented the zendo, before her job had taken over her life. With a small brush in one hand and a magnifying glass in the other, she began to search the rice mats for any trace evidence that might explain what Beka had been up to. Except for a few more strands of dark black hair and a few daddy longlegs, there was nothing out of the ordinary or out of place, and Devon wasn't sure that anything would have been different had she gotten there before Hans cleaned up.

"Any idea what time Beka came here last night?"

"We went up to the North Fork about nine o'clock."

"What time did you get home?"

"One-thirty or so?" Hans's hands were folded neatly in his lap as he answered Devon's questions.

She gathered the hair follicles and a few other pieces of trace fibers, then they walked out of the meditation room in awkward silence. She turned to the door to the anteroom. "Anything happen in there?"

Beka always chose to sit in the smaller room. She had always loved the way the sun came in through the round window, and in the summer she loved the way the roses bobbed their peach and pink heads outside. She loved it most though because it was the room of the Weeping Buddha.

The Weeping Buddha looked diminutive, swallowed up by the twilight and perhaps further burdened by the weight of death on its shoulders. Smuggled out of Tibet in the 1960s, it had journeyed long and hard to reach such an affluent resting point, but the Weeping Buddha did not look serene. Carved out of teak, its spine and ribcage were so finely detailed that Devon found her own ribs aching at the sight of it. Captured in time, this Buddha was somehow bowing forever over his legs with his forehead touching the floor and the flat of his hands pressed against his eyes in what could either be prayer or despair. From where she stood Devon felt compelled to bow, remembering the motion as most Catholics remember how to cross themselves—automatically. Her knees buckled as she knelt to the floor and touched her forehead to the ground. Palms upturned, she raised her hands to the sky as she breathed in the faded scents of hay, mildew, and sandalwood incense. Three times she knelt in *gassho*.

Hans waited silently.

She could almost see Beka sitting in front of the Weeping Buddha, imitating the painful posture of submission. Submission had never been one of Beka's strong points, Devon mused.

It had been a stupid fight.

Devon sighed. She did not bother explaining herself to her Zen teacher.

The past still haunted them, but it was past. If Devon had learned anything back in 1984 it was to always tell those you care about how you feel, just in case you never see them again. It may have seemed like a fatalistic philosophy, but it was practical considering all they had been through. How could she have forgotten such a simple rule? Why hadn't she called Beka and apologized?

She turned away from the figure and looked the monk in the eye. "Do you think Beka could've killed Gabe?" she finally asked.

Hans's sigh was long, almost labored. "Who can say what one is capable of when provoked?"

"Was Gabe provoking her in some way?"

"She wanted to talk to me about something. It could have been her koan. It could have been anything."

"What koan was she working on?"

Hans stepped into the room with the Weeping Buddha, pulled a book out, and handed it to her. Devon opened the book randomly, read from something called "*Chao-Chou's Mu,*" then paraphrased aloud, "Has a dog the Buddha-nature?" She looked at him and laughed. "That's a koan?"

"*Mu.*"

"Moo?"

"*Mu.* It is the word of all words, in Rinzi. It is like *Ohm* in Tibetan Buddhism. *Mu . . .*" The sound resonated through his mouth from deep within his chest until the vibration filled the room with two tones. She felt the furrows on her forehead relax and she shut her eyes as he chanted the holy word. When the sounds finally died away the silence around them had changed into something deeper and substantial, as if silence itself had become a sentient being. They stood in the foyer of the zendo barely moving.

Hans opened the book to the section on more advanced koans, and read out loud:

A monk takes a vow of silence to remain in a tree at the fork in a road until he reaches enlightenment. However, a traveler does not know which direction to take, and asks the monk for directions. In order to fulfill his *dharma* the monk must tell the man which direction to take, but to tell the man which way to go means instantaneous death. If the monk doesn't tell the traveler his path, he will live but never fulfill his reason for being.

It seemed like a waste of time to ponder for long. Devon knew that koans, like any puzzle, had a trick to them and that any sharp-minded intellect—with or without enlightenment to aid it—could solve any koan. The question was, did she care?

She had a lot to do in the next few hours: sleep, eat dinner, go back to work. She smiled to herself: You must solve a murder case but do not have time to eat or sleep, but if you do not eat or sleep, you cannot solve the case. That was her life's koan.

"Can I keep this for a few days?" she asked, referring to the book. He nodded. "Detective Brennen and Detective DeBritzi will need to speak with you."

"Any time is a good time."

"Is that a riddle or are you telling me the truth?"

"What is truth?" His eyes twinkled at her, then he added, "I'm up by five." He turned off the lights and placed his hand on the small of her back as they headed outside. Such a simple gesture, yet she felt stronger, and the weight of Beka's death seemed somehow lighter.

"What would you have done, Hans? Give directions and die?"

"One only knows what one would do when faced with the decision."

"Beka died, did she leave me directions?"

Hans bowed but said nothing.

Walking back across the courtyard to the edge of the privet, Devon thought only that she needed to call Loch and tell him what she had not found. It suddenly seemed to her that the clues for what had happened to Gabe and Beka lay in what was not there—not in what was.

"Come back to us anytime, Devon Halsey." She heard Hans's voice amid the wood chimes and tree limbs clicking in the wind.

CHAPTER TWELVE

The Four Vows: Sentient beings are numberless; I vow to save them.

—The Four Vows in Zen

Loch answered Devon's call on the first ring. He was disappointed that the prints on the knife appeared to be Hans's and even more disappointed that there was a logical explanation for them being on the weapon. It looked like the zendo was not a crime scene per se, but perhaps it was the last place Beka had visited. According to Devon, Hans and his wife had left for the Buddhist ceremony of two hundred gongs, held at a North Shore zendo. So why would Beka Imamura leave her house on New Year's Eve to cut her hair in an empty zendo, and then return home and kill her husband? "Why, if she was really a Buddhist, wasn't she up on the North Shore with the rest of them?" he wondered out loud.

"I don't know." Devon sounded as confused as he felt. "Hans says that in Japan, a woman cuts her hair when her husband or a loved one dies."

"But Beka cut her hair before Gabe was dead."

"Exactly." Her phone hiccuped, cutting off his next words.

". . . any reason . . . cut her hair . . . you can think of?"

"None." She tried to stress the possibility that someone might have cut it for her; although there was no proof of another's presence, Devon did not want to rule it out completely. "Hair floats, and despite Hans's clean-up I found enough hair in the vicinity of the altar to indicate that she cut, or had it cut there." He appreciated her keen eye. Her voice sounded suddenly distant, as if she was driving through an underpass.

"Thanks for taking care of that scene so quickly," he said loudly. "Gary and I will follow up with this monk character in the morning. Get some rest." Loch hung up the phone and scribbled in his notebook. Did Beka drug Gabe, then go to the zendo? But why drug him first, unless that was her initial m.o.? What if the drugs hadn't worked on him? She came home. He confronted her. They fought. She finished him off, realized she'd screwed up, and killed herself to save face—that's what they called it in Japan, right? Saving face? He stopped writing and started making doodles on the page, his mind busily working through the ins and outs of three different scenarios at the same time.

If that was the way it had happened, then that meant she had pre-meditated bringing the knife from the zendo. He scribbled in a circle until it was black. The zendo knife bothered him—it didn't quite work as the weapon. He could see her planning an OD, going to the zendo, and cutting her hair—perhaps that was going to be her alibi, but Hans had left already. Had she then returned home only to find Gabe not only conscious, but irate? He began to write again. She might have killed him in self-defense, but why kill herself if that was the case? But what if Gabe had been out cold? That didn't make sense—why so much violence if he was already dying? Unless she was staging something . . . Was that it? Had she staged a scene, choreographed it down to the last detail—the aria on the stereo? He hated theater people, give him a cop any day, anything but an actress or a dancer, they were just too high-maintenance. Everything rested on the toxicology report and he wouldn't have that until late the next day, at the earliest . . .

* * *

Devon had kept a few strands of hair from the scene unbagged so she could check them under her microscope at home. It was specially equipped with a high-powered lens for just this kind of work and she was eager to use Loch's Christmas present. She checked the hair, which was plated and secured, then took the scissors she had borrowed from the zendo and began to cut her own hair at the angle she saw in Beka's sample. She peered at the follicles, one black and belonging to her best friend, the other pale in comparison. She tried to follow the line of the hair, but Beka's follicle seemed frayed or blunted—she needed a better match. Someone with Asian hair to compare with, not her own frilly locks. She stared at the hair, willing it to be the clue that would answer all of her questions. If only she knew . . . A cold wet nose pressed against her hand. Boo sighed. It was time for bed.

She was tired and knew that she'd never find any answers if she couldn't keep her eyes open tonight, when her shift began. She barely felt Boo jumping in beside her. He propped his head on her hip and stared at her for so long that she had the feeling he was trying to tell her something.

"Go to sleep," she whispered. He picked up his head and placed it back on the bed atop his paws. Just like a kid, his tail thumped softly on the down comforter. Devon suddenly felt the enormity of regret—everything she should have done to make up with Beka—and now it was too late. Her mind swirled, flipping memories like flashcards: the first time she met Beka, their last argument, the dorms where they roomed together senior year of high school, their first New York apartment, the summers they'd spent at the Halsey farm in Sagaponack, back to the first time they met . . .

The dormitory hallways were packed with trunks and bicycles and girls caught between puberty and adulthood trying to find their rooms. Devon was already settled and unpacking her record collection when the new girl burst through the door dressed in a long flowing silk skirt and scarves. They stared at each other, neither sure what to make of the other.

"*O-hayio*," Devon had said, and bowed from the waist.

"Ohio? Is that where you're from?" Beka looked at her quizzically.

"No. I just said 'Hi' in Japanese." Devon spoke slowly, making sure to enunciate her words for the foreign student.

"Get outta here! That was Japanese?" Beka laughed. "How come you speak Japanese?"

"How come you don't?"

"Because I'm American," Beka said matter-of-factly, and ran over to the window to look out at the expansive oak whose branches just reached their window. "How far to the boys' dorms?"

Within minutes they were the best of friends, planning their escape route across the tree's limbs and their future husbands' lives. Beka told Devon all about living on Oahu, and Devon told Beka she had been born in Honolulu when her father was stationed there.

They couldn't believe they had a Hawaiian connection. Devon had only lived in Oahu until she was two and the family moved to Taiwan, though. She had never been back. Beka felt it was her duty to change all of that. For the next four years Beka spent Thanksgivings in the Halsey household in the Hamptons, and Devon spent New Year's in Hawaii with the Imamuras.

They had always seemed more like sisters than friends, and as they grew up they had grown apart somewhat, as sisters often do, until they were bound by a common past but little else. Still she had not really noticed the distance between them until this past year.

Devon fell asleep and woke up, fell asleep and woke up again, until her dream and waking states were indiscernible, a blend of near and far past, a montage of what she dreamt and thought. And between these two states, Beka and Todd floated in a realm she could barely reach with her mind.

* * *

Velvet hung on the walls of Beka's bedroom to help stop the drafts outside from coming through the bricks. Still, wind wended its way into the room, and Devon felt like she was camping outdoors. She could see her breath in the air.

Beka stirred in the loft bed above her head. "He's not back."

"How do you know?" Beka could blow an arctic wind across a guy's heart and never even notice the frostbite on his face.

"You tell the guys you like to leave you alone and they do. And the ones you can't stand won't go away no matter what you say! Why is that?"

Devon knew Beka enjoyed feeling like the shark, stalking her prey in the dangerous waters of her bed, until no one was safe from her hunger. She wasn't really like that, she just pretended to be—that's what she was upset about. Todd had taken her rejection seriously.

"What do I have to do, be easy?"

"You're already a slut; wouldn't want you to be easy, too," Devon teased from the futon below. Beka dumped a pillow on her head as Devon sat up and looked at the clock. It was one in the afternoon.

"He probably went back to Yale."

"Did you sleep with him?"

Beka didn't answer. Devon knew she was busy experimenting with everything in the meat department. It sort of fit the image dancers carried around with them—loose morals and even looser limbs. Devon had seen and eavesdropped enough to know that it didn't matter if it was true or not, most guys thought dancers were the perfect lay.

Devon's own mother had asked Beka once, "Why is it men look at you like they want to fuck you?" Every woman Devon knew had seen the lust in strangers' eyes, as if she was being subconsciously stripped. Beka was so sensitive, maybe she felt it more than most. Despite her attempts to appear tough, Beka wasn't—she felt things deeply. Devon had seen her come home crying because a stupid pigeon got hit by a cab—how could anyone live in New York City and care about pigeons? Maybe that was why Devon had always felt so protective of her. It was the pigeons.

"He said he wanted to marry me!" Beka's laughter was brittle in the cold. "My first proposal just dumped me."

"You told him to get lost, didn't you?" Beka's boyfriends needed an instruction manual to figure their way through the maze of tests she made them pass—an emotional obstacle course she designed to keep love at bay. She was nicer to pigeons than she was to her love interests.

"Maybe I should be a lesbian."

"Maybe you should!" They both giggled.

Devon finished the scenario for herself as she threw off the covers and felt the first bite of cold when her feet struck the wood floor. The plastic over the windows breathed in and out with a life of its own. Winter was in the room, and the view outside was bleak. Now that she thought about it, Todd had seemed desperate to get drunk last night. She'd seen guys lose it over Beka before—Godwyn had certainly been in that position and probably Josh as well. She had seen Beka disappear into the bathroom with one guy and go home with another. The only men she was nice to were guys she had not slept with. Look at poor Godwyn; she had slept with him twice last summer, been awful to him ever since, and now could not get rid of him. He drove her nuts.

"Todd was sweet," Beka said, looking down from her loft bed.

Devon did not ask why she referred to him in the past tense.

"What am I going to do with a nice guy who wants to be a minister?"

"Why are you so terrified someone's going to fall in love with you?" Beka didn't answer. "I thought that was the whole point." Devon rolled her futon bed back into a couch, fluffed the pillow, and tossed it up to her friend. A ghostly mist swirled around the World Trade towers making them look as sober and cold as she felt. "Are you so afraid of love that you can only sleep with strangers?"

Beka leaned over the edge of her loft bed. "I spend so much time being 'a dancer,' I don't know who the real me is anymore."

"Beka, there are people in this world who care about you no matter who or what you are. You could be a secretary and we would still love you. Maybe Todd would, too."

Beka's eyes lit with fear—the thought of being like everyone else terrified her more than anything else. Performers had to want to stand out in the crowd or they would never be able to handle the stress of the stage, but Beka also seemed panicked by the idea of being singled out. Her desire for fame was equal to her longing for anonymity, and it was an inner struggle that seemed to be taking its toll on her. Devon was more concerned about the self-destructive tendencies that Beka's career brought with it than Beka becoming a world-renowned dancer.

"Todd's just like everyone else. He even has my autograph."

"He told you that?"

"See, I'm nothing. I'm just a fantasy."

"Well, *Fantasia*, when you come back to earth we mere mortals will be in the living room." Devon walked down the hall leaving the diva to ponder her life. Alex, Maddie, and Godwyn were already up and working on a pitcher of Bloody Marys, and the furnace blasted semi-warm air across their heads as Devon sat down to join the hungover group.

Alex handed her a glass. "Hair of the dog?"

"Any news?" Devon took the drink.

"Sam is still looking for him," Alex muttered, so quiet Devon almost couldn't hear her.

* * *

Somewhere in the tangle of thoughts Devon lost all sense of time and slept. Her thoughts were entwined with nonsensical dreams, but something awakened her.

She'd forgotten to call Alexandra. The clock said ten-thirty p.m. It was time for her to get up anyway. Boo's tail thumped against the bed as Devon reached over and rubbed the spots on his head. She picked up the phone and called Alex's number in East Hampton. The answering machine picked up. "Alex, I'm working 12-to-7s this week, so I'll have to meet you in the city tomorrow. I'm going to go in straight from work. See you about one." She didn't say Happy New Year and didn't mention anything about Beka and Gabe—that wasn't the sort of thing to leave on a machine, especially if Alex hadn't heard yet. Tomorrow the papers would have the story and everyone would know. The less Devon had to talk about it, the better.

She had just enough time to stop and get a bite to eat on her way to work. She called Concha D'Oro's and ordered a meatball sub to go, then got dressed for another night of work. She kissed her dog's forehead and patted his ears. "I'm off, buddy. See you tomorrow." She always talked to him intelligently.

His gold-brown eyes stared up at her inquisitively.

"Does a dog have Buddha nature?" she asked out loud. He tilted his head as if to answer her question with complete comprehension. "It doesn't take months of meditation to know the answer to that koan." She rubbed his ear so his right lip curled up in a smile. "Just a really great dog."

CHAPTER THIRTEEN

Deluding passions are inexhaustible; I vow to destroy them.
— The Four Vows in Zen

Hair? Lochwood mulled over the problem of Beka's hair. He was anxious to interview Hans but didn't feel it was appropriate to drive all the way out to the East End and conduct the interview without his partner. The information Hans had would wait until Gary came back on at midnight—not everyone could work like Lochwood did, on two or three hours of sleep a night.

He flipped through his notes. The other interviews they had conducted with the neighbors had not been helpful. The Imamura-Montebello's closest neighbor lived over a quarter-mile away and was not a busybody. No one had seen anything. He had run the crime through all the standard scenarios, but so far the favorite was murder/suicide; nothing else added up right. As artists, Beka and Gabriel may have had their enemies, but enough for this kind of revenge? This was the age of guns: quick, easy, deliverable death that was completely impersonal. Knives were rarely used in pre-meditated crimes anymore; they were the instruments of impassioned rage, and as hard as it was to believe that Beka had stabbed her husband to death, finding someone else to fit that scenario was even more unlikely.

They still had to track down the staff at Beka and Edilio's Pilates studio in Sag Harbor; that was the problem with holidays—no one worked. The chance of a disgruntled staff member committing such a bloody murder was unlikely. The murderer, if it wasn't Beka, had to be familiar with sword strokes, and know enough about forensic evidence to cover both tracks and anything else that might have left a trace of his presence at the scene. And this mythic kind of criminal would have wanted both of the victims dead, very badly, and would have had to devote enormous amounts of time and energy to the task.

Such a murderer had to have known them well enough to get access to the house with no struggle, and manipulate the scene so it looked like Beka Imamura was the guilty party. It wasn't impossible; it was just more likely that Beka had blown a gasket and killed her husband.

The question Loch was currently mulling over in his head was when and how to ask Devon about Beka. He had to question her; they both knew that, but he wanted to get her when she was rested and clear-headed. He thought about beeping her, then thought better of it. She needed her sleep; besides, she'd be at work in an hour or two. Shutting the case file, he leaned back in his chair. His mind slowed along with his breathing and in a few minutes his head fell forward onto his chest. After twenty-eight hours, Lochwood Brennen, infamous for his insomnia, finally fell asleep.

The next thing he felt was the warm breath of a kiss on his neck. "Sleeping on the job?" Devon's voice was husky and low.

He smiled. "Two hours ago."

"About the time I woke up," she teased him gently, familiarly.

He hadn't realized how worried he'd been about her until he heard her voice sounding lighter and more animated. "Sorry we missed dinner."

"I needed to regroup. Did you go home?"

He nodded. "Briefly. Brea's moving out." He saw the light of hope leap to her eyes and watched as she smothered the internal glow. Every once in a while he glimpsed these moments and wondered what would happen to them—five years was a long time, like a marriage. He tried not to think about how hard it was for Devon to be in love with a man who already had a family. He'd never lied to her about his situation, and she'd never forced him to make any decisions. But she was waiting for him, he knew that, and from the look on her face he'd just given her a reason to hope that the wait might soon be over.

"She's growing up." She sounded so understanding.

"I'm not ready."

"You never will be. Oh, I forgot—there's a reunion. Tomorrow." His face fell. Loch was not big on socializing. "The loftmates are getting together. We're meeting at Number One Chinese Restaurant for dim sum."

The food was tempting but Loch nonetheless declined. "There's so much to do."

"I just want you to know that you're getting out of it only because I'd rather you stay here and figure out that Beka did not kill Gabe. Work all day." She smiled at him good-naturedly.

"Thanks." He was genuinely relieved. "We have a number of people to interview in Sag Harbor, especially her business partner Edilio." He looked at his case notes. "And we need to get hold of their lawyer. Do you know him?"

"Some New York City muck-a-muck, Goldberg or Goldstein."

"Goldstein. I might come into the city later to interview him." He felt insecure suggesting he meet her in the city and wasn't sure why.

"That'd be nice. He also has a place in Sag. Ask Aileen—she walks his dog."

Maybe she didn't want him to come in and meet her.

"Have you notified Beka's uncles yet?" she asked.

"I called the local authorities in Honolulu and asked them to contact the family in person. They called to let me know that the Imamuras have been informed and are expecting our call. I was waiting for you to come in." He reached over to the phone, punched the speaker button, then dialed the number.

She cleared her throat as the phone rang.

"Hello?"

"Mr. Imamura?"

"Is this the detective in New York?"

"Detective Brennen, yes sir. I'm sorry for your loss."

"We can't believe our Beka is gone."

"Biz?" Devon's voice wavered as she said his name out loud. "It's Devon."

"Oh my, Devon. You're there, too?"

Her eyes filled with tears. "I'm on the case, Biz."

"Thank god. Will you find out what happened?"

"I'm going to try, Biz."

"You know, we waited at the airport for an hour but she wasn't on the plane," Bismarck shouted into the phone. "She was supposed to be on the seven o'clock plane this morning, but she never arrived."

"Why was she flying New Year's Eve?" Devon asked.

"She couldn't get an earlier flight."

"Mr. Imamura, we didn't know she was coming to Hawaii. You're sure about that?" Loch asked.

"As sure as we can ever be with Beka's plans. She tends to change her mind a lot, and she always flew on the family buddy pass, so . . . But she was leaving Gabe and coming home." He spoke quickly and loudly, as if the phone line was going to go dead any second or the operator was going to bust in and ask for another quarter. "I never liked him. Such a bastard. She didn't tell you about her plans, Dev?"

"No."

"What was up with you two? She used to tell you everything, then she tells me you aren't talking to her."

"We had a disagreement, Biz. It was nothing."

"Must have been something for her not to tell you she was leaving Gabe."

"I've been real busy lately."

"You mainlanders always too busy."

"Mr. Imamura, do you know why she was leaving Gabe?" Lochwood asked.

"Hated him." He spat the words out.

"Was there any abuse, or violence?"

"I dunno. If she'd made it home she might have told us what was going on, but you know Beka. She'll bite any bullet for a good show."

Devon nodded. She had stopped in at rehearsal once when Beka and Edilio were working with the International Dance Company and seen the creative director screaming at them. Beka was sitting on the floor squeezing her toes, tears streaming down her face while the creative director ranted and raved about some mistake she had made. Then she silently got up and tried the sequence again.

"How's Edilio taking it?" Biz asked.

"We haven't been able to locate him yet."

"He's not dead too is he?"

"No, why?"

"He was supposed to be with Beka on the plane."

"He was coming to Hawaii, too?" Loch was making notes quickly but had time to catch Devon's eye.

"They were going to start a Pilates studio here."

"If you hear from him, would you notify us, Mr. Imamura?"

"Yeah-yeah." He used the colloquial yes, merged into one word, that was common to the islands. "Bert and I are catching the morning flight to New York tomorrow. Your parents are picking us up at JFK, Dev. We'll be at their house."

"Good."

"Yeah, your mother is helping us arrange a memorial service. Detective Brennen, the coroner is holding Beka's body. Can you get them to release her?"

"I'll see what I can do about that, sir," Lochwood assured him.

"They may still be looking for forensic evidence to prove her innocence," Devon added.

"Innocent of what? Killing that bastard? He deserved whatever he got and I'll tell you what, I hope Beka was the one to give it to him."

She couldn't believe what Biz was saying. "But they were friends before they got married, Biz."

"You never been married, Dev, what you know about vengeance?" The phones crackled as if the distance were a strain on them. "Besides, Beka was Gabe's idea of a tax write-off. He may have immortalized her with his art, but she paid a price for the privilege. You find out what was really going on."

"Okay, Biz. See you at Mom's."

Lochwood interrupted. "Mr. Imamura, one last thing, can you think of any reason Beka would have cut her hair?"

"Cut her hair? No way. Why?"

"It's not a Japanese thing?" Loch asked.

"I dunno, we're American."

Another voice broke into the conversation. "Biz." It was Uncle Bert. "She cut it off when her parents died, swore she'd never cut it again."

Loch made a note: *She cut her hair once before due to death in the family*. Was she anticipating her husband's death? Or, like he had thought earlier, was she trying to give herself an alibi after slipping Gabe a Mickey? "Thank you, sir, you've been very helpful."

"See what you can do about getting our girl outta that morgue. Beka wouldn't want to stay in there long. We got a place for her all picked out, right on the hill overlooking the bay at the Byodo-In Buddhist Temple."

"She would have loved that," Devon said.

"Yeah-yeah, if it's the only way we can get her home then that's what we'll do. She never should have left the island. No offense, but you mainlanders are crazy."

"Have a safe flight, Biz. See you soon." Devon leaned forward over the desk and punched the speaker button off.

Lochwood looked like a bloodhound with a scent; his eyes were glazed and his lips moist. Now there were two more things nagging him—the hair and the fact that no one, not Devon, not Jenny O'Doherty, knew that Beka was leaving her husband.

Why had it been so secret?

That was the scenario for an abused wife—to flee in the middle of the night with no one the wiser. But from what Jenny O'Doherty had reported, it was Beka who was the more violent and volatile of the two. She was the one who broke the front door by slamming it too hard, smashed a set of plates—a wedding gift from a local artist—and an expensive raku vase. But when Loch had asked what the rows had been about, Jenny's response had been noncommittal, as if flamboyant fights were a regular occurrence. It seemed like they loved to fight and they loved to make up publicly.

"What about this Edilio Ferraro? What do you know about him?" he asked Devon.

"Dance partner. Business partner. She started working with him when she joined the company in '82. They worked their way up until they became partners in '84." He fingered the case file. "You need to ask me about Beka," she said. It wasn't a question, and he didn't say a word. "Come on, let's do it."

"You sure?"

"I wouldn't offer if I wasn't. Let's get it over with so I can get to work." She sat down in his spare chair, propped her feet up on his desk, and leaned back.

He paused, scanning her face for any unwillingness, then asked her directly, "Why would Beka cut her hair?"

"The question is not why but where." She felt like Hans.

"Huh?"

"Her favorite room to sit in was the small one, not the main room. If she were doing some kind of ritual she would have performed it for the Weeping Buddha."

"You sure about that?"

"That's the only thing I feel sure of."

"Despite what happened between you two?"

"I have samples of the hair from the altar and the garden. I want to test the samples . . ."

"What did you two fight about?" he asked suddenly.

"It has nothing to do with the case. As I was saying, I'm going to run some tests to see how it was cut."

She could be so bull-headed. "Beka told you everything, then she stopped. You two barely spoke in the past six months."

"We didn't speak at all," she corrected him.

"Why?"

"Ask me something else."

He decided to give it a rest and come back to the question. "Was she ever violent?"

She stared at him. "Where's that coming from?"

"It's a different question."

"She had an artistic temperament."

He thought about asking Devon if Beka's temper was anything like hers, but fiddled with his pencil instead. "Do you think she would have told you if she was having problems with Gabe?"

"A year ago I thought Beka told me everything. Right now, I'm not so sure. "

"Which brings us back to your argument."

"I promise you it has nothing to do with the case."

"Then you won't mind telling me." Her eyes were busily looking at something under his desk. His face flushed angrily. "What the hell did you two argue about?"

"You! Okay?" she yelled back at him. "You!"

He was stunned.

"Beka thought I was wasting my life with you. Said the only reason I've been with you for five years is because you can't marry me!"

He felt his face fall. It had been said, the unspoken stated. "What'd you say?"

There was a knock at the door; Frank poked his head in. "Just got *Newsday*." He held up the front page: "*Murder of the Millenium—Black Widow of Bridgehampton Leaves Behind Blood Bath.*"

Hurley had landed the lead story, and the cover photograph was none other than Devon looking stricken with Loch's arm around her comfortingly—the caption left nothing to the imagination: "*Best friend and Suffolk County's first female Crime Scene detective, Devon Halsey, of Sag Harbor, is overcome with emotion after leaving scene. Can she handle her job?*"

Devon hid her face in her hands as Frank continued to read the article out loud. "Retired star of the International Contemporary Dance Company, Beka Imamura, and her husband, artist Gabriel Montebello, died New Year's Eve around midnight, according to the county coroner. Local fixtures in the East End art community, Imamura and her husband were well-respected and liked by all. Friends and neighbors are shocked by the events that began the year . . ."

Devon couldn't listen to any more and headed for the ladies' room, where she locked the door and sat on the toilet. Her body shook, tears stung her eyes, but still she could not cry.

No one had cried when Todd first disappeared. They had simply hoped for his spontaneous return—a bit naïvely in retrospect—but it had never occurred to any of them that Todd Daniels was gone forever. And now Beka and Gabe were gone as well. After the immortality of youth, mortality had been a jarring sense of cruel reality. They had gotten over Todd's disappearance, but it still haunted them, as any unanswered question did. She could remember bits and pieces of the party, the nights they searched for him, but she could barely recall anything physical about Todd. Only his essence remained.

"Why'd you do it, Beka? Screw the suicide or the murder or whatever, just explain the hair to me. Why'd you cut your hair?" she whispered. Then she had a feeling that she knew. She yanked down on the industrial size roll of toilet paper and ended up with one tiny square of sandpaper-textured tissue in her hand to try and blow her nose in. It was Todd who had died, not Gabe. Todd. But why had Beka cut her hair this year? Why not last year, or the year before? What had she learned about Todd that made her grieve his loss this New Year's?

CHAPTER FOURTEEN

The Gates of Dharma are manifold; I vow to enter them.
—The Four Vows in Zen

Devon did not return to Loch's office. She wasn't interested in seeing or hearing anything more about the *Newsday* article. All she wanted to do was find out what happened to Gabe and Beka and get on with her life. What part did she want to get on with? Wasn't there more to life than her job? What about that nagging sensation in the back of her mind that time was running out? The clock. She had always scoffed at women who felt that way, but she was thirty-eight and that was exactly how she herself was beginning to feel. It wasn't that she had a yearning to procreate or mother the world, but she did long to grow old with someone.

All she and Loch did every day was work. He gave new meaning to the word *workaholic*, and if he did leave Marty and marry her, would it be any different? Would he come home after his shift, or fall asleep at his desk as he had tonight? And after one too many nights of being left alone, would she still wait up for him, or would she be at her own desk catching Zs? And where would they live? She loved the remoteness of Sag Harbor, while Loch liked to be inundated with urban activity. She and Beka used to joke that someday they'd be the mah jong mavens of some retirement village—now, she didn't even have someone to joke about that with. How had this sudden loss of plans, of life, of friendship happened?

* * *

The Find Todd Daniels hotline and headquarters had been based on the second floor of First Presbyterian Church on Fifth Avenue, and it was in full operation by the fourth night of Todd's disappearance. An assemblage had organized itself quickly into volunteer groups including New York parishioners, the Daniels family's congregation, Todd's schoolmates from Yale, and local volunteers. Devon and the gang arrived around seven p.m. and watched the bustle around them in quiet amazement. Devon thought they had done an excellent job of searching for Todd in the previous four days, but nothing had prepared her for the kind of systematic order of search-team deployments across a grid of the city. Every quadrant, from Fourteenth Street to the Staten Island Ferry, was sectored off, and each had its own little push-pin, color-coordinated to signify which areas had been searched and which ones were still open territory. Neighborhood watch groups were covering the areas they knew best and showing up, like the loftmates, after the regular workday to help find Todd. It was with a mixture of regret and relief that Devon watched these newcomers to the crisis. Refreshed, invigorated, and looking highly efficient as well as rested and hopeful, they wore little name-tags and carried clipboards as if organization alone would bring Todd through the doors of their headquarters.

"Hi, I'm Paul. Night manager for FTHQ, that means Find Todd Headquarters." He handed them forms to fill out. "Just put your names and addresses here and we'll put you into groups with a leader who's familiar with search techniques." He was a bright know-it-all.

Beka curled her lip and looked askance at Devon.

"We also have phones to answer for the ladies, if you'd rather not be out in the cold." He looked at Devon as he said it.

She laughed, but no one else seemed amused. The loftmates stared at the young man as if he'd just flown in from Mars—or Connecticut, which at that moment seemed as distant as Mars.

"How many hours should I sign you up for? We usually try to rendezvous about ten-thirty, in time for the eleven o'clock news, so we can give the anchors any new developments. And we have walkie-talkies! One for each group. Did you hear about our request for volunteers on the evening news?"

Josh flopped his arm casually over the night manager for FTHQ and announced, "Paul, we're from the loft. We've been at this for days, not hours. We know what to do. Now, why don't you just tell us where to go."

The silence was deafening. It was quite clear where Paul wanted them to go.

His tone was riddled with blame and accusation. "I should have recognized you." He looked disgustedly at Beka. This pious young man must have been their age exactly, but acted sincerely as if God was on his side, not theirs. "Obviously, your techniques didn't work. I guess I'll have to divide you up with some of our neighborhood watch teams."

Todd's smiling face looked down on them from the FTHQ flyer with the hotline number on it.

"Hey! We are a team!" Josh retorted, pushing the guy back with his forefinger. "We were out there with Sam as soon as we knew Todd was gone!"

"Too bad he wasn't in one of the local bars you searched."

"We went everywhere he might have gone!" Alex defended their actions.

"Drunk." Paul's righteous eyes blazed.

Devon saw Todd's mother look up from where she was answering phones, her tear-stained face and tired eyes echoing their own hopeless faces. Devon stepped back from the group; this was not her fight.

Beka pulled herself up to new heights, her sinewy body lengthening like a snake ready to strike its prey. "You weren't there, so don't tell us what happened," she hissed in his face.

"Come on, guys, let's go." Alex opened the door. "We don't need this shit. Sam knows where we'll be tonight—where we've been every night since New Year's. On the streets . . ." She walked up to Paul's pompous face. ". . . looking for Todd." They all turned to leave.

Devon looked back as the door shut behind them—the room had not stopped its activity. Todd's mother was still on the phone; Paul had simply turned around and gone back to the map.

The next day she went back and volunteered formally. She was not overly surprised when she found Josh in the back room answering phones, but that no one else from the loft ever came back disappointed her. She had hoped they would band together in this crisis; instead they fell apart.

"You used to be an artist." She could still hear Beka's rage, as if becoming a cop had been a personal act of betrayal. There were days, especially days like the last two, when Devon wasn't quite sure why she had joined the force. Financial security had played a role in the decision—her dad had been so proud when she told him she was going to take the civil service exam—but there was something more to the decision . . .

After Todd disappeared she had felt—as they all had—that there wasn't much more time left to get it right, and trying to help Sam and his family find Todd had been a kind of self-awakening. There were two kinds of people—those who got involved and helped and those who didn't. The day she went back to FTHQ she decided that she wanted to be the kind of person who helped. Maybe it was as simple as that. She liked working at Find Todd Headquarters, and while she could not stand that guy Paul, he was gone after the second week anyway. Most people did not have the staying power that it took to search for something—someone—after hope faded.

Devon was there to the end. She helped them break down the office, two months later, when everyone conceded that if Todd was coming home it was on his own volition or as a spring floater. When neither happened, despair, like a shroud, fell over the loft. Beka began doing drugs in earnest; Alex took a job in California; Godwyn moved to Chelsea where photographers were supposed to live; Maddie disappeared herself for a few years, calling only on holidays; Josh moved uptown; and Sam went to grad school in a less urban area. Devon moved back home, began studying, and passed her civil service exam in the highest percentile in the state. By the first anniversary of Todd's disappearance, Devon Halsey was a member of the Suffolk County Police Department.

She sat down at her desk and looked at Beka's hair samples. Her head ached with pressure. There was so much to do and such a multitude of things to figure out that she wasn't even able to begin prioritizing all her responsibilities.

Frank came in and sat down at his desk without saying a word. She looked at the clock on the wall; the lieutenant would be in any second to update them on overtime and the lab situation. He always made an appearance twelve minutes into a shift so he could see who was late.

His door opened. It was 12:12 a.m. "Good evening, gang. Sergeant Houck says that Hematology and Toxicology will be open at eight a.m.," he announced. "This is the priority tonight. Don't do anything but process this scene so we can close the case, quick-quick."

"That's what we're doing, lieutenant, unless something else comes up," Frank reminded him. Lieutenant Whittaker was newer to the unit than Devon and had been an unfortunate bureaucratic assignment, yet another political move that compromised the department's integrity but made somebody upstate happy. He had never worked in the Crime Scene Unit and both Devon and Frank had to walk him through procedure to make sure he didn't make mistakes, rather than the other way around.

"No, no, this is priority, Frank." Frank tilted his head down and cast a disparaging look over the rim of his bifocals at the lieutenant. "Unless, of course, something else comes up."

He was such an asshole. Devon pressed down too hard on her mechanical pencil; the lead snapped. "Halsey, the sarge wants to see you in his office." She followed her superior officer out of the room and headed back upstairs.

Sergeant Houck was sitting at his desk with the window open, despite the cold and Lochwood standing in the corner. He smiled as soon as she came in and motioned for her to shut the door. The faint odor of cigarette smoke lingered in the room—*no smoking* did not apply in Houck's office.

She tried to read the atmosphere in the room, and smelled conspiracy as rank as stale tobacco fumes.

"Halsey, I'm sorry for your loss," Houck began, "and even sorrier about the asshole reporter that put you on the front page of today's paper." It wasn't even one in the morning and already everyone knew about the headlines. She had no doubt the chief of police had been awakened for the second night in a row by this case.

"Thank you, sir." She sat down across from him, wondering what to expect.

"We're going to have to cap this quick, and the best way I can think to do that is to take you off the case."

"I take exception to that decision, sir."

"The department doesn't need this to be higher profile than it already is."

"I can handle the heat if you back me up." She put the ball in his court; she knew how to play the game.

"The pressure's on."

"It's never been off, sir. Excuse me for saying so, but everyone in the department and the precinct has been watching me since day one, so what difference does a little press make?"

"You and Frank are one of the best teams we've got. I'm behind you." She knew he was lying but let him. "This is coming from higher up."

"I'd like to stay on the case."

"We've already got a handle on it." Lochwood added his show of support. "It doesn't make sense to change teams now."

"But I'm the one taking the heat if there're any more indiscretions."

"Are we responsible for the press' indiscretion?" she asked. Loch winced.

"You know what I mean, detective." Houck stared at her hard over the rim of his bifocals. So, he knew about them.

"There won't be," Lochwood said.

"No, there won't." He looked out the window, still undecided. "Okay."

She felt like a broken record, repeating herself. "Thank you, sir. Is there anything else?"

"Keep away from reporters."

Excused, Devon returned to Crime Scene feeling as if the sword of Damocles was now hanging over her head. Frank looked up at her as she came through the door but didn't say a word. "Houck's behind me," she told him.

He groaned. "Watch your back."

She walked over to the evidence locker and started to open it, then stopped. "Hey, Frank? Thanks for not asking me how I am."

"Anytime."

She pulled out two evidence bags and signed their names on the sheet.

* * *

Loch did not see Devon for the rest of the night, although they spoke several times on the phone to keep him abreast of the evidence they were processing. Nothing new came up. It still looked as if Beka had killed Gabe, just as Lochwood expected, and if everything went well with the interviews today he'd have the case closed, and Houck and the rest of the assholes upstairs would be happy.

He and Gary arrived at the zendo shortly before dawn. The service began later in the morning than the regular morning sit, but Devon had told them the best time to reach Hans was before six a.m. As they walked up to the house the detectives could see him through the kitchen window, looking very un-monklike in a pair of boxer shorts and a paint-spattered sweatshirt, drinking a cup of coffee with the *New York Times* and *Newsday* spread out in front of him. Loch tapped lightly on the door.

"Come in!" Hans waved to them. "Come in. My wife's still asleep. She likes to sleep in, so we can talk in here if you don't mind." The detectives entered the kitchen and introduced themselves. Hans bowed to them ever so slightly and held up the *Newsday* article.

Loch rolled his eyes. "We've seen it."

"I know Tom. Thought he had better taste."

"You'd be surprised what people will say for a dollar."

"I grew up in Sweden during the war, nothing surprises me. Coffee?" The aroma of some foreign dark roast permeated the air and Lochwood surprised himself by accepting a cup. Gary followed his lead. Hans handed them their cups of coffee and placed a small container of cream from the local dairy on the table.

Loch had never seen a table like it. Twelve feet long, roughly oval, as if it had been sliced out of an oblong tree; bark clung to the edges but it had been sanded and polished to a sheen so pure that the rings of the tree circled beneath their cups in slow spirals of a lost time. Loch reached down to touch the finish as Hans motioned for them to sit down. "Devon said you had some questions for me."

"Yes, but we want you to know that we respect any privileged information that you need to keep private as Beka's spiritual advisor," Loch told him.

"Catholic?" Hans asked.

"Excuse me?"

"Raised Catholic."

"Yes."

"So was I." Hans motioned for them to sit. "Don't worry. Buddhist monks and Catholic monks are two different animals—I can have sex." He chuckled heartily. "And no one comes and confesses anything to me. Buddhism has karma. You screw up, you pay. One lifetime or another, does not matter. Only active meditation and conscious acts change one's karma."

"So, in other words, Beka didn't tell you anything about herself to unburden her soul."

"Beka told me things were not"—he stumbled on the words—"turning out as she planned. She was Gabriel's *objet d'art*, or a doll, I think was the word she used."

"Did she tell you any specific incidents?" Loch asked.

"If she got so much as a flu-bug, he would make her sleep in the guest room until she was well. It also had become an obsession for him to be making molds of her body. I am an artist as well. Gabe's techniques intrigue me—casting, mold-making. He was very successful." Hans's English was awkward and his accent made it even harder to understand, but Lochwood was slowly following the monk's meaning. "He had her pose and then wrapped some sort of thing on her legs or arms—I am not sure how to call it, but he was trying to capture an essence of movement."

"That doesn't sound like grounds for murder, though," Gary mumbled.

"No," Hans agreed.

"What about her hair? Would she have cut her hair to anger him?" Loch asked.

"Possibly."

"You think she cut it out of grief?" Gary asked. "Doesn't cutting hair mean something in Zen?"

"Ah, to renounce one's attachment to vanity and worldly things. I do not think Beka was ready for such an act." He smiled. "She liked being beautiful."

"So, you don't think it sounds like a murderer's last statement before dying?"

"Perhaps." Hans was too noncommittal for Loch's liking. "But Beka would not kill a mosquito, why would she kill a man?"

"Perhaps the man bothered her more than a mosquito." Loch was starting to get the hang of monk-speak.

"To kill, who can fathom what it would take?" Hans stopped, then shut his eyes and added, "She was very angry at him. "

"Why?"

"There was a mold. I'm not sure how to say . . . I am a carver. Gabe likes to cast . . . It was like plaster sculpture, in the barn, that made her mad. She was so upset."

"When was this?"

"A few days ago. She told me she had just destroyed something Gabe had made that was not art."

"What was it exactly?"

"The question you should ask is *who*." Hans sipped his coffee and waited.

Loch waited for the monk to continue. He looked as if he had slipped into deep contemplation, though, and wasn't about to answer anything unless he was asked the correct question. "Okay," Loch finally asked, "who was it?"

"Ah, who, that is the question. Someone she'd known years ago. Todd something."

* * *

Devon and Frank loaded the vials of blood samples into a tray and walked them over to Hematology precisely at eight a.m. Murray Wu was waiting with a cup of coffee in one hand and a clipboard in the other. "How many vials?" he asked.

Devon stared at his head.

"Twenty," Frank answered.

"Shit, sounds like a real mess."

"It was." They began the paperwork to verify his receipt of the samples while Devon reached out and touched Murray's hair.

"What gives?" He backed up and looked at her suspiciously.

"Murray." Her voice was soft and sexy.

"Help me, Frank." Murray looked at the older man pleadingly.

"Can I have a sample of your hair?"

"What?"

"Just an inch or so." She pulled out a pair of scissors from her back pocket.

"What's this crusty old stuff?" Murray asked, holding up a bag and trying to ignore her.

"I found it way up inside the hilt of a samurai sword, one of the weapons at the scene."

"Cool—old samurai blood?"

"Or Chinese," Frank suggested.

"Not as cool, but hey, it could be some white guy's, too!" Murray winked at him.

"Can you tell how old the blood is?" Devon asked.

"Sure, might take a while, but it'd be fun to find out."

"You're so sick, Murray." Frank signed off on the form and handed the tray over.

"No sicker than you folks." Murray took the tray from the detectives. "Okay, I'll get with you tomorrow morning. The older samples may take longer to run. What are we looking for?"

"Anything identifying," Devon said.

"Type, illnesses, diabetes . . . the regular run-through?" He moved away from her again. "Back off, Halsey."

"It's for a good cause."

"All the specs," Frank assured him. "Thanks, Murray."

"Frank, don't leave me alone with her."

Frank ducked out the door as Devon made her move. She snipped a chunk out of his hair and slipped around the counter before he could feel the hole she'd made in the back of his head.

"Halsey!" She fled.

Devon returned to the Crime Scene lab and pulled out the scissors she had bagged from the zendo. She held up Murray's hair and compared it with the hair Hans had found at the Buddha and inside the zendo. She had already verified that it was Beka's hair in both places, but she was interested in something else and that was the way the hair follicle had been cut. What bothered her was the cut seemed dull, not crisp and sharp like Beka would have wanted. Even if she was cutting her hair off in grief, Devon could not see her friend making it a hack job—yet that's what this was.

She studied the angle of the cut on Beka's hair, then snipped Murray's donation in the same direction and slipped it into a slide. There was a slight difference but she wasn't sure it was something to base a case around. She had used the same scissors—actually, she assumed she had used the same scissors. Maybe there was another pair somewhere; she asked the secretary for her pair and repeated the experiment. The secretary's scissors were much sharper than the zendo pair she had first used to cut Murray's hair, but both scissors gave his hair an almost clean edge, while Beka's hair seemed frayed and split. She cut a piece of paper with both pairs of scissors and studied the trim—the zendo scissors were definitely dull, covered with wax from cleaning candlesticks and cutting incense sticks in half. The secretary's scissors cut clean and sharp.

"You got anything?" Frank asked.

"Yeah, plenty of nothing." She got up from the microscope and went to the evidence locker. If she couldn't solve the case that way, she would solve it another. "I'm heading into New York; if you see Loch, tell him I'll be at Gabe's loft around five or six."

"Try to have a good time, Dev."

"I'm going to work," she reminded her partner.

He smiled at her. "That's what I meant."

She dialed Loch's cellphone as she headed for her car and left a message for him. "I'm on my way to the city. I can't believe you let me get sandbagged by Houck. Call me later on my cell and let me know if you're coming in so I can kill you in person. Remember, honey, never mess with a Crime Scene detective. We know how to get away with murder." She paused, trying to decide if she should say anything else, then clicked *send* and returned the phone to the breast pocket of her blue Crime Scene jacket. She threw her backpack in the front seat, complete with her portable crime-scene kit, toothbrush, and a change of clothes. Devon had a motto, one she and Beka had adopted during the '80s: Always carry a toothbrush, you never know where you might spend the night (or with whom). Since then, Devon had amended the motto to include her crime kit, because you never knew when you were going to find a nice crime scene. She pulled out of the precinct parking lot and headed west to the city, instead of east.

* * *

Hans walked into the zendo as usual. There were no hairs on the altar, a relief after yesterday's surprises, and he set about sweeping with his usual concentration and focus. Deep inhalations, deep exhalations, he counted his breaths with his broom strokes. At seven-thirty a.m., the door to the zendo opened and Jenny O'Doherty arrived to take on the role of *Jikido* for the morning service. They bowed to each other and Hans left the rest of the preparations for service to his acolyte, then went to get dressed in his robes and *kesa*.

The gongs began the moment he walked through the door. Everyone bowed three times in unison as he knelt in three full prostrations before Buddha.

"The *Great Prajna Paramita Heart Sutra*," the *Ino* intoned. The *Makugio* began to beat the hollow gourd that kept their chanting in perfect time while Hans began the series of rituals that always cleared his mind, if not his heart.

"O *Sariputra*, all things are expression of emptiness . . ." The congregation sounded sleepy at first, but soon their voices cracked into the smooth timbre that made Hans's bones vibrate. His own voice resonated through the room. ". . . not born, not destroyed, not stained, not pure, neither waxing nor waning . . ." Hans thought of Beka—destroyed? Beka—gone or eternally recycled in the karmic flow of reincarnation—who or what would she come back as? ". . . supreme, perfect enlightenment . . ."

He usually achieved a deep level of meditation while chanting, but this morning, as he bowed and carried the incense around the shrine of Buddha and bowed again in *gassho*, he found his eyes checking the chanters around him. Could one of them have so much hate in their heart as to kill Beka and her husband? He wasn't even sure why he would think such a thing, but from the questions Loch and Gary had asked he had gotten the feeling they weren't completely sure what had happened or why her hair had been left as an offering at the zendo. ". . . by which all suffering is cleared. This is no other than truth." It made more sense, in Hans's opinion, to look for a murderer rather than to assume Beka was guilty, but then he knew Beka. She was like a daughter to him. His voice bellowed deeply across the room as he felt the emotions of his loss rising to the surface. "Set forth this mantra and proclaim: *Gate, Gate, Paragate Parasamgate, Bodhi Svaha! Gate, Gate, Paragate Parasamgate, Bodhi Svaha!*"

The group grew silent as the *Ino* began to recite, "The absolute light, luminous throughout the whole universe, unfathomable excellence, penetrating everywhere . . ."

Hans pressed his head into the floor and raised his hands above his head, as if propelling the universe to take away his burdens and answer the unanswerable.

"We especially pray for the health and well-being of . . ." The *Ino* read the same list of names from the zendo rolls. Hans knew each of the names by heart, some of whom had been on the list for a year, all of whom he had written down himself. "Edna Harmon, Leonard Peltier, Rena Gelissen, Devon Halsey, and . . ." The *Ino* paused so each member could quietly name the person in their thoughts to whom they wished serene health, perfect enlightenment.

Hans almost forgot what he was doing. What was Devon's name doing on the list? And who had written it there?

The service was over; everyone bowed to Buddha, then turned to face each other, bowing as Hans made his way out of the zendo. Ten seconds later, he was back inside the chamber and looking at the dedication. "Did you write this, Peter?"

"No, *Roshi*." Peter, the *Ino*, looked at the handwriting at the bottom of the list. "I always let you add the names."

"Jenny?" Hans asked.

"No, *Roshi*. I know who Devon is, but I didn't think she needed our prayers." He held up the list so the others could see it; everyone shook their heads.

Hans nodded, stared at the way Devon's name had been scribbled, and acknowledged, "This is not my writing."

CHAPTER FIFTEEN

The Buddha-way is supreme; I vow to embody it.
— The Four Vows in Zen

Lochwood explained who Todd Daniels was to his partner as they traversed from Northwest Woods through Sag Harbor and up to Scuttlehole Road. Yellow police tape still encircled the perimeter of the Imamura-Montebello house, and would until Loch gave the okay to have it removed, but he wasn't going to do that yet. He and Gary drove up the driveway and parked the car on the periphery of the scene, then signed the roster so their presence could be recorded. He was pleased to see local authorities following precise protocol procedures—he'd been nervous about leaving the scene open to snooping neighbors, but because of the location of the estate and the holidays, regular rubberneckers had been kept to a minimum.

"How you guys doing? Quite a scene here, eh? It's our fourth stabbing—hell, I guess its our fifth, too—in thirteen years." Aside from being overly chatty, the duty officer seemed to be doing his job.

"Crime is up," Gary mumbled.

"So it is. Exciting. Course, you boys get all the fun."

Lochwood wasn't sure how much fun he was having, but knew what the guy meant. He could never spend his day kicking pebbles around and watching tape flap in the wind. Being stationary for too long drove him crazy, that's why he didn't like to sleep.

"A lot of history to this place. Folks been wanting to get on the premises for years. Lots of strange happenings. You know, artist types." Loch didn't answer in hopes that silence would discourage his monologue. "You going to check out the house again?"

"We're heading up to the barn," Gary told him.

"Ah, that's the artist's studio." He pointed. "Right up that hill. You can't miss it."

"We've been here before. Thanks for the directions."

"Sure, anytime, glad to be of help. Anything you need just whistle. I'm on night duty, every night." No wonder the guy couldn't stop talking. Loch excused him with a brief nod.

The chalk lines where Beka had breathed her last had soaked almost completely into the dirt, and Lochwood stopped to study the shape of the fading lines one last time. The lines sans the body almost formed an arrow, as if she had been pointing to something besides heaven.

"I can't see Halsey hanging out with these people." Gary was looking across the compound.

"Why not?"

"It's like the guard says, weird artists."

"I think Beka had the same thing to say about Halsey hanging out with us."

Loch headed toward the end of the barn and looked out the back door. There were uninterrupted fields softly rolling to the west lined with forest on both sides that seemed dense and untampered. He remembered Devon telling him that Gabe and Beka were considering donating the land to the Nature Conservancy, but there was a large realtor's sign posted in the middle of the acreage so it could be read from the road—sixty-five acres, zoned for development, with the realtor's name and number underneath. Loch wrote down the information.

"What about that trash bin?" Gary pointed out. "It doesn't look like it's been dumped in a while."

"Your idea. Your search." Loch held out his hands for a leg up.

"Prick." Gary ignored Loch's proffered hands and stepped up to the garbage bin to look inside. "Looks like a lot of crap."

"That's because it is crap. Get in it and stop acting like a pussy!"

Gary sighed, climbed over the rim, and stood on the trash heap. "Look, more crap!"

"Whatta surprise." Loch watched as Gary gingerly went through the motions of a search through garbage.

"Wait a minute, here's something." He held up a slightly flexible Plasticine that looked like it'd been cut in pieces.

"I bet that would hold a print," Loch suggested, but he wasn't sure what the print would mean if they couldn't put it into context. "Any plaster in there?"

"There's some very wet and mushy stuff at the bottom. Looks like nasty mashed potatoes. Here's another strip." Gary pulled out two more pieces of the material that seemed to hold some kind of shape and crawled out of the dumpster. "Everything else is garbage and this probably is, too, but what the hell."

They lined them up on the ground and looked at them, then Loch turned them over. "Look at that indent and crease, that's an eye."

Gary turned over another piece. "You lookin' at it backwards, or inside out?"

"Both."

"That would make this a chin?"

"Looks like it. Do they belong together?"

"No telling without the missing parts." Loch glanced at his partner. This time he would help.

Together they pushed away some lumber resting on top of the heap. "Got something!" Gary held up a partial chunk of plaster. It was pocked slightly from where the snow and sleet had pelted it, but the form was unmistakable—it was someone's face. "You think this is what she broke?"

"Only Halsey can tell us for sure."

Fifteen minutes later they had found only two more pieces of Plasticine and a number of smaller pieces that were too torn to make much sense of, but Loch wanted all of it. "We'll put Halsey or Landal on this when we get back."

"Who knows, it might be something."

Loch paused to think for a moment and Gary let him alone. "Why would Gabe do a sculpture of a missing kid?"

"Maybe he was jealous."

Gary put the pieces into an evidence bag and looked at his watch. "We should get hold of Jenny O'Doherty again, find out if she knew whether there had been any legal separation proceedings, and if so, who instigated the separation." Lochwood was still staring out at the fields, so Gary punched O'Doherty's number into his cellphone and continued talking to his partner while the phone chirped.

"Then let's swing by that exercise studio and find Beka's partner, Edilio."

The path from the barn led past a pond, frozen and austere in the early morning air. On the other side of the water, probably a half mile away, was a road. "Did we check around the pond and the road on the other side of the pond for any tire marks or footprints?" Loch asked.

"A local team was over there yesterday morning."

"What did they find?"

"Deer tracks."

Gary stopped speaking as O'Doherty picked up. Lochwood headed back down the path and started to sign them out. A scrap of red moved behind the mountain-laurel hemming the pond shore, then darted back into the trees. "What was that?" he wondered out loud.

"Looked like a fox," the duty officer informed him.

"There's fox out here?"

"There's lots of wildlife out here; course, not for much longer the way the developers are taking over the land. You boys find what you're looking for?" He pointed at the bag.

"We found something."

Gary joined them and shook his head as Loch looked up at him. "O'Doherty didn't know anything about a separation."

Loch pointed across the pond. "Is that Scuttlehole Road?"

"Yep." The duty officer stuck the clipboard under his arm.

"And the pond is . . . ?"

"Daniels' Hole. It's actually more of a scuttlehole than a pond. That means it disappears and reappears depending on the rain and snowfall each season."

"Daniels?"

"It's a family name round these parts."

"Looks like a pond to me," Gary observed.

"It's been getting bigger for years. Mr. Montebello tried to fill it in; had to go to the town board to get permission, but it was a fool's dream. You can't go changing what's natural. I think there's an underwater spring feeding it," the officer explained. "They can't stop it from growing. Between the ocean and the marshes, in a few hundred years this whole area will be underwater."

"I bet the property values will drop then!" Lochwood said ruefully. They turned away from the scuttlehole and headed back toward their car.

* * *

Maybe it was an unconscious New Year's resolution to be on time that had caused Devon to arrive in Chinatown so early; she wasn't sure. Normally, she was never on time for social functions. She placed the white placard—*Police Business*—in the front window of her car and left it parked outside of One Police Plaza, along with a number of the others who had *Police Business* cards in their windows. She stared up at the row of windows on the third floor of Police Plaza.

It had not occurred to her earlier, but perhaps she should stop inside. In 1984, the Missing Persons Bureau had been stationed up there. She wondered if they had moved the unit. The building wasn't open to the public on Sundays, but Devon stopped in the employee entrance and showed her badge to the guard.

"What can I do for you, detective?"

"I'm doing some follow-up on a Missing Person's case in Manhattan that may have impact on a case I'm working out on the Island." It wasn't the absolute truth but it sounded reasonable. "Is there anyone upstairs today?"

"Step over there and I'll call up." She allowed the guard to make the call and waited until he signaled for her to come over to the metal detector. "You armed?"

"Two guns, officer." She showed him her arm holster and the gun she kept secured to her waist against her back.

"Sign here."

He pointed to the elevator.

"Is it still on the third floor?" she asked. He nodded.

It was surprising how quickly it all came back to her as she stepped onto the elevator—the same smelly old lift she had ridden up in 1984. The hallway did not look as if any time had passed, and the same rows of fluorescent lights lined the ceiling and reflected into the hard wax shine of beige linoleum floors. She felt as if she'd opened up a time capsule, and walked toward the Missing Persons Bureau door feeling the same trepidation she'd felt all those years ago when they'd brought her here for questioning.

Joey Zambini had been the male detective's name; the female—some flower-type name—had interviewed her with him. It had been Zambini who showed her down to the conference room, an informal feeling for an interview, and she knew now it was where you put people who you want to relax, not suspects you want to intimidate. Zambini had brought her a cup of coffee, and a reverend from Todd's church had joined them. They had chatted, almost amiably, about New Year's Eve. She could not remember what she had said now, she'd been too nervous for that, but she remembered watching the female detective and wondering how long it took her to make the grade.

She saw the same woman through the glass of the Missing Persons Bureau door. Her hair was grayer and her face more faded, but it was the same detective Devon had met before. She opened the door and stepped inside. "I'm Detective Halsey from Suffolk." The woman stared at her but didn't say a word. "I'm interested in reacquisitioning a copy of an old case, from 1984." Still no response. "The Todd Daniels file?"

"You what?"

Devon waited for the Missing Person's detective to shut her mouth and quit staring at her in shock. "I'm interested in seeing the case file on a missing college kid back in 1984," she repeated slowly. "Todd Daniels."

"I'm sorry to appear so stupid," Detective Carol Freesia explained. "It's really not in my nature, but you're the second person this week to ask to see that file."

Now it was Devon's turn to look and feel stupid; her mouth dropped open. "Somebody else has been here? You mind?" Devon pointed to a chair.

Freesia motioned for her to sit down.

She pulled the chair out and sat by the detective's desk. "Was the first person Detective Lochwood Brennen?"

Detective Freesia shook her head. "Nope. Why are people in Suffolk County all of a sudden so interested in this case?" Devon knew Freesia was avoiding her question. "It's stone cold, believe me. That kid isn't going to float up out of the East River any day soon. He's just bones now."

"Who asked to see the file?"

Detective Freesia raised her eyebrows in a silent challenge. "They didn't get to see it, so why should you?"

"Let's just say it'd be a personal favor."

"Cop to cop?"

"Something like that."

Detective Freesia looked at Devon's badge. "It's still an open case, I don't have to let you see it, and unless you have information to help close it, I can't see much reason to help." Devon knew the pissing game and waited for Freesia to finish marking her territory—they'd worked around men for too long not to act like them sometimes. "Halsey. Why's that ring a bell?"

"I just made C.S.U. in Suffolk." She used the abbreviated term for the Crime Scene Unit.

"That's right! They finally let a girl into the boy's club. Congratulations, but that's not it and you're too young for much else." Devon did not feel that young but it was all part of the game; she waited until Freesia was done. "You know, I worked the Daniels case."

Devon's eyes burned but neither of them blinked. It was like having a staring match with a cat—one of the big cats in the Bronx Zoo, not your standard house pet. "I know," Devon finally said, holding her gaze steady. "You interviewed me."

They both blinked.

"Good one." Freesia chuckled, then shook her head. "Poor Todd. He must have been a nice kid for so many people to care after so long. All I knew was his name, his face, and that he was big news. Good Long Island family. Honors student. Every parent's dream. And I couldn't tell them what we really thought because his brother was a part of that crowd." She looked at Devon hard, her eyes narrowing. "Hell, so were you. What were you doing mixed up in the downtown drug scene?"

"I was a kid."

"Is that a real excuse?"

"Did you interview Beka Imamura?" Devon asked.

"And to make up for your ways you became a cop who likes to solve things, but can't let go of the one you couldn't?" She gave the younger detective a discerning look. "Zambini and I did."

Devon had liked Freesia's partner and looked over at his desk. "Zambini, where is he?"

"Cancer."

"I'm sorry."

"Me too. He was one of those rare Brooklyn boys who could work with a woman like she was an equal." She smiled fondly, then jerked her chin up into the air. "You know, I was the first female Missing Persons detective, big hoopla in 1983. Is everyone at Suffolk's ivory tower watching you like a black kid walking through Bensonhurst?"

Devon nodded. "Every piss and shit I take. Every man I talk to."

"Some things just never change, even in a new millenium. Gene Roddenberry would have been disappointed. Tell you what, you can look at the file in this office but I can't let you walk out of here with a copy of it."

"I fill out the forms, how long will it take for records to pull it and get it up here?"

Freesia smiled strangely, as if enjoying some secret joke with herself. "Not long."

"Next week?"

"How about today or tomorrow?"

"Records is open today?" Devon asked, stunned.

"I have ways of getting what I want." There was that smirk again.

"Well, if it's possible, I'd like to take a glance at Imamura's interview, and if it proves informative I might come back tomorrow, if that's okay."

"Why her?" Freesia was noncommittal about tomorrow's date.

"She's dead and so is her husband, Gabriel Montebello."

"What happened?"

"We're not sure yet. She called and left me a message about Todd."

"Now, that *is* interesting." Freesia was finally engaged, and

Devon had a bargaining tool. "I always thought she had something to do with Todd's disappearance. Something just didn't add up. We couldn't find a trace of that kid anywhere."

"But this is New York City. He could have fallen into an elevator shaft or been murdered and dumped in the sewer."

"I know, I know. It still galls me, though. We dragged both rivers." She reached over to a metal-wire vertical file and pulled out a folder. She placed the file on her desk and Devon found herself staring at Todd's name.

It had been written in red indelible ink that had barely faded with the years, the edges were worn and slightly tattered, there was a coffee stain at one corner—it was all that remained of Todd Daniels.

"You interviewed all of us."

"That we did." Freesia tapped her pencil on the manila folder.

"So what are you doing with this at your fingertips?"

"You want to see it or ask questions?"

Devon held out her hand to take the folder.

"You can use that desk over there." Freesia pointed to an empty desk across the room where the nameplate *Zambini* was still sitting in its place. He must have died very recently, and Devon suddenly felt sorry she'd never gotten to speak to him again. "You know, I've had a lot of disappointments on this job, but Todd was my first," Freesia said a little sadly.

Devon took the file out of the senior detective's hands. "We always remember our first."

She skimmed through the initial documents and quickly assessed that much footwork had been done on Todd's disappearance but there was no evidence to indicate what had happened to him. No evidence anywhere to even hint at a reason for his disappearance. "Freesia?" Devon asked. "How many missing persons do you get a year?"

"Over a thousand." Freesia's eyebrows arched, as if amazed at the number herself.

"And how many get solved?"

Freesia shrugged. "Hard to say. Reports and what we end up investigating vary. You know, some call if their teenager's an hour late for dinner and others don't notice for a week that their kid's a goner."

"I remember telling Sam to report Todd's disappearance right away, but we couldn't make a formal notification for forty-eight hours. It took a while for anyone to take us seriously."

"He was a college kid. We don't want to tie up officers on a bogus report. What if he'd slipped off with some girl?"

"Beka was the girl he would have run off with," she reminded the detective, then turned her attention to the transcription.

Case: Daniels, Todd
Number: 84101-1001
Relationship: Friend
Date/Time: 1/6/84, 12:05
Interviewed: BEKA IMAMURA
Transcribed: 1/7/84

The first page was more like an introduction of the basic information—nothing vital—and Devon skimmed through the text until she found the meat of the interview.

Det. Freesia: Where were you when Todd Daniels disappeared?
Imamura: Well, we aren't sure exactly when he disappeared. I was probably dancing. I danced all night.
Det. Freesia: Can you tell us what else was going on at the party at the time of Todd's disappearance?
Imamura: Besides dancing? Drinking, popping off firecrackers. Is that what you mean?
Det. Zambini: Actually, Ms. Imamura, we're looking for something a little more definitive. For instance, did you see anyone dealing cocaine or passing vials at your party?
Imamura: There may have been some pot on the roof but I really wouldn't know. I'm very careful about what goes in my body and don't smoke at all.
Det. Freesia: So what can you tell us about the evening or about Todd that might help us find him?
Imamura: Nothing much, I was dancing with him when he ran

downstairs. The next thing I knew Sam and Josh were asking us to help look for him.

Det. Zambini: Were you having an affair with Todd?

Imamura: No. (laughter) He was too young for me.

Det. Freesia: That's not what his brother says.

Imamura: Sam was jealous. He has a crush on me, but he told me to leave Todd alone so I did.

Det. Freesia: Miss Imamura, please don't lie to us. We know enough about the party that night to know that you were involved with Todd Daniels.

Imamura: Involved, but an affair? That's what you have with a married man, not a college student.

Det. Freesia: So you slept with Todd?

Imamura: Just once.

Det. Zambini: Was that on Saturday night?

Imamura: No, Friday. I'm not known for my discretion and Todd was going to be a minister. So, Saturday I was into somebody else.

Det. Freesia: You were protecting his reputation?

Imamura: Well, I certainly don't have to protect mine!

Det. Freesia: You said was.

Imamura: I said what?

Det. Freesia: You said, "was going to be a minister." Do you know why you said was?

Imamura: I wasn't aware that I said was. I guess I mean is. I mean, what's the right tense for someone who's missing and may or may not be dead? He might be, right? And if he is dead then was would be correct, wouldn't it? If he's just blown us all off and disappeared or dropped out of school . . . would it be was or is?

Det. Zambini: We didn't mean to make you so upset.

Det. Freesia: I was just curious why you used the past tense in referring to Todd.

Imamura: I don't know. He's gone isn't he? I mean, where is he, if something horrible didn't happen to him? Why would he leave me on the dance floor like that and never come back? Why wouldn't he call and let Sam or his parents know where he is?

Det. Freesia: We were hoping you might tell us.

Imamura: I was hoping you might tell me!

Det. Zambini: Is there anything else you can tell us that might be of assistance?

Imamura: I performed at Yale two years ago, Todd started catching my performances whenever he could. He was some kind of dance groupie. I'd never met him before last weekend but he said he was in love with me and had been in love with me for like two years. He got really drunk and kept telling me he was going to drop out and move to the city for me. I told him to go screw Katiti.

Det. Zambini: Who's Katiti?

Imamura: A diva. She slept with Josh the night Todd disappeared, really bad taste I thought.

Det. Freesia: You don't like her.

Imamura: What's to like?

Det. Zambini: Tell us more about that, the party.

Imamura: What about it? It's 1984; we were so blown by that. The world's supposed to change big-time this year. All the psychics say it. Things are going to be different, and they are. See? Everything has changed. It sucks now more than ever.

Det. Freesia: He said he was going to drop out? Any idea where he might have gone if he did that?

Imamura: His girlfriend's? Yeah, he has a girlfriend! Don't I feel like a fool. Listen, is there anything else? I have to get to rehearsal.

Det. Freesia: You'll call us if anything comes up that might help in the case? And we'll call you if we have more questions.

Det. Zambini: I'm a big fan of your work.

Det. Freesia: You might call him a dance groupie, too.

Det. Zambini: Where are you performing next?

Imamura: The People's Republic of China.

Det. Zambini: Amazing.

Imamura: Yeah, we're the first modern dance company to go into a communist country in like twenty years or something. They've commissioned me to choreograph a piece for the concert. The pressure's on.

Det. Zambini: You should be proud.

Imamura: Yeah, proud.

Det. Freesia: Joey, this is being taped.

Det. Zambini: What are you choreographing about?
Imamura: Todd.
End of Tape.
End of Transcription.

Devon dabbed the tears leaking out of the corners of her eyes. She could see Beka's crestfallen face—and remembered the first time she had seen the dance Beka had choreographed about the disappearance of Todd Daniels. She had called it "The Weeping Buddha." They had all just wanted to have fun, all of the time. There was nothing sinister about the loft; it was just a party place like so many others back in the '80s. Wasn't it? They weren't innocent, but they weren't world-wise; they actually thought that cocaine was not addictive, or fatal, or any of the things they knew about it now. Back then it was called a "designer" drug, like ecstacy in the '90s—safe, until you died.

Devon flipped through the pages of transcription until she found her own interview. A quick glance up at Freesia told her the detective wasn't bothered by her presence. It would only take a few seconds to read what she had said back then. It was strange, but it was beginning to feel like yesterday.

CHAPTER SIXTEEN

But the torture dragged on as good fortune.

—J. BRODSKY, *About the 1910's*

Detectives Brennen and DeBritzi stood in front of a plate-glass window on Long Wharf in Sag Harbor and found themselves watching a strange ritual of exercise. The wind whipped up off the bay, but inside the health club people were sweating and women and men alike seemed to be in all manners of oddly erotic positions.

"What the hell is this place?" Gary exclaimed.

"Pilates, the latest exercise craze that started fifty years ago."

"Looks like S&M."

"That would explain the modern interest," Loch surmised.

Beka was a partner in the studio, more silent than anything, Jenny O'Doherty had said. Evidently, Beka had backed it financially for two reasons—to help her old dance partner and to have a place where she herself could exercise. It had ended up being a cash cow, though, with articles in *Vogue*, *In Style*, and other magazines; the studio now had a waiting list of over a hundred Hamptonites wanting to come exercise one-on-one with exclusively trained Pilates instructors.

"Well, this is going to be anything but routine," Gary muttered. They opened the door and entered, uncomfortably aware that they were the only people in the room fully dressed. And it wasn't just their leather shoes and winter parkas that looked out of place amid the more scantily clad people in leotards and gym shorts; it was the surprised looks on both of their faces. Lochwood kept trying to erase the smile creeping around the corners of his mouth, but the mirrors on every wall reflected his failed attempt to wipe off his amused grin; and Gary was doing no better in hiding his mirth. They would have been more comfortable in a gay biker's bar.

A woman moaned loudly while an instructor leaned her body

weight into the client's thighs. The exercise salon was full of almost medieval-looking contraptions: Tables on wheels slid back and forth with people lying on their backs moving their legs from open to closed positions in midair. There was something that looked oddly like a bed-and-rack combination holding a man's legs in metal springs and leather straps.

"Hello, did you want some information?" A woman in her mid-thirties walked away from a man closer to Lochwood's age, who groaned as he tried to stretch over his pale white legs while sand-wiched between a box and a board. "Here's a brochure." She handed Lochwood a glossy tri-fold with the words, *Change Your Body, Change Your Life* embossed on the cover above a color photo of Beka per-forming some exercise that looked particularly tortuous and, to any straight red-blooded male, sexually suggestive. "If you want to sit down and watch I can talk with you in a minute, just as soon as I get Harold over to the bed." She turned back to the groaning man. "Come on, Harold. Drop those heels! Drop your head. Suck in your gut and get your shoulders down."

No wonder there were so many men exercising here, Loch thought. Where else could you get pretty women to stand on you, or better yet, stand over you and yell, "*Drop your head!*"

"I wonder how much they pay for this kind of torture," Gary whispered to Loch.

"Seventy for your first session, three hundred for a series of five," the woman piped in. "I can answer all of your questions in a minute."

"Actually, we aren't here to, um, work out." Loch wondered if that's what they called it. "We're looking for Edilio Ferraro."

"So are we. Harold, focus on your body, not what's going on around you." She leaned on the man's back to press his chest closer to his thighs—it hurt Lochwood just to watch. "He was supposed to come back and open this morning, but I guess he decided to extend his Christmas vacation."

"Where did he go?"

"Can we do this later? It's crazy today without Edilio here and with Beka's misfortune . . . We should have closed, but everyone wants to work out now that the holidays are over, and I'm not being paid to rearrange the schedule."

"Imagine," Gary commented in a low voice to his partner, "expressing your grief by changing your appointment."

"Harold, did I tell you to get up? Come on, one more exercise. Stomach control!" She was no longer interested in them and her body language made that plain. She planted a fist into the man's stomach as he tried to sit up. "Exhale! And inhale!" Loch wondered if her clients called her *Mistress*, but decided not to ask—she scared him.

"What time is good for you?" Gary inquired.

"We're booked solid till three and the last client is done at quarter after four."

"Fine, we'll come back then."

They left by the same door they'd entered and walked out onto the pier. "What a trip!" Gary laughed. "I felt like I was doing undercover work on the West Side Highway in the '80s."

"At the Ramrod or Bull and Chain?" Loch chuckled. "Come on, let's go someplace that's more our speed and get some French onion soup at the Corner Bar." He led the way from the docks and up into the small town where Devon lived.

The Corner Bar was dark, as usual, and seemed full of regulars. Two famous authors sat at the oak-hewn bar. Loch recognized one of them from his book jacket and the other from his mug shot—a DUI, Christmas 1999. He couldn't remember either name but they were already fairly sloppy and he hoped they were walking home. He and Gary took a seat by the window and ordered two French onion soups and coffee.

"Guinness on tap," Gary said thirstily. "Want a draft?"

"When was the last time you saw me drink?"

"Don't remember."

"That's cause you're the one with all the vices."

"Well, somebody in this partnership has to be human!" Gary paused, then waved to the waitress. "Can I smoke in here?"

"At the bar."

"I hate puritans." He stood up and walked over to the bar a few feet away. One of the authors held out his hand, mistaking Gary as an approaching fan rather than one of the country's illiterate. "So, what do you think about this Edilio character?" Gary did not even notice the hand proffered him.

"Don't know enough to think anything."

"Odd, though, disappearing right after they croak?"

"Right before, actually, and being on vacation doesn't equal disappearing."

"He doesn't call in?"

"He could have called Beka and told her he was extending his trip and she never told, or got the chance to tell, anyone at the studio."

"Why not just call the studio himself—there's an answering machine at the desk."

"Maybe the machine was full of messages."

Gary stabbed his butt into the ashtray and returned to the table. "You're so good at negating theories, how about coming up with one?"

"What if he ordered a hit and got the hell out of Dodge?" Loch smiled at Gary's stunned face. The tureens of soup arrived, thick with bubbling cheese, and they set about digging out the beef broth and French bread hiding beneath its surface.

"A hit. That would explain the scene," Gary finally admitted.

"Too messy?"

"Yeah, it seems contrived. Too many clues that don't add up to anything concrete. That's not how a hit usually is."

"You sound like Halsey. Either it's clean and professional with one, maybe two mistakes, or it's an open book. This story has too many possible endings."

"So, you're not married to the murder/suicide scenario?"

"I'm not married to anything, Gary. You know me."

"Let the evidence speak for itself." Gary mimicked Loch's voice as if by rote. "I took your course back when I was a rookie detective hoping to pass the test."

"And I passed you?"

"You're such a prick."

* * *

Case: Daniels, Todd
Number: 84101-1001
Relationship: Friend
Date/Time: 1/6/84, 15:20

Interviewed: DEVON HALSEY
Transcribed: 1/7/84

Det. Freesia: What do you do for a living, Miss Halsey?
Halsey: I'm an artist.
Det. Freesia: You were a friend of Todd Daniels?
Halsey: I know his brother. I met Todd last weekend when he was staying with Sam.
Det. Freesia: And you last saw Todd?
Halsey: He was dancing with Beka. He looked like he was going to be sick and someone was in the bathroom, so he ran downstairs. Sam and I followed. He and Sam talked a bit, that was when Todd decided to go for a run around the block. I think he thought the fresh air would sober him up, and it was pretty cold out so it should have. That's what I keep thinking about.
Det. Freesia: What?
Halsey: He wasn't so drunk he couldn't hold a conversation with his brother. And everyone keeps saying he was so drunk that he could have slipped into the river, or an elevator shaft, but I don't see how he could have been that drunk.
Det. Zambini: Who's everyone?
Halsey: At the party.
Det. Zambini: Was he on something else?
Halsey: I could smell pot on the roof, but didn't notice anything else. There was a lot of activity in one of the bedrooms but I didn't try to go in, so I don't know what that was about.
Det. Freesia: Dare to hazard a guess?
Halsey: No.
Det. Zambini: So you and his brother were the last people to see him?
Halsey: I guess so, except for Broadway Bob. He lives on the grate outside the A train. I think he saw Todd after we did. He said something about an alien taking Todd up in the air. I didn't think much of it at first, but now I'm not so sure.
Det. Zambini: What changed your mind?
Halsey: He said they flew away, but now that I think about it he could have been pointing down Howard Street. Only we walked

down Howard right after that and didn't see anything.

Det. Freesia: What do you think happened?

Halsey: Sam says he worked at soup kitchens and was very inter-
ested in street people. That's probably why Bob saw him, I bet
Todd stopped to say Happy New Year. Maybe he tried to help an
unfriendly type. Ever since Reagan released all those people from
Bellevue there are a lot more psychotic people on the streets now.
Bob warns Beka about them all the time.

Det. Freesia: How do you mean?

Halsey: She likes to go for walks late at night and Bob always tells
her when the bad aliens are out and which streets to avoid.

Det. Freesia: If this "bad alien" got Todd, where's his body?

Halsey: That's your job, officer.

Devon smiled at her past self; she sounded so young, and she
had made the typical mistake of calling a detective "officer," something she'd never do now. Yet even then she had an eye for observation, albeit untrained at that time. She bet if they'd had her on the
case in 1984 they would have found out something about Todd. Of
course, she was forgetting that techniques for finding evidence had
changed enormously in the past ten years, and the department back
then was probably even more understaffed than it was now. Plus,
this was a big city with a lot of people—Todd had probably been one
of several to disappear that week.

She closed the casebook on Todd and stood up from the spare
desk. "Thanks, I owe you." She walked over to Freesia, handed her
the folder, and watched the detective place Todd Daniels back into the
vertical file amidst a number of other worn and semi-worn folders.

"Are those *all* of your unsolved cases?" Devon asked in disbelief.

"Lord, no! We have a roomful of those. These are simply the
boys who have disappeared on New Year's Eve."

"How many?"

"Eight. Only three were ever found. Spring floaters."

"That college kid two years ago?"

"He was the last one."

"Any sign of foul play?"

"There was something."

Devon's eyes narrowed, silently demanding that Freesia share the information with her.

"We don't know for sure. He was pretty well gone by the time we found him, and so were the other two," Freesia said. "I really thought Todd would be a floater."

Devon looked at the folders in the vertical file. "Why do you keep them out?"

"The similarities—their age, Ivy Leaguers, New Year's Eve in the city. I keep looking for some other connection, but they all belong to different frats, come from different areas in the tristate."

"And you have five more that never came up, including Todd?"

"Five, yes." Freesia fingered the files tenderly, rubbing her fingers on the tabs of the folders. "And it's happened almost every other year—except for the millenium."

"Too many undercover cops to get away with much," Devon reasoned. "What does Homicide think?"

"That I'm looking for a promotion out of here."

"Are you?"

"I like what I do; at least my folks are alive—sometimes." Freesia leaned back in her chair and cocked her head as if to say, that's more than you can say.

"I think I'd like to come back and read more tomorrow. Okay?"

"Suit yourself, detective."

"What shift are you on?"

"Seven to three."

"Great, I'll get here at seven-fifteen."

Freesia stopped what she was doing and looked the younger detective straight in the eye. "You know, your information was one of our only leads."

"What was that?"

"Broadway Bob. Zambini talked to him the day of your interview and thought that maybe his aliens were real people." She opened the file and read Zambini's notes. "Bob accepted a bottle of bourbon from the party-goers and maintains that he saw one of them go off with an alien. When asked what the alien looked like he said, 'All aliens look alike—short and dark. Everybody knows that, and antennas, they all gots antennas.' He then started waving at somebody walking by and screaming, 'There's one now.' The man was Chinese, about five foot seven with black hair." Freesia looked up at Devon. "Unfortunately, Bob started slipping halfway through the interview and screaming at a few more aliens who were trying to use the A train."

"His brain was fried."

"Yeah, well suddenly being cut off from a daily dosage of Thorazine does that to people. Zambini went back the next day to talk to him. He was dead."

"Dead?" Devon was stunned. Why hadn't she noticed Bob's absence from his post? Why hadn't Beka ever mentioned it?

"Froze to death."

"Was there an autopsy?"

"If I remember correctly, he died of heart failure and exposure. Common enough."

"Poor Bob. I wish I could have done more."

"You became a cop."

Devon stood in the doorway and looked at the detective who had forged her way through departmental red tape, making it easier for women to get promoted and titled. "So, are you going to tell me who else wanted to see Todd's file now?"

Freesia didn't answer.

"It might help me."

"I don't see how. She didn't get to see it. We can't let civilians look at open cases, can we?"

Devon did not have the energy for any more games. "Just tell me who it was."

Freesia fiddled with her pen and raised her eyebrows once more. "Your friend, Beka."

CHAPTER SEVENTEEN

Today one often confuses passion and vice. Cigarette smoking,
cocaine, and the vigorously esteemed recurrent need for coitus
are, God knows, no passions.
       —ROBERT MUSIL, *The Man Without Qualities*

Gary and Loch walked out of the Corner Bar and headed down
Main Street and into the town of Sag Harbor. Shop windows still
decorated with remnants of Christmas blinked cheerily and the town
seemed to hum with people waving to each other from across the
streets and wishing one another a Happy New Year. Loch pointed
out all the local points of interest—the police station, the firehouse,
Emporium hardware.

"What is this place, a movie set?" Gary, a Brooklyn boy who
thought Coney Island was the country, marveled. "Something out of
Mayberry RFD. Where's Opie?"

"It's a real homey sort of town."

"Except for those people all strapped up in springs and leather."

"Some summer people never leave." Lochwood could hear a
dog barking behind him; it was a joyful bark, familiarly demanding.
It got louder, moving up the street closer and closer to them. Loch
turned around to see what the commotion was about and saw Boo
dragging his pet-sitter up Main Street toward the object of his affec-
tion, himself.

"Brennen! What the hell are you doing here?" Aileen tried to
catch her breath as Boo madly wiggled back and forth, his left lip
curling upward, baring his teeth in that look only Dalmatians, or
very happy dogs, can pull off.

Gary backed away.

"Aileen." Loch kissed her cheek. "Gary, here's your Opie!"

She socked him in the arm. "I'm not that short!"

"Yeah, you are, but who's measuring?" He knelt down on the

sidewalk and began rubbing Boo's ears and received a thorough face-licking. "Good boy, good boy. It's good to see you, too." He continued to pet Boo while performing introductions. "Aileen, this is my partner, Gary DeBritzi. Gary, Aileen." He gestured to the one hundred and one spots vibrating in front of their eyes. "And this is Boo, Halsey's dog. Aileen is Halsey's pet-sitter and roommate."

"How you doing?" Gary shook Aileen's hand, then gingerly patted the dog on the head. "I thought he was gonna bite my leg off!"

"Nah, that's a smile!" Aileen laughed at him. "Not a dog person, are ya?"

"Aileen's known for her keen observations of people . . ." Loch said as he stood up, ". . . and dogs."

"Yeah, well so am I. How come you and Halsey's dog are so chummy?"

"How was your New Year, Aileen?" Loch evaded Gary's question with one of his own.

"I worked. You guys here cause of Beka?" she asked. Loch didn't answer. "Oh, can't say nothing, huh? Well, I hear Edilio's taken a runner. You think he might've killed them?" Loch had always thought Aileen had missed her calling; she had a way of getting information that even the best cops would have struggled to find out.

"Who are your sources, Aileen?" Gary asked.

"Sherm at 7-Eleven!" She laughed. "It's the only place besides the post office to find out what's really going on. But, hey, it's none a my business and I shouldn't have asked. I just wanted to make sure you knew the latest, and I couldn't tell Dev this morning cause she went straight into the city from work. Hey, you know when she's coming back?"

"I have a feeling she's staying in for the night."

"I would if I were her. It's such a long drive to go back and forth in one day, but Dev loves to drive."

"We gotta get going, Leenie." Loch patted Boo one last time on the head. He and Gary started back down the street, even though Boo was whining to join him.

"Why don't you guys stop by later? I'll make you some tea and give you the rest of the neighborhood scoop."

"Wouldn't miss it!" he yelled back at her. They continued down the street past Concha D'oro, the bustling Italian restaurant where he and Devon enjoyed Lena's meatballs and garlic knots almost every Friday night.

"So," Gary started in on him, "you not only know where Halsey lives, you know the people in her town, and her dog greets you like you're his long lost daddy. What gives, Brennen?"

"None of your business."

"Fuck you. How long has this been going on?"

Lochwood smirked; he couldn't help himself. "Five years," he admitted finally to his partner.

"You ol' dog." Gary slapped him on the shoulder. "I should have known. There's been talk, but there's always talk about Halsey."

"Which is why we keep it quiet. She doesn't need people thinking she slept her way up the ladder."

"Hey, it's not like you're a sergeant!" Gary teased.

"Which you keep reminding me of." Loch did not seek positions that stuck him behind a desk—he liked action, not politics.

"But you know how people are, they think what they want." Gary looked at his watch. They had reached the end of Main Street in less than three minutes. "So this is all there is to this town?"

"Nope." Loch stopped and laughed. "We have to walk back to the other end."

"I don't believe it, the new hot-spot of the rich and famous is barely long enough for a parade."

"Parades start by the Getty gas station on the edge of town; it's almost a mile from there to Long Wharf."

"This town's too small to get crowded."

"Not in the summer it's not."

They started to cross the street as a large 4 x 4 was cutting down the lane. Gary slowed but Lochwood kept walking; the car stopped to let them pass. Gary was dumbfounded. "Pedestrians have the right of way here?"

"Don't it beat all?" Lochwood was enjoying showing off the little town where he and Devon had fallen in love.

The first time she had invited him out here they had walked up and down Main Street and Loch had been amazed at how quaint and civilized Sag Harbor was. "Wait until summer," Devon had warned him. "Barbarians at the gate." But in that first summer, and every summer thereafter, they had holed up in her house, swam in the bay, and avoided the crowds by working weekends. The summer of love for Loch and Devon was in the '90s, not the '60s.

He and Gary began walking back down the other side of Main Street. "Five years?"

"Five," Loch affirmed.

"No wonder Halsey doesn't date anyone at the precinct. And all this time the guys thought she was a dyke!"

"Didn't you learn anything in the cultural diversity course?"

"It's just you and me." They passed Variety, the local five-and-dime where a T-shirt, still on sale from the summer, was hanging in the window. It read: *"Sag Harbor, a Drinking Town with a Sailing Problem."* They then passed one of the three liquor stores Sag Harbor sported. At Schiavoni's, the only grocery store in town, they crossed the street again to get to Long Wharf without having to navigate the traffic circle, although traffic was barely an issue the day after New Year.

* * *

Devon sat on one of the red chairs next to the gold lion with a ball under his foot and watched the doors to Number One Chinese Restaurant swing open and shut. Open and shut. Everything reminded her of the case and all she could think was, this isn't open and shut. A sea of Asian-American faces in large groups, families, and the occasional Caucasian passed through the foyer and headed upstairs. The twang of Chinese music amid Cantonese and Mandarin chatter from the dining rooms above trickled down the long stairwell; Devon wished her group would arrive. Then, at one o'clock, Maddie Fong, looking stylishly '80s in head-to-toe black, came through the door. She should have leapt up to greet her old friend but she heard Broadway Bob's description of aliens and found her words deserting her. True, he could have been talking about any number of people in Chinatown, but she could not ignore the fact that Maddie Fong was also short, dark-haired, and one of the people from the loft—so was Beka, for that matter.

"Devon!" All five foot two inches of Maddie Fong squeezed her with surprising strength. "You look great! My god, country life must suit you."

"I guess, but I miss the speed of things in the city."

"Not me, I can't stand New York anymore."

"Where are you now?"

"The not-so-trendy North Fork."

"Doing what?"

"I run a restaurant."

"What kind?"

"Chinese. We have dim sum on the weekends. I told Alex and Beka to bring you up there sometime. They must have forgotten."

"Is that one of our crowd?" Devon pointed to a tall, light-skinned black woman with a cascade of curls tumbling down around her face who had been staring at Maddie but now turned and seemed to be looking through the crowd of people for someone in particular.

"Katiti!" Maddie jumped up and ran out the door. "Katiti!"

Katiti shook her head so the tangle of curls that was her hair half hid her face then swayed her hips from side to side like an island girl carrying fruit atop her head. Beka might have been the dancer in the bunch, but Katiti was the actress. "Maddie? Oh my god, I thought it was you but you still look twenty-four. Josh is parking the car. Alex is with him. I wanted to make sure we got a table."

"You remember Devon, Beka's best friend?"

"We've met. I came after you were a regular at the loft, though." They shook hands while studying each other's faces.

"I remember you, too." Devon tried to sound as if it were a pleasant memory, but that would have been a lie. The territorial war between Katiti and Beka—who would be reigning diva of the loft— had taken its toll on everyone. "Are you still dancing?" Devon asked.

"I have my own company but I don't perform as much anymore. I heard about Beka."

"What about her?" Maddie piped in.

Devon could feel the blood leave her face.

"Are you okay?" Maddie asked.

"It's Beka," Devon stammered.

"She's not coming?" Maddie stamped her foot. "I knew it. It's just like her to have something more important to do and stand us all up! It's not fair, especially to you, Dev! We could have met at my place and avoided coming all the way into the city!"

Katiti reached out with her talon-like fingernails to grab Maddie's arm and stop her, as Devon's mouth somehow formed the words, "Beka's dead. So is Gabe."

"No . . ." Maddie stuttered. Devon nodded. Maddie sat down hard on the gilded chair next to the lion. "I knew something was wrong when I saw you. I was sure you would come in together. Katiti, you knew? Why didn't you call me? When did it happen?"

"New Year's Eve," Katiti said.

"Like Todd?" Maddie began to cry. "Why didn't I know about it?"

"It was on the news," Katiti informed her.

Devon wasn't ready to deal with everyone else's emotions regarding Beka's death and began to think she'd made a mistake in coming. How could Maddie have managed not to hear about Beka? Something that Maddie had just said made her ask, "Why is it like Todd? Todd disappeared. Beka and Gabe are dead."

Maddie continued blubbering.

"I tried to call you, Maddie, but you weren't home, and this isn't the sort of thing to leave on the answering machine." Katiti seemed rather nervous as she spoke, as if she were trying to justify something not yet asked for.

Devon mused. Maybe she had not made a mistake coming to dim sum, it might turn out to be more than a little informative—if she could just stay objective and keep her own emotions in check.

"Alex had *Newsday* in the car. I only read the *Times* myself, but you know Alex—three papers a day." Katiti added, "It's terrible what they said about you at the scene, Devon."

"You were there?" Maddie almost screamed her outrage. Devon nodded but remained silent. "Oh my god, how could you do that?"

"I did my job and tried not to think about who they were." She felt amazingly cool and collected as she responded and tried to assess whether or not Maddie was over-acting. And why was Katiti tossing her head back and forth, looking out the door every few seconds?

Katiti caught Devon watching her and struck a catlike pose. "Where's Josh?"

Devon shrugged and made two mental notes: first, if Beka had actually set up this reunion she would have missed it anyway, because she was supposed to be in Hawaii; and second, Beka had not invited her, Alex had.

"Was it really a murder/suicide?" Katiti asked softly, but something in her tone of voice made Devon doubt her sincerity.

"It's an open investigation, and I didn't come here to tell you guys what I know. I came here for some support and some . . ." Tears welled up in Devon's eyes; she would be able to observe them better if everyone treated her as the poor grieving friend and not an investigator on the case.

"This is worse than Todd," Maddie whispered, "much worse."

* * *

Hans was stuck. Usually he found comfort when chiseling his great wooden sculptures, and often answers came to him unawares, as if he were sitting *zazen* rather than working through chips of bark and pulp. Seeing Devon's name on the prayer rolls had disturbed his serenity. He pounded one section of the wood slab he was trying to mold into shape, then paused to caress the wood and check the contour.

He had called and left a message for her at home but she had not returned his call yet, and impatience nagged at his consciousness. He tried to remember what Beka had said about the boy Todd, something about Todd and Gabe? Or was it Edilio and Todd? There were so many people that she used to hang out with that he could not be sure. Beka had run with a faster crowd than Hans was accustomed to, but he had never held it against her. He never held anything against anyone, but the more he thought about it the more he wondered if that night back in 1984 had anything to do with the reason she was now dead. And was what had happened pertinent to Devon Halsey's safety?

Like one of the Titans, he lifted his mallet and hewed a chunk out of the wood he was sculpting. Why else would her name be on the prayer rolls?

CHAPTER EIGHTEEN

Wu Wang: Innocence (The Unexpected).
By turning back one is freed of guilt.

—I Ching, 25

"There's Josh and Alex." Katiti pointed outside the doors of the restaurant. The newcomers saw Devon at the same time, but neither smiled. Alex hugged Devon tightly, stifling a small sob, as Josh squeezed her shoulder. They had all been such good friends at one time, why had they all drifted apart? What had happened? Then Devon remembered—Todd had happened.

Godwyn's cocky British accent flitted over the Asian heads bobbing past them as the lanky Ghanese photographer, whose blue-black skin seemed to shimmer in the winter sun, grabbed Alex from behind. In seconds everyone was hugging each other—or were they clinging? Desperation as real as death's sickle grabbed at their shoulders and necks as if trying to keep a grip on the past that was slipping through their fingers. They stood apart then and looked at one another, judging the bits of gray hair that Clairol was covering, the softer faces that were pre–face lift age but post-youth.

"Who would have thought after all these years we'd all still be alive?" Godwyn said. The group looked at him, shocked by his words.

"Almost all of us," Devon said quietly.

"Where's Sam?" Maddie asked.

"Screw Sam, where's my Beka?" Godwyn looked up and down the street. "She come with you, did she, Dev?" They were standing inside the foyer now, blocking the arterial flow of pedestrian traffic up and down the stairwell of Number One Chinese Restaurant, as a sudden rush of reality whirred in her ears and Godwyn's face grew ashen.

Devon reached for his arm. "She's gone, God."

"Gone where? Hawaii?"

Devon stared at him. Had he known about her trip?

"She's dead, mate." Josh squeezed his ex-roommate's shoulder.

"That's not bloody funny." His eyes narrowed as he pulled away. "Helluva joke!"

Alex took his other arm. "It's no joke, God. She's dead, and so is Gabe."

* * *

Loch and Gary got to the Sag Harbor Pilates studio just as one of the instructors was heading out the door. She was coifed in a tightly pulled-back ponytail and looked to be about twenty-four years old. "Excuse me, miss?" Loch took the opportunity to waylay her outside. "You work there?"

"Yeah, but I'm pretty new. Pam can explain things better than I can." She seemed inordinately nervous, or perhaps just high-strung. Dancers all seemed to be high-strung.

"This isn't about exercising," Gary tried to explain.

"We're with Homicide." Lochwood discretely showed her his badge. "This is my partner, Detective DeBritzi. I'm Detective Brennen."

"It's about Beka, isn't it?" Her eyes seemed to glaze over.

Not the brightest bulb in the lot, Loch figured to himself, and decided to be as gentle as possible with her. "What can you tell us about them?" He used his most soothing voice.

"Edilio and Beka?" She looked up and down the wharf, tensely, then said, "Everyone knew they were breaking up because they had a fight right in the studio just before Christmas."

This was interesting news and Lochwood did not want her to know that he had been referring to Gabe and Beka. "They were breaking up their business partnership, or something more?"

"I don't know, I wasn't there. Pam could tell you for sure. But I heard that Beka told him she wanted him out of the business and out of her life."

"What day was that?"

"Just before he left for vacation."

"Do you remember her exact words?"

"Yeah, 'Go away and don't come back. I'm sick of you taking advantage of me.'" She paused.

"Any idea where he was going for vacation?"

"Hawaii." She stamped her feet in an effort to warm them. "Can I go now? I wasn't supposed to work today and I have things to do."

"Can we get your phone number? We might need to ask you a few more questions."

"Sure." She rattled off her number and sped down the pier toward Main Street.

Gary looked over at his partner. "Do you think there was something between Edilio and Beka?"

"Sounds like."

"Then why didn't Halsey tell us? I thought they were best friends."

"Maybe they weren't as close as she thought," Loch said, more to himself than to his partner. He looked at his watch and wondered where Devon and her so-called friends were at that moment.

* * *

Feeling like the odd one out, Devon unwrapped her chopsticks slowly, gathering her thoughts together as she watched the group's dynamic. They were sitting at a large round table staring at each other, awkwardly waiting for one of the many carts to make its way toward them so the feast could begin, and yet no one seemed eager to eat. Katiti poured herself a cup of tea; Devon silently disapproved. Traditionally, it was proper to pour tea for the people sitting next to you, then pour your own. Devon poured Alex's tea before her own, and saw Maddie reciprocally pouring Godwyn's first and then reaching across Katiti to fill Josh's cup.

"Are you going to tell me what happened?" Godwyn's voice trembled as he looked almost accusingly at Devon.

"She can't say anything about the case," Katiti informed him.

Devon judged Godwyn's grief by her own, and wondered if it was sincerity or fear lurking behind his obsidian eyes. It was no secret he had been in love with Beka years ago and perhaps still was, but he and Maddie had also been an item back then. They used to refer to Godwyn as their generic lover—it had seemed funny back then.

"I never thought anything good would come of marrying Gabe," Josh said. He draped his arm around Devon's shoulder, but was looking at his wife. "If you need anything, please call us. We're practically neighbors now." He smiled at Katiti, but Devon could not make out if it was a *fuck-you* smile, or *don't-you-agree-honey* smile. "It was Katiti's idea for us to become East Enders."

Katiti's eyes flashed with wicked daggers at her husband's head, and Devon recalled that Josh had also been one of the generic loft lovers.

Josh nodded at Godwyn. "A little more upscale than the London East End, though."

"I can't believe she's gone." Godwyn shook his head as if to clear any possibility of tears from his eyes. Josh's attempt at conversation having failed, they once again stared at each other across the table.

"We love the East End." Katiti tried to support her husband. "Especially the summer. There are so many parties."

Godwyn's half-lidded eyes glared at Katiti. "A bit too posh for us real people. I haven't been out there since Beka's last big bash. Now that was a party, wasn't it, Dev? Course, Beka knows how to throw a party."

Devon was thinking about his choice of words. He had just let Katiti know that she hadn't been invited to Beka's summer event in as unsubtle a manner as any Hamptons socialite might. He had also just gotten a dig in at her, for the party in question was the party Beka and she had fought at, and Devon had a sneaking suspicion Godwyn knew that. She wondered where he had learned to wield such deadly skill.

"Remember how she would dance for hours all alone in the center of the room?" He began to reminisce, and Devon found herself unwillingly touched by his sentiments. "We were lucky to know her. Lucky to be the ones she performed solo for." A tear fell from Godwyn's right eye.

Devon caught Alex watching her watching them; a quizzical look passed across her brow then vanished as a cart passed within striking distance. "Waiter!" Alex shouted like a Hollywood producer on a movie set at the almost-empty cart of food that seemed destined for the kitchen. "I have low blood sugar and have to eat." She snatched two plates of cold-looking fried dumplings. No one else seemed eager to imbibe, but Alexandra ravenously devoured three in a row, then sighed with relief as the conversation veered away from Beka and Gabe and drifted into the still waters of Todd's disappearance.

"Isn't it strange that Beka and Gabe should die on the anniversary of Todd's death?" Maddie leaned forward on the table like a carnival fortune-teller.

"Death?" Josh asked.

"Well, you can't believe he just disappeared anymore, can you? He'd have come back by now." She looked at him disbelievingly.

"Is it a coincidence, Devon?" Alex asked abruptly.

Devon did not answer.

"Remember when they brought the dogs to sniff for Todd?" Godwyn asked, sniffing a dumpling and making a face.

It was almost as if Todd's file were still open on Freesia's desk as the loftmates, with very little prompting on Devon's part, pulled out old items from the past and rehashed them out loud directly before her eyes. It was better than reading transcripts—it was virtual reality without the CD-ROM.

"I'll never forget the way he lunged at you." Alex recalled how Josh had run upstairs and practically crashed right into the nose of the German shepherd.

"I'll never forget the way he growled at your crotch!"

"The damn cops started laughing!" Josh reminded Godwyn.

She was intrigued. "What breed?"

"I think one had pointy ears and one was floppy-eared." Maddie was obviously not a dog person.

"A shepherd and a bloodhound."

"How do you know?"

"We use them in Suffolk, too, Mad Dog." Devon exhumed Maddie's old nickname from the 1980s' grave of misplaced anamnesis.

"I haven't been called that in years!" Maddie did not look pleased. In fact, she looked remarkably like a rabid mongrel when she was upset, thus the name.

"Maddie 'the Mad Dog' Fong," Godwyn mocked.

"What'd you have in your pocket, Josh?" Devon asked.

"I dunno. Keys?" Maddie and Alex looked at each other but didn't say anything.

"Well, if you can't remember I can't tell you what I know about police dogs." Devon held her cup close to her lips and shut her eyes as the steaming tea softened her face.

"I know what you had," Maddie said.

"I don't care what you know, Mad Dog," Josh's voice threatened.

"Maybe Detective Halsey does."

Devon listened to their exchange while breathing in the fragrance of green tea. "Maybe Detective Halsey already knows," she said calmly. Her eyes opened. They were all looking at her, stunned. "Shepherds sniff for drugs. Bloodhounds, bodies. I'm assuming you didn't have any body parts on you." Josh shook his head.

"We didn't do drugs," Maddie said.

"Cut the crap."

"Just recreational drugs," Josh justified.

"There are no recreational drugs, only illegal drugs."

"It was harmless," Maddie agreed with Josh.

"So harmless that Todd Daniels ran around the block and never came back?" Devon put her cup of tea down and looked at their faces. "I don't think so."

CHAPTER NINETEEN

*If you cannot find the truth right where you are, where else do
you expect to find it?*

—DOGEN

The last client was just putting on his street clothes as Loch and
Gary entered the Pilates studio for the second time that day. "You
came back!" the woman who had asked them to return later greeted
them. "I'm not Edilio, but maybe I can answer any questions you
have. My name is Pam. Did you read the brochure?"

"Actually, we're with Suffolk County Homicide."

"Oh," she gasped, and turned one shade off of sea-foam green.
"Thank you for not saying that earlier. It could have been very awkward." She sat down and motioned for them to have a seat on the
only two normal-looking pieces of furniture in the studio. "Dana,
can you stay a few minutes? These gentlemen probably need to
speak to everyone who works here."

"Sure." Dana picked up two yellow rubber balls and a metal
ring with knee pads somehow stuck on the side and came over to
sit on the floor with her legs spread wide open. She smiled at
Loch, then laid her chest flat on the floor. The sound of bones
popping sprung from her body. "Ah, that felt good. My hips are so
tight." Loch didn't think they looked tight at all, but he didn't say
anything.

"All of our clients want to know what happened, but we're not
saying much," Pam began. "We have a couple of clients who are
reporters."

"They called first thing this morning to see if we could squeeze
them in. As if we didn't know what they really wanted." Dana
stopped and looked at Pam, as if for permission to continue.

"We're trying to keep the press out of this as much as possible
as well," Gary assured them.

"Well, good luck. That man who just left works for *People*."

"We understand there was a fight between Edilio and Beka sometime before Christmas."

"I don't know why Edilio put up with her," Dana said softly.

"They were lovers?" Gary asked.

"I thought they were," Dana piped in.

"No, they weren't," Pam said quickly. "They acted like it but that's all."

"I overheard him on the phone one night and I know it was her, because the number was on the phone screen." She jumped up and hit a few numbers. "See! If I punch in a number it shows up on the screen."

"And you recognized Beka's number?" Gary inquired.

"I know it by heart," Dana said proudly.

"What did you overhear?" Lochwood wrote down what she was saying as inconspicuously as possible.

"Love talk. You know, 'I can't stand not seeing you tonight . . .' blah, blah, blah, '. . . but I'm supposed to be here until seven o'clock.' He asked me if I'd stay and close for him."

"How long had this been going on?" Loch wondered out loud.

"If it was ever going on," Pam reminded them.

"I don't think it ever ended," Dana said. "They were touted as modern dance's answer to Fonteyn and Nureyev, Barishnikov and Kirkland."

"Who?" Loch and Gary asked at once.

She shrugged her angular shoulders as if their lack of dance knowledge was truly tragic. "Never mind, I think they just kept the flame. She married Gabe for security but it was an open relationship."

"Open?"

"You know, you can sleep with other people if you want. Open!"

"Thank you for enlightening us." Gary stood up and began looking around the studio.

"Do you think she would have closed him out of this studio?" Loch asked.

Pam coughed. Both detectives looked at her. "He said everything had been worked out."

"How much money are we talking?"

"We're just hourly employees, we don't do the books, but the ledger's right there."

"You want to take a look?" Dana jumped up off the floor and ran to the desk.

Loch smiled encouragingly. "That'd be very helpful." He and Gary eyeballed the numbers for the past month. It was a good business from what Loch could tell; steady, but they weren't getting Hamptons-rich. Still, they charged a lot for private sessions and only paid out about fifteen percent to their staff. With four clients an hour, Loch surmised they were pulling in lawyer's rates.

"Where was he heading for vacation?" Gary asked, while Loch flipped through the numbers.

"Tahiti via Hawaii first."

"He and Beka were talking about opening a studio in Honolulu," Pam added.

Lochwood caught Gary's eye—the U.S. can't extradite from Tahiti. "You've both been very helpful." They wrote down their phone numbers and said good night.

"Think I could call one of those girls up for a date?" Gary asked, once they were back on Long Wharf.

"You're such a slut, Gary."

* * *

As usual Devon had hit her mark. Detective Freesia had been right in assuming the loft was involved with the downtown drug scene, but what, if anything, did that have to do with Todd or the present? Beka had started doing cocaine shortly after Todd disappeared—or so Devon had been told. Had her habit started sooner?

"There's Sam. Let's not talk about Todd or Beka anymore," Katiti suggested in a hoarse whisper. "Let's just make the rest of the day fun."

Devon snorted through her nose. Fun? How much fun could they have when topics like Todd, Beka, and Gabe stood larger than pink elephants in the center of every room they entered?

Sam looked wrung out. His eyes were red-rimmed and his cheeks puffy. "Sorry I'm late." He walked straight over to Devon. "I just can't get over it." She stood up and hugged him. "You're the real reason I came today," he told her, while looking directly into her eyes. "How are you?"

"I'm dealing with it as best I can." He nodded understandingly, in the way Lochwood might have when he tried to comfort someone who had suffered a loss. His manner was almost professional, as if he were her therapist, not a friend who was going through the same mixed array of emotions surrounding death.

Josh came over and began pumping his hand up and down and hugging him in a pounding-male sort of way; their exchange exactly the opposite to what she had just experienced.

"I'm sorry I didn't call each of you and let you know about Beka and Gabe," Devon apologized to the group.

"No one expected that of you," Alex assured her.

"I've been so busy trying to figure out what happened that there hasn't been time for anything else."

"It's okay, Dev. Sit down, Sam." Maddie poured him a cup of tea.

Sam's arrival once more eclipsed the arrival of food at the table, so after everyone had finished hugging him and settled back to their chairs, the group still sat with nothing but cups of tea, Alex's cold, unappetizing dumplings, and awkward silence. Dissatisfied with the lack of fare, Alex looked hungrily around again, but it seemed as if all the carts had abandoned them, migrating to the far side of the room.

* * *

Loch dialed Devon's cellphone from the car but got an out-of-range message. "That's funny, I wonder if my phone's working?"

"You think Edilio could've killed them?" Gary asked.

"What's the motive?" Loch tried her number again, got the same message, and hung up. "He was going to start a studio in Oahu. Why kill his connection to that town and his backer?"

"What if she left the studio to him?"

"That doesn't explain the affair. Why kill her if he's having an affair with her?"

They headed back down the driveway to Lochwood's car and got inside. "For a small town things sure move fast," Gary quipped.

"That's because everybody knows everybody else's business. Listen, Devon's house is just down the street, what do you say we pop in before heading back to the precinct? I need directions to Rysam Street and can use her phone to see if mine is working."

"Sounds good to me, will that cute dog-walker be there?"

"Why do you think we're really going?"

"Oh, so you're trying to set me up with Aileen and solve this case at the same time? Don't you do anything simply, Brennen?"

"No." Loch started the engine and hung a left onto Bay Street.

* * *

All of them except Katiti were what she would call *observers*, but it had been Beka whom everyone watched. She had never thought of it that way before: Sam was a therapist who specialized in art and dance therapy; movie producer Alex had started shooting and selling videos of Beka's performances; Godwyn had been the first one to document Beka in black and white, just as Gabe had used bronze and oils. It always came back to Beka. It was as if she were orchestrating their reunion from the beyond, still the center of the group, holding their attention even though she had just taken her final curtain call. Everyone was staring at everyone else but no one was saying a word, and the dumplings in the center of the table looked as greasy and unappetizing as the past they had been discussing.

Godwyn pulled his camera out and slowly aimed it around the table, quietly clicking the shudder. Devon knew his reputation, but she still couldn't help feeling like the group was part of one of his life studies that she would rather be left out of completely. She could also tell that Godwyn was just as uncomfortable being observed as she was. She didn't need a camera to study a person, just her mind, and she turned her focus on him.

In defense against her stare, he raised his camera and aimed. She shoved a dumpling in her mouth and made a face like a chipmunk. He clicked.

With a voice as flat as the sea at low tide, Sam began to speak about the years of searching for Todd. Loss of affect, Devon surmised. That's what psychologists called it when someone was so separated from their pain that they sounded cold and unfeeling. Across the table Godwyn was now focused on Sam's stricken face and clicked.

One, two, three. The only thing that was missing was the flash.

Devon blinked at the memory of orange and red spots dancing in front of her eyes, blinding her and Todd and Beka and Gabe, Edilio . . . One, two, three. She stared across the table at Godwyn, the emerging realization only just beginning to seep through her consciousness—of the five people dancing in the center of the room when he snapped their picture in 1984, Devon and Edilio were the only ones left alive. "Why'd you take it?"

"Take that?" Godwyn pointed at Sam's still frozen face. "A study on surviving tragedy. *Time/Life* loves those kinds of pics." Had Godwyn really become as cold and commercial as he sounded?

"Are you still at T.K. Psychiatric?" Josh was asking Sam from across the table.

"Yep, after living with you guys, working with the mentally insane seemed a natural progression." Sam forced a laugh that surprised her. It sounded too unnatural and contrived for someone of his psychological reputation to succumb to, but then Sam was as human as the next person—just because he could treat people did not mean he could deal with his own circumstances.

She looked back at Godwyn. "The picture at the New Year's party. Why'd you take it? You knew Beka hated flashes while she was dancing."

"I don't remember."

"Get off it," she shot back in a hushed tone.

"I was pissed. Flirting with him right in front of me." He began to rewind his film.

"She'd broken up with you," Devon reminded him.

"Yeah, well, just cause a bird breaks it off don't mean you're over her." His cockney accent matched step with his ire.

"You made Todd sick from the flashes!"

"I didn't know that, did I?" He maneuvered his camera back under his arm uncomfortably.

"Can we *not* talk about this?" Katiti interjected vehemently. What had been a quiet spat between the two of them suddenly came to the attention of the entire table.

"Go on, God," Devon continued her interrogation, "tell us why you not only took those photos but why you sold them to the *Post*."

"You took those fucking pictures?" Sam's voice was raw with rage. "I can't believe you did that to me and my family!"

"I was broke. I needed the money!" Godwyn retorted angrily.

"You made Todd look like a drunk monkey."

"I thought he looked happy," Alex defended Godwyn.

"Of course he looked happy! Beka had her leg next to his ear!"

"It's not like your family wasn't already making Page Six," Maddie reminded him. "For god's sake, your father had just purchased the largest parcel of land on the East End to develop into a golf course, or was it a subdivision?"

Devon looked at them calmly. The emotions around her escalated and their voices grew louder. Everyone was yelling about their own agenda and perspective on the solitary event that had changed their young lives.

Maddie was saying to Alex, "You don't know everything," who in turn reminded Maddie, "You slept with him, too!" Devon wasn't sure who they were referring to and wasn't sure it mattered.

"I can't believe you sold Beka and me out!" Sam glared at Godwyn. "Hell, you'd sell us all out for a buck!"

Across the table, Katiti seemed to be enjoying the bedlam. Her arms were folded and she watched the ensuing argument with a glint in her golden eyes as Josh, unaware of his wife's joy, just kept repeating, "We didn't know what was going to happen! We just didn't know . . ."

"Drugs were fun, not dangerous," Maddie was saying.

At the other end of the room the electric piano began to chime in with "Yesterday" as a Chinese woman sang Lennon's words in her twangy nasal voice—a Cantonese version of the Beatles classic.

"*Oh, I berieve in Resterday.*"

The tension between them shattered—first Sam, then Alex and Maddie, even Godwyn began to laugh. Devon found herself carried with the wave, slightly at first and then more fully as the laughter took hold of her body and shook until tears began to fall.

Josh waved to the fried crab-ball cart and Maddie beckoned to one of the waiters.

"Beka would have wanted us to have this party in her honor. She would want us to eat a lot and talk about her," Alex reminded them.

They had ejected their pent-up rage and gotten at least a few things off their chests, so that by the time the carts of food arrived on their side of the room their appetites had also returned. Soon the table was full of stacked bamboo steamers full of fresh, hot dumplings, shrimp toast, fried milk, and platters of fon dripping with oyster sauce.

Devon whispered, raising her cup of tea, "To Beka."

"To Beka," they answered in unison. The room suddenly seemed lighter as if her spirit had finally appeared—late as usual—and ordered Tsingtao beers for the lot of them.

CHAPTER TWENTY

Zen is the unsymbolism of the world.

—R.H. BLYTH

Loch peeked through the kitchen door window and saw Aileen wave them inside. A moment later he was receiving the official spotted welcome as Boo bounded through the back door. Loch knew Boo's grumbles were Dalmatian for *"Where the hell you been?"* but Gary, unfamiliar with the language of dogs, ducked behind the wagging tail and into the kitchen where Aileen was filling the tea kettle in the sink. Loch watched from the back porch as his partner chatted her up, taking his time to rub Boo's ears before coming inside.

"So how come you like dogs so much?" she was asking his partner when Lochwood finally came through the door.

"I don't know that I do." Gary still looked a bit unnerved by Boo's reception.

"He's just talking at you." Aileen laughed at him.

"I've never heard a dog talk before."

"Your partner's cute when he's scared, Brennen."

"Hear that, Gary? You're cute," Loch teased.

"Shut up. Only Aileen can call me that."

"I hear you been all over town asking questions. You guys going to interview me, too? I'm gonna be really hurt if you don't give me the good cop, bad cop routine." She pouted at them.

"Which one of us you want to be bad?" Gary asked.

She chortled and pulled three cups out of the cupboard. "What kind of tea you want? I got Lipton's and Earl Grey."

"What's the difference?" Gary asked.

"If you have to ask, you get Lipton."

"Can I use your phone, Leenie?"

She looked at Loch. "What is this? You asking cause your partner's here? Just so you know, he never asks permission for nothin'."

172

Loch walked over to the phone and began to dial Devon's cell-phone one more time.

"So I guess you knew Beka, too?" Gary said.

"Sure, we all go way back. Devon started bringing Beka out here every summer in high school. That's almost twenty years ago. Oops! Dating myself. I mean ten years ago." She put the kettle on the stove and turned up the flame.

"How're you taking it?"

"I'm not thinking about it, that's how I'm taking it. But Beka and me weren't close like Dev and her. We just knew each other, you know? Hell, she was a fixture around here. At least until they had that stupid fight."

Loch hung up the phone, perplexed, and looked at them both. "I thought it was my cell that wasn't working but I just got the same recording."

"Maybe she's out of range," Gary suggested.

"I've reached her in the city before," Loch replied.

"Didn't you say she's staying at Gabe's warehouse?" Gary asked. "Maybe the walls are distorting the frequency."

"I've called her there before, too." Loch proceeded to beep her.

"That's right, I keep forgetting! Can you believe this, Aileen? I just found out about these two today."

"Should have come to Sag Harbor sooner; we've known for years."

Loch sat down by the fire. "So, anything else unusual happening in town today?"

"Well, let's see, Barry Goldstein and his wife are leaving for St. Barts. There've been reporters all over town trying to get dirt on Beka and Gabe. Everyone's mad at Tom Hurley for the article he ran on Beka, and there are two Homicide detectives asking a lot of questions. I didn't know you guys went to the Corner Bar for lunch."

Gary whistled. "Jeezus, that's scary!"

"And you had French onion soup!" She laughed. "You sure you don't want breath mints instead of tea?"

"I told you, Aileen should be the cop! What about Edilio?"

"Now, him nobody knows anything about! But he's top on the

list of possible murder suspects at 7-Eleven." The teapot began to moan. "General consensus at the post office is Beka did it."

"You knew Edilio?" Gary asked.

"Aileen knows everyone." Loch checked his watch; Devon should have returned his page by now. He didn't like not being able to get in touch with her.

"I met him a few times but he wasn't much interested in getting to know me," Aileen was saying. "I'm just a small-town girl, unimportant in the Hamptons' scheme of things."

"That couldn't be true." Gary was winking at her.

"When you grow up out here you get used to being passed over by out-of-towners. The only way we get ahead is if we inherit and sell the property to the next golf course developer."

"The question for you, Leenie, is did you know she was leaving Gabe?" Lochwood cut in.

"No shit. I knew Gabe had the place on the market, but I thought it was more to piss Beka off than a real threat."

"Interesting." Loch smiled. She was probably right.

She brought over a pot of tea and set it down in front of them. "Now, if you're going to be here for a while I'll run down to Schiavoni's before they close and get something for my dinner."

"You're not going to stay and have tea with us?"

Gary is such a flirt, Lochwood thought.

"If you're still here when I get back, I'll have a cup with you. But Schiavoni's closes at five and I can never get out of there quickly. If you guys go before I get back, don't lock the door."

"Is that safe?" Gary exclaimed.

"What? The raccoons are going to break in and steal the garbage?" She chuckled. "Actually, that's happened to me before. This is the country!" She grabbed her coat and gloves. "Devon ever tell you about the lady who wanted her money back last summer because there were raccoons in Sag Harbor? Said she couldn't relax this close to wildlife, so she went back to New York City!" Aileen guffawed.

Loch held out his hand to stop her. "Hey! You know where this attorney Barry Goldstein lives?"

"Sure, yellow Lab—Pretzel's house . . . Take a left on Bay and go down three streets; it's the biggest house on Rysam Street. Gotta go, it takes me forever to get out of that damn store!" Aileen left them to the fire and Boo's occasionally tapping tail demanding more belly rubbing. Loch poured the tea.

"I never thought I'd see you looking so domestic, Brennen," Gary scoffed.

"Once in a while it's okay."

"Does Frank know?"

"Halsey can trust Frank more than I can trust you." He still wasn't used to calling her by her first name in front of his partner.

"I resent that!"

"You have a big mouth, DeBritzi, and I want you to keep this one to yourself. Devon's got enough to deal with."

"Hey, if she was going to sleep her way to the top, she'd do Houck!" Gary joked.

"She wouldn't find that funny."

"Sure she would. Halsey would crack that one herself. So what about this Aileen?"

"Rough childhood, her parents owned the local fish store but died in a car accident when she was nine, her guardian was an alcoholic fisherman who couldn't swim. She's known Halsey since they were kids . . ."

"I don't want a profile, asshole. I want to know if she's dating anyone."

"Oh." They drank their tea peering at the fire. "I don't think so."

Loch checked his watch and wondered where Devon and her Chinatown cronies were now. "Here, boy." He tossed the cookie into the air, watched Boo catch it, and settled back into the rocker to stare at the fire. It was good to be home.

* * *

Whenever she and Lochwood went out for Chinese food they ended up arresting someone, Devon thought, as she pushed the soy sauce around with her chopsticks. Empty plates along with tin and bamboo steamers were stacked in the middle of the table. After the initial rush of trying everything the servers brought them, the group had slowed down and eaten more leisurely, but now everyone was stuffed.

Josh and Maddie were comparing the quality of the dim sum with her own restaurant's fare when Maddie announced, "You know what the *I Ching* said today?" Everyone looked at her expectantly. "*Wu Wang*. By turning back one is freed of guilt."

"I never understood how a bunch of lines could say anything," Josh countered.

"Do you still read the tarot cards?" Alex asked Maddie.

"Not since that day at One Police Plaza," Maddie answered between bites of barbecued chicken feet and one hundred-year-old preserved egg.

Devon's ears pricked up and she turned her attention to their conversation.

"God, remember that?" Alex tried to balance a stuffed eggplant in black bean sauce on her chopsticks. "What did he accuse you of?"

"Black magic."

"Who?" Katiti asked.

Sam stopped eating and looked up at Maddie. "Reverend Brown. Man, did you piss him off."

Maddie began to play with a crab claw, dragging it through the soy until it was soaked and dark brown. She left it there and looked at her former roommate. "Yeah, well, he told me that I was evil." Her eyes looked across the table as if into the distance. "I believe his exact words were, 'It's because of you that Todd's gone. If you hadn't touched the devil's cards, we would have found him by now!' Detective Freesia came out and told him to leave me alone and he said, 'She's a witch!' 'She's a witness!' she yelled back at him. 'Leave her alone.'"

Maddie looked at her friends; they had stopped eating. "I kept telling myself that he was wrong, that it wasn't my fault that Todd was missing, but I couldn't help wondering . . . I can't help but wonder . . ."

"We all feel responsible—guilty, if you will—on some level," Josh told her.

"A lot of hocus-pocus, Maddie." Sam reached his hand over the remnants of their meal and took hers. "I asked you to do the cards, remember?" She nodded as he took her hand and smiled at her. "Christians can be just as superstitious as pagans if you ask me, but that doesn't mean they're right. I never held you or anyone else at this table accountable for Todd's disappearance, except maybe for Beka." His eyes caught hold of Devon's. "If she hadn't given him that coke maybe he wouldn't have gone off like that."

There it was again, drugs.

"Are you guys going to tell me what was going on, or am I going to have to squeeze it out of you?" Devon asked. No one volunteered any information.

CHAPTER TWENTY-ONE

What do you do when the show is all done?
Where do you go when the people go home? . . .
But what do you do with the leftover wine?
— MELANIE, "Leftover Wine"

Once outside the gang spread out from a semi-solid nucleus and blended in with the busy sidewalks as they moved at a quick pace through the late-afternoon crowds of Chinatown. They passed fish vendors and vegetable stands, little metal carts serving jook and dumplings, and stores selling trinkets, perfume, and electronic equipment. Every one of the vendors had a deal and hawked his wares at the passersby.

"Five dollar, sunglasses. Very nice. Very expensive." "Ten-dollar watch. Real gold plate, Cartier." "Fresh terrapin!" "Sushi. Fresh mackerel!" Devon stopped. Her eyes teared up as she inhaled deeply.

Alex shook her head and chuckled. "You're the only person I know who gets sentimental over the smell of piss and dead fish."

"We used to call each other *Saba* Sisters because we both loved mackerel sushi."

"Beka always said you were more Asian than she was."

"An egg." Devon recalled the slang term for a Caucasian who acted Asian.

"You grew up in Taiwan, right?" Alex asked.

"Maybe that's why I miss Chinatown so much."

"Sam could tell you. He's the psychologist." They had stopped at Josh and Katiti's Land Rover, conveniently parked on Mulberry Street next to Lung Moon Bakery. Devon ran in and bought some coconut rolls for breakfast the next morning, just in case Loch showed up, then returned to the gang outside.

"Anyone need a ride uptown?" Josh offered.

Katiti pinched him. "Honey, remember, we have errands to run."

He reneged on his offer.

"This has been like *The Big Chill* meets *Friends* in *Bright Lights, Big City!*" Alexandra reduced the entire group to a media stereotype.

"Except there are black people," Katiti pointed out.

"All we're missing is a Hispanic and Native American component to be completely PC," Alex added.

"I'm one-eighth Shinnecock," Devon told them. "Sherman Alexie might not like me saying that, but he's not here."

Katiti held up her perpetually tan arms. "And I'm here to represent the Latin quarter as well as black."

"You're brown sugar, Katiti. I'm black." Godwyn held his perfect ebony arm next to her honey-toned skin.

"God, you're beyond black! And god I love saying that!" She laughed raucously.

"I wonder what our ratings would be?" Alex was in full-swing producer mode now.

"Who gives a damn what we are?" Sam swore. "We're here and that's all that matters!"

"I wish I had my camera," Alex said wistfully.

Devon had not thought about it before and turned to look at her. "Do you still have the videos?"

"The whole lot." Alex's eyes drifted up and down the street as if she was looking for an angle to shoot.

"What video?" Katiti asked.

Devon watched her reaction. "I'd love to see New Year's 1984."

"You have that one?" Katiti hissed at her.

"It's in storage in L.A."

Devon squeezed her arm tightly so as to get her attention. "I want to see the tapes. I'm serious, Alex."

"Why do you care about 1984?" Josh piped in.

Alex pulled her hand through her short-cropped hair and squinted at Devon. "What's this about?"

"Closure," Sam answered for Devon. She smiled at him, but his approval of her request made her feel uneasy for some reason. She wasn't sure she wanted anyone else knowing that the tapes were still in existence, but now they all knew. It occurred to her that if one of them was a murderer she had just put Alex and herself into jeopardy. Unless Alex was the murderer, and then she wouldn't let Devon have the tapes.

Alex squeezed her hand. "I'll have my assistant find them. They're yours."

Devon watched as the others began to stare longingly at the filthy pavement of Canal Street under their feet, and another awkward silence shook their reality. They could only share brief moments of tenderness before the quick clouds of New York's hard-edged brusqueness tumbled back across their lives and their faces. "There's going to be a memorial service sometime this week," she announced. "Call my mom for the place and time. We're in the book."

They hugged each other good-bye, then began to move off down the street, each going their separate ways as they had so many years ago, only to be reunited by death or birthdays: Josh and Katiti on errands, Sam to the Hamptons-bound jitney bus, Alex to a friend's loft in Tribeca. Maddie and Godwyn disappeared into the crowd and suddenly Devon found herself alone on the street, the words to one of Beka's favorite Melanie tunes playing in her ears: *What do you do when the show is all done? Where do you go when the people go home? . . . But what do you do with the leftover wine?*

She headed down the street unable to make out any familiar places—Chinatown had been renovated in the past few years and seemed strange with its shiny new exterior. At Lafayette she stopped and looked up. There were the windows to the loft hanging high above the holiday crowds. She hadn't planned to, but she found herself looking into the vendors' shops for the way into 255 Canal Street.

* * *

Hans's mail truck pulled partway up Devon's driveway, then stopped. Aileen's car was not parked there and he recognized the detectives' car immediately. He let the engine idle in neutral and eased up on the brake, coasting back down the drive before shifting into reverse to turn around on Bay Street. There was only one cop he cared to speak to at that moment and it wasn't either of the two in her house. He turned right on Bay and headed for home. Devon would call—he knew that. It was just a matter of time.

* * *

The loft's windows were above her but the entrance to the loft seemed to have evaporated. She stuck her head inside a jewelry vendor's booth and saw the familiar old mailboxes on the wall just behind where the booth stopped. It was completely obscured from the outside. Beka would have loved it; she had always hated anyone being able to find where she lived.

Devon climbed the first two flights of stairs past the beauty salon and electronics store. She could remember many nights looking down that long stretch of stairs, feeling the slightest hint of vertigo. They had counted the stairs once, sixty in a row. One thing they hadn't needed when living in the loft was to work out on any Stairmaster machines. On the landing of the third floor she caught her breath and tried not to acknowledge to herself that she was out of shape. One more flight of stairs and there it was—the same old glossy black door that had once led to their home.

She reached for the doorknob with the strangest certainty that the door would still be open even after all these years. She could not imagine the loft ever being locked, and the past swung open as easily as if it were on hinges. Devon called from the bottom of the stairs, "Is anybody home?"

"Come on up!" a shockingly young voice answered.

"Sorry to bother you, but I used to live here. I thought I might stop by and see the place, do you mind?"

A girl about twenty jumped up off the couch and stared at the stranger who had intruded on her home. Something about Devon must have assured her, though, because she sat back down. "Sure, come on in."

In the corner of the stairwell was the parking meter Todd and his brother had found on the street the night before he disappeared. It had taken two of them to carry it home, and they needed Josh's help to get it upstairs. It was so heavy no one had ever bothered to move it again. The "*Toys*" sign was still on the wall, but Josh's neon "*Kosher Meat*" sign was probably casting its greenish haze on Katiti nowadays.

"You should lock your door," Devon told her.

"That's so cool! When did you live here?"

Devon told her.

"Wow, I was five years old!"

It had seemed long ago before, now it seemed that an eon had passed. Devon wanted to pinch herself; this girl could have been any one of them just a quick back-step in time. She had been replaced by a younger—hopefully less screwed-up—replica of herself.

The loft had changed. The ceiling was no longer covered with a parachute and twinkling lights but had wallboard that smoothed out the rough edges of the room. The way to the roof was a stairway instead of a metal ladder, and there were skylights in the ceiling for extra light. The brick walls once covered with Godwyn's murals of Ghana and street people were now painted bright white, along with the ceiling and the kitchen and the bathroom. The totally black and mirrored bathroom was bright and shiny with positive colors; the black couches, tables, and chairs that had made the place look so mod in the '80s were now replaced with gentrified Pottery Barn furniture, trying too hard to look hip. It had never occurred to her why black was the color of the day back then, but now it seemed obvious—cocaine would have been invisible on white counters and tabletops.

The floors had been sanded and polyurethaned into a glossy finish that held no resemblance to the rough, splintery wood that used to shred under Beka's heels when she spun and twirled for them. The loft was as different as they were now, and like the loftmates, it had cleaned up its act. Devon looked around the space. When they lived there they had filled it with friends and parties so they wouldn't get lost in the space. And here was this young girl alone on a Sunday afternoon waiting for life to take her on its ride. Was she fearful of what the future might hold? Devon felt as if she were looking back in time and already knew what was in store.

"Who has the front room on the right?" Devon asked.

The girl jumped up as if Devon had just invited her to join in a trip down memory lane. "That one's mine!" Devon followed her into Beka's old room.

"There used to be a loft-bed up there." Devon pointed above her head to where Beka had once slept.

"Awesome, I was thinking of putting one in," the young girl said. "It's like synchronicity."

"Yeah." Devon moved to the window, leaned her head against the glass, and looked out at where the Twin Towers had once reigned supreme, letting her breath fog the glass.

"Are you okay?" the girl asked.

"Just thinking."

"Did you have my room?"

"Um, no," Devon faltered over the words, "my best friend did."

"Shoot, that'd be so cool to meet her. What'd she do?"

"She was a dancer."

"Awesome. I'm a dancer, too! Was she anyone I would know?"

"Beka Imamura?"

"Are you kidding! I saw a tape of her in my dance-history class! She used those ropes and pulleys to dance off the ground."

"Beka hated gravity."

"Me too! Isn't that awesome? It's like synchronicity!"

"Just like it." Devon started down the hallway.

"I wish she was here today," the girl said dreamily.

"So do I." Devon looked at the stairs to the roof. "You mind if I go up?"

The girl sat down on the couch cross-legged and opened up the magazine she had been reading when Devon first arrived, then nodded to the stairs. "Help yourself."

The air on the roof was colder than it had been on the street, but there wasn't a strong wind and she peered across the haze of Manhattan, inhaling what seemed like fresh air. Leaning over the edge she looked down at the hundreds of people milling below. They looked like a river of molecules moving at the same rate of speed down one of New York's main arteries. "*Koyaniskatsi*," she mumbled under her breath.

* * *

Beka had been doing a line of cocaine along the edge of the railing when Devon caught her with the straw up her nose. "Beka, what are you doing?"

"Nothing."

"Bullshit."

"Nothing's right, that's what's wrong." Beka sniffled as if she had a cold. She had been sniffling a lot lately.

"What's this mean?"

"Every night I have a dream that Todd calls me from that phone." She pointed to the booth outside of Diamond Lil's strip bar, on the other side of the street. "I go to the window and yell for him to wait for me, but he laughs and runs down the street jumping over parking meters. Sometimes it's so real that I run downstairs . . ."

"I was talking about drugs."

"Where is he, Dev?"

"I don't know, Beka. We'll never know."

"What if they had found his sweater, or even a shoe?" Beka ignored her statement. "Do you think we would have found him then?"

They stared out at the cityscape, silent except for Beka's incessant sniffling. "I just want to die." Tears were brimming in her eyes, but none fell.

"So, you going to jump or OD?" Beka had looked at her aghast. Devon pushed the coke off the railing and into the air. "You're so upset about Todd, choreograph a dance for him. He deserved more."

"I'm afraid."

"We all are, Beka. It's what you do with your fear that matters."

Beka had moved out of the loft that week and come out to stay on the East End with Devon's parents. She got clean and started to work on "The Weeping Buddha," the dance that would thrust her into the spotlight and make Todd Daniels almost immortal. It wasn't until today that Devon had realized that the loft was directly connected to Beka's drug use, though. Beka had stopped using as soon as she moved out, and that meant one thing—one of the loftmates had been Beka's dealer. Was that person also responsible for Todd's disappearance?

There was the distinct sound of metal grating against metal, either opening or closing, she could not be sure, but her first thought was that the girl had decided to lock her up on the roof. Devon spun around. The entrance was still open. On the neighboring building, however, a door was now opening, and Godwyn stepped out of the interior shadows.

"Hullo, Dev."

"God." She walked over to the edge of the roof. "What are you doing?"

"Checking out Beka's old escape route." He shut the door behind him.

"Escape route?" Devon remembered seeing Beka go up to the roof on New Year's Eve, right after Todd had taken his fateful run around the block, but she didn't remember seeing her come back down.

"She brought some guy up here once," Godwyn told her, "then leapt to the other side. When he wouldn't follow her she told him to meet her downstairs—so they could go to his place. By the time he got downstairs she had locked the outside door and the inner door automatically locked behind him. Then she came back across the roofs and went to bed. He was locked downstairs all night."

"She loved to mess with guys," Devon said.

"I'll miss that. I never understood how she and Gabe ended up together."

"Stranger things have happened."

"I thought Gabe was gay."

She glanced across the roofs of Tribeca. "I don't know what to think anymore." She wondered why he had actually come up here, and if her presence had thwarted some plan.

"Well, I'm off, see you later." He walked back to the door and gave the knob a turn. "It won't give."

"Is it locked or stuck?"

He jiggled the knob. "Locked. Bloody hell."

"I guess you'll have to jump across."

"God help me."

"Or I could." He smirked at her and she smirked right back at him. Godwyn took a few steps back and started his run toward the edge, but hesitated a few inches from the ledge. He looked into the crevice between the buildings—it wasn't even a full alleyway. "Shit, when you're young and immortal you can do anything, but when you get older . . ."

He turned to face her on the other roof and began his approach faster this time. "I'm too old for this shit!" he yelled as he leapt into the air between the two buildings.

He landed on the edge of the roof. She grabbed his arms and steadied him there for a moment. "Don't let go, mate." Devon tightened her grip as Godwyn's torso wavered.

"It's amazing any of you survived this long," she said under her breath, pulling him onto the roof with a heave.

The girl started off the couch as they returned together, but found Godwyn's appearance quite humorous when Devon informed her that he had also been a loftmate. The fact that there was another entrance was not of great importance, Devon told the girl, since it could not be recommended as a safe mode of travel.

Godwyn stood in front of the whitewashed walls, his face stricken with grief, and placed his dark hand on the chalk-white brick. "The world's gotten so bloody white. I never thought I'd see this loft so fucking clean. Remember how we used to leave the door to the roof open and watch the snow fall inside?"

"I bet it was wild!" The girl was jubilant.

Godwyn encouraged her. "You have no idea."

"We should get going," Devon said, looking over at the small alter ego on the couch.

She stared back at them for a minute, sizing them up and probably deciding that despite their age they might have some inkling of hip left in them.

Godwyn headed downstairs while Devon hung back, wishing she could say something to make this young woman's life in New York City safe and promising. She looked at her for a moment, trying to remember what it was like to be her age.

"You got any advice for living here?" the girl asked.

Devon stopped on the once-black stairs. "Yeah, don't do drugs."

CHAPTER TWENTY-TWO

I have gained insight into my real nature once, that is enough.
—Zen phrase

Loch and Gary got tired of waiting for Aileen to return. And it was already getting dark when they stopped by the largest house on Rysam Street to see if Gabe and Beka's attorney was in. He was, and he was busy packing his Mercedes.

"Looks like they're leaving town," Gary surmised. "Nice to know Aileen's information's accurate."

"Mr. Barry Goldstein?" The detectives flashed their badges and smiled in the friendliest way they could, considering they were dealing with a lawyer. "We understand you might have some information on the Sag Harbor Pilates Studio, and we need to ask you a few quick questions about ownership of the business."

"This regarding Beka and Gabe's deaths?" He did not look surprised. "Such a shame and a shock, of course my vacation would coincide with tragedy. What do you need to know?" He sighed with resignation.

"Did Ms. Imamura and Mr. Montebello have a will?" Loch began the questioning.

"They did."

"There's some question as to the circumstances around their deaths, sir. We'll need to know who the recipients are."

"Of course, there weren't many. Just two in fact."

"And who would they be?"

"Edilio Ferraro and Devon Halsey. Halsey is the executor."

"Halsey?" Gary asked.

Loch tried not to shudder; if the press got hold of that information the department would really be tied to the whipping post. "How did it break down?" He chose to focus on their suspect.

"Ferraro gets the bulk of the estate with a stipulation for an arts foundation to be started in their names. Halsey gets a small percentage of the estate property. I am the executor."

"Shit." Loch, normally well in control of his emotions, cussed and kicked a rock down the driveway.

Goldstein leaned against the trunk of his car. "In the event that their heirs have predeceased them, there is a stipulation for the land to be preserved for wildlife. The buildings are to be used to house poor artists, who can apply for one-year residencies through a fellowship that will be administered by my law firm and funded by the sale of Gabe's art." He lit a cigar and chuckled. "Of course, they both wanted their names to come first, so Beka finally figured out a way to make that possible: The Montebello-Imamura Center for Art and Movement Exploration and the Imamura-Montebello Wildlife Preserve."

"How much is the estate worth?" Gary asked, as he too kicked a stone across the driveway. "And are there any liens on it?"

Loch liked the question and looked at the lawyer closely—the motive for most murders was money. Where was the money?

"No liens. Property is worth much more than money out here, detective. The land itself is worth millions—not including his other properties and the sale of his art—who knows how much."

"Jesus," Gary cussed under his breath. "Excuse me."

"Quite all right," Mr. Goldstein said. "It's a lot of money."

"Quite a motive for murder," Loch mused.

"Don't get me wrong, detectives, I like Edilio Ferraro just fine, but if he inherits the estate, the provisions for the land are null and void. He could, if he chose to, litigate against the provisions of the will and do just about anything he wanted to with the property, including sell it to the highest bidder."

"Any idea why Gabe put the land up for sale?"

"It's a feeding frenzy out here, gentlemen. My client wanted to liquidate his assets in case of a messy divorce and reinvest in something more secure, like Switzerland."

It was Loch's turn to chuckle—that sounded like Gabe. Most artists weren't businessmen as well, but Gabriel Montebello had been both—Loch wasn't so sure he had ever been an artist. "Just a few more questions if you don't mind." Loch glanced at his notes. "Had any legal separation papers been filed?"

"Not that I was made aware."

"And the value of his art after death?"

"It will go up, and then it will go up more."

"Why Edilio? He was Beka's business partner." Loch could not imagine everything going to the man his wife was sleeping with.

"Gabe was very fond of Edilio and didn't have any family, or none that he cared to speak of."

"Where are you going?" Gary asked casually while indicating the bags in the trunk.

"St. Barts." He smiled, disarmingly. "Here's my card if you need to reach me."

"You'll be taking care of the estate when you return?"

"Or after your investigation is done. Between FedEx, faxes, and email, no one will even know I'm gone. This is the information age, gentlemen."

"You've been very helpful," Loch lied. He was more confused now than before.

"Sometimes we lawyers can be." Goldstein flicked the ash of his cigar across the driveway and watched the detectives head back to their car.

* * *

Devon and Godwyn came down the last steep flight of stairs from the loft slowly, somberly.

Godwyn stepped back and took one last photo of the fire escape above them, then began to rewind his film.

"This whole day has been a reunion of ghosts," Devon whispered.

He turned to look at her.

"It is, God. I can feel Beka watching us. And Gabe. And Todd. We're standing in the very place where Sam and I last saw him." A pain shot through her eyes, warning of a headache. They walked down the street, barely jostled by the thinning crowds as dark descended over the city. Shops were disappearing as quickly as the light faded and soon, except for the fast-food joints, Canal Street would look almost exactly as it had in the '80s.

"Why wasn't Edilio here today?" Godwyn looked at Devon with narrowing eyes. "What aren't you telling us?"

"You don't know where Edilio is, do you?" Devon asked.

"No, but he must be devastated. They've been lovers for years."

"Edilio and Beka?"

"No, Edilio and Gabe. Beka never told you?" Devon stopped cold. "I used to live upstairs in Gabe's building, remember? You'd be amazed at the boys who tromped through Gabe's building."

"Did Beka know?"

"Beka was never prudish. She got everything she wanted, money and prestige, sex on demand. Gabe was very bisexual."

"Beka just wanted someone to love her," Devon said sadly.

"Love wasn't enough for her. It never is for performers."

They continued down Canal Street to Broadway Bob's old sub-way stop. He kissed her good-bye—not the same kiss he had planted on her all those years ago, but a gentle quest for friendship during a confusing time. She kissed him back and watched as he headed down the stairs to catch the A train to Chelsea.

Without the entourage in tow, Devon stood outside the subway entrance looking thoughtfully at the place where Broadway Bob had once sat on his grate with his brown tweed suit coat wrapped tight around his distended belly, smoking his cigar.

"'Dem Aliens come and take him," he'd said.

She missed the man Beka had dubbed the guardian angel of the street; who would warn her of danger now? She knelt down in the corner where Bob had been on New Year's Eve, then pointed in the general direction he had pointed. All she saw were a few stars wink-ing into an indigo sky and the row of buildings at the end of Howard Street. What had he really seen that night?

Voices drifted up from the stairwell below—Godwyn had met someone in the subway.

"Did you tell her?" It was Maddie.

"No. I don't think it's any of her business."

The tile walls must have been amplifying their voices; Devon leaned back and listened.

"Cops," he said. "Keep 'em out of it. You comin' with?"

A train heading downtown rushed into the station, its brakes squealing painfully. After a few moments it started off again toward Wall Street. There were no more voices. Curious, Devon walked around the corner to see if they were still there. The platform was empty.

She walked back up the stairs to the now virtually empty streets. Dark had descended suddenly and the downtown street lights seemed yellow and dull, barely lighting her way. Devon was alone in Chinatown, faced with nothing but Gabe's building at the end of Howard Street. She reached into her pocket and pulled out the key. Beka had told her to stay there whenever she needed to and that's exactly what she planned to do.

CHAPTER TWENTY-THREE

We awaken to Reality suddenly, and are perceiving phenomena right now.

—Zen phrase

Devon opened the front door to the building on Mercer Street with trepidation. She could not help remembering Beka say that sometimes the place gave her the heebie-jeebies. "It feels haunted," Beka used to complain, "and Gabe is always teasing me because I'm scared to stay here alone, but it's so big."

It was big. Each floor was a 2,600-square-foot loft, not including the ground floor where his sculpture studio was located. The place was worth well over a million dollars now, but Gabe had bought it back in the '70s for thirty thousand cash. He had always been smart with his money. When he won the International Sculpture Competition grant money, he invested in real estate and rented out the third floor to make sure he always had a steady income. Since then, he'd had some tough times, but he was never broke and never hungry; that's what had enabled him to continue, he always said. He never had to sell out to survive.

He also didn't have to give away his commission to a gallery if he didn't choose to; he used half of the second floor of his building as a gallery and lived in the other half. On the bottom floor was the studio where he worked on his heavier pieces—he had a welding torch, huge buckets for mixing plaster, and a contraption that helped him pour the contents into molds. There was even a loading dock, which made it easy to ship cumbersome bronzes to clients around the world. When he'd met Beka she was in need of rehearsal space so he shared the top floor with her—the front half functioning as a dance studio, the back half as his place to paint. The basement studio was too dark for painting, and sharing the studio with Beka gave him a chance to observe dancers in their element. Gabe had been better known for his sculptures, but inspired by Beka he had started selling color-splashed abstracts of the human form dashing across an expanse of canvas in the same way she dashed across his fourth floor studio. Like an artist with the Midas touch, his oils had sold as well as his sculptures.

Devon turned on the stairwell lights. It was a typical warehouse, nothing glamorous or sophisticated about it. Not much different than the loft, actually, except there was no one else inside. She started up the stairs, avoiding the old building's elevator—she wasn't about to get stuck in that with no one else around.

No exhibit was up on the second floor, and if she remembered correctly, Gabriel had not used his gallery in over a year. But there were paintings propped up against the walls, as if someone had been deciding which order to place them in, shuffling them like oversized playing cards to find the perfect combination. Only one sculpture was on display and she'd seen it before. *Having Hand* was the current title, in honor of a dating joke from the retired sitcom *Seinfeld*. The piece had changed over the years. One hand grabbed hold of another as they crept upwards in a vertical kind of bronze-ascension. Gabe had told her that it was about getting to the top.

"But it's just casts, Gabe," she had told him. "You didn't carve the hands; they're molds that you cast. What's creative about that?" She had always disliked the piece and didn't know why Gabe insisted on keeping it *on hand*.

"It's what they say, their shape. I tell my model to think of something, like they're drowning, and then attempt to cast that emotion."

"He's always trying to capture emotions, Devon," Beka had warned, "don't try and figure it out. He lives with me because my art is temporal but he spends all of his time trying to capture it in bronze or oil."

"Aestheticism is concrete," Gabe explained.

Beka disagreed. "Aestheticism is ethereal."

Devon had to admit that the detail on the sculpture was better than it had once been; his materials must have improved over time, but it was still just a bunch of bronze hands. And the latest addition looked as if it were grasping for nothingness between its fingers. "It's depressing," she said out loud. "Sorry, Gabe. I still don't like it."

Having Hand was never for sale—Beka said it was always a work in progress and that he never finished it so he could always say he was working on a piece, in case he ever hit artist's block. It was an interesting idea. Not dissimilar to Hemingway's theory of never stopping at the end of a chapter, *Having Hand* had been Gabe's perpetual first sentence for the next day's work. Despite her personal dislike for the piece, maybe it had done its job; Gabe had certainly never suffered from artist's block. She wondered how much it would bring now that its creator was dead, but could not begin to fathom the fickleness of the art world. She owned three Montebellos herself, and with Gabe's death might have just become rich.

She turned off the light in the gallery and headed up to the third floor where Beka and Gabe had lived after he stopped renting it out. There were dishes still in the sink, crusty with old marinara, and two goblets with dried-up wine at the bottom of the glasses. Spontaneously, she pulled out her dusting kit and quickly pulled the prints off each glass. One set was definitely Gabe's, the nick in the right forefinger was there, and the other set appeared to be a man's hand as well. She continued through the kitchen and into the living area. A coffee-table book of dancers was lying face up, opened to a photograph of Beka and Edilio wrapped seductively around each other like the limbs of a tree entwined with monkey vine. Devon touched the photo sadly, so lovely. She could almost feel Beka's presence in the room.

She sat down on the couch, hugged a pillow to her chest, and stared at the photograph. "What happened, Beka? Tell me what happened." But there was only silence and the occasional thump of the radiators circling steam heat through the cold pipes of the building.

The ground floor was more like a basement. It was dark, windowless, dank, and smelled of resin and plaster dust, as well as rat turds and mildew. It was not the sort of place she would want to spend the night, and when she turned on the lights half of the fluorescent bulbs in the ceiling flickered out. Still, she could see well enough to make a search.

She wasn't sure what she was looking for, maybe it was just a feel for where Beka and Gabe were in their lives more than anything else—some hint as to why they were now dead. It was simply a natural progression after combing the Hamptons house to go through their place in the city; sooner or later Loch and Gary would have had to do it anyway.

Next to the sink there were six Tyvek paper suits hanging neatly on hangers, just like the ones she wore on a crime scene to keep her clothes clean and to keep herself from leaving trace evidence. The studio was strewn with body parts—plaster casts of limbs and torsos—all shapes and sizes. Mostly men's bodies from the look of it. She shuddered. Was this Gabe's next stage in development? In dripping black brush strokes he had written on the wall, *"The Greatest Work of Art is the Human Body."*

She moved to the back of the studio where the welding, soldering, and casting were done. Much of his work was commissioned by the Japanese, but it hadn't occurred to her until this moment what a boon being connected to Beka must have been for him. Maybe she had been more than a muse—maybe Beka had been a cash cow.

Devon knew they hadn't married for love, but she thought there'd been something more to it than business. Maybe she'd been wrong. Maybe that's what Beka had really been angry about, that Devon was with someone she loved. Even though they weren't married, she and Loch had an equal partnership that surpassed what most married couples ever attained—passion and equality. Devon could hold her own against Loch in any given situation. He had never had to save her and never would.

* * *

Loch tried Devon's cellphone two more times and finally left a message.

"It's probably her battery," Gary suggested.

"She has a spare."

"We've been working around the clock, Loch. And she just lost two friends; don't expect her to be Superwoman this week."

Lochwood silently agreed with him and hit the gas as the car sped toward the LIE. He wasn't worried about her, it was just that she usually followed up on his calls fairly quickly—unless she was in the middle of something important—and that's what he was really afraid of, missing something.

* * *

Every move she made sent a chill down her spine, and she felt as if she were being stared at. She reached for her shoulder holster and turned slowly to her right.

Beka was staring at her, a sightless dummy in plaster.

Devon snorted air through her nose, angry at her own lack of nerve, then tossed a drop-cloth on top of Beka's white head. "Sorry, Beka, but I don't need more ghosts than I brought with me."

She picked up a bag full of a fine dusty powder. Alginate. It was what dentists used to make molds of teeth—no wonder he was getting better detail in the *Having Hand* sculpture. She picked up a mold that, broken, looked like it had been the original for the last set of hands. She let her own hand hover above the portion of the mold she'd found; the hand was larger than hers and the fingers looked well-muscled and full of creases, denoting someone who worked hard. There was also the indentation of a ring in the mold. She knew she'd seen it in the top pair of hands in Gabe's sculpture upstairs but she'd seen the ring elsewhere as well; she just couldn't place where or on whom.

Pulling her cellphone out of her breast pocket she noticed that her beeper was missing from her belt. She knew she had put it on last night; she had changed clothes before coming into the city but could not imagine leaving it behind in her locker. Stress was taking its toll on her memory. Her cellphone had a tiny picture of a letter— she had missed a call. The building must be messing up her signal. She pressed the buttons for voice-mail and heard an angry beep. Her battery was out. That was strange; she had replaced it this morning . . . or was it last night? She could not remember. There was a spare upstairs in her crime kit, but that meant turning around and walking up three flights. Feeling cut off from the world, Devon stood in the middle of the room trying to decide what to do.

A buzz overhead made her look up. The fluorescent tubes in the ceiling flickered twice, faded to brown, then black. She blinked. Orange spots appeared in the darkness.

"Shit." She turned around as the door to the studio slammed shut.

The wind must have closed it, she reasoned, and took a step forward in the darkness.

The exit sign glowed dangerously red at the front of the room.

She steadied her breathing and took another step. There was a definitive click of the barrel of a gun being cocked. A shadow seemed to pass under the exit sign. Were her eyes playing tricks on her?

Then there was a slight crunch of plaster beneath a foot. Not hers.

Reaching for her gun, Devon backed up slowly, peering through the pitch black of the room.

CHAPTER TWENTY-FOUR

*I have experienced great satori eighteen times, and lost count
of the number of small satoris I have had.*

—DAIE OSHO

Loch dropped Gary off at his car with the Plasticine parts they had
collected at the crime scene. "Get Frank on that in the morning," he
told his partner. "I'll call you from the city." He tried Devon's cellphone one more time but still got the out-of-service message. The
one thing Lochwood Brennen could not stand was having things
beyond his control, yet his entire life seemed to revolve around circumstances that were out of his jurisdiction. It was things like his
daughter's life decisions, Marty's illness, and phones that did not
work that made him nuts!

Deep in thought, he cruised west on the Long Island
Expressway toward New York City. What did it mean if Edilio and
Beka were having an affair? Did it really change anything? Did it
change what happened on New Year's Eve or further muddle the
details? If what he and Gary had learned was true, and they always
kept an open mind to the truth, it didn't explain why Beka suddenly
decided to kick Edilio out of the business.

Loch disliked the conundrum, which, like misfit pieces to a
puzzle, only fit halfway in and on the other side stuck out. He
couldn't force things to match, but he couldn't figure out what
exactly was out of place. The only thing he was definitely sure of
was that something was not clicking. He flipped open his notepad,
keeping one eye on the road as he read his scratches and scribbles
regarding the case. There it was, he had to keep reminding himself
of that tidbit Beka's uncle had shared—she had cut her hair once
before, after her parents died—that might explain Gabe's murder,
and an affair with Edilio, but did it explain her subsequent suicide?
And if Edilio was in on it with her? Money. It had to be financial—

two dancers would always be broke, but one dancer married to a wealthy, successful man could take care of the other. If that was true, why would Edilio change the scenario and get rid of her? And why hadn't he shown up to play the part of a grieving business partner and collect his due? Where the hell in this scenario was Edilio Ferraro now?

Involuntarily his foot weighed on the accelerator until he was speeding along the LIE at eighty-five miles per hour; he could be in the city in forty-five minutes, he'd done it before. That was one of the advantages of being a cop—speeding. He wasn't really worried about Devon, just irritated that in this not-so-new information age he could not reach her. And in finding himself cut off from her, he suddenly found that he missed her terribly.

He began running the license plates of cars in front of him on his police computer. One never knew when a car thief was going to pass by, which was why Loch had more accomodations than anyone else in New York State—he worked even on his drive to work. After three clean sweeps he got bored and decided to call the other woman in his life, his daughter. He punched in another plate as the phone rang twice then went into answer mode. "Brea? It's Dad. Pick up."

"Loch?" It was his mother-in-law's voice on the other end. "Where are you?" She could be so demanding and critical.

He shuddered. Family was more terrifying than twenty Joel Rifkins. "I'm in the middle of a murder investigation, Ruth." He hadn't meant to sound so defensive and he felt bad that as soon as he heard her voice, he bristled. "Where's Brea?" he asked more gently.

"She's spending the night at Sabrina's." There was a pause on both ends, then he heard her quietly say, "She wants to move out."

"I know."

"Well, I don't think it's a good idea."

He didn't either but he was damned if he was going to side with his mother-in-law. "She just wants to live a normal life and that's not going to happen living at home, Ruth." As if it were a reflex, he punched in another license plate.

"That's why I want Marty institutionalized," she said.

"That's not what people do nowadays."

"Then whatever it is they call it. I want her to go someplace where she can get help! We can't anymore. We've done our best, Lochwood. It's time to let go."

He could tell that it was hard for her to say those words by the way her voice trembled. "I know," was all he could say.

"It isn't living, and we're hurting Brea." It was the first time he had listened to her in a long time, and it was the first time she was making sense. They had a history and not a pleasant one—she had blamed him for Marty's illness, threatened to take Brea away from him, and fought her daughter's diagnosis by taking her anger out on her son-in-law. Since then, though, they had developed a working relationship based on a mutual need to protect and help Brea and Marty. Now that same woman was saying, "We can't help Marty, but we sure as hell can help Brea. I called T.K. Psychiatric. They have a group home that can take Marty and offers a day treatment program for the long-term care of the mentally ill. It's a good place, Lochwood."

He was in shock. "You called them?"

"I know you said you would do that, but I took care of it. Maybe it's time her mother made some decisions and stopped leaving it all up to her husband." He couldn't help but wonder what had facilitated her change of heart, but he couldn't bear to ask, so he listened. "I don't want to lose Brea."

Neither do I, he thought, but instead he said, "We both love them, Ruth."

"It's just that we got Brea through high school and I thought now we could relax and be a family, but she wants to run off to Colorado somewhere. Wasn't Ted Bundy from out west?"

"Joel Rifkin was from Long Island," he reminded her.

"But you caught him, Loch. She's safe as long as you're around. How can we protect her all the way out west?"

"Marty's your daughter. If you think she'd do better in a group home, then let's do it. Together—you and me." He felt an invisible weight lifting off his shoulders. Armistice had been declared and as in so many wars, his ally was none other than his former enemy.

"Do you think it's too late to change Brea's mind?"

"I'll talk to her, Ruth. Don't worry," he assured her. "Maybe we can take her out to Boulder together and encourage her to look around at other schools. We'll let her make her own decisions and hope she stays close to home."

"You're a good father, Loch." He was speechless; she had never said that to him before.

"I gotta go, Ruth." He clicked off the call and tried not to think about all that had been said; even his desire to run license plates had faded.

* * *

Devon could see nothing but red streaks dancing in the dark under the exit sign which she knew, from the hair rising on the back of her neck, was not where she wanted to go. She knew she couldn't trust the color red—of all the colors in the spectrum, red moved the most, any art student who'd taken the Physics of Color knew that. And the exit sign was no different; it wiggled and shifted in the dark like an angry serpent.

She listened for something more definitive, the sound of breathing, a footfall. There was nothing. She had to evaluate what her advantage was against this unknown intruder, and she had to figure it out quickly. She knew she had the advantage of darkness and familiarity with the area she had just walked, and she decided to wait for the other person to make the first move. If the intruder shot blindly at her, she'd know exactly where the bullet was coming from and drop him.

She also knew there was another exit at the far end of the studio—she'd seen Gabe open the door when he was working with toxic fumes and in need of cross-ventilation. So, she wasn't trapped. The dark befuddled her mind, though, and she began to fancy that the wind had shut the door and she had imagined the cocking of a gun. She kept her eyes peeled to the spot just under the exit sign where she thought she'd seen the first hint of movement, but she was going to have to trust her ears more than her eyes, and she steadied her breathing to a deeper, slower rhythm.

There was a scuffing sound against the cement at the top of the loading dock, like someone dragging his feet. The sound stopped and moved toward her again—this time more quietly. She took a spontaneous step backward and reached for the plaster bust of Beka, placed it on the floor directly in front of her, and backed up slowly and quietly. She made a mental map of the studio based on her last visual recollection before the lights went off, and knew she had distance on her side. But if the person stalking her in the dark knew the studio better . . .

She began to count her steps backward. At step ten she reached out for something to place in her path again. Her hands floated through the darkness, careful not to knock anything over. She found a stool; it wasn't an ideal choice, but she couldn't reach anything else. She heard the quiet crunching of dust and dirt on the steps as someone came down the steps to ground level. Aware that her own shoes carried dirt on them as well, she quickly slipped them off her feet. Then she picked up the stool and placed it on the floor, cringing as the metal legs grated against the concrete. She knelt quickly to the floor in case the intruder decided to use that noise to aim and shoot. The sounds of someone moving toward her stopped.

She reached through the darkness with her mind and body, using her eyes and ears to keep her balance. Shoes in hand, she was able to roll her feet silently from toe to heel, softly padding across the concrete floor more quickly now. Devon kept moving backwards, counting her paces, just as Hans had taught her when they did walking meditation. Her breathing slowed and she performed what was almost reverse *kinhin*—as her awareness heightened, she felt the floor and room around her. The footsteps in front of her started again, then stopped; Devon did not falter. She heard a few more hesitant steps, and knew she'd confused whoever it was by her silent movement. At forty-five steps away from Beka's bust she felt the brick wall behind her back and, gun in hand, stretched her arms out as far as she could on either side. The door was not there.

She did not panic. Instead, she quietly took a deep breath to steady her nerves and moved to the left a few feet, felt nothing with her right hand, then moved a few more feet to the left. Nothing. She did not give up; she knew the door was on one side or the other.

Where had she seen the broken plaster in the studio? By the Tyvek suits. She moved a few more feet to the left and felt the corner of the room—dead end.

There was a crunch of plaster.

She whipped around in the dark in order to face her opponent and moved quickly back along the wall, keeping her gun aimed into the darkness. Just as she felt the cold metal of the doorframe under her fingertips, the plaster bust of Beka toppled to the floor with a thud.

The intruder was forty-five paces away from her.

Devon reached for the knob. It was cold in her hand and turned easily, but the door did not open. Of course, it was bolted. Her hands flew directly above and below the chain handles that double-bolted the door. She was going to have to coordinate her movements quickly and, as much as she didn't want to, turn her back on the stalker. She holstered her gun, grabbed the bolts' chains in both hands, and pulled simultaneously up and down. The sound of the metal scraping against metal was deafening.

The bottom one gave. The top one did not.

The stool crashed to the floor behind her. Thirty-five paces away.

Tugging on the top bolt one more time to no avail, she grabbed the chain with both hands for one more good hard yank. It popped and the door swung open. Devon dashed outside, spun around, and hit the alley wall with her back, ready to face her stalker—gun drawn, cocked, and ready to fire.

The door banged against the outside wall. She backed up carefully, making sure she had plenty of maneuvering room. Nothing happened. She began to count one-one thousand, two-one thousand, three-one thousand.

Her gun arm wavered. Why would someone tracking her through the dark not face her in an alleyway, unless that person knew she too had a gun. And how would her stalker know that unless he knew her? She kept her arm steady and tried to think. If she ran around to the front of the building the intruder could escape through the back door the same way she had. But to go back inside through the alley door was unthinkably stupid—she'd be back-lit and an easy target. Her stocking feet were damp and cold. She steadied her gun arm and listened carefully for any noise coming from inside the studio, but it was silent. The door slammed shut. Her finger trembled on the trigger. It was just the fickle wind playing tricks on her—no one burst through the now-closed door.

Across the alleyway was a garbage can; Devon picked it up and quickly wedged it under the doorknob. She saw the knob turn and waited to see if the door would hold. It did.

"*Gotcha*," she hissed under her breath, and started up the alley, racing around the block to the front of the building.

She punched the power button on her cellphone hoping for a little juice, but heard the sickly beep of the dead battery. Without a partner to help her seal off the building or a phone to call for back-up, she knew she was in a high-risk situation. She couldn't believe her battery was dead. Free of the alley she hooked a right on Broome Street and finally made it to Mercer—there was no one on the street. The front door, which she had locked when she entered the building, was now swinging in the wind, and footprints thick with plaster dust led away from the scene. Gun raised, she scanned the surrounding area again. Nothing moved.

Inside, Devon turned on the stairwell light and found the studio door open and more dusty footwear impressions. With just the ball of the feet to mark the trail, Devon figured the person had left at a dead run as soon as she secured the garbage can under the door knob. She went back to the doorway and stared up and down Mercer and then up Howard—there was no one on the sidewalk and the streets seemed oddly quiet. She looked at the lock to see if it had been picked, but there were no scrapes around the keyhole. She didn't want to go all the way back into the studio without backup and decided to call Loch from the upstairs phone, but there was no way to secure the premises from someone who had a key. She locked the door to the studio from the outside, wishing there were an inside bolt for the front door. She'd just have to be on her guard.

Her heart was still pounding, and for good reason. Whoever had come into the studio when she was here had a key to the building. But who? She hadn't told anyone at dim sum that she was coming here. Could one of the gang have followed her? Or had her presence foiled someone's plan to rob the place? A random robber with a key? Not bloody likely, as Godwyn would have said.

Devon headed upstairs slowly, her gun now uncocked but still drawn. She scanned the second floor. It looked undisturbed, which made sense considering the person who had entered the building must have come from the street and directly into the art studio. She would have heard someone on the stairs—or would she? It was a solidly built warehouse—the thing Gabe had loved about it was that Beka could dance on the fourth floor and he wasn't bothered on the third. But what if the intruder had been on the fourth floor? That was the only floor she hadn't checked. There hadn't been much point since she knew it had been unused for several years, ever since Beka retired. She locked the second-floor door from the outside— she wasn't having any more surprises tonight—took a deep breath, and headed up to the third floor.

The lights were still on, just as she'd left them. She moved quickly to the phone and dialed Loch's cellphone. The line was busy—he was probably trying to reach her. "Loch, it's me. I'm at Gabe's building. I hope you can get over here if you're headed this way; if you are, please hurry."

She thought for a second about her next move, locked the third-floor door, and started up to the fourth. The only thing she could think was that someone had been up there when she came in, and had waited until she was in the studio.

As she started up the stairs she could hear the faint sound of dripping water. She pulled her gun again and turned the doorknob. The tumblers shifted, slipped, and shifted again. She jiggled the knob and pulled on the door; it seemed stuck. She pressed against it with her body weight, pulled back, and almost fell over as an invisible force rushed out at her and sent her reeling.

Her hand flew to her nose, but it was too late. The smell ensconced her and the entire fourth story. She knew what she was going to see even before she turned on the light—it was *who* she was going to see that she wasn't sure of.

The sweetness of decaying flesh permeated the air until she could feel the heaviness of its scent clinging to her own skin, as if the smell itself could make her own body begin to decompose. *Putrefaction* was the only word that sprang to mind, that and *gas mask*, the one thing that would have made the scene bearable. The room was almost completely empty, but Devon could have shut her eyes and followed the smell.

On the Cadillac, a piece of Pilates equipment that Beka had sworn she could not live without, rested the shadow of something hanging as if strung up on a trapeze. The room was dimly illuminated by the street lights outside, and, still on full alert, Devon pulled a pair of gloves from her back pocket. With the flick of the switch the room was swiftly illuminated and she could see how Pilates springs had been tightened around his neck, and bound his arms and legs together. The head was tilted back and away from her, but as she got closer she began to make out the features. It was Edilio Ferraro, and from the stench she guessed he'd been dead for about a week.

She opened the window, leaned her head into the alleyway so the fresh winter wind could slap her face, and breathed deeply. Sometimes all there was to be grateful for was fresh air.

She went back to the body. There was nothing she could put over her nose now that wouldn't smell like the corpse, so she didn't even try and mask the smell. She had more important things to do. The torso was carved over the heart, just as Gabe's had been, with deep lines that were now soft and fraying around the edges from decay. Although the spring had been tightened around his neck the face was not blue, as it would have been from suffocation. She knelt closer to the chest wounds—no blood, they were made postmortem.

A door banged shut down below and she could hear heavy footsteps, like those of someone wearing boots, coming up the stairs. She grabbed her gun out of its holster, ran into the hall in her stocking feet, and positioned herself around the corner of the stairwell. She had the advantage of surprise and not being winded; of course, whoever was coming up those stairs would know what floor she was on by the light she had just turned on.

Cocking her gun for the second time that night, she waited calmly. She could tackle a 240-lb. felon and had—she was not worried. The sound of heavy breathing ascended the last flight of stairs. The intruder did not slow down until the last three steps, then stopped. Whoever was there seemed now to be listening as well.

CHAPTER TWENTY-FIVE

"Devon, is that you?"

She peered around the corner, just as Loch was holstering his gun. "What would you have done if I'd been someone else?" she asked.

"I know the sound of your breathing."

"I have a surprise for you."

His hand was already at his nose. "I can smell it. Did you know that Edilio and Beka were having an affair?"

"Where did you hear that?"

"At the Pilates studio."

"Your sources are almost right." She led him into the room. "Edilio was queer as a three-dollar bill, but I don't think he's having an affair with anyone right now." She pointed to the Cadillac and stepped back to give Loch a view of the body.

He looked at the once-handsome face of Edilio Ferraro. "Well, that blows that theory."

"And according to Godwyn Kamani, Gabe and Edilio were spanking the monkey more than Beka and Gabe." They opened up a few more windows for cross-ventilation.

The open-relationship theory had seemed implausible, but this new theory had possibilities. Loch could see Beka ending her business partnership with Edilio now, and the anger escalating into violence against her husband—as the aftermath at the crime scene had illustrated. Even the suicide became more logical. How could she live with such betrayal? She might have felt she'd failed as a woman, or maybe she just couldn't continue the charade anymore. He began to whistle; even the spousal abuse made sense. If Gabe was in the closet and repressing his natural tendencies, it could have come out as inappropriate behavior. Loch had seen it before. Hell, he'd seen everything before.

He stepped over to the elaborate-looking bed with springs and leather straps on either end—it was exactly like the one he had seen in the Sag Harbor studio, only this time it looked like it had been used for its original intention, torture.

"Something else happened tonight, Loch," Devon interrupted his thoughts. "I had a run-in downstairs."

"Well, you certainly didn't walk into a murder."

"No, but I'm thinking somebody may have been checking up on their work."

"So, what happened?" The fresh air was not helping him breathe any easier.

She gave him a brief rundown of events and waited for his response. "The question is, how can we work this scene and still turn it over to the NYPD?"

He winced and nodded, looking miserable at the thought of letting another Homicide team come in on what he felt should be their case even if it wasn't their jurisdiction. "We simply have to make sure we get all the information we need before we turn it over to another Crime Scene and Homicide unit." He paused to think about the quickest and easiest way they could accomplish this. "I'll get the camera. You can't dust before they do, or they'll know. But we can certainly get our own set of film before they get here."

"We have two scenes here, too. What if I don't make a report on the break-in?"

"If it relates to the murder, we've suppressed evidence," he reasoned. "Okay, we start up here. Then I call it in, while you process the studio downstairs. We let them do their thing, and I feel out the lead on their team. When you've had enough time downstairs on your own, I'll let them know what we've got down there and make sure you're in on the processing. I don't think we'll have any trouble proving there's a link between Edilio and the other two. I'll call Houck in a minute and make sure he's ready to back us up."

"Sounds like we have a plan!"

She was looking uncommonly chipper, and he felt it was his duty to bring her back to reality. "This doesn't prove anything. This is way over the top, but she was still alive when he died. No way you get this kind of stink from a day-old body."

He headed downstairs to grab her camera, leaving her alone to think about the events of the past two days. If Loch could schmooze the lead detective while linking their investigation into Beka and Gabe's deaths to Edilio's, they would be allowed to view the autopsy and Devon could get Edilio's prints more quickly. She felt pretty certain the city would work with them since it was going to be high-profile all the way around. The only real problem would be that Loch's schmoozing techniques were more than a little lacking.

He was back in a few minutes, camera in hand.

"I can always dust after they leave," Devon said, as she focused on the body. The bulb flashed. It was the first time in two days the flash of a camera did not send her reeling into recollections of the past. "When they're gone, I can pull the same prints they find."

"Yeah, that shouldn't bother them too much."

"Can you finish shooting the surrounding area while I run downstairs and get some paper and a pencil?"

"What for?"

"I want to sketch the marks on his chest. All day I've regretted that I didn't sketch those marks on Gabe and I'm still waiting for the photo lab to open."

He took the camera and started shooting the scene, something he hadn't done in years. She ran down to the third floor, unlocked the door, grabbed what she needed from Gabe's desk, then ran back up the stairs, her heart pounding with excitement. She started sketching quickly and deftly as Loch finished one roll of the film and inserted another.

"I think we can take our time calling this in, seeing as nothing is fresh."

"Yeah, but the closer we stick to the truth, the better," Devon reminded him.

"We're cops. They'll expect us to hide something," he mumbled, more to himself than to Devon. "I wonder who's on tonight."

"Probably somebody you pissed off at one time or another." She was trying to figure out which stroke came first but couldn't tell. "I wish Jo could get a look at this body. I can tell that these marks were made postmortem, just like Gabe's, but I can't see how deep they are or if that matters."

"If they let us join the autopsy we can find out soon enough, but you're probably right, it'll be somebody I've pissed off." He bent over to see what she had sketched, then moved closer to observe Edilio's chest wound.

"We've never worked a scene alone together before." She pinched his butt.

"It's good to see you back to your old tricks." He grabbed her around her waist, squeezed her tightly to his chest, and kissed her in front of the sightless corpse.

"How romantic." She kissed him back with a little laugh, then pushed him away.

A half an hour later, Devon was locking the art studio door behind her so as not to be disturbed by roving police officers eager to do more than the job upstairs. She popped another roll of film in the camera, walked over to her shoes, and put them back on. She was proud of her escape and considered removing her shoes an inspiration from Beka—the shoe-hating dancer herself. How many times had Devon and Beka watched horror films where the heroine tried to escape some monster or murdering menace in her high heels?

"Take off your goddamn shoes!" Beka would yell. "Kick him in the balls! One good pair of spikes can incapacitate any man!"

With her sneakers now on, she began to comb the area more carefully. There was a good footwear impression in the plaster around Beka's now-shattered bust. The fact that there would be no more imitations of Beka in the world made Devon feel sad. She began snapping the footwear impression, but could tell that there was a bit of an imprint that wasn't going to reproduce well because the dust was so fine and white. What about the Alginate? It copied bodies and teeth in perfect detail. What about a mold made out of dust? She'd used Alginate before in dirt and mud, but something as fine as this powdery plaster? She went over to the sink, took one of Gabe's old mixing buckets, filled it a quarter full with water, then began to add Alginate until the mixture was just the right thickness. She took a metal ring from a container and placed it around the footprint, then poured the liquid on top. She stood up and glanced around the room; it would only take three minutes for the Alginate to set but she didn't want to waste any time. Looking at the foot-prints across the studio floor, she could see the path her socks had made, as well as the soles of the shoes of the intruder following her. The prints went all the way up to the alley door, and from the placement of the last set it looked as if the person had been waiting inside the door. Hoping she would come back inside?

He or she—Devon could not tell gender by the foot size—must have been trying to make up his or her mind when the wind shut the door that Devon had then secured with the garbage can. That move must have sent the intruder bolting for the front door—where the prints she had found earlier headed back to the front of the building. She pushed against the alleyway door. The garbage can was still holding it fast. It had been a good move on her part; she pushed both of the interior bolts back into place—to secure the building from the inside. Loch could move the can tomorrow.

It was time for the Alginate to come up; it peeled easily off the cement floor. *"Voila!"* She was very happy with her work; the imprint was a clean copy of the sole of a boot and the trademark, *"Dr. Martens Air Cushioned Sole,"* encircling a cross, with the words: *"Oil Fat Acid Petrol Alkali Resistant, Made in England."* "That narrows it down to 200,000 people in the village alone," she scoffed at herself.

There was a clean set of left- and right-handed prints right around the seat of the stool—aluminum always took great prints. She started to place the Searchie down over the dusty swirls, then stopped herself. They looked familiar. They were so evenly placed, not at all like someone who had bumped into a chair. She held her hands over the stool and recalled how she had reached for it. They were her own prints. The remnants of Beka's bust weren't going to show any prints either, she concluded. The intruder had been pro enough to wear gloves. She sat on a box and began to ponder what had happened, tracing the intruder's movements through the room. The first crunch of plaster she had heard was by the closet.

The Tyvek suits were still hanging by the sink in an open closet but they seemed looser than they had before, as if someone had rearranged them. She began to count: *one, two, three, four, five* . . . There had been six. "Damn!" She looked around the room, then closed her eyes and felt each suit, first with her gloved hands and then with her fingers. "You were here." There was no way the intruder could have known which Tyvek suit to take by touch alone, because they all felt the same. Whoever had come into the building must have been after one thing, and Devon wasn't it.

Her eyes blazed as she drew her gun and swept the room in one glance, looking for some kind of hiding place. It had not made sense at the time. She should have seen somebody running down the block—she'd known that on some level, but there had been the footprints outside.

She had turned on the studio lights and looked around the entrance of the room, but she had not gone back inside the studio, instead locking the door from the outside. The intruder had still been there, watching her. She scanned the space once more, gun aimed at empty space. It didn't make sense. She didn't feel another's presence and she normally was very astute that way.

How had this Houdini escaped?

She looked at the loading-dock door. It had a bolt that could be opened from the inside that would automatically lock again as soon as the door was shut. She twisted the chain and pushed it up with a clatter. There was a smudge under the grate where someone had rolled, and sock foot impressions on the metal dock platform where he had stood up and made his way off the dock.

She looked at her own feet. The intruder must have tripped over Devon's shoes in the dark, realized what she had done, then turned around and used her own trick against her. The footprints leading outside were a decoy—the intruder had backtracked into the studio in stocking feet, taken one of the Tyvek suits, and escaped after Devon had gone upstairs.

It had been stupid of her not to go back inside the studio and make sure no one was really there. Under normal circumstances, she would have acted with more sense. So much had happened lately, and now she had screwed up and possibly let a murderer get away.

CHAPTER TWENTY-SIX

Dancing and singing are the voice of the Dharma.
—HAKUIN ZENJI

There was a knock at the art studio door. "It's me," Loch said. Devon unlocked the door and let him in. "The M.E. just arrived. You almost done in here?"

"Just finished."

"Let's leave the door open so they can look around. Our lead guy is Marders and I just informed him of the B&E. He doesn't think it's related and since nothing was taken, I'm letting him think that way."

"Good, only something *was* taken." She headed toward the stairs.

"Where you going?" Loch stopped at the elevator.

"That thing is too small to trust."

"But it's four flights."

"I guess with half of NYPD here I can take it up, but the last place you'll find me is on that elevator when this building is empty. You could be stuck in there for days and nobody would find you."

"Such a morbid mind." He held the door open for her, and kissed her on the cheek as she pressed four. The doors clanged shut and the wheels above them began to grind. "Whose idea was it to paint the walls red? They vibrate."

"Stop complaining. This was your idea," she told him.

He closed his eyes and steadied himself on the side of the cadmium-red walls. "So, what's missing?"

"A Tyvek suit." The metal doors clanged open and they were suddenly amid a flurry of cops and detectives. "Later," she whispered, and stepped off of the contraption she had only ridden a few times before.

The floor was bustling with activity, although inside the one-time dance studio they were holding traffic to a minimum. Loch showed Devon through the small, professional crowd. "Detective Marders, this is Detective Halsey of Suffolk County Crime Scene." She noticed immediately that Marders was wearing his Crime Scene's gloves and did not stick her hand out to shake his.

"Halsey, I understand you know the owners of this building."

"*Knew*, detective, they're both dead."

"The New Year's Eve murders, Detective Brennen told me. What were you doing here?"

"I have a key and stay here whenever I'm in the city. I was meeting friends who knew the deceased and thought I'd spend the night."

"And snoop around to see if there was anything to help explain your friends' deaths?"

"That was a possibility."

"And does this body help explain things?"

"Not so much."

He smiled wryly. "Well, the M.E.'s about to give us his prelim. If these cases are linked we'll have to work with you, so you two might as well come on in." She signed the crime scene sheet just under Lochwood's name and reentered the room. It was well marked with number tags in all the areas where she would have put them, and a few where she wouldn't have; all in all, it looked as if the city Crime Scene Unit was doing a thorough job.

The M.E. wore a mask over his mouth and nose and circled the corpse with ease and familiarity, then moved in to examine it while he spoke to the detectives. "There's no bruising under the legs and no abrasion around the ankles. Fixed lividity is in the hands, feet, and legs, consistent with the body being strung up after death. He was not strangled; the ligature marks are not deep enough to have accomplished anything but surface bruising." He felt around the throat. "And the hyoid bone is intact. Good thing it was cold this week or this would be really nasty."

"How was he killed?"

"We'll have to get him down to find out for sure. From the eyes . . ." he pulled up the lids of each eye, "popped blood vessels and severe dilation, I'd say cardiac arrest. There are eighteen stab wounds, all superficial."

"None of these wounds was fatal?" Detective Marders reiterated.

"They were all inflicted postmortem."

"The carving as well?" Devon asked.

"The carving as well," the M.E. affirmed.

She turned and whispered to Loch, "Overkill." He nodded imperceptibly.

"Would you say the body was posed, Tom?" Detective Marders asked.

"Like the Lambroski case?" the M.E. replied.

"Yeah."

"Possibly. It certainly is a strange way to leave somebody."

"Isn't it usually serial killers who pose bodies?" a younger detective asked Detective Marders; Marders did not answer. "Would this be an m.o. or a signature?"

"I'd say a signature," Marders answered gruffly, "if we were looking at a serial, which we're not." He turned his back on the younger cop. "You see any similarities between your cases and this one, Brennen?"

"We had one body, fatally stabbed to death, with some carving in the same area of the chest. The other body appeared to be a suicide. We found the knife that did the carving in him, next to her. She had slit her wrists with it."

Devon moved around the body to watch the M.E. work and shot a look to Loch across the room. "Did you measure the chest wounds?"

The M.E. looked up at her. "We did that and took the photos already."

"If you don't mind, could you tell me the diameter of the carving area?"

He looked at his notes. "Six by eight."

She wrote down the dimensions for later use, although what she really wanted was a paintbrush, tracing paper, and a Kinko's to enlarge it.

"Any idea where your victims were last Tuesday?"

Marders's question arrested her line of thinking and made her thoughts flash to Detective Carol Freesia and the call she'd had from Beka. *"You're going to find out sooner or later, and sooner's always better . . ."* She started to speak, then paused; she hadn't even been able to tell Loch about stopping by Missing Persons yet. "Ms. Imamura was in the city last Tuesday, and one of your own can verify that she saw Detective Carol Freesia."

"What!" Loch almost bellowed at her.

"Why the hell did she do that?" Marders sounded stymied, too.

"I haven't had time to update you on everything, Detective Brennen." Devon gave Loch her sternest look. "But I did stop at Missing Persons. Detective Freesia headed up an unsolved Missing Persons case back in the '80s that Beka Imamura was evidently trying to get information on. She asked Detective Freesia to show her the case file last Tuesday afternoon."

"Interesting, Detective Halsey. Is there anything else you're keeping back from us?"

"Of course not, Detective Marders. Although I must say that this looks almost like a practice run for what happened on New Year's Eve. The same number of stab wounds, the carving, but all inflicted on a corpse. It's as if the murderer was preparing for the crime to be committed. What will be most interesting is if your Toxicology and ours match."

"What's in your Toxicology report?"

Brennen coughed uncomfortably. "We don't have those back yet. But from what our M.E. tells us, Imamura died of cardiac arrest, possibly due to a drug overdose. Montebello died from stab wounds."

"Were there drugs in his system?"

"We'll know tomorrow."

"I can't believe you didn't know last night," Marders criticized.

"Precisely what my sergeant's thinking right about now." Brennen smiled at him.

"What do you bet it's the same m.o. as here," Devon piped in, hoping to save Suffolk County's face. "If you can get Toxicology back by tomorrow we'll all know at the same time."

The M.E. stepped back from the corpse. "Bag him." He packed up his things and followed his assistants downstairs.

The police from more than one precinct, as well as captains, sergeants, and lieutenants, milled around the building for a few more hours until there was nothing else they could do but go home.

Then, as reluctant to leave the scene of the crime as the paparazzi are a Broadway opening, they began to filter through all four levels of the building until they were finally on Mercer Street and out the door. Loch and Devon, no better than the rest, hung out in the hallway with police personnel and watched as others worked until about three-thirty in the morning, when the last of the detectives made their way downstairs.

"Where you folks staying tonight?" Detective Marders asked.

"On the third floor," Devon told him.

"Make sure you don't cross the line upstairs."

"Of course." She handed him her card as the elevator took them down to the bottom floor.

"I had my guys go over the art studio just in case something is consistent between the two scenes. I have a feeling you did the same." He looked at her but Devon did not blink. "I hope you'll keep us up to date."

"Of course, detective." Devon offered her most disarming smile. It didn't work on Marders; he grunted and looked at Lochwood.

"What time's the autopsy?" Lochwood asked.

"The M.E. said he'd squeeze it in early, about noon." They shook hands for the first time as Detective Marders headed out into the street. Devon locked the door behind him.

"We'd better get there at eleven. No one does an autopsy at noon," Loch grumbled.

"You think he'd lie to us?" Devon thought he looked like a little boy who didn't want the other kids to go home yet.

"I know it. He doesn't want to work with us. He doesn't think we can handle the case."

"How can you say that?"

"I know how he thinks. I'm the same way."

She started up the stairs without even looking at the elevator. He followed her, willing to give her the benefit of the doubt.

"So now that we're alone, are you going to tell me about the Tyvek suit?"

"I'm almost embarrassed to." She paused. "I fouled up bigtime."

"I doubt that."

"No, I did. Whoever was in there with me made it look like they had escaped, and then hid inside. I should have gone back in and made a thorough inspection of the floor."

"Alone? Right. What do you want, a bullet in your back?"

"That would not have happened." She would have caught the intruder; she knew it.

He stopped on the stairs and looked at her. "So, if you had gone into the art studio rather than locking the door and going upstairs to call for backup, where would you have looked first? The truth, don't edit your answer. Your heart is pounding and you're out of breath. Where would you have gone first?"

"Cautiously toward the back."

"The lights were on?" She nodded. "And this person was hiding where?

"Under the loading dock."

"Behind you." She nodded again. "And this person may be a murderer and not just a thief. You really think this person would have let you look around?"

"I would have heard him move and popped him off in one shot."

"Or you'd be wrong and I'd be really pissed off." He took her hand. "We already have three bodies; let's not make it four. You did the right thing." He kissed her forehead.

"Don't patronize me."

"I'm not!"

"Oh yeah? What would you have done?"

"I'd probably be the one who was dead now. On a more practical note, I don't think murder was the purpose of the visit."

"Why would someone want to take just one suit?"

"Maybe the murderer left it here," he suggested.

"That would be stupid, unless the murderer was trying to frame Beka for both murders and realized after the fact that trace evidence on the suit would prove Beka's innocence instead."

Spontaneously, he kissed her on the cheek. "Very plausible. I'd better call Gary. I want the rest of those suits at the barn checked." Even as he said it, though, he knew the murderer had probably goofed once, but not twice.

They were halfway up the second flight of stairs when she

stopped. "Loch, what if someone wore a Tyvek suit, booties, gloves, and hair-net to commit a double murder?"

"Hypothetically?"

"What kind of scene would we have?"

He instantly saw where she was heading. "We'd have a scene with no trace or fiber evidence, no footprints, and no fingerprints."

"Unless prints were planted specifically to confuse us."

He spoke without thinking and immediately regretted opening his mouth. "But who would let anyone into their home dressed in head-to-toe Crime Scene gear?"

Her face paled. Her hands began to tremble and then shake uncontrollably. "Oh my god!" She sank to the stairs. "Oh my god . . ." Loch turned around and stared at her. "Beka thought it was me."

CHAPTER TWENTY-SEVEN

Those who hear not the music think the dancer's mad.
—HALLMARK CARD

Fortunately, scent rises like smoke, so the smell had not fallen to the lower floors. And except for the fact that the third floor had been searched and processed for evidence, Devon and Loch could spend the night without too much unpleasantness. They stood in the doorway for a moment perusing the scene. It was not in total disarray, but everything seemed to be covered with a thin film of gray dust. The dishes in the sink had been fingerprinted; the coffee-table book, too. For the first time in Devon's life she had an inkling of how it felt to live in a home where a crime had been committed, and was shocked at how violated she felt. It had never occurred to her that the police perpetrated their own presence upon victims' privacy. She looked around the room she knew so well—this was how others felt when she and Frank left a scene after doing their job, not more secure and safe, but abandoned and unprotected.

Loch poured Devon a glass of red wine and undid the laces on her shoes. "You need some rest," he said, gently massaging her toes, the arch of her foot. She lay back on the overstuffed sofa and nestled into the pillows.

"So much death all around," she whispered.

"It isn't your fault."

She did not respond.

"We're going to get to the bottom of this, Dev. Just hang in there." She nodded and shut her eyes, letting his hands work the tension out of her feet and up the calves of her legs. "Last night you had more to tell me," Loch reminded her.

"I did?"

"Why did you two fight about me?" He wasn't a detective asking the question, but a lover.

Devon didn't know if she should tell him the truth or not, but she didn't have the energy to keep the secret any longer, and maybe it was time to bring up the topic of their relationship. "She didn't think you were good enough for me," she said.

"I'm not."

She reached up to muss his hair, but stroked his cheek instead. "She thought I deserved someone who isn't already married."

"You do." He was afraid to go further, but how else could he get to the truth? He didn't want to ask her but he had to know, for himself, not the investigation. "So what did you tell her?"

"I told her I loved you, Loch."

He stopped massaging her feet and ankles.

She waited but said nothing as the emptiness inside her yawned, ready to swallow her whole. "I feel like I'm floating away from you."

"I won't let you go." He wrapped his arms around her, cradling her against his chest, weighing her back to earth. She kissed him desperately, then deeply, then urgently, her desire commingled with her grief. He returned her questioning lips with tender assurance.

They made love slowly, cherishing their bodies, their togetherness, the life flowing between them. When she came, it wasn't with screams of ecstasy, but tears. She wept in his arms and buried her head into his shoulder until his kisses on her hair and forehead drew her out of her sorrow, drew her back to him.

"Don't ever leave me," she whispered.

"I'll never leave you," he answered. He fell asleep nestled in the turbulence of her dark blond hair and she followed him into her own world of dreams, where there were no murders or murderers, no lost boys or death. It was a pleasant world—a dream world.

She awoke two hours later with Loch snoring in her ear.

Extricating herself from his limbs, she walked softly over to her jacket pocket where she'd put the sketch of the marks on Edilio's chest. Somewhere, she knew, Gabe had a Japanese ink brush set. She looked through the drawers of his desk and found extra paper and an ink block; the brush was in the pencil jar on the top left corner. She filled a raku cup with water, dipped the squirrel-hair brush twice, then swirled it around the ink block until there was a black cloud of water at the tip. It took her a few sheets of paper to get the strokes right, but finally, when she felt she had a sense of the line, she was able to copy the scratches in Edilio's chest, line for line. When she was done, she was certain she had something. But what? She reached for the phone. It was six a.m.

He answered on the first ring.

"Hans? It's Devon."

"Ah, I've been waiting for your call. Someone wrote your name on the prayer roster."

"Me? Why?"

"I don't know. I am afraid for you."

"When did you find my name?"

"Yesterday morning's service. I am the only one who adds names to the list and I didn't write yours."

"Maybe someone thought I needed your prayers."

"But no one admitted to writing your name."

"I'm in the city right now; I'll come take a look as soon as I'm back out there. I called because I need to know if you can you read *Kanji*."

"No."

"Do you know anyone who can?"

"Isshu can. He used to sit with us."

"Does he have a fax?"

"I believe so."

"I'm sorry to make this so urgent, but I need someone who can read *Kanji* right away."

"Let me call him and get the fax number for you."

"Thanks, Hans." She gave him their number in the city, then sat back and waited for three full minutes before the phone rang. This time she was the one to pick it up on the first ring.

"He's home and waiting for your fax."

"That's great, what's the number?"

"011-813-3282-0201."

"Where's that?"

"Kyoto. He's there now."

"You called Japan?"

"Sure. You coming to the sit this afternoon?"

"I don't know. What day is it, Hans?"

"Tuesday. Are you okay?"

"Just a little discombobulated." She could not believe it was Tuesday already; she was still stuck somewhere between New Year's Eve, Monday, 1984, and this year, which one was it?

"We sit at five o'clock. You could look at the list."

"I'll try."

"Take care of yourself, Devon. You'll think more clearly if you can take the time to focus on the present." It was as if he had read her mind again. She hung up and turned to the fax machine. It only took a few minutes for the fax to decipher the lines and spit them out across the international dateline to Kyoto. Devon went to the kitchen to make a pot of coffee.

Forty-five minutes later, as a hint of gray was cracking over the dismal edge of lower Manhattan's empty skyline, the fax returned an answer to her question. She stood by the window reading what it said and staring out at the empty sidewalks of Mercer Street. Someone had been here last night and she knew now that that someone was Gabe's murderer as well.

Loch thrashed and moaned on the couch, his breathing quickening until he sounded as if he were hyperventilating. She had grown used to his night terrors and watched calmly as his subconscious wrestled with unknown demons. Most people thought Brennen had this supernatural ability to stay up all night, working twenty-four hours a day with only a few hours of sleep sprinkled here and there. She knew better—sleep took more effort than staying awake. She waited for the dream that tortured him to end; she had only awakened him once during an episode and would never repeat that mistake. She watched his tormented face, the mouth gaping open as saliva gathered at the corner. The scream, a little boy's scream, erupted from inside his chest and escaped through his throat. "Ahhh!" He sat upright, staring about the room in confusion.

"You're in Soho, at Gabe and Beka's loft," she said softly.

He nodded in response, but his eyes were glazed over as his brain tried to figure out the particulars of what she'd just said. He sighed deeply, like a modern day Jacob—worn out from wrestling with his angel, or was it his devil? "It's been a while since I had one of those. Don't you ever get tired of me waking you up like that?"

"You didn't wake me up. I've been pulling a Brennen—working

on the case while you catch a few Zs."

He folded his hands behind his head and looked at her almost proudly. "See, that's why I love you. Where else could I find a woman who can process a corpse without getting queasy, make love like nobody else on earth, and solve a case while I'm napping?"

"I didn't say I solved anything, but I did find out something. We need to get those photos from the other scene back today." She held out the fax from Japan, then stopped. "Did you say *love?*"

"You heard what I said." He tried to snatch the fax out of her hand but she held it higher over his head. "What's it say?"

"I'll tell you just as soon as you repeat what you just said, so I can hear it!" She straddled his hips and sat down on top of him to make sure he was pinned to the couch. He looked at her, then at the fax. It was a toss-up, so she kicked him to help him decide.

"Love you," he mumbled teasingly. "So, what's it mean?"

"Lochwood Brennen, you cad!"

"I know." He grabbed her and pulled her on top of him. "Now, it means . . ." he began the sentence for her.

She bit his ear and faked a German accent. "Ve are returning to zis line of questioning, detective. Ve have ways of extracting information from ze likes of you."

He squeezed her tightly and gave her a deep and longing kiss. He had won.

"It's a Zen koan." She snuggled into the crook of his arm contentedly.

"What the hell is a Zen koan?"

"*Shi moshi hito kentetsu sureba. Shin no, dai joba, to nazuka,*" she said in very bad Japanese.

He grabbed the fax from her to read what it said for himself.

"Death. She whose insight penetrates here is a truly great woman, He whose insight penetrates here is a truly great man."
This is a famous ink drawing done by Master Hakuin Ekaku, who lived in the sixteenth century and is revered as the organizer of koan practice in Rinzai Zen. It is strange someone not Buddhist should be so familiar with our practice.
—Isshu

Loch reread what the Zen master in Japan had written, then looked down at Devon's head.

"Hans is *Rinzai*?" She nodded in answer. "Okay, then whose insight? Beka's?" He started to sit up.

"It's a koan. It's not supposed to be clear."

He ignored her Zen instructions. "If Beka killed Edilio, the woman is you. This is a message for you."

"*If* the murderer was Beka," she reminded him.

"Or if the murderer is not Beka, the murderer knows you." He had just negated yet another theory and could hear his partner chiding him; it was one of his talents—blowing holes in others' theories. Lochwood was not convinced that this was anything more than a trick that could have been left by Beka after she cut her hair and left it at the Buddha. He let the events of the past few days play through his mind. What if someone was still out there who had killed Beka, Gabe, and Edilio? What if Devon was right?

"You're being too linear. Koans are never that linear." She brought two cups of coffee over to the couch and put them down on the table.

"I don't even know what the hell a koan is! I'm a recovering Catholic!"

"The Virgin Mary giving birth to Jesus is a koan in a way—how is it possible for a woman to give birth and remain a virgin?"

"God works in mysterious ways?" Loch laughed.

"So does Buddha. A koan doesn't make sense until you reach enlightenment, when for some reason it then makes sense."

"Why's it make sense?"

"When and if I ever reach enlightenment, I'll tell you."

"Please do." He looked down at the fax. "So this koan could be about you, meant for you, or have nothing to do with you?"

"Exactly." She sighed and let her chin dip toward her breastbone. He took her face in his hands and kissed her tears before they could fall. She had been debating whether to tell him about her name being on the prayer rolls at the zendo, but now decided it was absolutely necessary.

"Someone thinks we're playing a game here."

"A game? It's too insane for a game. None of it makes any sense."

"Just like a koan." His eyes lit up as he laughed. "The game's afoot, Watson!"

She stared at him. "That reminds me, have you seen my beeper?"

"How does that remind you of your beeper?"

"Have you?"

"*Nada.*"

"I don't know what happened to it. Oh well, I'm going back to look through Freesia's files."

"Good idea. Whoever planned this obviously knows about Todd."

"*Whoever?* You didn't say Beka."

"She's still number one on my list."

"At least now there's a list." She kissed him good-bye. "Call my cell if you need me. It's working now." She handed him his cup of coffee. "And don't get into too much trouble while I'm gone."

CHAPTER TWENTY-EIGHT

Three men testified about the tortoise, so that makes it a turtle.

—ZEN PHRASE

Devon had only just left and Loch was already bored. He poured himself another cup of coffee and headed downstairs. He wanted to peruse the building without any interruptions from Marders's people, and he knew they'd be back. He carried his cellphone with him and sipped his coffee, walking through each floor slowly and deliberately, but nothing untoward leapt out at him. He looked through the Tyvek suits and poked through the rubble of Beka's bust, then walked across the art gallery, not bothering to look at any of the art. He stopped at the fourth floor and winced as the putrid fragrance of Edilio's body assaulted his still waking nose.

His cellphone rang. "Brennen here."

"What's up, partner?"

"We had some interesting developments last night, among them a new corpse." Loch looked out the top-floor window and down at Howard and Mercer Streets.

"Sorry I missed the excitement."

"It was Edilio Ferraro."

"No shit!"

"He's carved up like Montebello," he told his partner.

"You think we got a serial?"

Loch did not answer. "Imamura was still alive when Ferraro was killed, but this is way over the top. Oh, Edilio was gay."

"We were just wrong all over the place. You think he was doing Gabe?"

"Evidently."

"Did Gabe kill him?"

"And then get killed the same way? I don't think so."

"What if Gabe killed Edilio and Beka killed Gabe in exactly the same way? Maybe she found Edilio, figured out what happened, and decided to get back at Gabe."

"Why? With Gabe prosecuted for murder she'd be one rich lady. And it's not like she didn't know people on the force. You can't do better than that?"

"Maybe she was afraid for her life," Gary suggested.

"Anybody who can commit these kinds of murders can't be too scared."

"So, what do ya want me to do on this end?"

That's the offer Lochwood had been waiting for. "I need Houck to call Homicide here and make sure we get included on the autopsy this morning. Second, I want you to fax me the pictures of Montebello's chest wound as soon as you get them. Devon hit on something this morning."

"It's seven, Loch. It is morning."

"She's been up since five."

"God help us, she's getting like you."

"The lines on Ferraro's chest are Japanese for whatever you call how they write."

"Hey, remember how I said it looks like Sanskirt or something?" Gary was obviously impressed with his own powers of observation.

"That's San*skrit* and yeah, you're a regular Detective Morse."

"Hey, he screws up a lot!" Gary protested.

"My point exactly."

"You sure are feeling your oats this morning. What'd you do, get lucky last night?"

"Get to the damn photo lab!" Loch countered. "And call me as soon as Frank gets that mold glued together."

"You did get lucky! Am I good or what?" Gary laughed into the receiver.

"Or what. Oh, and put us in for more overtime."

"I'm on it."

Loch hung up and started pacing the floor. He wanted to figure it all out *now*; he didn't want to wait for the pictures or for Devon to return from Missing Persons, and the autopsy was going to waste hours of valuable time. He wanted it all to happen immediately, and since there was nothing else he could do, he decided to do what he could to speed things up. He picked up the phone again and called the number Detective Marders had given him.

Detective Marders was at his desk but did not sound pleased to hear from his nemesis so early in the morning. "What do you want?"

"Haven't had your second cup of coffee yet?" Loch asked brusquely.

"I'm too busy for coffee, what's your excuse?"

"I was going to share some information with you, but maybe you don't need it."

"You hindering our investigation now, Brennen?"

"You hindering ours, Marders?"

There was silence on the other end of the line. "I hear trouble follows you wherever you go, and your reputation has preceded you. Just because you can sniff out a corpse like a damn bloodhound doesn't mean you're on your own turf now."

"Doesn't take a bloodhound to smell a corpse, Marders, just a good cop." Loch loved busting balls and this conversation was giving him more of a kick than his last cup of coffee. "It also doesn't mean that the crime I'm investigating and the one you're investigating aren't connected. Let's be candid, Marders. If we don't wrap this up quick the Feds are coming in to do it for us—this murderer has crossed county lines."

"And I'm thinking your dead girl is the murderer and the case is closed."

"I didn't think you were that dumb."

"Cut the crap. We don't have any bodies that prove she didn't do it. That's how it plays for me—sounds like she snapped, offed her business partner, offed her husband, offed herself."

"That chicken scratch on his chest . . ." Loch dangled the bait to see if Marders would bite.

"What about it?" Marders didn't sound interested or apprecia-tive enough to warrant handing over the information so easily.

"It means something. See you at the autopsy." Loch hung up.

* * *

Devon arrived at One Police Plaza at seven-ten and was upstairs and in Detective Freesia's office by seven-fifteen. Freesia looked up from her desk and acknowledged Devon with a brief nod. "I left the file at that desk. Coffee's over there. Make yourself at home."

Devon had questions, though, and sat down at the senior detective's desk. "You gotta second?" Freesia half nodded. "I'm curious, did Beka tell you why she wanted to see Todd's file?"

"She asked if it were possible. I told her no, and that was that."

"How'd she get up here?"

"She didn't. She called from the front desk. No one gets upstairs unless they're escorted, or, like you, on the force."

"And that was what day last week?"

"I already told you." Freesia wasn't interested in playing any games.

"That's right, Tuesday." Devon walked over to the desk and opened the folder. She still wasn't sure what she was looking for and flipped through the pages of the case file until something caught her eye—a news clipping. In the photo Todd seemed surprisingly young, untainted by the world and its problems, yet there he was with Beka's leg by his ear. On the outskirts of the picture Gabe, Edilio, and Devon were looking on. She read the article and realized it was more about Beka's seduction of the innocent Yale Divinity student than anything else. Thanks to Godwyn's photographs, the press had grabbed the story and run with it. There hadn't been any dirt to drag out on Todd, only Beka. Times hadn't changed much; Beka was still the one the press dogged.

Devon turned past the news articles to start with Josh's interview. She tried to remember what Josh was like back in the '80s before he was a self-assured doctor, back when he was only a self-assured intern. She wondered if he had fidgeted in the chair, or if he had been suave enough to disguise his discomfort.

> *Zambini: So, the last time you saw Todd was?*
> *Shapiro: Dancing with Beka at our party. He and she were, you know, cutting the rug.*
> *Freesia: A bit of a local celebrity, isn't she?*
> *Shapiro: More than local, but yeah. Anyway, Todd seemed to get*

dizzy. You know, he was a little green when he took off down-stairs.
Zambini: And that's the last time you saw him? For the record, Mr. Shapiro just nodded. We're recording, Mr. Shapiro, if you could please state Yes or No for the transcript.
Shapiro: Yes.
Zambini: Were there any drugs at your party?
Shapiro: No way. I'm pre-med. I wouldn't allow drugs where I live, you know?

What a crock that was, Devon thought to herself.

Zambini: Was Todd drinking heavily?
Shapiro: We'd all had a few, it was New Year's.
Freesia: You know, Josh, I don't know one party nowadays that doesn't have pot on the fire escape, poppers on the dance floor, and toot in the bathroom. You telling me that with all your medical expertise you didn't see as much as a joint at your party?
Shapiro: There was probably some pot . . .
Zambini: And?
Shapiro: That's about it. We had punch with a little extra punch in it, champagne, firecrackers, and cigars, but nothing illegal.
Freesia: Thanks for being frank with us. Tell me, is there another entrance to your building?

Devon could almost hear the acerbic tone in Freesia's voice—Freesia must have known he was lying to them.

Shapiro: Just the door on Canal Street.

Why had he evaded that question? Semantically, he'd answered truthfully, but why hadn't Josh told the detectives about the passage over the rooftops?

In the column of the transcript, someone, probably Freesia, had made notations: *"Check out other possible entrances to the loft. 1/5/84."* A later notation, dated 1/8/84, stated: *"No other entrance could be found."*

Devon flipped to Alexandra Parnel and found that the Reverend Brown, about whom Maddie had spoken at dim sum, had also sat in on Alexandra's interview. He had alienated Alexandra much quicker than he had Maddie, and his first mistake was to ask her if she was Christian. Alex didn't look Jewish but she was, and she made it quite clear that she didn't appreciate his line of questioning.

"None of your damn business," Alexandra had replied. Devon checked the date and time at the top of the page as well. It was a few hours after Maddie Fong's altercation with the man of the cloth. The likelihood that Maddie had called Alex after her interview explained Alex's flippant answer, although generally Alex didn't need much prompting.

From Detective Freesia's notes in the margin, Alex was the first loftmate to cry over Todd's loss or to show any emotion. But the rest of the interview seemed unremarkable. Alex told them about the elevator shaft, the party, the crowd; she denied that there were any drugs, just like they all had . . . Devon flipped back and forth a few times to make sure it wasn't there. But on the second read she was quite sure Alex had avoided telling the detectives that she had recorded the entire party. She wondered if Alex would really call L.A. and have her assistant get the videotape out of storage. Devon hoped so; she wouldn't like to have to take a warrant out on Alex, but she would if she had to.

Devon had almost finished reading the entire case file. She just had Maddie's interview to go, and skipping the preliminary information the detectives had to gather, it only took her a few seconds to read the two brief pages of text.

> *Fong: I drank a lot of punch that night.*
> *Freesia: We understand a lot of people did.*
> *Fong: Yeah, but . . . I don't know.*
> *Freesia: Come on, what don't you know?*
> *Fong: Anything. I don't remember anything that happened.*
> *Zambini: You were there, right?*
> *Fong: Yeah, I was there, but it's all a blank. I'm listening to everybody talk about what happened and can sort of put it together from that, but I don't know if I actually remember anything*

myself. You know?

Freesia: Not really.

Zambini: Ms. Fong, it sounds like you're saying that you were in a blackout.

Fong: Oh god. I hope not. That sounds so serious.

Freesia: But is that what you're saying?

Fong: No, I just don't remember anything. That's all.

Zambini: What is the last thing you remember?

Fong: Waking up next to Godwyn. I don't even remember if we did it or not.

Freesia: Godwyn? Godwyn? He's not on our list.

Fong: He used to live in the loft like I did, on a couch.

Freesia: Are there a lot of people living there who sleep on the couch?

Fong: Sure. Last month we had three people from Iceland staying there as well as God and me. We're a generic crowd.

Zambini: We have more people living in this place than a homeless shelter.

Fong: It's like a shelter for artists! God—that's what we call Godwyn for short—moved into Gabriel Montebello's building just after Christmas. He got a great deal. Pays two hundred a month for the fourth floor, and caretakes the place when Gabe is out of town.

Zambini: I take it Godwyn was at the party?

Fong: Yeah, God was at the party.

Rev. Brown: I object to that phrase.

Zambini: I'm sorry, reverend.

Freesia: Was this artist Montebello there?

Fong: Everyone was there, but Gabe left early, about two or so.

Zambini: Two is early?

Fong: I'm sorry I can't remember more. I don't even remember Beka almost falling into that elevator shaft. It's like we're cursed.

Rev. Brown: Cursed.

Freesia: I doubt that very much, Ms. Fong. If anything does come back to you, be sure to tell us.

Fong: Sure. I don't know why it happened. It must have been the grain alcohol in the punch.

Freesia: Or maybe you drank too much, period.
Fong: No, I think it was the grain alcohol.

Right after Maddie had admitted to not remembering anything, she told them what the tarot cards had said about Todd being in the river. No wonder the Reverend Brown went ballistic in the hallway—he must have been furious with her for being too drunk to help them with anything more concrete than psychic, whatever that meant, intuition. Devon felt angry, too, just reading the interview.

She rubbed her eyes; they were dry and tired from the early-morning sleuthing, and reading the transcripts had only made her feel more deeply the emptiness of the situation they had found themselves in back then. She walked down the hallway, looking for some way to get a breath of fresh air, but all the windows were sealed to prevent escape. She stopped outside of the interrogation room where they had conducted the interviews of each loftmate and close friend. This was the hall where Reverend Brown had verbally accosted Maddie, and Maddie had left with the beginning of an understanding that she had a drinking problem. She wondered if Maddie 'the Mad Dog' Fong had ever stopped drinking and realized she didn't know. She didn't know anything about these peoples' lives now, and yet back then her life had practically revolved around theirs. It was difficult to fathom how fast a track they had been on then; they seemed to have grown up despite themselves.

"What are you doing out here?" she heard Detective Freesia ask.

"Just taking a break." Devon looked out the window at yet another bleak winter day. "I don't see Godwyn or Gabe in the file."

"Notebook. We interviewed them in the Mercer Street building. We only brought people who actually lived at the loft at the time in for questioning."

"And Gabe?"

"Didn't know anything. He left the party almost immediately after Todd disappeared and didn't even recognize the photos of the kid. Dead end."

"You know, we went to the loft yesterday, after I met you; a kind of loft reunion at a nearby restaurant that ended up being an impromptu wake for Beka and Gabe. At the loft, Godwyn Kamani jumped from one side of the roof to the other and showed me how Beka used to get downstairs from the other building. Of course, the door was locked and he barely got across, but evidently, Beka enjoyed leaving that way quite a bit."

"I'll be damned. Joey said Beka had a scam but we couldn't figure out how she did it," Freesia said, referring to her previous partner.

"You sat on the loft?"

"They were dealing top-of-the-line coke, real high-quality stuff."

Devon was stunned.

Freesia flipped through her calendar impatiently. "I wondered why Shapiro lied. Something about this does not add up here. And I don't know what it is."

"One of the guys in Surveillance out on the Island used to work for the Sanitation Department; he says you could dump a body in the sewer and never leave a trace."

"We get a number of things down there but most of them aren't attached to much that's identifiable. We could probably clear more than a few cases if we could match them with someone in our files. Unfortunately, people who go missing aren't usually DNA-tested before they disappear, so we can't do much with the bones the sewer guys find—although, sometimes they're over a hundred years old. Occasionally we get lucky with dental impressions, and technology has certainly helped clear more cases than we used to be able to clear. But then society's gotten more violent and volatile. We have more cases than ever."

"I don't think I could stand your job."

"What do you do, pick up traces of blood and bodily fluids? You see stuff I'd have trouble stomaching."

"I doubt it. It's all technical. Your job, that's emotional."

"I guess we're all cut out to do different things. Listen, I'm in the middle of a case meeting, so I'll be tied up until nine. If you finish before I get back, leave the file on my desk."

"Would you mind if I looked at the other kids who went missing on New Year's?"

Freesia glanced down the hall as if to make sure no one was listening. "No, go ahead, just promise me you'll let me know if you find any dots to connect."

"You bet. Thanks for your help." Devon stared out the window at the people hurrying down the street toward the courthouse; some heading for work, some heading for justice. Was there any real justice? Even if she found out what happened to Beka and Gabe, even if she proved that Beka didn't kill her husband, even if she figured out what Beka was looking for in Todd's case file, would they ever be sure what had happened to Todd Daniels? She knew the answer, even as she asked herself the question.

Todd was, would always be, an unsolved mystery.

She walked back down to Freesia's office and nonchalantly pulled the eight other cases out of her vertical file, then sat down at her desk.

CHAPTER TWENTY-NINE

A thousand grasses weep tears of dew;
A single pine tree murmurs in the breeze.

—ZEN PHRASE

Lochwood's beeper went off at the same time the fax began to ring, then purr. He still didn't understand how faxes worked, and didn't really care; the fact that some guy in Japan, a day-and-a-half away, could analyze information and get it back to them in an hour was beyond his ken. "Hey, Gary," he said into the phone, "I'm watching it come out."

"How soon can you get back to me?"

"I need Devon to ink it in, then we need to fax Japan."

"There's got to be somebody closer who can interpret this."

"You know any Japanese people?"

"Just that dead broad."

Loch almost burst out laughing. "And she couldn't have read it if she were alive."

Gary chuckled at himself. "Don't her uncles read Japanese?"

"Great idea, let's bother the grieving family! Besides, they're third- or fourth-generation American, Gary. What are you, second?" Loch enjoyed instructing somebody else on the subject of America's melting pot—it was usually he who got the lecture from Devon.

Gary ignored him. "Okay. So, Frank's in here working on the rest of the photos and our mold. It looks like something out of a sci-fi movie—one eye, part of a mouth, a nose. There are no nose holes. Evidently, when you cast someone's face you stick straws up the nose so they can breathe."

"Intriguing."

"Almost. Frank thinks it could be the mold of a dummy and that's why there're no air holes. Problem is there's hair in the

Plasticine . . ." Loch started to speak but Gary interrupted. ". . . It's already at the lab."

"Sounds like you don't even need me there."

"We'll keep you for entertainment value."

"Is Tox back yet?"

"Get this, they both had lethal doses of Norflex in their systems."

"So why the knifework?"

"Exactly."

"I bet Ferraro is the same." Lochwood wrote "*overkill*" again on his notepad. "Anything else from Hematology?"

"The blood on the sword is Gabe's, but there's also blood on there that's over two hundred years old. Too cool!"

"A little out of our jurisdiction." There was a lightness developing in his team that felt familiar, and it made Loch feel the swift excitement of his work that sustained him more than food. He'd been afraid that this case would be nothing but pain and sorrow—some were, but even in the really terrible tragedies, they usually managed to get above the horror. It had been hard to do that this time, seeing as it was one of their own suffering a traumatic loss. Devon had come out of her stupor smack in the middle of the night, though, pulling this amazing information literally out of thin air.

He could hear the change in Gary's voice and knew Frank was working happily on the photos, the mold, probably without even going on the clock. Solving crimes, fighting crime, was what nourished them. Love and sex were good, too, but justice had a fix that nothing else could bring, and his team felt the same way. They liked being the good guys. There was a reason he had hung that sign in the Homicide Squad's break room: "*Our Day Begins When Yours Ends.*"

Ten minutes later Lochwood had six photos laid out on the coffee table and was comparing the marks on Gabe and Beka. He placed a piece of tracing paper over the photos and began to sketch the lines, but he wasn't an artist. All he could make was more scribbling than sense. He'd have to wait for Devon. He called her now-charged cellphone—no answer—wished she hadn't lost her beeper, and began to pace the room once more.

* * *

Freesia poked her head into her own office and offered, "You want to get a cup of coffee with me in the break room?"

Devon followed her down the hall and sat in one of the plastic prefab chairs allotted by the city for detectives to relax in. "This is harder than I thought, going back and looking at it all."

"It doesn't solve the case, does it?" Freesia handed her a cup and pointed to the sugar and Coffeemate on the counter. "I don't know how you like it."

"Black is fine, thanks."

"Back when I was new on the job, every once in a while I'd pull out my old cases and read through them. Picking scabs, that's what I call it."

"Every New Year's Eve Beka used to call and talk about Todd."

"And this year?"

"I didn't answer her call."

"That explains it." Freesia stirred her coffee slowly.

"Explains what?"

"Why you're really here." Devon looked at her expectantly. "Picking the scab for her." Freesia sipped her coffee and looked at the younger detective thoughtfully. "I get calls from downstairs all the time from parents and friends looking to see the unsolved case file of their loved ones. Beka was not unique. She just wanted closure, and no one could give it to her."

"Sam Daniels has gone on with his life. He hasn't been here asking for the file."

"How do you know?" Freesia raised her eyebrows and tilted her head down toward Devon, waiting for her to ask. "Around Todd's birthday. Anniversaries are hard on everybody, especially for family members, and his dad died last year."

"Death always brings it up again."

"Yep. Sam may be a psychologist who knows all about the range of feelings that go with the territory, but he was still here the week of Todd's birthday, looking for answers. You know, we recommend his book, *Unreconciled Grief, For Survivors of a Missing Person*. Ever read it?"

"I wasn't even aware he had a book out." Devon felt slightly embarrassed.

"It's an excellent resource . . ." As Freesia began to tell her about the stages of grief, Devon relaxed.

"If *you* aren't picking scabs, why is it that you have all the missing New Year's files on your desk?" the younger detective asked.

"*Touché.*" Freesia raised her Styrofoam cup. "I'm also looking for similarities."

"Are there any?"

"You tell me."

"Well, they all disappeared on New Year's Eve."

"After leaving a group of friends, or a party," Freesia pointed out.

"There's no trace of them, ever again, except for the three who were floaters."

"And no sign of foul play. That is, except maybe for the last one."

"What was different about him?" Devon's ears perked up.

"He had some marks that could have been made by someone, or they could have been made by garbage. There's lots of glass in the East River, especially on the bottom where he was rolling around for two months. But it was so cold that winter that he wasn't as decayed as the other two we found, so we could still see abrasions."

"What makes you think they're not random scrapings?"

"Edilio Ferraro." Freesia took a sip of her coffee, forcing a dramatic pause. It was Devon's turn to say *touché*, but she kept her mouth shut. "Marders called me this morning. That's what my meeting was about. The decay on last year's body was advanced but there were superficial wounds on his chest. I've requested the autopsy reports on the other two as well, but his was the only one with any scarring. There were no bruisings or other premortem marks to indicate violence or foul play."

"Were they wet deaths?" Devon asked.

"The fluid in the lungs in all three cases was consistent with the river."

"And there were no strangulation bruises or ligature marks?"

Freesia nodded. "You see the problem. How do you drown someone, leave no bruises, and then carve them up after they're dead?"

"I don't know," Devon lied. Her mind leapt to one thought

alone, *Norflex*, but she kept her revelations to herself. "Would you do me a favor?"

"Another one?" The corner of Freesia's mouth was upturned and Devon knew she was kidding with her.

"I have to go up to the coroner's anyway. Could you get me access to the photos from those three boys, Detective Free—"

"Carol," Freesia interrupted her, "call me Carol. What do you think you'll find?" They were definitely on the same page.

"Do you know what *Kanji* is?"

"Rice soup in Chinatown?"

"Actually, I'm referring to Japanese and Chinese characters," Devon explained. "I'd like to see if the body you found last year has similar markings."

"You don't think Beka killed Gabe."

"Never did."

"Marders thinks she killed all of them," Freesia warned her.

"Beka was a slut, not a black widow."

Carol laughed out loud, then stopped herself. "I'm sorry. I forgot she was your friend."

"That's okay. She was a slut with a great sense of humor." They smirked at each other and drank their coffee. "Beka had her own ghosts. She was haunted by Todd's disappearance, her parents' deaths. She was very superstitious, but she was no murderer."

"Her parents died? How?"

"Car accident."

"Maybe somebody should look into that."

"You trying to get into Homicide now?"

"I'd settle for a free trip to Hawaii!"

"Beka did not kill her parents."

"You sure about that?"

Devon stood up quietly.

"I'll help you get copies of the autopsy reports and the corpses. But Devon, these are my boys. They've been missing for years and these families have no idea what happened to their sons and brothers. I want in on anything you find."

"Carol, you're the one who's kept their memories alive. You'll be the first to know."

"Maybe it's all just a coincidence."

"You know what Detective Brennen says? Too much coincidence means crime." She looked down at the blinking message on her cellphone. "I'll be at the coroner's office in an hour." Detective Freesia smiled and nodded.

They shook hands and Devon handed her new colleague a Suffolk County business card. She headed down the corridor and stepped onto the escalator. She had ridden it down to the lobby all those years ago, when she'd left One Police Plaza for the first time, and she wanted to repeat the experience. She wasn't sure why, but she had a feeling it had to do, like Freesia had said, with closure.

CHAPTER THIRTY

The practice of Zen is just like making a fine sword . . .
—NANSHINKEN

Lochwood was standing outside of Montebello's building, tapping his foot and checking his watch, when her jeep pulled up to the curb. "You took long enough." He sounded irritable.

"Take a pill. It's not even ten-thirty." She rolled her eyes.

"Gary faxed the photographs from the scene and I can't make any sense of them." He could be as impatient as a teenager.

She thought about telling him what she and Detective Freesia were working on, but kept her mouth shut. He was too cranky.

The photographs had been distorted by the fax resolution, but Devon thought she could make an accurate rendering and began to trace the lines on Gabe's body. She outlined each mark, then went back to Gabe's desk and began to paint the lines in thick ink strokes. She didn't worry about getting the stroke positions wrong, she just let her wrist float above her hand loosely, the way she'd been taught to hold the paintbrush in school. *"Don't hold it like a hammer! It's a feather, the wingtip of a bird, your lover's hand!"* Kermit McBride had yelled at them while they tried to relax and incorporate his instructions.

Lochwood began to stride back and forth along the windows. It was taking longer than he wanted, she knew that, but she was not going be rushed. She ignored him with all of her powers of concentration until his constant pacing and the weight of his feet against the wood floor got the better of her.

"You're driving me crazy!" she yelled. He sat down on the couch and didn't move. "I mean it, Loch. If you don't get out of here right now, I'm going to stop what I'm doing."

He crept out of the room and down the stairs, but she didn't resume her brush strokes until she heard a door slam. She shook her wrist again to ease the flow of blood to her left hand and began once more. When she was done, she knew for sure that she had seen one of the ideograms in Hans's book at the zendo, but she couldn't recall what it meant. The rest she didn't recognize. She stuck the three sheets of paper into the fax machine and dialed Japan. Now it was her turn to pace.

She went downstairs and sat on the stoop with Loch. "We've got time to kill. I have no idea what time it is in Japan right now. Why don't we head up to the autopsy and stop back here on our way home? If I haven't heard from him by then he can fax us at the office."

"I wish there was a quicker way to do this."

"There probably is, but there wasn't at six this morning. Come on, let's go." She stood up and locked the front door. Fifteen minutes later they were at Bellevue, and the city mortuary.

* * *

"You're early." Detective Marders was standing in front of them almost menacingly.

Great, Devon thought, this will really improve Loch's temper.

"Didn't want to miss anything," Brennen told him.

"Yeah, well, I knew you'd show up no matter what time I told you."

"You were right. Now, you gonna include us in this shindig or are we shut out?"

"Your C.O. called my C.O."

"Fancy that."

Devon stepped away from them—Homicide detectives had complex personalities different from any other species. They could be egotistical but sensitive, observant yet tunnel-visioned; they were intelligent about human nature but idiots when it came to love; they were temperamental workaholics who could be intuitive, creative, and analytical, but she wasn't sure they were human. They reminded her of artists, maybe that's why she felt comfortable in both worlds.

At the information desk she asked which way to take for archives and decided to wait until after the autopsy—she didn't want

Marders to know what she was up to yet. Detectives were sneaky, too.

"So, you gonna tell us what you two came up with this morning?" Marders was asking Loch.

"Just as soon as we hear what the M.E.'s got to say." Lochwood wasn't giving Marders any gifts. They went through the security scanners and headed down the hallway to the morgue elevator.

"Detectives," Ron Smithers, Chief Medical Examiner for the city of New York, began his autopsy formally, "what we have here looks like a strangulation accompanied by postmortem wounding."

"So it looks like torture but it wasn't?" Marders asked.

"You're a regular whiz kid," Loch quipped.

"The cause of death is OD."

"What was the drug in his system?" Devon asked.

"We had the lab run that, detective—" He paused.

"Halsey," she introduced herself.

"Well, Detective Halsey, it was Norflex."

"That matches our m.o. in Suffolk," Lochwood confirmed. "Both of our victims there were drugged, one was stabbed to death but the other died of cardiac arrest from an overdose—that victim also had slit wrists."

Even as he said the words, she heard the warning voice in her head, *overkill*. Both victims—all three, if one considered Beka a victim and not the perpetrator—were classic overkill scenarios, when a murderer bent by rage inflicts wounds after the victim is dead. It was a not-uncommon phenomenon but it usually occurred when a perpetrator knew the victim and wanted to make certain that the victim did not come back to life. She had seen it in domestic abuse cases as well as serial murders.

She caught Loch's eyes again. She knew he was putting it together the same way, but wondered if he saw that Beka had been killed twice as well, with an overdose and the slit wrists. Jo had pointed out that some suicides like to make sure of their success, but those cases were usually male suicide victims, not female.

"The indentation of the springs in the flesh and the lack of bruising in those areas are consistent with postmortem additions to the body. The carving of the chest was done immediately after or upon death—the blood was still clotting. He had eaten prior to his death and had had a glass of wine." The M.E. finished his commentary on Edilio's wounds and concluded that he had been dead about one week.

"Put that with Beka Imamura's presence at Missing Persons last Tuesday and we've got our murderer all wrapped up and in a morgue already," Marders announced.

"Excuse me?" Devon was outraged.

"It's pretty self-explanatory," Marders said as they left the autopsy room.

Devon could not believe what she was hearing.

"The person who murdered Edilio Ferraro had time, motive, and an agenda. That person had to own or live in the building in order to take the time to kill him in this way, since what we've just heard proves that it was not a random act. And Norflex takes time to work, three hours before coma and cardiac arrest. Furthermore, if what you're saying about this Japanese stuff is true, we have m.o. and signature. It had to be Imamura."

"All you guys want to pin it on the Asian 'chick' because she's convenient," she fumed at him. "I knew her!"

"Yeah, well, maybe you didn't know her as well as you think!" Marders yelled back.

Devon didn't flinch. "What about the break-in?"

Lochwood took a step back and let her go. Marders did not know how flawless her logic could be and Loch planned to enjoy the utter emasculation of his rival under Devon's tirade.

"You don't know who it was any more than we do. It could have been a random act; someone who reads *Newsday* or the obits in the *Times*, someone who knows the building."

"Right. A random thief who stole only a Tyvek suit, when there were original paintings worth tens of thousands on the second floor?" she said frostily.

"Hey, I like Imamura for the murders. You don't? Prove it."

"Fine, we'll need copies of the fingerprints you pulled." She had him where she wanted him; now he had to hand her the prints without any delay.

"And we'll need the same from your scene to run against the prints we pulled last night."

"If you want to expedite things, I can take your prints with us and run them in Suffolk." Devon knew he wouldn't go for her idea, but couldn't stop herself from trying.

"I'm not letting you walk off with any prints. I don't trust you," Marders said, snarling.

"That was unnecessary." Loch stepped in to defend Devon.

"I don't care what you think, Brennen! She just told us her friend—the only suspect in my opinion—is innocent!"

"You both have your own agendas for this case."

"Hey, I don't even know what she's doing on this case. You guys short-staffed or what?"

Loch punched his forefinger into Marders's chest. "Don't put your own incompetence off on my detective, Marders, just because you think women should only be meter maids."

Marders stuck his own finger out at Brennen. "Just cause you're boffing her doesn't mean she gets special treatment in this county!"

Loch grabbed him by the collar.

"Good work, Marders." Devon laughed as she slapped Lochwood on the back of the head. "Too bad you can't figure out who the real murderer is. Now why don't you two boys go piss on a few poles and get it over with!" She headed down the hall for the elevator.

Lochwood was still steamed but his voice was calm as he shoved a copy of the fax they had just received from Kyoto into Marders's hand. "You really think she'd have figured out what the carving meant if she weren't interested in finding the truth?"

"Imamura still could have done it."

"She didn't read or write Japanese."

"And Halsey does? Imamura could have copied them just like your sweetheart did." Marders snorted at him and headed back toward the morgue.

Devon was halfway down the hall and about to leave Loch behind. He followed her down a corridor and a back stairway, which led to a more-than-tomblike attachment to the county morgue—Archives. Freesia had done her part; all Devon had to do was sign for the receipt of the duplicates. Twenty minutes later they were sitting in Loch's car and looking at photos from Eric Heron's autopsy—the first sign that someone may have performed this kind of mutilation before Edilio and Gabe.

"You know, Marders is aware of this report," Loch sputtered.

"Of course he is. But he thinks Beka did it and I know she didn't."

"And why is that again?"

"Because Beka hasn't come into the city for New Year's Eve since 1984." She wiggled her finger at the ignition so he'd start the engine. "Let's hurry up and get this to Japan."

CHAPTER THIRTY-ONE

For eighteen years I could not return;
Now I've forgotten the road by which I came.

—ZEN PHRASE

The fax pages were lying on the floor next to Gabe's desk when Devon and Loch arrived back at the loft. But the Zen phrase Isshu Koga had quoted back to them was about as clear as any koan could be: *"For eighteen years I could not return; Now I've forgotten the road by which I came."*

"What the hell's that mean?" Loch asked.

"It's been eighteen years since Todd disappeared. Think of the stab wounds, Loch. I was right . . ." She looked at the second sheet of fax paper but had to re-read what Isshu had written. "This all links back to Todd." She handed the fax to Loch and sat down at Gabe's desk one more time to begin tracing the photograph she had gotten from the city morgue's archivist.

Loch watched her bend over the tracing paper and begin outlining the marks left on Eric Heron's corpse, then stepped silently out of the room and headed downstairs before she could yell at him. He figured he could pace on the second floor just as easily as the third and maybe learn something about art while he was at it.

Having Hand was a stupid name for a sculpture. Loch walked around it and peered out the window at Mercer Street. His hand rested on the bronze momentarily. Cold. He started to move away but felt a semi-fascination by the chill creeping up his arm. He stared at the work of art, puzzled. Was this what Devon meant by the "art experience"? That some works touch you in a deeply personal way? But this one had physically touched him, and it wasn't personal at all. The sculpture felt exactly like a cadaver—cold, waxy, unmoving. The detail on the hands was perfect, right down to every wrinkle around the knuckle and crinkle at the joints, every ridge . . . The top set of hands had a ring on the left ring finger that looked familiar. He had seen it before, recently. It was one of those sacred hearts—two hands clasped in prayer holding a crown. He squinted and searched the recesses of his mind—where had he seen it? Then he recalled; it was Edilio's ring. But was it Edilio's hand? He knelt down and looked up at the piece. There they were, every ridge and whorl and indentation necessary for a fingerprint, and as Loch stooped lower he could see more fingerprints embedded into the bronze.

"Devon!" He leapt up, ran out of the room, and tripped up the stairs yelling, "Devon! Where's your print kit?" She raised her head as a disheveled Lochwood burst into the room. "The kit, where's the print kit?"

She pointed at the tackle box sitting next to the couch. "What's up?"

"I'm experiencing art!" he yelled. "You were right. It *is* exciting." He ran back downstairs.

"Not that exciting," she mumbled under her breath, while inking in what looked like chicken scratch to her but might be a decayed ideogram.

Loch hadn't pulled prints in a long time—it wasn't part of his job—and he enjoyed the practical application of dust to the sculpture, watching it adhere to the detailed bronze and then cling to the Searchie paper. He numbered the hands from the bottom to the top, and even though some were sealed or only had one or two fingers free he printed them all. He was able to get one or two prints for almost every hand and about ten complete sets. He took pictures as he went, chronicling the sculpture from the base up and making copious notes about the position of the hands. He wanted to know who these people were whom Gabe had cast. Were they friends, models, or a collection of acquaintances that had come through his life? The way they were cast was curious—the desperate, clawlike gestures each hand made as if grasping at invisible straws. He felt the heat on his back of someone watching him and turned around.

Devon was standing in the doorway, a bemused look on her face.

"Hiya." He was too chipper.

"Whatcha doing?" she asked.

"Printing this monstrosity."

"You *are* bored."

"No, I'm serious. There're prints in the molds."

"Really?" She came over to the bronze and knelt down to the floor in order to look up at the piece. "How'd you find these?"

"I thought about what you said that day you dragged me to the Guggenheim, 'You have to look at art from every angle, not just the one mounted in front of you, to understand it.' Remember? We were looking at a Jackson *Polack* and I thought it was glamorized spin art?"

"It's Pollock." She studied the prints he had pulled. "I've been avoiding this sculpture for years because it leaves me cold."

"Well, that's what made me think about it! Close your eyes and touch it."

"Do I have to?"

"Come on, experience the art around you," he mocked.

She did and shuddered. "It feels like a corpse."

"Exactly! One that's at least six hours old, full rigor, and no body temperature left."

"And we care, why?"

"Edilio's hands are the last set cast."

She looked at the hands and the ring, then eyeballed the prints. "Shit, you're right."

"I know!" He kissed her. "Let's run the prints I've pulled and see if anyone with a record let Gabe cast them for posterity." He handed her the print cards and grabbed the kit. "You get the fax off to Mr. Isshu Koga?"

"Sent. He'll fax us back at the office."

"Great!" He hugged her.

"I don't know if what I sent him says anything, Loch. The body was pretty deteriorated by the time they found him. It might just be decay and garbage from the bottom of the East River."

"Anything on the other two corpses?"

"*Nada.*"

"Then how come this one is all scratched up and the earlier ones aren't?" She hadn't thought of that. "Everything's shaping up. Can't you feel it?"

"I feel pretty overwhelmed."

"But things are moving. We're onto something here. Last night was not a random B&E, and don't be fooled by Marders; he doesn't think it was either. He's just trying to throw us off."

"The jerk."

"Yeah, he's a lot like me."

"He just wants Detective of the Year. You know, you really ought to try sharing that award sometimes." She liked saying things like that to Loch; despite all of his awards he could be so hard on himself, and she was inordinately proud of his achievements.

"Why should I share the honors? It fits my personality to win. Anything else we need to do here?"

She shrugged and looked at the last pages she faxed as if the secret could be unlocked from the ideograms. "Nothing that I can think of."

Loch pulled her into his arms. "It's going to be okay."

"You sure about that?"

"Trust me."

"You're crazy." She turned her face up to his.

"I love you." He kissed her lips tenderly.

"You just like the way I fax." She suddenly found it difficult to return his gaze and wasn't prepared for his sudden confidence, or was it a confession? Wasn't this what she wanted, to be held, secure and confident in his presence?

He locked her in his arms, searching her eyes as she had so often searched his. "I mean it."

She gently extricated herself from his hold and walked across the room to get her coat.

See, I was right! You are afraid of intimacy! Beka's voice seemed to be yelling at her from the corner of the room. Devon spun around. "What did you say?"

"I love you?"

"No, I heard . . ." she stopped midsentence.

"A ghost?" he asked.

She put her coat on, walked back across the room, and kissed him back. "I love you, too." She turned to the place where Beka's voice had emanated from. "Is that better?" she asked out loud. When there was no reply, she looped her arm around Loch's waist and walked with him out the door and downstairs to their respective cars.

CHAPTER THIRTY-TWO

It is like a water buffalo passing through a window lattice. Its head, horns, and four hoofs have all passed through. Why can't its tail pass through?

—Goso Hoen Zenji

They tailed each other as they drove out of the city. First Loch led, then Devon passed him. She switched lanes and let him move in front of her to avoid a suddenly slowing cab. He returned the favor. They drove like experienced jockeys through the rat race of Manhattan. On the eastern side of the Midtown Tunnel, just as they passed the BQE, Devon's cellphone sounded. "Just wanted to make sure it was working," Loch's voice came over the cellular. "What do you think about that black Beamer in front of me? Hot?"

She pulled into the lane next to him to check out the car ahead. "It's hot alright, Loch. But I don't think it's stolen and we don't have time to find out." She could hear him punching the license plate into his police computer as she spoke.

"Registered to Amil Ababbi. That look like Amil to you?"

"Yes! Would you behave?"

"Just wanted to have some fun." His car darted across all three lanes to avoid Amil's heavy-handed lane shifting. "What's the connection that pulls our three victims together, besides the fact they knew each other and were at that New Year's Eve party in 1984?"

Devon chased his car across the lanes and thought for a second. "Art, dance . . ."

"What else?"

"There's the Pilates connection. There might be a connection between art or dance and Pilates, but why the koans then?"

"So, Zen has to be a part of it." He dodged a white Ford Mustang convertible, owned by a Peter Olsen from Oakdale. "You'd look great in that car."

"I'm more of a '57 Thunderbird girl." She could hear him chuckle in response. "There's no apparent connection between the Pilates studio and Zen except for Beka's association with both, and there's no correlation between Gabe's art and Zen. Although a number of artists frequent the zendo," she thought out loud.

"You frequent the zendo."

"Not that frequently."

"You go, though, and you've studied Zen in the past. When I first met you, you referred to yourself as a Buddhist. I thought that was weird."

"Zen is nonviolent. You thought I was weird?"

"Weren't the samurais Buddhists? And look at the Chinese Buddhists against the Tibetans. Buddhism isn't any more pacifist than Christianity." Loch had a point.

She suddenly wished she could conference-call on her cellphone, but since she couldn't, she excused herself from their conversation. "Just thought of something, call you right back!"

"What?" His voice was desperate to be included.

She hung up on him, then pulled out the business card Detective Freesia had given her and punched in the number with her right hand while holding the phone in her left hand and steering with her left knee. "Carol? It's Devon Halsey."

Freesia's voice came crackling over phone, "Detective."

Devon halted. So, they were detectives again and not on a first-name basis. She wondered what had happened, then decided it wasn't any of her business. "Why wasn't Edilio Ferraro ever interviewed after Todd's disappearance?" she asked.

"Why would we have interviewed him?"

"He was Beka's dance partner in the '80s and he was at the party."

"Did he live with them?"

"No."

"Well, if he didn't live in the loft and no one gave us his name, we wouldn't have interviewed him. Why?"

"He was in the photo the *Post* ran."

"That's Ferraro? Beka told us she didn't know who he was."

"She wanted to protect him . . . but why?" Devon wondered.

"Those kids led us around by the nose with all their fake stories.

The more I think about it the more I think they are responsible for Todd's disappearance, indirectly if nothing else."

"I was one of those kids."

"You told us everything you knew; they didn't. We had nothing to go on except what was told us."

"Maybe there really was nothing to go on."

"I just wonder if Todd knew about the coke. What if he threatened to tell someone?"

"Oh my god," Devon stammered. She could see Loch's curious face trying to lip-read her conversation while still maneuvering through the traffic. "Carol, I'll get back with you. You just reminded me of something."

"Devon?" Freesia's voice had faltered.

"Detective?"

"I'm catching heat here for helping you." Devon was sorry but didn't apologize. "But my day off is coming up; thought I might come out for a visit. My husband can take care of the kids for once, I need a day off from the politics of police work."

Devon had to laugh. "Don't try and fool yourself, Carol. We both know why you're coming out and you're welcome. We can use your expertise."

"Too bad we aren't partners."

"We could wrap a few up." Devon thought about Frank. He and Carol Freesia weren't far apart in age and here Devon was, the youngster in the crowd, benefiting from their years of experience. "I'll fax you directions to my house, but get there early, it's hard to find after dark."

Devon got off the phone with Freesia and waved to Loch as she called Maddie Fong. Loch pointed to his phone, she stuck her tongue out at him. Maddie was not home so she called information for Godwyn's number and called him. "God? It's Devon."

"Hello, luv."

"Don't luv me, God, I need to know what you and Maddie are hiding from me."

"Don't know what you're talkin' about."

"Sure you do, you were talking about it in the subway last night."

"You were in the fucking tube?"

"What happened at the party with the cocaine?" It was a shot in the dark but she had a feeling she had hit her mark. "And if you don't tell me right now, I'll have NYPD at your door in twenty seconds to bring you in for questioning." She could be a good liar.

"I told Alex and Josh it would all come out now."

"Todd?"

"He saw us cuttin' the ounce we got for the party. We had all invested in it and had to turn it around fast, you know, to pay rent."

"Sounds like more than rent."

"Todd was really upset, but Beka cooled him down and got him to try some blow. It wasn't a big deal."

"Everything is something, God."

"That's not what happened to him."

"How do you know?"

"I just don't think that snortin' coke is why he vanished."

So Todd had tasted forbidden fruit. "What about Sam?"

"Sam thinks Beka screwed up, but then Sammy-boy was in love with her, too. You don't have to tell no one, do ya, about the coke?"

"Sure I do, God. Confession is good for the soul."

"Guv? You sure you didn't know about the drugs? It wouldn't look good to have that spread all over the news—that you used to hang out with amateur drug dealers. Might could ruin one's career, a slur like that."

"Are you threatening me, God?" She hung up on him and called Loch back. "There are three party guests of our four in the photo that ran in the *Post* who are now dead, and one most likely dead but certainly missing. And the loft had a business on the side that may be related to this stuff."

"Yet another connection?" Lochwood was enjoying all these leads. This was like playing that card game *Spite & Malice*—everything was getting stacked up, but nothing could be done without that all-important ace. Once the ace appeared, the cards would fall into place. "Who else is in the photo?" She didn't answer. "Devon? Who else is in the photo, and who took it?"

"Me. God."

"God is in the photo?"

"No. I'm in it. God took it. Godwyn Kamani."

Loch swerved out of the fast lane into the slower middle in order to digest what she had just said. The pieces of the puzzle had shifted and one or two dangling pieces suddenly seemed to fit in with segments of fact. "What else besides the party, Zen, and the photograph do these murders have in common?"

"Cocaine."

"I keep tossing them at you and you keep hitting 'em!" Were drugs the cause or simply the effect of Todd's disappearance? Beka had gotten clean but had she stayed clean? What if . . .

"There's something else that these murders have in common that you haven't thought of," he said quietly.

She couldn't think. Her mind was whirling—unable to touch on anything concrete—and she wasn't sure why. "What's that?"

"You." She stared hard at the road, knowing he had hit on something as soon as he spoke. Why hadn't she seen it sooner? "You were on call the night Beka and Gabe died."

"But not when, or where, Edilio died." She breathed more easily—maybe he was wrong.

"But it was a logical conclusion that Edilio would be found after Beka and Gabe. Suffolk County Homicide was going to have to make a trip to their building. Why not send you?"

"And that's what you did." Devon pursed her lips and took a deep breath, then began the list. "Maddie Fong lives on the North Fork, and I think she's Buddhist. She was definitely one back in the '80s. She was the one that started us all going to the temple in Chinatown."

"Where is she now?"

"I have no idea, but she was in the city yesterday with Godwyn."

"How about the rest of them?"

"Alex, Josh, and Katiti live in East Hampton. Sam is in Westhampton." She was speaking as Sam had at dim sum, without affect or variation in the tone of her voice. "Alex and Josh are Jewish. I don't know what Sam is. But all of us used to study Buddhism, and we all had access to koans." The traffic had stalled suddenly, as it did so often on the LIE. Devon called it congestive traffic failure, or traffic farts, depending on the length of time they spent sitting in one spot. Usually Loch would dart over to the access road or put on his portable siren and coast down the median, but today they just sat side by side talking on their phones and looking at each other through tempered glass windows.

"What's the motive?" he asked.

"I don't know yet." She needed him to lead—the significance of what he'd just said was only beginning to settle on her.

His car crept forward a few feet then stopped again. "Let's look at this slowly—the murderer impersonated you to get into their house. But how did the killer drug them?"

Devon could see where he was going and answered, "Beka and Gabe had to know the killer, and the killer had to hang out long enough for the drugs to take effect."

"So, pretending to be you may have looked like a practical joke to Beka and Gabe, and a practical application for the killer."

"That means the killer had to be about my height, Loch."

"Good point."

"Godywn has to be six foot one and black as ink—Sam probably around five-ten and blond, like me. Josh is the shortest of the guys and he's got dark hair."

"What about the girls?"

"We're all about the same height except for Maddie—she's a Smurf—five foot one or two."

"And they were all in the city yesterday afternoon when you were alone in Gabe's studio."

"But why kill Edilio first?" She had to ask the question—it was one of those sticky wickets that just did not fit, and yet to the murderer it must have made perfect sense. "If we're talking about an experienced killer there would be no need to practice, which is what Edilio's murder looked like, a practice run."

"You think we have two killers?"

The traffic had begun to breathe again; it had only been a traffic fart, much to Devon's relief.

"The New Year's boys seem to create a pattern—it's too perfect not to be planned. But are our victims connected? I don't know."

"There's something else, Loch." She paused before continuing. "God just threatened me."

"That's it. We're tracking these people down so they can feel the heat of a real murder investigation, not just some Missing Persons chat." Loch paused. "We need to have a team meeting as soon as we get back to the precinct. If Beka's not a killer, someone has murdered three people in five days, and we may not have much time before he strikes again. I'm going to call Gary and get him to set up a room for us. Think we can be there in fifteen minutes?"

She was about to say no, but he had already hung up and put the siren on the roof of his car. Cars darted out of his way and some came dangerously close to accidents as they decreased their acceleration from eighty miles an hour to fifty-five. Loch loved creating havoc and then leaving it in his wake. He roared off.

She sped after him like a water-skier clinging to the towrope of a crazy man. So strong was her pull toward him that she almost felt as if she could shut her tired eyes and let him carry her back to HQ. Fatigue was lurking around the fringes of her consciousness. It didn't make sense yet, and she wasn't sure she was going to be happy with the outcome, but at least they were moving in the right direction—she could feel it, with all the dread and hesitation that facing the truth brings.

CHAPTER THIRTY-THREE

My brothers, since the beginning of the summer I have done a lot of talking. Look, have I any eyebrows left?

—SUIGAN

At the precinct, Devon left Loch and headed for her own department to pick up Frank. He had been there all day, despite the fact that it was their day off, and he smiled ruefully at her as she walked through the door. "My wife can't wait for me to retire. She says next year she wants me home and all to herself. I don't know what she wants to do with me but if I mysteriously die next New Year's you'll know it's her."

Devon sympathized with him, but Frank was one of the few detectives who had not gotten divorced and she thought Louise was a gem to put up with Frank's hours. "Takes a lot of patience to be a cop's wife."

"Or husband," Frank reminded her, and held up the cast he had built. "I got the negative mold pieced together. We're just waiting for the plaster inside to dry."

She looked at his handiwork but couldn't tell a thing from it. "What about the prints we brought?" She flipped through the photographs and read Frank's notes, adding extra details before they went upstairs. She got stuck looking at the photo of Beka's body. She had not taken in all the details, and now was her chance to scrutinize the scene from a physical distance, even if it was through the lens of Frank's camera.

* * *

Loch and Gary set up Homicide's break room, a double entendre if there ever was one, so the team could meet to discuss the latest developments on the case and the more confusing elements of the crimes. Frank and Devon laid out the photographs in sequence, Edilio's murder scene first.

Gary pulled out the dry-eraser set and drew a timeline on the board, leaving space under each murder for specific details that might tie the murders together. They stood over the photos on the table silently for a moment, then Lochwood began the meeting. "Okay gang, this is what we're looking at. From what Detective Freesia says there have been a number of disappearances on New Year's Eve in the past eighteen years. And while these disappearances started with Todd Daniels, it wasn't until last year that any marks were found on a body that might indicate foul play." He picked up Gabe's photograph. "Has Gabe been stalking young men and popping them off one by one over the years?" He let his premise sink in, then added, "And if that is the case, why is Beka dead? This is the problem. We don't have any proof that this was Gabe's m.o., enticing young men to his lair by using Beka as bait, but it is possible."

"Beka couldn't have known," Devon told him.

"But if that scenario is true, then we are most likely looking at Beka's death as a suicide."

Devon did not agree with him, but she kept her mouth shut. He knew where she stood and she knew she needed to follow his train of thought.

"Perhaps Beka figured out what was happening and couldn't take it—the shame, the betrayal." Devon raised her hand again. Loch shook his head. "Let me finish. The problem is there are only eight people who knew there was a signature on these bodies. Four of them are in this room right now, three others are with NYPD—the eighth is our murderer. There is no way Beka Imamura could have known Gabe carved his bodies unless she was a part of it, and that means seeing the bodies after they were carved, and being able to decipher the ideograms, which even our guy in Japan has had trouble reading. I think we all find that scenario hard to believe. There have been plenty of wives in the past who were semi-aware of their husband's indiscretions, but she should have known, on some level, that the bones in the backyard belonged to his victims. But for Beka to know this would have made her an accomplice because of the detail of the koans. She had to know what he wrote, in order to copycat him." He paused and looked at his team. By the glint in their eyes he knew they were following his every word. There was no need to go back over any detail or explain the obvious.

"Therefore, we very likely have a murderer who has planned this out to make it look like Gabe is the guilty party, and make Beka out as kind enough to rid the world of his menace—despite the fact that she could have called her best friend, told her what he'd done, and received our full protection."

"What if Gabe was guilty?" Gary asked. "Could this be a revenge killing? Take Beka out like Gabe took out Todd?"

"Doesn't play. Beka died after Gabe," Loch challenged him one more time.

"Why kill Edilio? What's the motive?" Frank wondered.

"Maybe Gabe and Edilio were a team. Beka the bait." Gary was good at presenting possible solutions to a problem; Loch, good at shooting holes in them.

Devon sighed deeply.

Frank looked over at her. "Is this bothering you?"

"I'm just trying to put together what Gary is suggesting with what I found in the Missing Persons report," she assured him. "I think it's possible."

"If these kids were targets of a sick mind, I think Detective Freesia is right in thinking that these young men were marked for a reason," Loch said. "This murderer likes taking his victims unaware, and isn't looking for a struggle. Then a few years ago, the desire to leave a mark, a trace on the victims, began to influence the killings."

"What about that sculpture?" Gary asked, pointing to the photograph of *Having Hand*.

"We don't know yet," Frank answered him. "But we're working on it. Thanks to Todd Daniel's application for the Peace Corps, his prints were on a government database, and Detective Freesia got them for us. Todd's hands were fourth on the sculpture, Beka's prints are the second pair of hands, and Edilio's are the last. Gabe's hands are first. Because of the way some of the molds were welded together, not every set is complete. There are about thirty pairs of hands in the piece that are still a mystery."

"That's the first order of business, to get the prints run from that piece. I'm sorry I couldn't bring it with me, but New York City isn't our jurisdiction. I hope I was thorough enough."

Frank chuckled, "I'd like to see you do anything half-assed, Brennen."

"I think he cast the hands of his lovers, his conquests," Devon suggested.

"What's Todd doing there then?"

"What if Gabe came on to him?" Devon began to think about that possibility. In her mind it played something like "Ode to Billy Joe." Had Todd jumped into the Hudson River, like Billy Joe McAllister had leapt into the Tallahatchie after being forced to have sex with a dirty old man? Of course, Gabe was not an old man.

She wished she had that damn videotape so she could see if Gabe had spoken to Todd at all during the party in 1984. If Gabe had made a pass at Todd, it probably would have freaked him out. He might have taken off. But she had been dancing with Gabe just before Todd went on his walk. Hadn't Gabe gone out for cigars soon after that? Broadway Bob had been smoking a cigar. What if Gabe had given it to him? She remembered Beka asking Bob if he'd seen Todd on the street. Broadway Bob had pointed upward, or so it had seemed at the time, but what if he had actually been pointing to Gabe's building? Could they have gone back there? What if the whole time they had been looking for Todd he was in Gabe's studio? She shivered. Her mind raced in fast-forward, but there were no answers in her memory—the answers were locked away in the past or on the videotape that was, hopefully, on its way via FedEx.

She retraced her thoughts back to the idea of Todd and Gabe. What if Todd had turned Gabe down? What if he had fled Gabe's loft? Was Gabe the alien, or was there someone else with him who fit that description? What if he ran into someone who comforted him, made him feel like a man again? He would have been so vulnerable . . .

"Loch, we've discussed the possibility of a male killer, but what if your profile was applied to a woman? Would anything change?" she asked.

"There are very few female serials."

"Amuse me."

"We'd be looking at a woman who had a deep-seated resentment toward men. She would toy with them, act willing to please, and then strike. In her mind, she would be innocent—it would be their fault."

"What would she be like in the beginning, before she got in the practice of killing?"

"She might act out, be promiscuous, volatile, and temperamental."

"Sounds like every girl I ever dated," Gary mumbled.

"Then she'd lose it one night. Get out of control and *voilá*, an impulse killing. The fear mixed with the power would be intoxicating and could set up a desire to repeat the pattern—this is the same pattern we see with male serials. We don't have much information on female serials. They're not common. The only one we've really had information on is that chick in Florida who popped off truckers who picked her up. In her case, which might fit ours, she enticed men into sex, then killed them for raping her because she had no way, psychologically, of discerning between the act of consensual sex and rape."

"Was Beka ever raped?" They all looked at Devon.

"She was attacked when she was in junior high, that's why her uncles sent her to a private girl's school on the mainland."

"All serial killers spend a great deal of time fantasizing about ways to kill. Over time, the fantasy takes control and becomes a subconscious way of planning a murder, so when the opportunity presents itself—i.e., the first murder—it occurs almost involuntarily, but it also starts the cycle so the fantasy has to be repeated."

"Every New Year's Eve?"

"Or every other," Gary suggested. "Maybe the numbers are divisible by something meaningful. I think the dates of these murders, if we're right in this assumption, are deliberate."

"An anniversary of some sort," Frank suggested.

"Perhaps a celebration of that first murder. We may be looking for someone who lost someone dear to them, or someone they hated, on New Year's Eve." Loch continued, "After that, if our perp got away with the initial murder, the pattern and lust for power and control over another's life would satisfy him or her more than sex or love. He or she would begin to act out more and more regularly and then want to leave a trace or mark that he or she had been there—proof that these accidental deaths or disappearances weren't haphazard as the police presupposed. He or she would enjoy getting away with it at first, then begin requiring credit for such brilliance, something more than mementos, trophies. That's when the decompensating begins and our perp gets sloppy."

"So at this current stage of development, psychologically, there wouldn't be much difference between a male or female."

"The justification might be different, but that's all I can say for now. I really don't know much about female serials. No one does." Lochwood smiled. "Frank, you're on the prints. Devon, you're on Isshu—find out if he was able to discern anything from that last fax and let me know as soon as you hear from him. Gary, you're with me. We've got a few loftmates to interview."

Everyone stood up and made ready to clear the room. Frank and Devon were putting the photographs in order as Gary erased the words *bait* under Beka's name and *Serial Couple?* under Edilio's and Gabe's. Slowly the other suspects' names were also erased: Alex, Maddie, Godwyn, Josh, and Sam . . .

"I was just thinking," Devon said hesitantly, "what if *Having Hand* was a collection of Beka's conquests, not Gabe's?"

"Beka's a serial killer?"

"I didn't say that." But she was thinking it, again. She couldn't help herself.

They walked down to the Crime Scene lab where Frank's mold was finished setting and watched as he peeled back the Alginate from the cast.

"Is that Todd?" Loch asked.

Devon knelt down and ran her hands over the plaster-smooth skin of a face she had only seen once before, in a photograph earlier that day. "No. It's Eric Heron," she whispered. The boy who had gone to watch the ball drop in Times Square on New Year's Eve two years ago and wasn't seen again until spring thaw. "There are no holes to breathe through at the nose."

"Call Japan!" Lochwood ordered. "I want to find out what those cuts on his chest mean. Now!"

CHAPTER THIRTY-FOUR

*Today's students are like blind men who have thrown away
their staffs, calling them useless baggage.*

—Zen phrase

The farm fields just past Bridgehampton looked fallow in the winter
light and bordered *"closed for the season"* farmstands that barely
looked as if their presence were justified. Each stand offered different specialties: one had silver-queen corn and homemade bread,
another, pick-your-own-strawberries or watermelon; in the fall
there were pumpkins. Sunflowers would tilt their heads skyward and
lines of traffic would clot Highway 27 once summer started and the
locals began their harvest of tourists. Gary and Loch passed
Poxabogue Golf Course and turned right on Sayres Path. "We're
looking for Osborne Farm Lane." Gary jerked his partner out of
what looked to be a stupor, but was really quiet reflection of the
countryside around them and a constant review behind that of all
that had happened. "What area is this?" Gary asked, as he opened
up the Suffolk County road map he kept in the backseat and tried to
read it while driving down the treed lane.

"Wainscott," Loch grumbled, and took the map out of Gary's
hand so he could figure out where Alexandra Parnel lived before his
partner wrapped them around one of the oak trees he seemed so in
awe of.

Rows of shake-shingled houses were nestled behind the mature
trees shading the street in the summer, but looked remarkably stark
and bare now against the steel-gray of the sky. "Quaint little houses," Gary observed.

"Yeah, one million . . . quaint." Lochwood felt as surly as he
sounded; he was not sure why he'd suddenly launched into such a
bad mood.

"No way!"

"No joke." He traced his finger down the line of Sayres Path. "Take the next right. We're not far from where Devon's parents live. How convenient." They pulled up the drive of a rather new house that faced farm fields of winter rye and went up to Alexandra Parnel's door.

She was not what he expected—hair cropped close to her head and two black-rimmed coke bottles with an aluminum-bar bridge for eyeglasses. She was dressed in head-to-toe black linen and looked un-ironed but extremely comfortable. Behind her a large-screen TV glared at them in bright blue with the white word *"Pause"* in the bottom left-hand corner.

"Lochwood Brennen!" She sounded overly pleased to see him. "I've been hoping to meet you, but Devon seems to be hiding you from the rest of us. Or maybe you're just shy." She stood back to allow them inside. "I suppose this is your partner?" She held out her hand.

"You act as if you were expecting us," Gary observed.

"I do? Let's just say I hoped you'd come by. It makes me feel important after yesterday."

"What happened yesterday?" Lochwood was positive Devon had not spoken about Edilio Ferraro to anyone, and was curious how Alexandra could know about the crime all the way out on the East End already.

"Don't you read the *Post*?" She flipped to page six and showed it to the detectives.

The main photograph showed Edilio Ferraro's body being removed from the Mercer Street building. The headline read, *"BLACK WIDOW STRIKES AGAIN."*

"Why the hell didn't we hear about this sooner?" Now Lochwood was in a really bad mood.

"I didn't know about it," Gary answered.

"Somebody at the precinct must have."

"Why's it a problem?" she asked.

He was not about to tell her, but found it the height of unprofessionalism. Somebody must have gotten the story from NYPD, but he did not recall seeing any reporters at the scene last night. Lochwood's first inclination was to call Marders and ream him a new asshole. No wonder he was so distrustful earlier, and Loch had thought it was just bad manners. Someone had tipped off the *Post*, but who? He turned to Gary. "I want you to call and find out who took that picture."

"Tom Hurley wrote it," Alex told him. "Devon was complaining about him yesterday at brunch. He could have tailed her."

Or the murderer could have called him and let him know about the body after finding Devon in Gabe's building. Loch considered the possibilities.

"I knew Devon was up to something when we left her in Chinatown," Alex was saying, as they followed her through her modest but comfortable home. "I should have stuck around. It would have been more interesting than the jitney ride home." Then, without prompting, she pulled out a white stub. "Here's my ticket. So you know I was on the bus when Edilio was murdered."

He took her ticket and made a mental note that she seemed unaware that Ferraro had died a week earlier. At least the article did not have all the details; maybe the leak had not come from NYPD. Maybe Tom Hurley was receiving phone calls about the crimes from an anonymous source. If he was, that source could very well be the murderer. He motioned for Gary to come closer and whispered in his ear that he wanted him to contact Hurley now. Gary excused himself and went outside.

"Okay then," Alex began. "Let's see, New Year's Eve I was at Nick & Toni's for dinner and drinks with a few of my colleagues. I'll write down their names and numbers for you; I have plenty of alibis at the restaurant. I'm well-known there." She stopped.

"Where were you last Tuesday? We'll need an accounting for most of the day," Lochwood said.

"Whew, let's see. Tuesday . . ." She opened her palm pilot and began to punch in something on the tiny keypad. "I had an appointment in the city at Widow Productions on Fifty-ninth Street. It was a budget meeting, all day. We ate at Café des Artistes, a two-hour business lunch, and wrapped it up about four. I took the five o'clock jitney back, got caught in traffic, and home around eight. She pulled out another ticket stub and handed it to Loch—the date and time corresponded with the ticket, and she had paid with a credit card so it was more than likely she had been on the bus.

She smiled at Loch and flopped back into a wingback chair. The entire room was decorated in black or white—there were no neutral tones anywhere. He looked up at a pair of astonishingly large oil paintings, one over the couch and one over the fireplace. There were several sculptures and a few smaller paintings.

"No one saw me after I got home," she confessed. "I watched some TV—I don't know what—then I watched *Law and Order* on A&E. I love that show. Does that work for an alibi?"

"Are these Montebellos?"

She looked at the walls and nodded. "I'm a collector."

Gary stepped back into the room and handed Loch a slip of paper that read, "*Hurley got an anonymous tip. Marders already talked to him.*"

Loch was more than a little steamed that Marders had not kept him in the loop, especially when it involved the press, and could not recall what he had just asked Alexandra Parnel.

"I'm developing a new show. A cop show." She leaned back and looked at both of them. "Devon inspired it, but it would be great to put you and her together."

"Just what we need—another cop show that doesn't know crap about police work." Loch did not approve.

"Facts don't matter as much as story," she informed him.

"Facts *make* the story."

"Want to be a consultant? I could pay you three times what you're making now."

"But I wouldn't have the joy of busting criminals."

"Is that why you do it? I've always wondered." She motioned for them to sit while punching something else into her palm pilot.

Lochwood wondered if he'd just helped her develop her character and felt even more uneasy.

"So, you like being one of the good guys?" Loch did not answer. She made herself comfortable in an oversized couch, put her palm pilot down, and held up her hands in mock surrender. "Okay, enough banter. Ask your questions."

"You've answered most of them, except why do you think someone would want to kill Beka, Gabe, and Edilio?"

"I assume from your question that Beka is no longer the primary suspect?"

"We're reserving our judgment." Lochwood wasn't about to share any information with her.

"Ah, well . . . Offhand, I can't think of any reason someone would want to kill them. Beka was in the middle of a lawsuit with the Pilates people, but I don't know that that was a reason for murder. And I don't know why Gabe would have been a victim in any crime."

"This is the first we've heard of a lawsuit."

"Yeah, the exercise technique was named after the guy who created it but the name was never copyrighted. A few years ago somebody bought the copyright to the name and has been trying to get studios that were already in business to pay him a fee for using the name. Beka headed up a countersuit to retain rights to use the Pilates name, stating that it was synonymous with the type of exercise. Sort of like how Cuisinart can't be separated from the food processor, Pilates can't be separated from the technique."

"Interesting, but we're looking for someone who had access to Beka and Gabe's building, as well as a motive for murder."

She stood up, walked across the room, and reached her hand into a pot. "You'd better check the lot of us, then." She tossed the key through the air. Gary reached out and caught it before it could land on the coffee table.

"Good catch, detective! Beka gave those to me a few years ago in case I ever needed a place to crash in the city. Maddie has one, Sam may. She never gave one to Katiti—they didn't like each other—but Josh probably has one from before he married Katiti."

"What about Godwyn?"

"He used to live there, and Gabe never changed locks."

"Edilio?

"Definitely. They rehearsed upstairs all the time."

Could Edilio have brought someone who did not have keys into the building? Loch briefly wondered. But the door to the building was locked when Devon arrived, and there had been keys in Edilio's pocket when they found the body. That meant their murderer must have keys.

Alex looked at her watch and announced, "My break is over, guys. I have to get back to work." She pressed play on the remote control in her hand. The big-screen TV across the room suddenly filled with the video version of "The Weeping Buddha." Beka, always ageless, was almost soaring through the air with the help of ropes woven above her head that created the set Gabe had designed. Her long black hair trailed after her, sweeping around her shoulders and waist as her legs once more took flight.

"A little grainy—processing and tape quality has improved so much since then," Alex reflected. "We're going to digitize it. I've been on the phone all morning with PBS; they're going to run a retrospective on her work. I just made the deal to edit the program. It's my epitaph to her."

Loch watched as Beka's body seemed to hang in the air. Gary leaned forward to watch the dancer.

"How could anyone hurt such light?" she murmured. Tears streamed down her face. "Catch who ever did this. Please, get them—she wasn't just Gabe's muse. She was mine."

"One last question." Loch interrupted her reverie. Alex pressed pause again. "How much money do you think your art collection is worth now?"

"Enough to finance a small film." She pressed play and turned her attention back to the screen. The music swelled as Beka became airborne above the stage. Loch watched for a moment, then left the house without Alex bothering to show them the door.

* * *

Lochwood began fuming as soon as he and Gary stepped outside. "Fucking Marders!" He slammed his fist onto the roof of the car.

"Hey, it's not like we're being open and honest with him."

Loch glared at his partner, then laughed. "We'll beat him at his own game." He dialed Marders's office. "So, what you got on Hurley?"

"He used to go to school with your girlfriend. She leak this news to him?"

"You're such an asshole."

"So are you, Brennen. And if I find out Halsey's feeding the press, I'll hang her out to dry."

"Did you trace the call?"

"A payphone on Canal Street, a block from Montebello's building."

"Any prints?"

"Lots of them, but no one who uses a voice box to disguise her voice is going to be stupid enough to forget gloves."

"You sure it's a woman?"

"No, the bitch had a box. But your girlfriend is the only one who knew about his body."

"Except for the murderer."

"The murderer is dead," Marders snarled.

Lochwood hung up the phone.

* * *

Devon held her breath as the fax came out of the machine.

"What's it say?" Frank asked impatiently from over her shoulder.

"I don't know yet." It seemed to be taking forever. Finally, the second page came out. Isshu wrote that he could not be sure if he had rendered the ideograms correctly, but it was a line from a poem attached to a koan that had been written by Setcho Juken in the year 1000—"*Will the clear pool reflect, cold?*"

Isshu had sent the entire verse to Devon and she read it out loud for Frank to hear:

When the frosty heaven's moon has set
And midnight nears
Whose shadow with mine
Will the clear pool reflect, cold?

Isshu had gone on to say this came from the *nanto* koans, or the very difficult koans. And the verse was written in response to the koan, "*When men of today look at this flower, it seems to them like a dream.*"

It certainly seemed like a dream, the deaths of yesteryear and the deaths of yesterday. She was about to call Loch to give him the good news, then paused; was a serial killer ever good news?

CHAPTER THIRTY-FIVE

The dragon-hum in the dead tree, the eyeball in the dry skull.
—ZEN PHRASE

Josh and Katiti Shapiro's house was not one of the great East Hampton homes. In fact, it wasn't even one of the old refurbished barns that were so popular now—theirs was a brand-spanking-new domicile that smelled of new money and even newer carpeting. From first glance, Loch guessed they'd lived in it for one summer season. They received the detectives at the door, a little less gracefully than Lochwood would have expected from a respected physician and his wife. Loch and Gary introduced themselves and were semi-cordially shown into the living room. "I don't know how we can help you detectives, but we're willing to try," Josh assured them.

For Lochwood, that statement alone had come to be a cliché suggesting guilt.

"You're here about Beka and Gabe, no doubt." Josh gestured to a leather divan that was the color of honey butter and remarkably close to his wife's skin tone. In fact, the whole house seemed color-coordinated.

"Did you know Edilio Ferraro?" Gary began the questioning while Loch took notes.

Josh was studying Lochwood. "Are you Devon's friend? I think she mentioned you yesterday."

"I work with Detective Halsey," Loch affirmed without further comment; he did not appreciate the doctor's lack of discretion in a professional situation and doubted whether Devon had said anything about him. "Now, about Edilio?"

"We haven't seen each other much in the past ten years—even though we all live out here."

"You've been out here for ten years?" Loch asked, surprised.

"Well, we rented first. Not everyone is as lucky as Devon to inherit property in Sag Harbor," Katiti informed them. "She's not south of the highway, of course, but when her parents die she'll get the proverbial farm and a house in Sag Harbor. It's enough to hate her, but we don't! We love Devon. Of course, you know, we never saw Beka much. We moved in different social circles."

Loch wondered which circle was the snootier and decided they must be tied. Katiti fidgeted in her chair and crossed her leg up under her body. Loch recalled that she was a dancer, like Beka, and wondered where she exercised when they weren't in the city. "How about you, Mrs. Shapiro? You were a dancer. Did you know Edilio?"

"*Ms. French*—I kept my professional name. And no, I did not know Edilio professionally. I know who he is, of course."

"Of course." Loch didn't know why she said *of course* but he wanted to make her feel at ease. Dancers always thought everyone knew who they were. "And you knew Beka professionally?"

"I knew her through Josh, but she's older than me and was fairly established in her career by the time we met."

"My wife and Beka had a healthy rivalry," Josh added. Katiti's eyes flashed angrily at him.

"Too many divas spoil the party?" Gary asked. Neither Katiti nor Josh laughed.

"Why are you asking about Edilio, detective? Has something happened?" Josh asked.

So clever, Lochwood thought to himself, as if we wouldn't notice his attempt to take the attention from Katiti. He hated the clever ones and ignored Josh's question by asking his own. "How tall are you, Dr. Shapiro?"

Loch had caught him in mid-slouch and Josh sat upright before answering. "Five foot nine and a half," he said a little too emphatically, and from the bemused look on his wife's face, Lochwood knew he had exaggerated, probably by a whole inch. Josh pushed his fingers through a mass of curls atop his head at the same moment as Katiti did the same, and Loch wondered who had moved first. They were almost like puppets, and from their interaction, it was pretty clear who was the puppeteer.

"So, you two came back here last night?" Loch handled the redirect as he and Gary volleyed their questions at the couple, almost more interested in who answered and how than in what was said.

"Actually, we stayed in the city last night and came home this afternoon," Katiti answered. "Josh took the week off so we could just relax in the country."

"In the winter?" Loch wondered aloud.

"Is where we were last night important, detective?"

"Could be. Did you see anybody while you were in the city?"

"Not after we left Chinatown. Alex came back out here on the jitney with Sam, and Maddie and Godwyn went off together . . ."

"Like they used to," Katiti added cattily.

It was interesting how they took turns tag-teaming the answers; Lochwood made a scribble on his notepad to see which one of them would notice and take the defensive. Josh did.

"Sweetheart, the detectives don't need to know all the dirt from our collective pasts."

"Isn't that why they're here? Beka loved to dredge it all up and throw it in our faces. You should have heard her last week! She blamed Josh for Todd's disappearance. Said he didn't look hard enough because—because he was tired." Katiti began to massage her right foot.

"Beka called you last week?" Gary asked.

"She called everybody to make sure we were all coming to New Year's brunch."

"She didn't mention going to Hawaii?"

"No, but that would be just like Beka to arrange a reunion brunch and then not show up. And I know it sounds rude, but that's exactly what she did!"

Lochwood wanted to slap her, and except for the fact that she was so pretty, he could barely comprehend why Josh put up with her prima donna act. Prima donnas were a dime a dozen out on the East End; Josh could dump his wife and have another just like her in minutes. He watched her fidget with her toes and toss her curls from the right to the left shoulder, then said, "It sounds like you had a grudge against her."

"She was jealous that I married Josh. She liked to think she had a special hold on all the boys from the loft." Yeah right, thought Loch, as Katiti squeezed her husband's knee.

"Is that true, Dr. Shapiro?" Gary chose to use Josh's formal name. "Did Beka think she had a hold on you?"

"Only one woman has anything over me, detective, and you're looking at her." He smiled adoringly at his wife.

Loch thought he was going to be sick. What was this, Bad Acting 101? "For your information," he began, "Beka, Gabe, and Edilio Ferraro are dead."

"Edilio's dead?" Katiti screeched.

Loch continued, "We'll need to know your whereabouts on New Year's Eve and last Tuesday." He directed his next statement to Josh: "And I for one would like to know why you avoided telling the Missing Persons detectives about the second entrance you used into the loft back in 1984."

"Excuse me?" Josh looked stupidly innocent.

"Detective Halsey's been going over the transcription of Todd's case and tells me you were less than forthright about the second loft entrance."

"First of all, it wasn't a legitimate loft entrance." Aha, a doctor who can play the lawyer. "So I don't see that I was actually lying to anyone about it then or now."

"Nevertheless, it was a secret. Why?" Lochwood pushed him for an answer.

"We were at 75 Main for their New Year's Eve celebration," Katiti butted in. "A number of people there could identify us."

"Excuse me?" Lochwood was not going to let her sidetrack his investigation.

"You asked where we were New Year's Eve," Katiti replied.

Loch chose to ignore her. "Doctor? I'm waiting."

"It's no big deal. Beka used to get followed home sometimes from performances and liked to use that entrance to get away from the weirdos. She'd sneak in the wrong way and then they wouldn't know where she lived."

"Is that the only reason?"

"Is this off the record?"

"That depends."

"Honey, don't." Katiti fidgeted. Her movements were like a barometer for Lochwood's questions; the more uncomfortable she seemed, the closer he knew he was getting to some kind of truth.

"It doesn't matter now anyhow, Katiti." She obviously disagreed as her tangle of curls bobbed, disapprovingly, from side to side. Finally Josh added, "Let's just say it had something to do with extra-curricular activity and a quick way to pay back my student loan."

"I didn't think you chose Ear, Nose, and Throat out of the goodness of your heart."

"He's very well-respected in the field." Katiti sat defiantly upright.

"I'm sure he is." Loch had had about enough of this sparring back and forth with husband and wife.

"I've been clean for ten years, detective. You can't buy a house like this and toot up."

"I made him quit."

Loch had just been thinking that she had probably done the opposite—she was the kind of woman who could drive a man to drink and drug—but he didn't make any comments. "What time did you leave?"

"Leave?"

"75 Main." Loch loved catching suspects off guard by recalling statements they had made minutes earlier out of context and registering their reaction. From Katiti's look of panic, he knew whatever time they said they left would be a fabrication.

"Was it about two, sweetheart?"

"We'll check," Gary reminded them. "Are you sure?"

"I'm not positive about the time. It was at least an hour after midnight." Josh looked at his wife as if to make sure the time was correct. "Wait, I think it was later." She nodded in agreement, then switched her legs around so the left one was crossed underneath her instead of the right.

It was the way she moved that made Lochwood think it—the smooth fluidity of her limbs, as if she were floating above, rather than sitting on the couch. "Have you ever worked out at the Pilates studio in Sag Harbor?" he asked.

"No, why do you ask?" She stared so steadily at him without blinking that for a moment he wasn't sure if she was lying or not. He did not trust her, no matter what she said.

"Just curious."

"You are referring to Beka's studio?"

Loch nodded his answer.

"Beka and my wife were not close friends, Detective Brennen," Josh reminded him.

"It was Edilio's studio, too," Gary added.

"Of course, I forgot they ran it together."

Loch doubted that, and said as much. Josh Shapiro did not answer; instead, his wife jumped into the verbal foray.

"I go to a different Pilates trainer in East Hampton. One who's certified and has the legal right to use the term *Pilates*."

"Ah, the lawsuit," Gary muttered.

"It's quite the legal battle in the dance world," Katiti informed them. "Old-school against new. They were going to be deposed in a few weeks."

"Who?"

"Beka and Edilio."

"That's news to me," Loch lied.

She looked pleased with herself. "A class-action countersuit against using the copyrighted name. Have you checked out the defendant in that case? Maybe he's your murderer!"

"Is copyright-infringement reason for murder?" Gary asked her.

"Anything can be a reason for murder nowadays," she said triumphantly.

"But why kill Gabe? He had nothing to do with the studio."

"You're the detectives, but I bet it is the lawsuit and has nothing to do with Todd. I can't believe Devon would waste valuable departmental time reading through old files like that. I told you she was up to something, Josh."

"Class-action suits don't usually result in the murder of all the plaintiffs," Loch pointed out. "There'd be quite a number of people to x out if that were the case."

She fidgeted instead of replying, then tilted her chin up and, looking like a modern day Nefertiti, gazed out the window. "You don't think our lives are in danger, do you? I mean, what is this, *And Then There Were None?* What if this *is* about Todd?"

"This is real life, Mrs. Shapiro, not fiction. I doubt you're in any danger." Although, if there was anyone he would have liked to see murdered, it would have been her. He couldn't stand women who pussy-whipped their husbands; worse, he couldn't stand husbands who allowed it. Her fawnlike eyes expanded to deer-in-the-head-lights size as she stared at Josh, then Loch.

"You'll be safe," Loch assured her. "If anything else comes to you, please don't hesitate to call . . ."

Josh opened the front door for them, and much to Lochwood's surprise, Aileen was standing there in front of them, holding a leash with a dog attached to the end of it.

"Brennen, Gary," she greeted coyly.

"Aileen, I was just wondering when I was going to see you again." Gary stepped forward, not as afraid of this dog. "So, you know the Shapiros?"

"Aileen knows everyone," Josh told him.

"Except you." Aileen winked at Gary.

"Well, we'll just have to change that, won't we?" Gary smiled back at her.

Their flirting was making Loch feel sick. He had had a feeling when he introduced them that he'd unleashed a monster, but he wasn't sure who was worse, his partner or Devon's roommate.

"How was the reunion? Everyone have fun?" Aileen asked Josh and Katiti, as she made the dog sit and await further instruction.

"Why didn't you go?" Gary asked.

"I wasn't invited."

"Leenie's too good for us," Josh said, as Katiti rummaged through her purse.

Aileen handed Josh the lead. "He was good. Not acting out like he usually does. I told you he does better when you're out here. Don't spoil him, Katiti. I'll be back next week."

"We'll pay you then." Katiti must have seen the ire in Aileen's eyes, for she added callously, "I'm sorry. All I have are hundreds."

Aileen smiled too sweetly. Loch smothered his own grin, and they walked back down the drive together to Aileen's car.

"Can you believe her? She's got more money than God and can't pay me on time. Me, who lives from check to check. And they never tip." Aileen scoffed. "Beka set it up. Man, was that a mistake, but friends are friends. They think they're helping me out. But who needs help like that? It's not like I'm a charity case!"

"No, you're not," Loch confirmed.

"I got some charity for you. Why don't you and me go out sometime?" Gary asked suddenly.

She looked at him, pleasantly surprised, and jerked her chin in the air, sort of tough and sort of fragile. "You got my number, same as Devon's. Call me." She waved as she started her VW Rabbit and rolled down the window to yell, "See ya's! I gotta get my next dog. Holidays are hell!" Loch could not have agreed more.

Gary watched her move down the drive with an admiring tilt of his head.

"You're such a wolf, DeBritzi."

"I'm not."

"You are, but you know what they say about Sag Harbor girls?"

"No, tell me."

"Well . . ." They got in the car and headed toward the Halsey farm on Daniels Lane.

CHAPTER THIRTY-SIX

The good merchant hides his possessions well and appears to have nothing.

—Zen phrase

Loch had never met Devon's parents and entered the Halsey household for the first time in the company of his partner, not Devon. It did, however, seem strangely apropos that he should finally meet them while investigating a case. He introduced himself and his partner to the Halsey and Imamura families, then was welcomed into the kitchen where a fire crackled on the hearth. Lochwood felt his heart warm as he sat at a large wooden table built by none other than the monk, Hans. Evan Halsey told the detectives proudly, "Hans and me go way back to the '60s. He was a wild man."

"So were you, Ev," Lelia reminded her husband.

Above their heads copper pots and pans and bunches of herbs hung from exposed beams next to friendly cobwebs. The stone fireplace had an old wrought-iron kettle holder in it that had once been used for cooking, and the chairs squeaked as they settled into the wood—every object in the room had to be at least a hundred years old, including the ghosts (if Devon's stories were correct). Everything about the Halsey's bespoke history; Lochwood could feel the weight of it around them.

Her mother was as fiery and lovely as her daughter; her tresses had a redder tone to them than Devon's, but she had the same slope of a nose, the same smoldering eyes. Their eyes. Their eyes reminded him of the winter Atlantic with a nor'easter stirring up its depths, a steellike strength beneath their flash of blue. He wondered if her passions ran as deep as Devon's, and could not help but watch this woman who seemed to foretell Devon's stature in twenty years. His heart stilled in her presence, as if in glimpsing Devon's future-self he was seeing his own. Would they be together in twenty years? Were they one of those couples?

Evan Halsey was not the distinguished gentleman-farmer Loch had expected but a craggy-faced seaman with gently crinkling eyes. He could see his daughter in the man, but it was not the facial features or stance that told him they were related—it was the package, a strength of spirit, that reminded him of Devon. The stories she had told him of her father made sense when he looked at the man's face—here was someone who would fight for justice, could be brutally honest, and would rather hold sand in his hands than a drink. His daughter had the same qualities.

Evan Halsey shook Loch's hand heartily, and by the firmness in his grip Lochwood knew he was being sized up. In turn, Loch studied Devon's father without being obvious and, for the first time since he was a young detective, hoped he could live up to another man's expectations. He liked Evan Halsey immediately and wondered if they would ever walk across the twenty acres the family still owned and talk about their years in the service—Vietnam for Loch, Korea for Evan.

"We spoke on the phone. I'm Detective Brennen." He introduced himself to Bismarck and Bertram. Bert gave a small bow, but it seemed to be more of a reflex than a gesture of respect.

"I'm Bismarck Imamura," the taller of the two gentlemen said, as he shook Loch's hand without the slightest dip or incline in his posture. "This is Bert."

They sat back down at the kitchen table. They were in their sixties and sat with folded hands and straight backs, staring at Gary and Loch, the shock of sudden death covering their faces and eyes like a living shroud.

The fire popped and fizzled in the stone fireplace and Loch allowed the comforting sound of the burning wood to fill the room before beginning. "We're in the middle of this investigation and I can't offer you any answers yet, but I feel fairly certain in saying Beka did not kill Gabe."

"She didn't do it," Bertram said, slapping Bismarck on the arm. "I told you she didn't kill him, Biz. You and your scenarios."

"I was going to kill him if she didn't."

"Why is that?" Gary asked.

"He was as faithful as an un-neutered dog." Bertram cleared his throat. "In other words, he'd fuck anything that stood still long enough. Excuse me, Lelia, but it's true."

"Don't I know it. Beka told me what a hound he was, but I don't think she expected much more from him," Devon's mother told them.

"Beka said she was leaving him and coming home for New Year's?"

"Yeah-yeah, but she was always changing her plans. Busy girl, our Becky."

"You raised her after her parents died?" Lochwood was trying to be as gentle as possible.

"I'm her legal guardian," Bismarck said. "Her mother's brother."
"And Bertram?"

"Oh, we're married. Not that it matters in this country."

"Such a shame," Lelia commented, "to be together for as long as Ev and me and not have it legal."

"Uh-huh," Lochwood tried to agree, and hoped the surprise didn't register on his face, but it just wasn't the sort of thing one expected from their generation.

"No one thinks we're gay," Bertram assured him, his eyes twinkling as he began to speak more freely. "You know, people actually think Japanese people aren't gay! We have Kabuki theater but no faggots! Right!"

"We sent Beka away to high school so she wouldn't have to deal with the stigma of having two male parents," Bertram told them. "We wanted her to have a normal teenage-hood. You know how mean kids can be. On the mainland, everyone thought we were brothers and both her uncles. No one at her private school knew about our relationship."

"Devon knew," Lelia reminded Bismarck.

"Devon didn't care."

"What about Gabe?" Loch asked.

"I knew Gabe was a fruit the first time I met him and I told Beka to stay away," Bismarck said.

The politically incorrect statement jarred Loch, but he figured Bismarck could call Gabe a fruit since Bismarck was one, too.

"He was bi, Biz. There's a difference." Bertram patted his partner's knee.

"Not that much difference. Why couldn't Beka find someone like you? She was a pearl. A gift." Bismarck began to cry. "Maybe she was more comfortable with bi men than straight men. Maybe it was our fault." Bertram and Lelia reached for Bismarck at the same time.

"It wasn't." Lelia took his hand. "Beka loved you both, more than anyone. She told me she couldn't wait to get to Oahu and blow up 200,000 firecrackers outside your house."

Lochwood looked at Lelia expectantly. "When did she tell you that?"

"Last week. Just because she and Devon weren't speaking doesn't mean Beka didn't come talk to me. We were friends. She didn't have a mother so she adopted me by default, and I loved her like a daughter."

"Does Devon know you spoke with Beka?" Loch asked.

"Devon hasn't even returned my calls from last week."

"Did Beka tell you anything about what she was planning?"

"I knew she was thinking about moving back to Hawaii. If something else came up, she didn't tell me," Lelia said sadly.

"Any ideas?" Gary sat on the edge of his seat. The chair objected with a loud crack.

She shook her head. "You've got the talking chair. We think it's haunted. We mostly talked about you and Devon, Lochwood." The fire was suddenly making the room feel extremely hot.

Loch pulled at his collar and nodded his head as assuringly as possible, but the lack of information was frustrating and he wanted to get back on the trail. "Did she say anything else that day? It doesn't matter if it's important or not to you; it might be to us."

"I told her to call Dev and work things out because no one should let a grudge follow them into a New Year. I guess Beka never got hold of her."

"I wish she'd never married him," Bismarck said sadly.

"We just can't imagine life without Beka," added Bertram.

They all looked at Lochwood, dependent on his next move but unable to give him any more assistance than their prayers. "We have to go." He stood up abruptly. "I'm sorry, but we have a lot more work to do tonight. Thank you for your help."

Gary scrambled to his feet, trying not to upset the chair he was sitting on, and placed it carefully back against the table.

"We'll catch who did this, don't you worry," Gary assured Beka's uncles.

"Devon's supposed to be here any minute," Lelia said.

"We can't wait. We'll see her later." Lochwood spontaneously kissed Lelia's cheek, then headed out of the farmhouse door.

Halfway to the car he heard the sound of a throat clearing behind him. Loch turned around to face Evan Halsey as Gary scuttled away to the safety of the car. "Do you know what one acre of this land is worth? Values are all screwed up nowadays. It's all about money. Except for Dev; she likes making a difference." The man's eyes bore into Lochwood's. "Don't take her lightly, detective. You screw up, it'll be your loss. Not hers. Yours." He didn't point at him, or threaten him with any gestures; he stared out past Lochwood to the horizon and did not wait for a reply. The last glimpse Loch had of Evan Halsey, he was walking out across his potato fields, his Mackintosh open and flapping behind him.

CHAPTER THIRTY-SEVEN

The cold kills you with cold, the heat kills you with heat.

—ZEN PHRASE

Devon gazed nostalgically out the window of her car as she neared the family farmhouse. The final hints of day were casting ever-lengthening shadows over the last half-dozen potato fields in the neighborhood, and a lone pheasant strutted across the rough rows of broken-down corn, seeking stray kernels in the fallow winter ground. She had not grown up on this farm, but her father had, and she knew how painful it was for him to watch his childhood world change. This was country that had held out against nor'easters and drought, but the blight of chateaus which had descended upon the land was worse than a slew of natural disasters.

The mansions were encroaching upon all that her family loved and held dear. People who could care less about the delicate earth heaved concrete foundations upon the sand and paid town officials under the table for approval of Waco, Texas–like compounds, as if life itself were a danger to be shielded against. The architects of these monstrosities of poor taste refused to acknowledge the fragile ecosystem upon which they built, and instead of placing houses up on pillars, as once had been standard for beachfront property, they ignored the sea and constructed monuments to their egos which engulfed and eroded the dunes that had once acted as a natural barrier to the tides of change.

She could see him in his fields, walking against the wind as the fog began to roll in from the sea, looking as rugged and strong-willed as ever. Devon knew her Dad's thoughts were full of treachery and mayhem. The rape of Sagaponack had become Evan Halsey's obsession, and, while not a religious man, he regularly prayed for a big nor'easter, like the one in '65, to take away the barrier houses and return Left Left Pond, now renamed Peter's Pond by map surveyors, to its original size. Devon knew her father's dream was to see the kettleholes consume the larger houses in one large slurping belch that would return the once-gentle marshes to the egrets, osprey, and Baymen.

In the wake of skyrocketing real estate prices, many of the old families had succumbed to parceling off sections of their farms to make life more than a little easier. Devon's father could have been a very rich man if he sold the Halsey farm, but he wasn't giving up another inch of soil to outsiders. He rented the land to the few neighbors who still farmed so they could plow and till it into crops to sell at Sag Main Street vegetable stands and in town. Secretly, he liked to watch the plows kick clouds of dirt from his fields and hoped it filled estate homes with more dust than their maids and air filters could handle.

Her father used to tell her how as a boy he could walk straight across the field to the beach and on his way dig a fresh potato out of the warm earth, wash it in the ocean for flavoring, and eat it raw for lunch. Now, there was a kingpin who blocked his daily trek to the beach with gun-carrying thugs who threatened trespass violations against anyone who crossed the land. Devon believed in upholding the law, but couldn't help wondering if the guards shot pheasant and deer for trespassing on land that the animals had rights to long before human beings invaded the East End.

Sometimes she wished for those simpler times when fishermen, farmers, and a few eccentric writers and artists knew about the peace and beauty of the eastern shore of Long Island—before the nouveau riche. Of course, her family had come uninvited as well and inflicted their presence on the Shinnecock and Montauk peoples, but then Dad had married Lelia Haile, who was part Shinnecock. Halsey was an old name, and it had not gone over well when he married a girl with "Indian" blood. Evan had never cared much about society people, and had chosen to leave the area rather than place his wife under their ridicule. Working for the navy, the young couple had toured the world, and when he finally returned to head the local coast guard, his new family was embraced by the Halsey clan. His first love had always been the sea; Lelia's first love had always been the land—their daughter loved both equally. It wasn't the land's property value or anything that could be figured on paper—it was an emotional connection to the soil, the salty wind, and the way her heart soared whenever she drove across Little Bridge at Sag Pond toward Daniels Lane, toward home.

The Halsey farmhouse was badly in need of repair and a new paint job, the indoor swimming pool needed to be drained and re-tiled, the porch steps were collapsing and had to be rebuilt, but Lelia and Evan secretly relished being the eyesore of the neighborhood. Amid all the spanking-new mansions their house was a lingering reminder to the newcomers that in place of manicured lawns, crops had once grown; chicken coops had housed chickens, not stockbrokers; and ramshackle shacks had housed real artists, not copy-writers and graphic designers. While the rest of the world was consumed with a renovating mania to paint over the past and got their knickers in a twist about keeping up appearances, the Halsey's house peeled. Who was going to complain? The Halseys had helped found the damn town!

Her dad waved and moved quickly to the house, yelling something—probably to her mother. In a few moments, the driveway was full and she was hugging Beka's uncles and crying as her mother brushed the hair from her eyes and asked if she was okay. The smell of wood smoke hung in the air like a comforting blanket, anchoring her to her parents' home. Her only wish was that Beka were here to sit around the big supper table, just like old times.

"Uncle Biz. Uncle Bert." She squeezed Beka's uncles again, while her parents watched the reunion.

"Detective Brennen and DeBritzi were just here," her mother said.

"You met Lochwood?" Devon stammered.

"Yep. I think your father threatened him with a harpoon if he didn't treat you right, but I liked him just fine."

Her father hugged her.

"A harpoon, Dad?" Devon rolled her eyes.

"Just a small one. He's older than I thought."

"He looks reliable enough," her mother tried to be supportive.

"He's not a car, Mom."

"No, he's a man who has his eye on our most precious asset."

Her father slipped his arm around her waist as they walked toward the house, and she felt the deep pit inside her gut widen until she was overwhelmed by the desire to curl up in a ball and weep like a little girl.

Biz patted her back. "There, there. We're all in this together now. No one is alone in this."

Beka is, she thought to herself, but she did not say that to him.

Her mother opened the door and they walked in toward the kitchen table where cups of tea were set out on the table and the teapot was snug in its cozy. Her mother put out an extra cup for her daughter and, knowing how Devon liked her tea, placed the sugar pot nearby. The fire crackled in the hearth. "Honey, you look tired. Are you working too hard?"

"Mom, we're trying to find out what happened to Beka. Of course I'm working too hard."

"You can't solve anything if you're exhausted. I know Lochwood's an insomniac, but you need your rest, young lady."

Devon started to laugh, as all desire to be comforted faded. "You're making me feel twelve years old! I'm almost forty, Ma."

Lelia blushed and looked over at Bertram and Bismarck.

"Beka was the same way, argumentative," Bismarck reminded her. "Always refusing to take care of herself."

"She works late and sleeps late, or she did when she used to sleep," Lelia affirmed.

"Mom."

"It's my prerogative to worry. Evan, talk to her."

"She's a grown woman, Lelia. And I want her to catch Beka's killer."

"Well, so do I!"

"She's a tough broad like her old lady." He patted his daughter's shoulder but remained standing while the rest of them sat. There was a moment of almost silence.

"Bert, Biz, how are you doing?" Devon finally asked gently.

"They're releasing her on Thursday."

"You'll take her home then?" They nodded, both looking down at the table. "I'm so sorry about all of this."

"It's not your fault, Devon."

She did not answer. All she had been thinking for the past twelve hours was just how much of it *was* her fault. If only she'd called back when Beka beeped her. If only she had stopped by like Beka had asked. If only . . . Her thoughts started racing.

She wasn't actually sure Beka had beeped her. If what Loch said was right, the killer knew an awful lot about Devon . . . Did the killer have her beeper number as well? She jumped up from the table and ran to the phone.

"See that?" Lelia exclaimed. "Still working!"

"Mom! Please, this is important." She listened to the person on the other end of the phone. "Records, please. This is Detective Halsey. I need you to trace a beep I received at 10:45 New Year's Eve. I just want to know where the call was made from." She gave the operator her parents' phone number and hung up. "They'll know in a few minutes."

"Know what?"

"I don't know yet." She piled two teaspoons of sugar into her Earl Grey tea.

"Will you come visit when this is all over?" Bert asked Devon. "We won't have our girl to come and keep us in line; we'll be counting on you."

"Yeah-yeah." She reached across the table to take both of their hands. The room filled with the granite stillness of sorrow.

"You always have a home in Oahu. Just like Beka always had a home here. You don't know how many times she told us that you . . ." Biz looked at Lelia and Evan, ". . . made it easier for her to deal with the loss of her parents. She felt like she had a family here."

Lelia patted his hand. "She did, Biz."

"You know, I thought that was strange when Beka stopped by. She usually confides more in me, and this time she only talked about superficial things. It was almost like she had just come to say good-bye." She reached for a tissue and dabbed her eyes.

It was suddenly quite clear to her that her mother's tirade about taking care of herself came from her own reaction to Beka's death. Devon reached her hand across the table. "I'm sorry, Mom." Devon ran her finger thoughtfully around the rim of her teacup. "So, what'd you and Beka talk about?"

"You two."

The phone rang. Devon grabbed it and listened, said "Thanks" into the receiver, and hung up, disappointed. The call had come from Beka's cellphone, which they still had not found, and was probably so damaged by the snowfall that it had long since stopped working. Nor did it prove that there had been a third party. Beka could have thrown it into the woods before she killed herself, *if* she killed herself. She winced, then looked at Uncle Bert and Uncle Biz.

Her mother brought a tin of shortbread out of the cupboard. They ate thoughtfully while discussing the funeral. Hans had called and offered the zendo for a memorial service. Devon told them she planned to come to Hawaii for the funeral at Byodo-in Temple, and Bert and Biz decided to hold off on the dates until Devon could tell them which week she could take off from work.

Devon finished her tea and got up to leave. "I have to be at the zendo by five or Hans will be mad at me." She hugged them each good-bye.

Her father walked her out to the car. "Sweetheart, you and I both know your mother's just worried, but I think she has good reason to be."

"Why, Dad?"

"You don't sail the ocean without learning to listen to your intuition as well as the radar screen." He paused. "Watch your back."

"I will." She squeezed him, then got in her car and headed for Town Lane, the shortcut over to Swamp Road, and into the depths of the Northwest Woods.

CHAPTER THIRTY-EIGHT

The current of ordinary life;
But he, after all, comes back
To sit among the coals and ashes.

—PORTION OF A ZEN KOAN

Sam seemed to be expecting them and met Gary and Loch at the front door of his modest Westhampton Beach home, just a block from the ocean. He showed them the way through the house with little fanfare, but cordially enough.

"Nice digs," Gary whispered to Loch, then said to Sam, "You can afford this on a psychologist's salary?"

Sam looked surprised by the question, but answered without much hesitation. "It was my parents' first vacation house. They gave it to me after they moved to Southampton to be near Dad's golf course." The living room looked out across the dunes to a scrap of ocean on the horizon. "Please have a seat." He gestured to the couch and two chairs, cushioned in plaid, probably from the '60s. There was a scrapbook lying face open on the table with a newspaper article about Todd in it. "I guess you're here about Beka."

"And Edilio."

"I heard about that." A shadow of fear fluttered across Sam's face.

"How'd you hear?" Because of his credentials and everything he and his family had been through, Loch expected to feel empathy and perhaps an affinity for the man—he felt nothing. And searching Sam Daniels's face for some sign of emotive depth turned up nothing; even his body language seemed to lack emotion.

"Alex called." His voice was flat, but a tinge of anger seemed to creep into his words. "If I were you, I'd see if Godwyn took the photo. The *Post* loves Godwyn. They print him under the name Ian McGregor, although in this case I bet it's an anonymous photographer. Maybe Hurley will tell you who took it. No, he'd probably lie, too." Sam stopped himself from talking any further and looked at the detectives.

Sam Daniels obviously held no love for Godwyn Kamani, but Loch wondered if he had any notion of how strange he had just sounded.

"Any idea where he is?" Gary asked.

"God? His apartment in the city this morning. We had words." He wrote down the address for them and handed it to Gary, then sat and began flipping through the scrapbook on the table. "Yesterday's events brought up a few unpleasant memories for me. I couldn't even make it into work today." He looked up at the detectives and shrugged his shoulders. "Some shrink, aren't I?" He flipped the pages of the book again.

"Mementos?" Loch inquired.

"You could call them that. Anytime someone goes missing on New Year's Eve I follow the story. I can't contact the families directly, the last thing they want is to hear from someone who never learned what happened—my family is every family's worst nightmare." He went to the bar, picked up a bottle of Jack Daniel's, and poured himself a drink. "It's easier to have a corpse. That sounds cold, doesn't it, but you don't know how many times I've dreamt, wished, prayed that some part of Todd would wash up on a beach and give us proof that he's gone forever. The haunting is unbearable." Loch glanced over his shoulder and saw clippings of the last New Year's Eve case Carol Freesia had worked—Eric Heron's disappearance two years ago.

"You interested in Eric Heron?"

"He disappeared on New Year's Eve."

"Do you know if Gabe might have known him?"

"No idea, but he was a dancer." Sam's eyes seemed to narrow as he raised one eyebrow.

"He was?" Loch looked at the article more closely. Eric Heron had taught Pilates at a city studio and danced with the International Dance Company—the same company to which Edilio and Beka had belonged. He was not about to let Sam Daniels know that this information was news, though.

"Is it healthy to keep these articles around?" Gary asked.

Sam chuckled. "No, but it's human. Just call me a psychological rubbernecker."

"Do you mind?" Loch gestured to the book and caught Gary's eye.

"No, please. I left it out for you to look at." Sam handed it to him.

Gary continued the interview to take Sam's attention away from the scrapbook and give Loch free rein with the clippings.

"We think Beka's murder may be connected to the night your brother disappeared."

"Really?" Sam sounded interested and at the same time doubtful, as if the effort to hope had been worn down by the passing years.

"We're following up with everyone we know who was at the party and checking on their whereabouts this New Year's Eve."

Sam gestured to the scrapbook. "That's easy. I spent the night with my brother and a bottle of booze. I'm afraid my idea of a happy New Year's is pulling out that old book and getting rip-roaring drunk, just like we used to. Doesn't solve anything but it hurts the next morning, and I prefer pain to numbness."

"You're not married?"

"Divorced two years. She got tired of sharing me with Todd, too." The hardness in Sam's voice was like thin flakes of shale that could crumble if touched too roughly, but nick the flesh if rubbed the wrong way.

"And last Tuesday, where were you?" Gary redirected Sam's attention to the present.

"My office. You can check with the receptionist. I work at a day-treatment center for the mentally ill up by Port Jefferson."

Loch's ears perked up for a reason other than the investigation—Sam must work at the same place he and Ruth were considering for Marty. "How is that facility?"

"Professional interest or personal?" Sam asked.

"Both."

"It's excellent for treatment of critically, permanently mentally ill and PTSD or trauma issues. We have an art-therapy program, which is extremely effective for personality and psychotic disorders, like schizophrenia; there's a lot of one-on-one supervision. For those who don't have permanent issues I can think of more effective treatment environments; our clients aren't going to get miraculously better someday, but we try to help them cope with their illness in a safe environment where they can't hurt themselves or be hurt." He paused. "I sound like a brochure."

Loch appreciated his candor but didn't say anything about his own situation. He needed to keep Marty out of his professional life. But if Sam wasn't a murderer, he might prove to be a good contact at the program.

Gary looked at Loch for his lead, then asked, "Do you have keys to Gabe's loft in the city?"

"Me? No. Beka and I didn't stay very close after Todd's disappearance. I always sort of held her responsible. I think she knew that."

Loch's ears perked up again; Sam was the only person they'd interviewed so far who denied having keys, and that seemed strange. "What's this letter here?" he asked, holding out the first page of the album.

"Todd's last note to me. He left it on my door Saturday afternoon before the party."

Loch showed the note to Gary.

Bro. Went to Gabe's studio with Beka, you should come over.
Hang in there. Catch you later!
T

Sam walked over to the picture window and stared out at the tempestuous ocean. "It's like somebody is picking us off one by one."

"That's what Katiti French said."

"Well, normally I wouldn't agree with her, but in this case . . ." Sam pressed his head against the glass and sighed heavily.

Loch finally found the empathy and pity he had expected to feel at the beginning of the interview. There was no way he wanted to be in Sam Daniels's brain or place. Maybe this recent loss, despite his feelings for Beka, had taken one more toll on the once-young man. He seemed to be aging before their eyes. Loch turned his attention back to the scrapbook. There was a collage of Todd's baby photos and school pictures, the brothers in Boy Scouts together, Todd's high school graduation, and a photo of Beka looking lovingly into the camera—the date at the bottom of the photograph read 12/31/83.

"Why is she in here?"

"I dunno." Sam laughed, a little too ruefully.

CHAPTER THIRTY-NINE

Speech and silence tend toward separation or concealment.
How shall we proceed so as not to violate it?

—PORTION OF A ZEN KOAN

Devon left her parents' house and was at the zendo in less than ten minutes. There were a few cars parked along the side of the road when she pulled up, and Barney, the zendo dog, began his warning bark as soon as she got out of the car.

"Shhh, Barney." She held out her hand to quiet the overly zealous mutt. His barking became even louder and more repetitive. Finally, she reached the barn door and was able to escape into the quiet.

Inside, the whisper of socked and slippered feet shuffling across the pine floors behind the door muffled the noisy hound, although Devon wondered how anybody could focus with Barney keeping watch outside. She had missed the first sit at four-thirty, and it looked like she was the only new arrival for the five o'clock meditation. She slipped off her shoes and placed them neatly in the row of other shoes. It would be a few minutes before the door opened so she stretched her back and neck in the foyer. She was out of shape for everything but catching crooks and murderers, and wanted to be warmed up before attempting the lotus position for half an hour. Once she had finished stretching she pulled the rope handle to the door and stepped inside. A blast of heat from the small gas furnace hit her face. She shut the door behind her and waited until the circle had passed before bowing and joining the back of the line. She was just in time. The *Jikido* clapped once, and in unison they folded their hands in prayer. He clapped a second time and everyone found his or her spot; Devon chose a place close to the door. On the third clap they bowed and took their seats.

She placed her feet in the position Hans had taught her so many years ago—the left leg wedged into the right thigh and the right foot cradled by the left ankle—then she placed her left hand under her right hand and brought the tips of her thumbs together as the hands rested themselves near her naval. Three gongs emanated from the singing bowl and seemed to flow through the room, through Devon's body, and into her heart. Then there was only silence and breathing. Devon began to count her breaths, one to ten, one to twenty, up to one hundred. The candle at the end of the room seemed to illuminate Hans and make his aura vast and golden until it encompassed the altar. The floor turned to liquid as she breathed, and a fainter glow began to seep around the edges of the other meditators. She felt a beam of energy strengthen her spine, making her sit taller and straighter. She could almost see Beka sitting across from her.

Time must have passed swiftly because the chiming of the bell jarred her as if she had been rudely awakened from a deep sleep. She was conscious of her kinesthetic response to the sound—the tightening in her abdomen and shoulders—as if she were on guard, even in her deepest meditation. Having been absent from the zendo for so long, she had to pay extra close attention to the other Zen practitioners and follow their motions. She folded her hands in prayer and raised them before her face. Then she listened to the words they began to chant. *"Creations are numberless, I vow to free them . . ."* Hans's voice at the front of the room embraced theirs with his bass timbre.

"Delusions are inexhaustible, I vow to put an end to them." Tenors, altos and sopranos chanted in unison.

The last words were spoken in one final exhale, releasing every shred of breath inside and leaving her lungs as empty as her mind. *"The enlightened way is unsurpassable, I vow to embody it . . ."*

There were three more gongs and only after the resonance of the last one finished did the group stir. They brushed off their *zafus* and *zabuton* mats, shook their cramped feet, and stood facing each other. The *Jikido* smacked the wooden clappers together one more time, they bowed, and when they stood up everyone appeared to be human again—only Hans maintained his Buddha-hood.

"Everybody," he announced, "we are having a memorial service for Beka after tomorrow night's vigil. The vigil will begin at eight p.m. and end with the memorial service at eight a.m. We will sit on the half-hour with five-minute *kinhin* intervals. Please feel free to come for a few hours or the whole night. The sit is open to the public, as is the service."

Devon watched as the formality in the room dissolved and the group broke into more informal cliques. A few of the members came up and hugged her. "Good to have you back. I'm sorry that it was under these circumstances," Peter, the *Ino*, told her.

One woman hung back nervously; she looked familiar but Devon could not place her. After the small group around Devon cleared, the woman bowed to her and introduced herself. "I'm Jenny O'Doherty, Gabe's secretary."

Hoping to hide her shocked face, Devon bowed to the woman.

"Beka brought me here a few years ago, after you stopped coming. She didn't like to do things alone, and I needed something in my life besides work and my good-for-nothing husband."

Devon's brain began clicking—they hadn't really looked at Jenny O'Doherty as a suspect, and from what Loch had said, Devon didn't think she had an alibi for New Year's Eve. "You've been coming for a while then?"

"A few years," Jenny murmured.

"Did you ever go into the city with Gabe?"

"Whenever the gallery needed help getting organized. We were getting ready to open a new show of his work."

Devon nodded—the canvases propped against the walls. Her mind raced beyond the conversation to the fact that Jenny O'Doherty must have a key to the studio. She did not want to ask her too abruptly, though.

"I don't know what to do about this," Jenny was saying. "It's so horrible. Hans has been helpful, but it's such a shock."

Devon felt Hans's hand on her elbow. "Excuse us, Jen. I need Devon to look at something." He led her back into the meditation room and shut the door behind them. "Here is the prayer list."

"Who else has touched it?"

"Peter and myself are the only ones who should have; somebody else must have, though."

"Can you have Peter come in here so I can print him? I'll need to sort his prints from yours and anyone else's I find." Hans poked his head out of the door to call Peter. "Hans?" she added as if it were an afterthought. "I could probably use everybody's prints." He nodded and stepped into the foyer. She began dusting the cover and pulling the prints off of the black glossy cardboard folder.

Peter stepped into the room. "You needed my prints?"

"Thank you, Peter." She pulled out her inkless print kit and rolled his fingers quickly. "You're done, send in the next victim." He looked at her questioningly. "I'm joking." Sometimes she wondered if American Buddhists had any sense of humor; she knew the Asians did. Jenny O'Doherty came into the meditation room looking nervously about, even though she had just left the room a few minutes earlier.

Devon began to roll her thumb and found that her fingers were remarkably cold and damp. "Do you still have keys to the Soho building?" Devon asked nonchalantly.

"I have keys to everything," Jenny confessed. "I don't know what to do with them. I guess Robert Goldstein will tell me when he gets around to the will."

"Did your husband ever come home?"

Devon took her left hand and began to roll her thumb, then index finger . . .

"Excuse me?"

"Detective Brennen said your husband was missing on New Year's Eve."

"He wasn't missing," she said harshly. "He was drunk."

"I'm sorry."

"Not as sorry as he was when he finally showed up. I threw him out." O'Doherty looked at her feet. "I'm coming tomorrow night. I can't sleep anyway, so I might as well come here."

"Then I'll see you tomorrow."

Devon printed six more people, then asked Hans to come back in. "Can I keep this?" she asked, pointing to the prayer book.

"I recopied it so you could have the whole book. I thought you might need it."

"We'll turn you into a detective yet, Hans."

"And we'll turn you into a Buddhist! You're coming to sit tomorrow night." It was not a question.

"I feel like I need this in my life right now."

"Then you do." He hugged her, his arms solid and strong around her—the best hugger in the world, she thought. "Just on the East End," he whispered.

She blinked at him. Had he been reading her mind?

"You are my dharma daughter, like Beka was," he answered her silent question.

She headed down the path, following a few of the others through the dark, but stopped halfway. Barney was staring beyond her, without barking. She turned and saw Jenny O'Doherty standing at her car watching her with her mouth half open. Devon started toward her, but the woman quickly got into her car, started the engine, and pulled out into the road. It was only then that Barney began to bark.

* * *

Her cellphone was blinking with a message again; she knew it was Loch and punched his number on auto dial. "You rang? How'd the interviews go?"

He coughed. "These people were your friends?"

"Part-time friends."

"They're about as appealing as . . ." he paused, "I don't know what . . . something I detest . . ."

"Beets."

"Beets!" Loch laughed.

"They aren't going to warm up to you when you're thinking one of them is a murderer."

"Like I care." The sarcastic edge to his voice could not be muffled, even by the poor reception.

"Did you get everybody's fingerprints?"

"Already gave them to Frank."

"And what about alibis?"

"I thought I was the lead on this investigation."

"That's just for appearances, Loch. You know I'm really boss."

"Women always are."

"And don't you forget it."

"Alex seems covered. Josh and Katiti's alibi seems shaky; Gary's going to follow up. We haven't located Maddie or Godwyn yet."

"What about Sam?"

"Sam Daniels does not have an alibi for New Year's Eve. Evidently, he doesn't celebrate that holiday. He also has a fondness for bourbon, Jack Daniel's to be precise."

"You like Sam for this?"

"There's something funky there, Dev. He has a real grudge."

"Against Beka?"

"And Godwyn."

"What are you saying?"

"Nothing, I'm just thinking. Listen, sweetheart, I want you to go home and get some rest. Frank needs you to pick him up on the way to work. His car is in the shop. I think he's expecting you sometime around seven-thirty. Gary and I are checking alibis in the a.m., then I'm going to the North Fork to find Miss Maddie Fong and Gary's off to the city to find God—what's his last name?"

"Kamani." She looked out of her windshield into the impenetrable night. It was barely six-thirty and black as pitch. She could hear him shuffling papers on the other end of the line. "Are you coming back out to Sag Harbor?"

"I might squeeze you in between three and five," he answered.

"How about if I come get you?"

"Your mother gave me a mouthful about your health. Evidently, you need your beauty rest . . ."

"Lochwood Brennen!"

"She's right, you look peaked, and you were up most of the night last night and the night before . . ."

She did not let him finish. "I can't believe you met my mother without my being there to intervene! Did Dad really threaten you with a harpoon?"

"Now I really feel like it went well."

She laughed. "Don't worry, honey, if anything happens to you I'll make sure Dad is proved innocent."

"Why doesn't that make me feel any better? Go home and get some damn sleep. There's nothing more you can do tonight anyway."

"If that's true, there's nothing more that you can do either.

Come home with me." She could tell he was looking at the file by the way his voice not only withdrew from the line, but his presence seemed to disappear as well. He was going to work at his desk until he figured it all out or fell asleep sitting up. "I give up. Have fun with your casebook, but remember, when you wake up holding the picture of a corpse, you could be in bed holding me."

They hung up simultaneously and moments later her phone lit up with his numeric page, *999-9999*. Maybe she didn't need a beeper after all. She headed for home.

CHAPTER FORTY

The Arrival at Mutual Integration:
When two blades cross points, there's no need to withdraw.

—PORTION OF A ZEN KOAN

Devon made a fire in the fireplace and flicked on the TV while a can of Progresso soup heated up on the stove. She didn't know what else to do, and Loch was right, she was exhausted. She could actually count on one hand the hours of sleep she had had since New Year's Eve. Boo watched as she stacked the wood, his tail thumping on his pillow by the hearth whenever she walked past. She rolled up pages of newspaper leftover from the Sunday *Times*, which she hadn't had time to read, his head following her every move. Finally she lit the fire and he laid his head down to rest as Devon took her place on the couch.

It was nice to be home alone. Quiet, no one to bother her. The phone rang.

"Hey, Dev. I met your man today." It was Alexandra. "Not bad."

"Liar. He's mean as an old snake. Listen, did you get the video today?"

"It has to come all the way from L.A., Dev. I called my assistant and asked her to find it. She had to go to my storage locker, and things aren't in alphabetical order in there. I hope you appreciate it. She FedEx'd it this afternoon."

"So I'll have it tomorrow?"

"After ten."

"Great, can you call me when it arrives?"

The kitchen door opened and Aileen walked in carrying a bag of groceries. Boo jumped up from his bed to greet her with a wagging tail and a quick dab of his tongue on her hand, then returned just as quickly to Devon's side.

"Sure. What's going on, Dev? You're acting very mysterious." Alex's voice sounded hesitant.

Devon sighed heavily and kicked the pillow under her foot. "I'm in the middle of a murder investigation, Alex, that's what's going on. I'm hoping the video might help." Boo knocked her free hand with his nose so that it landed squarely on his head. She patted him involuntarily.

"We've looked at it before. Remember? I ran it for about twenty-four hours after the party. I never saw anything the least bit telling."

"We weren't watching it for information." Boo tossed her hand in the air again. She smiled, aware that she had stopped rubbing his ears a few moments earlier. "No one went through it frame by frame."

"Well, I did, sort of," Alex told her. "But I guess I was just looking for clips to edit into a larger abstract of Beka dancing. You really think it will help?"

"I don't know, Alex. My job is to collect the evidence; Loch's the one who puts it all together."

"Loch's going to see it?" Devon could hear the hesitation in her voice. "There's some stuff on there I don't want anyone but you seeing, Devon. You can't arrest us for illegal acts committed so many years ago, can you?"

Devon felt it was best for her to be completely honest and had to say, "If there was a murder on the tape, I could use it as evidence." It hadn't even occurred to her that she might need a court order to get the tape, and if there was something incriminating on it she wanted the evidence to be admissible.

"What about drugs, Devon? I mean, if you were just a regular Joe, it would be no big deal, but there was stuff happening at that party before it started that I taped."

"I can give you my verbal assurance that I won't use any of the drug use against you or anyone else on the tape. This case isn't about drugs."

"Are you sure about that?" Devon didn't answer. "I think I'd better discuss this with my lawyer."

There was another pause on the other end and Devon knew she

was in danger of losing the tape altogether if she didn't play the next few moments very carefully. "Alex, this is about Todd and Beka, and figuring out what happened to them. Nothing else. You want me to find Beka's killer?"

"Of course." Alex's voice grew softer.

"I know you did stuff you'd rather not have made public; so did I. It was the '80s. We're not going to punish you or anyone else for being young and stupid." She could feel the tension in Alexandra dissipating even though she couldn't see her. "Listen." She decided to change her tack entirely. "I'll be the only one to look at the tape unless there is something on it that proves insightful to the murders or Todd's disappearance. After I watch it I'll call you and let you know if I feel that Loch needs to see it as well. At that point we can bring in the lawyers, if that will make you feel better."

"That sounds reasonable, but I'll need a non-disclosure agreement from you first. Just in case."

She knew Alex would call her lawyer anyway as soon as they got off the phone, but in order to get Alex's mind off of legalities, Devon said, "Tomorrow night there's an all-night sit in honor of Beka and Gabe."

"What are you doing, praying for enlightenment on this case?"

"You could say that." Devon didn't want Alex knowing more than was absolutely necessary. "Hey, you don't know where Maddie and God got off to, do you? I wanted to let them know about the sit." Devon saw Aileen wave from the kitchen and point to the soup on the stove. Devon nodded, got up off the couch, and walked into the kitchen.

There was a click on Alex's line. "That's me, gotta go."

Devon had the distinct feeling it was Maddie on the other end. "If Maddie calls, tell her to call me." Devon rattled off her cell number.

Her soup was steaming in its bowl and looked not only good, but comforting. The theme music for some sitcom started and Devon began to sip her clam chowder, hoping to placate her mind with someone else's woes.

"How was the reunion?"

"You should have come."

"And hang out with all of the *nosous upliftous* crowd? No thanks."

Devon chuckled. She had forgotten how she and Aileen had given Latin names to all of the cliques in junior high—*burneous outus, jockeous sportus, cheereous leaderetch, nosous upliftous.*

Aileen flopped down in the chair next to her roommate. "You want to talk?"

"I want to be shallow for about an hour and not think about murder, death, or disappearing people."

Aileen poured them wine and settled back into the cushions of the chair to watch yet another pouty-faced dirty-blond actress with big eyes, and even bigger lips, fumble her way through her life's pitiful problems. Fortified by hot soup and crusty *ciabiatti* bread, Devon began to feel less shaky from fatigue and hunger. Aileen hit the mute button as a commercial invaded the atmosphere.

"What I don't get is why someone killed Edilio." Aileen obviously wanted to talk.

"I don't get any of it." Devon swirled the wine in her glass and watched the watery film catch the sides and drip down quickly—not a vintage year. "Not Edilio, not Beka and Gabe . . . How could someone I know do this?"

"How do you know it's someone you know?"

"There are indications."

Aileen leaned forward and stared at her friend disbelievingly. "Really?"

"Yeah, like my beeper going off. We still haven't found Beka's phone, but I think it could have been the murderer calling me."

"Oh my god . . . that means they know your number . . ."

"But it could have been Beka, too."

". . . and maybe where you live. Do you think you're in danger?"

"I can't believe I didn't call her back."

"Devon, are you in danger?" Aileen's eyes widened with fear.

They looked at each other—the words said more than either of them cared to admit.

"The only thing I'm in danger of is losing my faith in people. I feel like everything I knew for sure is no longer true, and people I thought I could trust are not—maybe never were—trustworthy." Devon pushed back a tear with her index finger.

"Remember that song Cindy Lauper used to sing, 'True Colors'?"

"I don't think this was what she meant by her lyrics."

"Yeah it is. Everyone lies."

"The law doesn't. It's there to back us up."

"You're an idealist," Aileen observed. "Now, Loch and I are cynics."

Devon chuckled; Aileen was right. "You know the worst thing about all of this? The cold-bloodedness. Loch's been working up a profile, and a killer like this would have to be totally anti-social. These people are nothing but socialites."

"Maybe they're not the way they appear."

"Obviously! But Aileen, I'm at the zendo tonight, meditating, and all I can think is what if it's one of them?"

"You're going to figure this out. I know you will. You always do. You're good, Dev."

"You're always so encouraging."

"Hey, you've always been in my corner."

"Not always."

"Well, almost always."

"You're my oldest friend." Devon stressed the words as she held her glass up to the firelight to stare at the flames through the blood-red of the wine.

"Great, now I'm going to get killed, too!"

"Don't say that."

"Here, have some more wine." Aileen refilled their glasses and they drank in silence.

Devon yawned. She could feel her energy running out of her spine like battery fluid. Last night she had felt like Loch, up all night, working and figuring things out, jazzed by the investigation. Tonight she felt like a damp rag wrung out and hung up to dry. As soon as she could get up off the couch, she would go to bed so that by the time Loch arrived, if he ever arrived, she'd be in dreamland.

They watched the rest of the show without much conversation until the theme song signaled the conclusion of their mental intermission for the evening. Devon started up the stairs, but stopped partway up. "Aileen, when was the last time you saw Beka?"

"Schiavoni's a couple of weeks ago. She was buying porterhouse and I was getting rump roast."

"Did she look okay?"

"She looked great, as usual. We just time-of-day'd it and talked about the weather."

"You guys were a lot alike in some ways," Devon said.

"Yada, yada."

That was Aileen's way of letting Devon know she had stepped too close—Aileen hated sympathy.

"Hey, that guy Loch was with yesterday?"

"Gary?"

"What's his story?"

"No story. Just divorced."

"You cops always have a story, but . . ."

"What are you thinking?"

"Nice ass."

"I hadn't noticed."

"We could double-date."

"Soon as this is all over."

"How about Saturday?"

"Aileen!" Devon laughed out loud. "You're as bad as Gary."

"What ya mean?"

"He was asking Loch the same thing last night."

"Then it's meant to be!"

Law and Order was starting—it was Aileen's favorite show, but Devon had had enough off both. She patted her thigh to signal Boo. He leapt up off his bed by the fire and pushed past her on the way up the stairs.

"I got one for you!" The lilt in Aileen's voice stopped her. "What's the Hamptons's theme song?"

"I give."

Aileen began to sing, *"Oh Lord, won't you buy me a Mercedes Benz . . ."*

CHAPTER FORTY-ONE

The master swordsman is like the lotus blooming in the fire.
Such a man has in and of himself a heaven-soaring spirit.
—PORTION OF A ZEN KOAN

Devon woke up and stared at the other side of the bed—empty. She knew Loch would stay at the office, or maybe he had gone home to his own bed. It didn't matter. The fingers of depression seeped into her consciousness like fog clouding her mind, making it hard to get up, get going. It was still dark as the middle of the night, not six in the morning, and she knew if she let her eyelids fall shut again she would slip into the welcome arms of sleep and not wake again until daybreak. She swung her legs over the side of the bed and onto the warm belly of Boo, ever faithful, still asleep by her side of the bed. She rubbed her feet into his form and watched his tail thump against the floor. He rolled to a sitting position and stared at her expectantly; this was one creature who never had trouble waking up. "Just a quickie," she told the dog. "Aileen will take you for a longer walk later." He jumped up excitedly.

Devon figured Boo had a vocabulary of about thirty words, *walk* being the first he had ever learned. He also knew the words *pig ear, bone, chew, baby* (the name of one of his toys), *go to bed, go to jail* (for when he was bad), and phrases such as *Cross the road, Go back home, What the hell are you doing? Get the hell back here* . . . The list of phrases was pretty long, too, Devon mused, although she wasn't sure if it was vocabulary or tone of voice that he understood. It didn't really matter, she wasn't a dog trainer like Aileen, but she considered Boo to be exceptionally intelligent because he was also, like herself, exceptionally stubborn.

She took him outside for a quick pee, and put him back in the house. He would bark indignantly when he heard her car starting and realized she was going somewhere without him—they didn't call them coach dogs for nothing—but there was no other way around it. Maybe she should have become a fireman, then her dog could have come to work every day. His outraged but muffled baritone sounded from behind the kitchen door as she started the engine; he would stop by the time she reached the end of the driveway. She looked both ways, more out of habit than necessity, and pulled onto Bay Street. The boats still moored in the harbor were real fishing boats; there were no yachts towering over the piers as in the summer, and the gentle tinkling of masts in the wind should have made her smile. She loved it when the town was still and empty. She stopped at the 7-Eleven, grabbed an extra-large coffee, and headed across the Sag Harbor Bridge and on to North Haven.

The sun was just beginning to break open the iron mass of clouds floating low over the bay and Sag Harbor Cove as she made her way past the inlets of water sandwiching Long Beach. Seagulls hung in the air almost motionless as they tried to fly toward the bay while the wind pushed them steadily back to shore. Steel-blue waves of surf curled and chopped across the pebbles and shells that made the beach rough on the tenderfooted. She slowed down and pulled over at the lookout point. Behind her a small herd of deer grazed on the marsh grass, raising their heads momentarily to check her out before returning to their foraging. Devon popped the lid off her coffee and took the first sip to wake her out of the stupor that had taken hold.

The sky began to show shreds of magenta and orange as the light filtered across her little town, and she felt the strongest desire to flee the investigation, flee it all and go to Hawaii the next day with Uncle Biz and Bert and Beka's body. She wasn't sure what was bothering her, and thought maybe she'd feel better if she had a little cry—but no tears came. She was too tired, too numb to feel much. What she really needed was a vacation. And that was the last thing she was going to get.

"Pull yourself together, Devon," she chided herself out loud, then cracked the car window to feel the comfort of salt air and wind.

The coffee made her feel more focused and alive. Maybe she could talk Loch into going to Oahu with her after they solved this case. Loch probably had thousands of hours due; she'd never known him to take any time off in the five years they'd been seeing each other. Hawaii. She looked at the surf and thought of the perfect azure and cool greens of Kailua and Kaneohe Bays. She could taste the salt water, smell the hot sand, and feel the cool shade of palm and banyan trees protecting her from the sun. She shifted her car back into drive and took another gulp of coffee—as soon as this was over, they'd go away. They'd sit on the beach all day and eat jabons and guava from Auntie Mack's garden and platters of carryout from Kozo Sushi. They'd snorkel at Hanauma Bay, or maybe just stay at the Imamura beach house on Kaneohe Bay and hitch rides on a boat out to the reef where they could snorkel and picnic until the tide came in and they caught a ride back home. She would take Loch to all the places Beka had taken her on their many visits to Oahu. They would visit Beka's grave at Bodyo-in Temple and set a ginger lei on the water at low tide in her memory. They would rest and make love on the dock and forget they were cops—they would make plans to retire in Hawaii. They would never come back.

It was a nice daydream, a gentle flight of fancy that soothed her nerves and made the day seem more bearable. She just wanted it to be over.

CHAPTER FORTY-TWO

Praise to you, violent god of the Yellow Hat teachings, Who reduces to particles of dust Great beings, high officials, and ordinary people . . .

—ZEMEY RINPOCHE

Tension was higher than usual at the station that morning. Lieutenant Whittaker was like an old hound on an even older scent, and followed them around the office as they tried to finish the Printrak search that had been running all night on the national fingerprint database system. There had been four hits out of the twenty full and partial sets of prints—two of them had been arrested on cocaine charges, one for male prostitution; the fourth was none other than Eric Heron.

Of course, no sooner had they discovered the connection than Sergeant Houck called Loch for a meeting to update him on their progress. It was almost as if the man were psychic when it came to breaks in cases—though Loch would have preferred waiting a few hours before he laid it all out for Houck. Unfortunately, a few hours was not what he had. The foursome arrived in Houck's office under the strictest orders from Loch to keep their mouths shut. Houck for his part did not allude to whether or not any of Marders's allegations against Devon had reached his ears. Instead, Houck nodded approvingly as Loch told him how it looked like Gabriel Montebello had been getting away with murder for almost two decades.

"I can't believe nobody saw anything!" Houck yelled when Loch was done explaining the prints they had found.

"I'm sending Frank and Devon back over to the Montebello estate as soon as we're done here," Loch explained. "But as for witnesses, even Gabe's secretary, Jenny O'Doherty, hasn't seen anything and she's worked for him for ten years."

"Something's not right."

"We're considering the possibility that he worked with some-one."

"Ferraro?"

"That would have been nice, except who killed Montebello then?"

"Did he have any other business partners?"

"Just Imamura."

"And you're still looking for a someone?" Houck's eyes narrowed. "Sounds like you have it solved. Tell me . . ." He looked directly at Devon. "Would you want to be married to this guy? Would you call your friend the cop and have him get off because of some legal technicality, or kill him yourself?"

"I believe in the law, sir."

"Did your friend?"

"We just want to make sure we don't miss anything," Loch reminded him.

"Sounds to me like Ferraro was his partner; she finally figured it out or got fed up with it and did what nobody else could. Is that a stretch or am I an idiot?"

Devon did not answer his question.

Loch was steamed but didn't let his ire show. "A few things don't add up, sarge."

"Make them." Houck nodded to Loch's team. "As much as you don't like it, NYPD may have this right. The mystery now is how many guys did this nut actually kill, not who killed the nut. Wrap it up."

Loch did not push the issue; he knew better than to do that when Houck was acting like the bureaucrat—clear the case and get good press—and not a cop. He followed his team out of Houck's office, but just as he was about to reach the door, he heard his superior add, "And Brennen, try not to piss off Detective Marders any more than you absolutely have to."

They were waiting for him in the hallway, waiting for his instructions. "Devon, Frank, you two are on the estate. Go over everything, the barn, the house. Find something that tells us what Gabe's sick little fantasy was. Gary, you head into the city to find this God person and see if you can stop by Marders's office and find out what they got on the Edilio Ferraro case." He shook his head at Devon. "I don't think Imamura is our killer, but until you guys come up with something concrete, she's the fall guy, so get busy." Frank and Gary headed down the hall but Devon stood in front of him, not like his girlfriend but more like a bad dream that won't go away. "What now?"

"I'm going to be at the zendo tonight." She told him about the all-night meditation Hans had planned.

"What do you mean—you sit all night staring at a wall?" Her plan to participate did not thrill him.

"We meditate through the darkest hours and when the daylight breaks we chant for the enlightened way," she explained for the third time. "I think if I can keep an eye on these people I can figure it out."

"And how many people are there at this little shindig?"

"Usually it's called *Soka Gakkai*, and anywhere from ten people to just me and the *Jikido* will be there."

"What's a *Jikido*?"

"I believe it's Jenny O'Doherty." She grinned at him.

"Were you going to tell me or just let me find out?"

"What do you think?"

"There's no way you're getting stuck in a room with her alone—she's a fruitcake and I haven't cleared her off my list of suspects yet."

"I can handle O'Doherty."

He stared at her, one eyebrow levitating toward his hairline.

"Hey, if she's the killer and attacks me, I'll have her. End of story."

"If she attacks you, she's a fool. And I think that's actually what you're hoping for. I won't have it. I'm fine with decoy surveillance—not on your own and without backup. I'll be outside in my car and you'll be on radio."

"No way!"

"Only way. You aren't sitting with your back toward anyone who might be a potential murderer, Devon. No one! You understand me? I won't have your safety compromised for an investigation."

"I'm going to be well aware of what's going on around me."

"Yeah, at four-thirty in the morning when your eyes get heavy, are you going to be so ready? The only way I can authorize this is if I'm posted outside."

"What exactly are you watching for?"

"It's an all-nighter in the middle of the woods not six miles from where the murders occurred, and almost directly connected to the crime. What do you think?" He was irritated with her; anyone else would be happy for extra protection, but not Devon. Well, he was damned if she was going to have all the fun.

"Okay, you have a point, but the real reason you're coming along is you're afraid you'll miss something and I know it. You can't stake the zendo out on the side of Swamp Road, though, people will see you."

"Let me worry about that."

"Maybe Hans would let you sit in the kitchen. Nothing's going on but a bunch of people sitting around with their eyes half shut—or half open, depending on how you look at things."

"What sort of vantage point would I get from the kitchen?"

"Your butt will stay warm."

"You have to be on radio in case something happens while you're meditating."

"Like enlightenment?"

"You have to be able to contact me if necessary."

"The equipment will be too bulky."

"Wear a big black robe like that monk of yours. I insist. I won't have you off radio."

"You're really nervous about this. Why?"

"Because I'm a good Catholic boy and not used to this mumbo-jumbo religious crap."

"Oh, and Catholicism isn't full of mumbo-jumbo?"

"We call it mysticism."

"So do we." She jutted her chin out and dared him to push the point any further. "Nothing's going to happen."

"That's exactly what I'm hoping for—a nice uneventful evening. We haven't been bored in days."

CHAPTER FORTY-THREE

*The Coming from within the Real: Within nothingness there
is a path leading away from the dusts of the world.*

— PORTION OF A ZEN KOAN

Frank and Devon pulled up the driveway of the Montebello estate
and waited for the guard to wave them in. There was a private guard
now, but they had free reign of the place once they showed him their
badges. They went through the house again but found nothing new
or remarkable. In the barn up the hill everything looked in place, the
Tyvek suits were still hanging and it felt like an art studio, nothing
else. Devon looked out the window at the pond. It was frozen but
not solid. Aileen had always said that the fresh spring that fed Trout
Pond, down the road, also fed Daniels' Hole on Gabe's property, and
neither completely froze over in the wintertime.

"Devon, what's this room here?" Frank held open a door that
led to a smaller room where the models could dress or undress and
sometimes warm up. The barn could get fairly cold in the winter
months, and while Gabe always used kerosene heaters, this room
was small enough that it heated quickly and held the warmth.

"I guess you could call it a dressing room." It was typical, no
windows or other exits. The door was remarkably solid and had a
dead bolt on the outside. There were pegs for clothes. She looked at
the doorknob again. It did not lock from the inside.

"Why are there meat hooks in the ceiling?"

"This was a working farm at one time, Frank. Maybe this was
the slaughter room."

They looked at each other and simultaneously pulled out their
spray bottles of Luminol from their waist pouches. She took one
wall and he took the other and in moments the room was glowing
with the residue of blood. They stood back and looked at their
work—cow or human? Could Gabe have killed his victims in this

very room? It had been cleaned remarkably well, but whoever had wiped down the walls had not used bleach to get rid of the protein residue. "How long does residue last, Frank?"

"Ten years max, and that's being generous."

"He bought this place the year Todd disappeared."

They called Lochwood and waited for him to arrive with Jo the M.E. in tow; a few hours later Devon walked past Tom Hurley without the slightest nod or indication that she knew the reporter. He was going to have to get his information from someone else; no one she knew would speak with him. Still, when Houck arrived on the scene his first statement to the press was as callous as they come: "We believe that Gabriel Montebello and his wife Beka Imamura may have worked as a team baiting and killing young men. However, the evidence as of yet is still inconclusive. Suffolk County detectives are working around the clock with New York City detectives to get to the bottom of this, but I think it is safe to say that the public is not in danger. We have been certain since the beginning that Beka Imamura killed her husband, what we did not know was why—I think that is obvious now."

"Obvious to whom?" Devon hissed under her breath.

She went up to her superior and said, "I need the night off to attend a funeral." Houck simply nodded and shook his head as she signed herself off the crime scene and walked away.

* * *

Loch had already parked in the back of the garage and was heading to the kitchen when the dog ambushed him with a series of critical barks and growls.

"Barney! Barney! Come on, boy," Hans called the beast off. "He only barks if he doesn't know you."

"Good watchdog," Loch grumbled, a bit too much like Barney.

"Not really. He never bites." Hans held the door open to the kitchen. "I've set up a break room in the foyer—coffee, tea, biscuits. Would you like some coffee?" Loch accepted the mug from the monk.

Devon and Aileen arrived together, walked through the privet past Barney and his wagging tail, then walked down the path toward the kitchen. Devon wasn't sure why she had come. She was still looking for answers, though, even if Beka was a murderer. Like Houck said, she had to know why. Maybe that's why she had chosen to sit through the night, wrestling with demons, or angels, or memories, until one of them gave her what she was seeking.

She stepped into the kitchen. "What are you doing here?"

Loch put his hands on her shoulders. "Did you really think I was going to let you come here alone tonight?"

Devon pulled the walkie-talkies out of her purse. "Here, I guess I must have known you'd show up, despite Houck solving the case." She took the robe that Hans was holding out for her to wear. It would help conceal her accoutrements—gun, radio, notepad, a pack of gum.

Loch took his walkie-talkie. "You going to meditate, Aileen?"

"Are you kidding! I been hearin' about you guys runnin' around arresting folks for too long—now I'm finally in on it." Aileen punched Loch's arm, her eyes glimmering with excitement. She picked up his walkie-talkie and pressed the button. "I always liked these gadgets. Calling all cars! Calling all cars! A bunch of unruly Buddhists are sitting in the woods—we need assistance here. We can't budge them!"

"It's not a game, Aileen. It could be dangerous."

"That's what makes it so cool! Hans, did you know these two are a regular, I don't know, Starsky and Hutch!"

"He's Starsky," Devon said.

"Hutch was the cute one," Aileen told Loch.

Loch rolled his eyes. "Are you responsible for her?"

"She's leaving early," Devon assured him, and tossed an arm around Aileen. "She hates to miss *Law & Order.*"

"I'll come back here around five. I'm always up by five."

"You should be the Buddhist," Hans teased. "Devon could never get up early enough for the morning sit."

"It doesn't make sense to sit anywhere at seven a.m. without a cup of coffee by my side." Devon kissed Loch on the cheek.

Aileen stood on tiptoe to peck his other cheek. "Don't worry, I won't let anything happen to her."

Loch laughed. "Just make sure she stays awake."

"Hans uses a stick for that." Aileen winked at him as they headed out the door.

* * *

The lights in the kitchen were off, and Hans had left the overhead light on outside as well as the motion-sensor light at the corner of the zendo so Loch could watch people going to and from the house for bathroom and coffee breaks. He approved of the set-up and hoped the night would prove to be at least spiritually, if not criminally, enlightening.

He had a picture of Maddie Fong and Godwyn, the only two loftmates he and Gary had not yet located, and someone was moving in the shadows. One quick glance at Maddie's photo told him she had just entered the courtyard and bowed to the Buddha under the privet. How had she known the Buddha was there? It wasn't easy to see, unless one knew where to look. Maybe she was familiar with the surroundings, he mused. Barney came out, took one look at her, and turned his back. The dog knew her—Maddie Fong had been here before.

Alex came through the gate, again Barney did not bark. She and Maddie embraced and whispered, then slipped through the barn door and into the zendo. Loch noted their actions inside the garden and scribbled down the time; it was 8:55 p.m.

Next, Josh came stomping through the underbrush; he was oblivious to the Buddha and his surroundings and seemed angry to be there, and yet there he was. Loch wondered if Katiti had put him up to it. Barney ran out of the doghouse growling and carrying on at him. Josh kicked him and kept walking. Interesting. Loch wondered if this was why Aileen was having such trouble training their dog.

Sam came through the fence just after Josh had gone inside, but elicited no response from the so-called watchdog. As far as Loch was aware, Sam was not a zendo regular. Wasn't he Protestant? Todd had been planning to be a minister, right? He made a note to ask Hans how well he knew Sam, and then began to wonder if he could count on Barney for an accurate read. It seemed as if the dog might ignore some people simply because they arrived after he'd made a big to-do over somebody else.

The only person still a no-show was Godwyn. Loch looked at his photographs and wondered where the Ghanese-Englishman had disappeared to. Gary was in the city staking out his apartment, but so far there had been no sign of Godwyn Kamani anywhere.

He kept his eyes peeled to the dark. It was almost time for the *Soka* shindig to begin. The next arrival, Jenny O'Doherty, burst through the hedge looking out of breath and flushed. She glanced nervously around, made a quick dip to the Buddha, and dashed inside. There were a few others who came through the gates, but Loch didn't recognize any of them. They were probably friends of Beka and zendo regulars. The first gong, warning those inside and out to hurry to their *zafus* and *zabutons*, resonated through the night air. It was time for *zazen* to begin and each of them to take their places.

CHAPTER FORTY-FOUR

*Even if you observe the taboo . . . you will surpass that eloquent
one of yore who silenced every tongue.*

—PORTION OF A ZEN KOAN

Inside the zendo, Devon watched Maddie hug Hans warmly. She
hadn't known that they knew each other and felt her skin prickling
with suspicion. As soon as Maddie and Alex moved into the inner
chamber, she cornered Hans to ask him how long he had known
Maddie.

"Beka brought her here after you stopped coming. Alex, too,"
he told her. The first gong sounded. He squeezed her elbow and
steered her like a child to the door. "Now go take your place, we'll
begin as scheduled whether our *Jikido* arrives on time or not."

Devon walked to her cushion, pondering how close Maddie and
Alex might be to Hans and the zendo, and saw Josh now sitting there
resolutely. He must have sneaked past her. Sam came in behind her
and looked a little lost as he found a place to sit. It was a good turn-
out; the meditation room was almost full. They were all in their
places when Jenny O'Doherty bustled into the room and took her
seat facing them, while everyone else turned his or her back toward
her. The hair on Devon's neck bristled, but her position was already
set and the room was now full. Jenny O'Doherty had a clear path to
Devon, and Devon had no other choice but to sit with her back to
the woman.

The other Buddhists arranged their clothing and their legs in
preparation for a half-hour of sitting stationary. The small heater
rattled like a bag of bones, sending dry heat through the room and
a faint odor of gas, masked only by a slightly stronger scent of sandalwood incense. To moisten the air, two shallow clay pots filled
with water, with three perfectly round black stones in each, rested
on the grill. The lights were on low and cast a golden glow through-

out the room. It was just going to be a simple ceremony, no chanting or ritual bells. It would be quiet through the depth of night and they would come out on the other side of darkness cleansed and free of illusion. Personally, her goal was to grieve in silence and clear her mind of the fog that had descended when she awoke that morning. Devon had not meditated all night since she and Beka had come to *Soka Gattai* in 1990 to celebrate Buddha's birthday.

It was one of those magical memories. Hans, sitting like a slab of black marble in his robes, rarely got up for *kinhin*—the man could sit for hours without the slightest movement. Through the quiet of the night they had meditated, until dawn—the symbol of Buddha's enlightenment shared with all sentient beings—crested the horizon. After twelve hours of silence, their voices had been rusty as they chanted in unison: "*All Buddhas throughout space and time. All Bodhisattvas-Mahasattvas, Maha Prajna Paramita.*" It was one of the most poignant and beautiful moments of her life. Perhaps that's what she was doing here now, searching for that kind of hope again. Maybe after a night of mindfulness she would see clearly, and either Beka's killer or why Beka had not told her Gabe was a killer would be made plain.

A monk takes a vow of silence to remain in a tree . . . Devon pondered Beka's last koan. What would a monk be doing in a tree?

At regular half-hour intervals the gong interrupted the quiet and the acolytes bowed to the wall, stood up, brushed off their cushions, and faced each other while the monks remained sitting, passionless and placid, staring into space. Devon envied their serenity. She stood with the others, waiting for O'Doherty to smack the wooden blocks together, indicating that she would take a short break to let the blood flow back to her limbs while the others walked single-file around the room like thoughtful zombies. Devon counted breaths as she walked and thought about the chant Hans had once whispered to her:

I don't know
But I've been told
Tibetan pussy sure is cold.

After five turns around the room, O'Doherty clapped the blocks together again and they returned to their *zafus*. They repeated the ritual of manipulating their legs into the lotus, semi-lotus, or kneeling positions, and waited for the gong.

The group was orderly and organized. There were four people she did not recognize, but she appreciated their presence and silent support. Hans was seated by the altar and around him sat Catri and Dorothy, the senior monks. Next to Catri's seat was Peter, then Alex, and across the aisle from her, Maddie and Josh. Devon sat between Aileen and the door, and Sam was at the end of the room. Maybe it was just her cop training, but she felt more at ease with her eye on the only exit. It also kept her in constant awareness of who was sitting and who was leaving the zendo for a break. This was more than mindfulness—this was a stakeout.

At eleven o'clock Josh made a scene by stretching and grunting as he took a break. Alex had taken a break fifteen minutes earlier and Aileen took her break about the time that Josh returned. Maddie and even O'Doherty excused herself around eleven-thirty, handing the clappers to one of the zendo members before she ducked out of the room. Sometimes people came back in the middle of the half-hour sit, others returned during the next formal *kinhin* break. The way people kept coming and going was almost lax. It reminded Devon of a math problem as she mentally made notes of their entrances and exits without the luxury of being able to write anything down. It was driving her nuts. Alex came back in with Aileen. Josh came back before Maddie, but after O'Doherty. It was siesta time. Devon could almost hear the toilet flushing in Hans's house and felt her toes fidgeting as she wondered what Loch was up to, then decided he was probably incurably bored.

* * *

Ennui. Monotonous. Dreary. Blah . . . The room was cold; the floor was cold; the coffee was cold but Loch did not want any more anyway. He fidgeted quietly. People dressed in black flowed in and out of the house like a zendo merry-go-round. He wondered what they thought about while they stared at walls and if more than a few took a nap while sitting upright. What did staring at a blank wall have to do with enlightenment anyway?

He could hear the toilet flushing down the hall and kept tabs on every person's entrance and exit to and from the zendo to the house and back again. There was only one section of the walkway where his vision was blocked by the front porch, but that was because of the overhang and he didn't figure that much could happen in those ten feet to the front door. Every once in a while he saw Barney exit the house through his dog door, lift his leg on a tree or fence post as if he were making a sweep of the grounds, and then return through his own entrance. Occasionally, Loch could hear him barking at someone coming into the house or out on the street—which he seemed to think also belonged to him—but Loch had a feeling Barney spent more time chatting up the neighborhood foxes than being a watchdog. As the hours progressed, fewer and fewer people remained, and keeping track of who was meditating and who had left became easier. Loch relaxed and hoped that Devon was enjoying herself, if enjoyment was what one was supposed to achieve. He felt like he was actively meditating himself, that's how bored he was: ennui; monotonous; dreary; blah . . . What he wouldn't have done for a little action, even a fox in the henhouse.

It was well after midnight when the acolytes finally settled into the rhythm of their breathing. All of the earlier activity subsided, and for the next two and a half hours no one exited the zendo—no one even coughed. The night dragged on. Around two-thirty some of the zendo regulars, including Catri and Peter, left, and sometime between three and three-thirty in the morning, Hans, Maddie, Josh, and Sam left during *kinhin*, so Devon was alone with Jenny O'Doherty in the room. Devon followed O'Doherty around the room in a grown-up version of "Follow the Leader," but as soon as she sat, her skin began to crawl. O'Doherty was positioned directly behind Devon and would be staring at her exposed back for the next half-hour. It went against her every natural and professional inclination to sit quietly, openly susceptible to a potential suspect. Devon could not concentrate on her breathing, nor did she want to. She wanted to be ready to pounce should O'Doherty move even a muscle.

Devon was suddenly very relieved that Loch was on the other

end of her walkie-talkie, but that didn't help her concentration. There was a scratching sound at her feet. Her body jerked to one side, her eyes widened, and her mouth opened, ready to yell for help. The scratches were the minute movements of a field mouse under the barn, making its bed after foraging for seeds all night. Something rustled behind her and Devon whirled around.

O'Doherty was sitting very still, her half-lidded eyes not divulging whether she was staring at Devon or not. Devon put her hand to her back and pretended it was a cramp, not suspicion, that had caused her to move, then turned back to face the wall.

She hated it. Hated the flat, white expressionless wall without a flaw or detail to hang her thoughts on—hated the way the blankness was slowly driving her crazy. What was she doing? There were no answers here. The answers to Beka's murder were in action, not inaction. No amount of praying was going to help her figure out who had killed her friend. Her hands were clenched in fists as her breathing got more and more shallow. Time crept by.

There was another scrape at her feet, but this time her nerves were steady-steel; she was not about to flinch. She was too pissed to be scared. She did not want to waste any more time sitting, but her training and knowledge of Zen etiquette kept her from standing up and walking out. She heard the rustle of cloth. O'Doherty was definitely moving. Good, Devon thought, if she attacks me I can cuff the bitch and go home. She clenched her hand around the gun nestled in her robes.

Tension was building behind her. The air pressure suddenly dropped. O'Doherty moved. Devon's hand twitched.

The singing bowl let out a long mournful gong. The wood sticks clapped together. Devon did not bow to the wall; she did not want to. Instead, she scrambled to stand up, stamping her feet against the hard wood floor and straw mats, trying to wake up the flesh that had fallen asleep despite the activity of her mind. O'Doherty clapped again for *kinhin* but Devon dashed out of the door, grabbed her shoes and coat, and shot across the lawn to the house.

A fog had descended as so often happened in the winter, and the privet hedge groped at her hair as she pushed through the gate and almost ran into Hans and Sam returning from their break. One look at the monk in his black robes walking through the mist was enough to completely unnerve her. "All you need is a scythe, Hans, and you'd look like death itself!"

He held up his finger for silence.

Devon bowed obediently as Hans and Sam disappeared into the zendo, then she headed for the thin halo of light hovering above the doorway to the house. Inside, the coffee set-up looked well used. A number of cups were in the wastebasket next to the electric pot of hot water, but no one was sitting there now. She went to the bathroom, but the door was locked. She figured Maddie or Josh must be in there, so she slipped into the kitchen. "Loch?"

"Right here."

She walked across to him in the dark and stared at the velvet mist outside the window. "Anything unusual?"

"Nothing." He sounded bored. He'd wasted the entire night sitting around watching trees disappear into the low-riding clouds.

"This is ridiculous. Let's just question Maddie. Gary's probably already talked to Godwyn."

"No. I just called him. He's on his way back."

"I want to get out of here."

"What about dawn and enlightenment?"

"Spirituality is all very nice, but it doesn't solve anything. Life still sucks. People kill each other and no one—*no one*—is any more enlightened now than they were back in Buddha's time. The illusion is that we think we've progressed."

"He doesn't bark at some people and barks at others, why?"

She looked out the window at Barney nosing around the garden again instead of sleeping like any normal dog should at this hour. "He recognizes the regulars here," she told him.

"Maddie Fong is a regular?"

"Beka brought her and Alex a few years ago."

He seemed lost in thought.

"Loch? I want to go home."

"You were right."

"What?"

"I think you're right to pray," he said.

"Since when did prayer take the place of cold hard evidence?"

"It didn't, they simply coexist."

"You're a Zen master now?"

"I just wish I had your faith, Devon. I lost mine years ago." He squeezed her hand. "Hans says enlightenment comes when you most want to run away."

"You've been speaking with Hans?"

"He came to get a swig of brandy for his coffee."

She almost burst out laughing, but heard footsteps outside the kitchen door; Loch held his finger up to his lips.

"Devon?" Maddie whispered from the hallway. "Are you in there?"

Loch stepped back into the shadows and pointed to her pocket. She patted her walkie-talkie, then stepped out of the kitchen.

"Hey, Maddie, I was just looking for something cold to drink. I always get thirsty in there."

"Listen, I'm going to go. I want to be fresh for the service tomorrow."

"We were looking for you earlier," Devon told her.

"Alex told me. I can talk to your boyfriend tomorrow after the service."

"Talk to me now. All we need to know is where you were New Year's Eve and last Tuesday." Devon tried to make her queries as nonchalant as possible

"Is that all? Okay, can you walk me to my car? I'm a little nervous to be alone." Illuminated by the sensor light, Maddie looked like one of Broadway Bob's aliens, with an aura of mist surrounding her body.

They walked out of the house together. Devon dug her hands deep into the borrowed robe so that she had one hand on her gun and one on her walkie-talkie. This was the kind of set-up a murderer might go for, outside and away from everyone else.

"I got out about one-thirty, I think. I spent New Year's Eve with Hans at the ceremony on the North Shore. That's where I study."

"I didn't realize you were so serious about Buddhism."

"You never asked." Her words hung awkwardly in the fog.

Devon knew she had withdrawn from many of her closer friends over the past ten years, but didn't let that sway her primary aim—to find out Maddie Fong's whereabouts last Tuesday.

"I don't remember what I did," Maddie told her. "It was my day off . . . Oh yeah, I drove back from my folks' place in Rhode Island. I was up there for the holidays. I took the Orient Point Ferry. I probably still have the stub."

"Which ferry?"

"Two o'clock, I think. I got home around five, so that sounds about right."

"See, wasn't that painless?" Devon asked her.

"That's all you needed?"

"Unless you know where Godwyn is."

"I stayed with him the night after dim sum and came out here this afternoon. He said he was coming out to see you this morning. You didn't hook up with him?"

"Nope."

They walked to the edge of the privet where it was darkest and the light no longer shone.

"That's strange." Maddie's hand reached into her coat pocket. Devon tensed. Maddie pulled out her keys. "I'm going to Alex's. I'll call Godwyn's cellphone and see if I can find him."

"Give him my number. We need to talk."

Maddie stopped and pointed her keys at Devon, who involuntarily took a step backward as if the keys were loaded and dangerous. "You really think it's one of us." It was a statement of fact. She put her keys into the car door and got in. "It must be horrible to go through life not trusting anybody." She locked the door behind her.

Devon watched the lights of Maddie's car merge with the darkness. "It is."

The woods were always silent when the fog came in, and only the dripping of condensation from the branches of the trees gave her any sense of place and time. She turned around to start back to the zendo but saw dark footprints in one of the last clinging strips of snow. The ice shimmered with moisture and wouldn't last the night if the air continued to warm; that in turn would create an even denser fog. She knelt to look at the prints and let her hand hover above them—size ten, men's, she assessed. They were fresh, too, not

overly soaked like they would have been if Hans had made them earlier in the day. And that was what was strange to her; she could
understand seeing Hans's footprints, but these prints weren't heading toward the zendo. This person had headed back behind the
house via an overgrown path that skirted Hans's property. This was
the path they took when they were dumping underbrush or wanted
to go straight to the backyard . . .

She hung her penlight around her neck in order to keep one
hand free. The walkie-talkie crackled at her; she pulled it out. It
would be such a waste not to use it at least once tonight.

She pressed the call button again and used her throatiest voice.
"Go for Devon." He didn't respond. "You just wanted me to say, 'Go
for Devon,' didn't you?"

"You sound so sexy on radio."

"You sound sexier." They were always punchy about this time of
night. She stared down the path and chuckled at how much it looked
like some horror movie with too much fake fog obscuring the monster in the woods. "Loch?"

"Go for Loch," he teased.

She tried not to smile but couldn't help herself. "Someone's
been back behind the house in the past couple of hours. I found
footprints, pretty fresh. I'm going to follow them. Just wanted to let
you know."

"Wait for me!"

"So you can ruin my fun? Forget it. Besides, you're staking out
the zendo."

She stooped under tree limbs, trying to avoid stepping in the
tracks. Heavy billows of fog drifted in and out of the trees. She could
make out the prints easily where there was still snow, but in other
areas she needed to use her light to find the trail hiding in the soft
ground. It was surprisingly light in certain spots, since fog always
reflected light in a luminescent way, whether it was reflecting the
moon, stars, or just the snow's own whiteness.

"Devon?"

She pressed the button and answered him in her throaty voice,
"Go for Devon."

"We should play with these in bed sometime."

"Good-bye, Lochwood."

She could barely see the house except for where the lights illuminated the kitchen and Loch was hiding. In fact, if it hadn't been foggy she could have made him out quite easily. He was actually backlit, quite nicely, by the outside light. She heard something moving behind her and stopped. A low growl sounded from the undergrowth.

"Barney. Good boy, Barney. It's me, Devon." She spoke in her most friendly and nonthreatening voice. Slowly she turned around. The growl came deeper from his gut and became even more insistent. She reached behind her for a stick or a tree branch to pull herself away from his teeth, but an unmistakable chill rose up through her arm.

A phone began ringing behind her. She wheeled around. Godwyn was staring at her in unblinking terror.

His eyes were glazed, his mouth had dried blood on it—he had been pierced through his chest with a fishing spear which held him securely up against a tree. From the touch of him, she deduced that he'd been dead at least four hours—rigor had set in. The phone rang again from Godwyn's pocket. It was probably Maddie.

Something moved in the underbrush.

Barney lunged through the darkness toward her, almost knocking her to the ground as he leapt in the air.

"Get him off me!" The voice was Josh Shapiro's.

CHAPTER FORTY-FIVE

*The act of wondering is more potent than the answer, but we
cannot really deal with human evil until we've come to terms
with ourselves.*

— Hans Hokansen, Senior Monk, Sagaponack Zendo

Jo was not happy to be up and about in the middle of the night for
the second time that week, and her huffiness was plain as her heftiness unwedged itself from her Town Car. "The body's down there?"
She pointed down the allée of privet and melting snow.

Loch nodded. "We've held back any activity until Devon could get
in there and pull the footwear impressions. It's a delicate scene, Jo."

"Fog's a big help, too." Jo grunted. "I better go back and put on
my galoshes. Why couldn't you two find another body in the city? I
like it better when you wake up their M.E. in the middle of the
night. It's as cold as the morgue out here."

"Next time we'll try to find a considerate killer who only attacks
in daylight and summer months."

"That's all I'm asking." She made her way back to the car to don
galoshes and heavier socks.

Devon made her way back up the trail to where she had wrapped
the yellow police tape. Frank had not arrived yet, and since working
a scene at its most fresh was paramount, she had already started.

"How's it going in there?" Loch asked.

"I found my beeper." He looked at her questioningly. "It was on
Godwyn's belt, with Beka's cellphone number on it."

"We'll need to search the Shapiro house to see if we can find
that."

"That's what I'm thinking. Anyway, I'm ready for Jo to come in.
I've taken a ton of pictures, but I'd rather not move him before
Frank gets here with the van."

"Videotaping in this pea soup may not be worth squat."

"I trust his eye." She began to walk Loch through the scene she was still busily reconstructing in her head. "Godwyn's prints are the tracks I followed in from the street. Did you find his car?"

"It's parked around the corner."

"I wonder why he was being so secretive?" she wondered, then returned to her recitation of facts. "We also have tracks coming out here from the house and then returning."

Loch looked at his notes. "Eleven o'clock, Josh took his first break. We'll know when Jo gives us time of death."

"The thing is, why did Josh come back if he'd already killed him?"

"He forgot something?" Loch made a note to grill the suspect on that point as soon as he got back to the precinct.

"The footwear impressions are definitely Josh's shoes. You can see here that the older impressions are less defined because of the melting snow, and here's an example of his tracks made later." She showed Loch the shoes she'd pulled off Josh before they carted him away to the station. Doc Martens. "There were Doc Martens imprints at the studio the other night, too. I'm not sure they're the same shoes yet, but they're the same brand."

"Hans says the spear is his." Loch filled her in on what information he had collected. "It was hanging by that whale pelvis in front of his house."

"Josh could have taken it on his way into the house, then gone out the back door."

"Did Josh know the house well enough to know where the back door was?"

"It's not rocket science, Loch."

"True, but every other murder has been meticulously planned, why not this one? And how'd he know that Godwyn was out there?"

"They must have talked."

"You think Josh set him up outside to watch the zendo so he could kill him?"

"That's your job."

"Never stopped you before."

She pointed through the mist to where the lights in the kitchen could now be seen. "From where I found Godwyn, I could see you in the kitchen. You were backlit, very nicely I might add. Maybe Godwyn was taking your picture."

"Without his camera?" he asked gruffly.

"I was staring at you when Barney attacked Josh." Devon was still following her train of thought.

"So they knew I was here." He had one eyebrow raised. "How?"

"I'm ready," Jo interrupted. She was not dressed in Tyvek whites tonight, but then neither was Devon, she had had to make do with what she'd been wearing inside the zendo.

"This way, Jo." Loch held back the branches of privet that led around the crime scene. "We're going through the garden to avoid making more unnecessary tracks."

"Great." She plodded after them, expounding on her displeasure with as many guttural sounds as possible. "No offense, Halsey, but I don't get the glamour of living out here."

"That's because you're only meeting the dead. Of course, they're nicer than the summer people!"

Jo pulled out her penlight and shined it into Godwyn's obsidian eyes. "Looks like he was drugged."

"Did you check that?" Loch asked, pointing to a green thermos lying on its side under Godwyn's body.

"I'm leaving it until the van arrives. I don't even have anything to bag with yet," Devon told him, pointing to Josh's shoes secured in a paper grocery bag.

"Probably Norflex, like the last two," Jo said under her breath.

"Probably." Devon appreciated Jo's acknowledgment.

Jo began her assessment. "Nice carving job. Just one thrust through his gut, like Gabe, only cleaner. No wounds around the eyes either."

"The murderer didn't know him as well as Gabe and Beka?" Loch wondered out loud.

"Josh and Godwyn are pretty close . . ." Devon started to say.

"Maybe he came back to make sure he was dead," Loch finished her sentence.

Jo pulled out her thermometer and checked the temperature of the air. "Twenty degrees." Then she stuck it in the ear of the body and waited. "Rigor is set and the body temperature is seventy-three degrees; I figure the loss is an average of five degrees per hour with this cold weather. It's five-thirty now. We're looking at time of death somewhere between eleven and twelve, but closer to eleven."

Devon checked Loch's list of times people exited the zendo during *kinhin*, and nodded as he pointed to where he had written, "*11:10-Josh. Back-11:40.*"

That was that.

"The other marks were made postmortem again?"

"Would you let somebody carve you up if you were still alive?" Jo quipped.

"Devon, make sure you get the ideogram on his chest. You can work on that here and fax Isshu from Hans's office."

"I'll come in and finish up," she told him.

"By the time you're done here it'll be time for the service. Frank will bring the evidence back to the labs and start processing it. You stay. It's all nuts and bolts from here. We won't need you," Loch said.

"I can skip the service."

"Would you follow an order for once in your life? I want you on the carving and the tape. Oh, and take Beka's uncles to the airport."

"That's not police work!"

"It's the most important part of police work, taking care of the victim's family. Check in with me after you get the videotape from Alex, there might be something else to nail into Shapiro's coffin."

"I can hear you two whispering!" Jo chided halfheartedly.

They moved away and watched silently as she finished her prelim. "I'm done. Get that thermos to the lab after you print it. Brennen, I'll see you for the autopsy. Early today. I'm going straight in. What time will you be there?"

"You tell me."

"Eight o'clock."

Devon opened her mouth to object but caught Loch's eye and kept quiet.

"Eight o'clock, then."

"We'll have this wrapped up before the Mr. Imamuras leave today." He patted Devon on the shoulder and motioned for Jo to follow him back around the perimeter of the scene. "And congratulations."

Devon looked at him questioningly.

"You were right."

Frank walked up to join them, mumbling something about never getting a night off. Jo stopped to mumble with him, then let Loch and Devon catch him up on the details of the evening. "So, where's DeBritzi?" he asked.

"Staking out Godwyn's apartment in the city."

"He's not there." Frank looked at the corpse.

"He's on his way to the precinct now to question Shapiro. I'm going to finish up with the folks in the zendo."

"Devon? Loch?" They could hear Aileen's frantic voice from the road arguing with the duty officer who was having trouble getting her to stay behind the police tape. "Let me in there! Is Devon okay? Devon?"

"Shit!" Devon looked at her watch. It was five-thirty a.m. She headed down the path and yelled, "Hey, Leenie I'm fine! There's been another murder, though."

"Oh my god!"

"How many others are going to do the same thing?" Loch whispered in her ear.

"A few, Maddie, Alex . . . a few regulars will come back, too."

"That makes it easier. I can get everybody questioned that way." He headed down the path toward Devon's friend. Aileen was visibly upset but Devon and Frank had work to do and moved away as Loch took her gently by the arm and led her into the zendo where he had the rest of the group waiting to be questioned.

Devon began to point out what she'd covered. "I've cast the footwear impressions but there are no prints on the weapon, or the thermos there. Do you have the black light with you?"

"You want to scan the area before they come to take him down?" She nodded.

"Bad way to go, skewered to a tree like that."

"If he was drugged maybe he didn't feel too much." She didn't believe what she was saying, but half hoped it was true and God had died without pain.

Frank began to walk along Josh's trail, stooping every few steps to pick something up with a pair of tweezers, which he then dropped inside individually marked bags that Devon held open for him. She labeled while he continued to search the area for any traces of hair, fabric, or blood that might prove helpful.

Devon borrowed a sketchpad and some charcoal from Hans and began to copy the carving on Godwyn's chest. His skin was so dark that Frank had to hold the light on him to illuminate the markings. Whether she was getting adept at Japanese characters or Josh had not finished writing the message, Devon was not sure.

* * *

The fog was finally lifting as dawn began to creep across the horizon, faintly at first as if still shy of the dark. Devon had to blink a few times to make sure the sky was changing and wasn't still black, but a definite film of gray was beginning to wrap over the black tree limbs still clicking in the wind. The breeze would push the fog back to sea and they'd be able to see much more clearly in a couple of hours.

"The motive still isn't plain," Loch surmised.

"If Josh was cast by Gabe in the *Having Hand* sculpture and if that meant he slept with Gabe, and keeping his indiscretions a secret was important to his career," she pointed out, "perhaps Beka found out about Josh, and Gabe, and Edilio. Maybe the whole serial killer idea was a mistake."

"Sounds like serial monogamy instead." They began to walk toward the road together, not like the mod squad this time. They were too tired to be cool.

"I don't think Josh could have done Todd, Loch."

"We may never know what happened to Todd," he reminded her.

Even if Loch and Gary proved that Josh killed Gabe and Beka, as well as Godwyn and Edilio, could they prove that he was responsible for Todd, or the other missing college kids Detective Freesia brought out of her files every New Year's? Was anyone responsible, or were they simply arbitrary, accidental deaths?

Sam Daniels was waiting for them as they came under the police tape and could barely contain himself as he demanded to know what had happened. Loch told him that they had Gabe and Beka's killer, then paused because he was not sure what else to say.

"What about my brother?"

"I can't promise anything."

"Nobody can ever promise anything!" He lashed out at a nearby car, kicking the tire and growling with despair. "It's not fair!"

Devon reached out to touch his arm but he shook her off and headed down the road. She was about to start after him, when she noticed the way Loch was watching Sam.

"He looks like a trapped tiger."

"What do you mean by that?"

"Didn't both brothers have a thing for Beka?"

"Yes."

"Get that videotape, honey. We may be looking at Todd all wrong."

CHAPTER FORTY-SIX

When you can do nothing, what can you do?

—Zen koan

The interrogation room was bare except for a desk with steel hooks on it for cuffing and a window with bars on it. Outside in the hallway was a metal kind of ballet beam, used to cuff prisoners while they awaited processing or interrogation. Every year at Halloween the officers handcuffed a mannequin to wait alongside the collars, and this year they had dressed it up like Santa Claus and left it out. Josh was cuffed next to Santa, despite his protests. Loch was not about to trust a killer, whether elf or surgeon.

"I told you," Josh complained again, "Godwyn told me he was meeting Devon behind the house. When he didn't show up at the zendo I got worried, and that's when I found him."

"Very plausible, Mr. Shapiro. Except for one thing: Why didn't you just ask Devon where Godwyn was if you were so worried?"

"He told me we had to act as if nothing was going on so no one would get suspicious. Besides, it's silent as a tomb in that place. Have you ever been inside a zendo? You don't just stop somebody and say, 'Hey, I thought you were meeting God out back.' They're Buddhists. They don't even believe in God!"

"Cute." Loch smiled evilly at his villain. "You've been practicing that one, haven't you?"

Josh was sweating. "When Devon came out, I figured I was supposed to meet her in the back. So I went back there and found Godwyn. I didn't know what to do!"

"Murderers rarely know what to do when they get caught."

"I swear the only reason I was there is because Godwyn told me to come and meet him."

"I was watching from the kitchen, Josh. Be very careful with your lies."

"Why would I lie? I could see you watching." Josh was beginning to sound panicked. "It's the truth!"

"Of course it is. Nobody ever lies to us, do they, Gary?"

"Never. We trust all of our murderers to tell us the complete and honest truth."

"Didn't the footprints in the mud show you I'd been there only once?"

"Actually, we have your tracks going to and from the zendo and then one set returning later. You took two breaks, Josh—one at eleven o'clock and one at three-thirty, remember?"

Josh nodded miserably.

Gary outlined the crime the way he and Loch saw it, laying it all out for their suspect so he would know they knew he was guilty. "The only thing I don't get is why you returned to the scene."

"I didn't."

"Were you stalking Devon?" Loch felt himself burning with anger at the very thought that Devon might have been a target of this sick man's mind.

"I thought she was the murderer."

"Right, Detective Halsey looks exactly like a murderer. Was it the long hair that gave her away?" Loch taunted him, hoping for some outburst that would show Josh for what he truly was, a psychopath.

"You're the murderer, Shapiro. Come on and admit it!" Gary slammed his fist down on the table. "You had an affair with Gabe and who knows who else, and you wanted to hush it up. Didn't want your showpiece wife to find out you jerked the sausage both ways?"

"I'm straight!"

"Then why are your hands in his sculpture at the loft in New York?"

"Because of Beka. He cast Beka's lovers along with his own, that's why he called it *Having Hand*."

"Did Katiti know about you two?"

"Katiti likes to think I was a virgin before I met her. She'd kill me if she knew about Beka. She's already pissed off about Alex and me."

"Is there anybody you didn't fuck?"

"It was the '80s! Of course not!"

"Gary, do you remember what we found in Godwyn's clothes? Something we might have missed in all the excitement?" Loch turned his back on Josh for two reasons—to make him feel uncomfortable as a nonentity and to entice him into an attack. Josh did not move.

Gary picked up the copy of the inventory sheet from Godwyn's belongings and began to read it out loud. "Keys, a wallet with twenty-five dollars cash, green card, New York State driver's license, matches, a pack of Dunhills, another set of keys, Devon's beeper."

"Did you think planting her beeper on your victim would throw us off?"

"I'm not stupid." Josh glowered at Detective DeBritzi.

"Two sets of keys? What do you bet one goes to Gabe's loft in the city?" Loch said to his partner.

"Stake my pension on it."

"Make sure Frank pulls the prints off those keys," Loch told him.

"Already on it."

"See, Josh? We already have you placed at the scene, now we're going to link this murder with the others. How many are there? Was Todd one of your victims?"

"God no."

"You went back to get the keys from Godwyn, didn't you? Why'd you need his keys, don't you have your own pair?"

"Maybe he borrowed Godwyn's set to kill Edilio," Gary suggested.

"I'm telling you, I only went once! When I found him." Tears filled Josh's eyes. "Wait! My shoes were damp when I put them on the first time. Someone must have taken them by accident."

"Maybe the real murderer tried to frame you—that must be it. Don't you think?" Gary turned to his partner and winked. "And you just now remembered this vital piece of information? Isn't it amazing how that always happens?"

"It's true!" Josh complained.

"Well that explains it, doesn't it?" Lochwood mocked him. "I for one am relieved. What about you, Gary?" The two detectives bantered back and forth as Josh squirmed in his seat, getting more and more uncomfortable.

"If Dr. Shapiro says its true, it must be, Gary. He is a doctor, after all. Should we release him? Obviously, he's telling the truth."

"Obviously."

There was a knock on the door. "This what you were looking for?" A uniformed officer handed DeBritizi a bag.

"Well, I'll be. Beka Imamura's cellphone. Do you know how long we've been looking for this, Mr. Shapiro?" Gary stared into the murderer's eyes.

Loch shook his head as if trying to get his thoughts around the discrepancies in Josh's testimony. They had footprints going to and from the murder scene right back to the zendo. Why had he gone back to the body? What had he forgotten?

Loch jumped up and poked Josh hard in the chest. "What were you going to carve on Godwyn? That's what's missing, isn't it! What was Godwyn's koan? You got part of it done, but something, or someone, disturbed you."

Josh glared at Loch, then uttered those four words Loch hated most in the English language, "I want my lawyer."

CHAPTER FORTY-SEVEN

When your activity of mind is exhausted and your capacity for feeling comes to a dead end, if something should take place not unlike the cat springing upon a mouse, then in a flash great livingness surges up.

—A ZEN MASTER

Devon lit a stick of incense and tried to say something about Beka, but the words stuck in her heart and only tears answered her desire to speak. Her mother stepped up to the front of the room and took her daughter's hand. She did not bow to Buddha or light incense, she simply turned to face Beka's friends and family and said with an almost whimsical smile, "What I will remember most about Beka is her dancing, on the beach, on Manhattan rooftops, in the potato fields outside our home. Anywhere she felt needed movement, anywhere that felt lonely, she danced. She was like a daughter to me and I grieve with you, Biz, Bert. I will always see her dancing out of the corner of my eye." Devon and her mother sat down, then Alexandra walked up to the front of the room.

Alex bowed to Buddha and lit the incense, then with a voice rough from crying spoke softly, "She was the last Isadora. That is all. She was the last—forever."

Others stood and spoke or read poems for the dearly departed. The scent of sandalwood infused the air.

After the memorial service Devon and her parents took Uncle Biz and Bert to the airport where the coffin carrying Beka's body awaited its final journey home. Devon promised to come to Hawaii soon, then returned to the East End feeling empty and worn out. She still had to deal with Alex and the videotape. Despite Alexandra's vulnerability and the soft words she had spoken at the service, she was a brutal negotiator when it came to retrieving the tape. It took two hours of haggling over the legalities before Devon finally got her hands on New Year's Eve, 1984.

She called into work to see if she should come in, but Frank told her everything was moving smoothly. "Stay home and watch the tape, Dev," he suggested. "We've got Shapiro on Godwyn, and it won't take much to prove he killed Beka and Gabe. Right now Brennen's more concerned about finding a link to Todd."

Josh, a murderer. She could barely believe it. They had already poked holes into his alibi for New Year's Eve, and it looked as if Katiti, while innocent, had lied about his whereabouts for the entire evening at 75 Main. According to the maitre d', he had ducked out for over an hour and tipped the man to keep his mouth shut. Josh maintained he was having an affair but wasn't able to produce the woman.

It was four o'clock when Devon finally made it home, and after a quick romp with Boo she was able to sit down, pop the video into her VCR, and collapse on the couch. Boo seemed overly concerned about her well-being and carefully sniffed her to make sure that she was all in one piece. Once his investigation proved she was whole and intact, he dabbed her with his tongue and laid down at her feet. Her body felt the way it did after she'd been in a boat for a long time, as if the earth were moving too fast for her legs. She'd been up for yet another thirty-six hours, the third time in six days, or something like that.

"What ya watchin'?" Aileen asked as she came through the kitchen door.

"The infamous videos—both of them. Alex finally let me have it after I promised to give her my firstborn."

"She didn't."

Devon brandished the legal waiver she had had to sign before getting hold of the tapes. "A testament to the '90s, if there ever was one. Sign, sue, or die."

The second tape was on the table waiting to be played, but the first was already running.

"So this is it?"

"In the flesh."

"That's so cool."

"If these disappearances are all linked it'll be cool, otherwise it'll just be depressing."

Aileen looked at the screen. "I can't believe Alex shot them tooting up."

There were lines on the table and Sam, Josh, Alex, Godwyn, Maddie, and Sam were snorting coke and laughing. "I think Alex shot them doing everything—at least that's what I'm hoping."

* * *

"Good stuff," Beka was saying on the screen. "Sometimes I feel like I could dance forever with shit like this."

There was the sound of a door slamming and footsteps coming up the stairs.

"What the hell is that?" Todd stepped into the camera frame as Sam tried to hide the stuff. It was too late. "Are you all idiots?" Todd yelled. He threatened to tell their parents, and leave for home at once.

Beka sidled up to him and handed him the straw. "Come on, Todd. It won't hurt. I do it all the time."

It took some convincing, but finally Todd did his first line, looked into the camera, and said, "I don't feel a thing. Should I try some more?"

Everyone—Maddie, Josh, Alex, Beka, even Sam—laughed.

"Go for it," Josh said.

* * *

Aileen put the kettle on the stove and threw two teabags into the pot. "So, Josh killed Beka and Gabe? Hard to believe."

"It is. I have to admit I'm grateful that it wasn't someone I cared for."

"But Josh? I mean, who'd have *thunk?*" Aileen stood up. "You gonna watch the whole thing?"

"Only time I've ever gotten to work from my couch and eat popcorn!"

"You could fast-forward to where he disappears."

"Might miss something. Was there something you wanted to watch on TV?"

"No, no," Aileen said in a mock-*Dragnet* voice as she headed for the kitchen. "Wouldn't want to interfere with police work. You want some tea?"

Devon nodded, slouched back, and draped her legs across the arm of the couch. "I can't believe they did so many drugs."

"Josh doesn't seem the type." Aileen wasn't listening. "I mean, I've been taking care of their dog for a year now and Katiti seems more like a murderer than Josh. He's too pussy-whipped to be a serial killer."

Devon laughed out loud. "Don't worry, they're picking her up for questioning, too."

"Loch's interviewing her?"

"Interrogating."

"I should go check on their dog. Katiti will forget all about him." The kettle began to whistle. Aileen poured the hot water into a pot, threw in a few teaspoons of sugar and a little bit of milk, and fit the tea cozy over it. "It's light and sweet like you like it." She placed it on the living room table in front of Devon, then brought her an empty mug.

"You've been a real godsend, Aileen. Thanks."

"It's the least I can do." She poured Devon's tea and handed it to her. "I'm going to drive over to the Shapiro house and tuck their dog in for the night."

"Take Boo with you, so I know you're safe. Oh, by the way, Detective Freesia from Missing Persons is coming out tonight for a little R&R. She'll be thrilled to know we solved our case, but not hers." Devon yawned. She wasn't going to be much fun when Carol arrived; maybe they'd order carryout from Concha D'Oro's.

Aileen moved to the door and grabbed the spotted leash that matched his spotted color. "Come on, Boo! Let's go for a ride in the car!"

Another phrase in his vocabulary—the dalmatian jumped up and raced out the door with all the abandon and excitement of a puppy.

Devon sat up, propped the pillows behind her back until they were in the perfect position for lounging, and sipped her tea. She inhaled the bergamot scent coming up from her mug. It was Prince of Wales Earl Grey, her favorite. The video had the time in the bottom right corner; it was 10:31 p.m. when she saw herself walk across the screen for the first time.

The picture on the screen slowly became more and more frenetic as the loft got fuller and fuller and the party began to wind up like a gathering storm of people and music, a maelstrom in the making. Alex must have time-lapsed some of the earlier scenes; if Devon remembered correctly, sometimes she let the camera record unattended, other times she walked around and shot handheld. The first tape ran out just after everyone kissed each other, popped champagne corks, and blew up the small arsenal of firecrackers on the roof—the digital counter on the bottom of the screen turned to 12:00. Devon put in the second tape, on which Alex had written: *"12:02 and Beyond."*

She poured herself another cup of tea, grateful for the copper tea cozy that kept it hot despite the hour that had elapsed. Devon liked to sip hot drinks while they were still steaming. Even though she'd spent years as a street cop, she had never gotten used to drinking anything lukewarm and despised cold tea or coffee, unless it was iced in the summer. Iced. God had been literally iced; Beka and Gabe were in deep freeze—along with what was left of her faith in friends.

She missed something on the screen and reached for the remote control, dropped it, picked it up, pressed search-rewind and watched Beka and Todd move backwards across the screen, then looked at her watch.

Time was playing tricks on her again, slipping through her fingers like so many grains of sand. It was still early, six o'clock, but Aileen had been gone for over an hour. She wondered if she should worry, but reminded herself that Josh was the murderer—there wasn't anyone running around loose anymore with a desire to kill the loftmates, or her friends. Her eyes teared spontaneously; she must be getting her period.

She poured the last of the tea into her mug and leaned back to watch more closely what she had missed a few seconds, or was it minutes, ago? She looked at her watch again, six-thirty. She was losing time.

What if something had happened to Aileen?

She didn't know what she'd do if she had to face the loss of another friend—have a nervous breakdown, probably. Another tear pressed out of the corner of her eye and dribbled down her cheek. Aileen was safe; Josh was the murderer. She was just walking Josh's dog. Everything was fine.

She felt a cold chill prickle across her scalp. They had picked up Katiti, hadn't they? She reached for the phone and called Loch's cell. "How you feeling?"

"Exhausted."

"Have you guys picked up Katiti yet?"

"They left a little while ago."

"How long?"

"Half an hour."

"Shit! Aileen left over an hour ago and she's not back yet."

"That's a long time."

"Loch, if something happens to Aileen . . ."

"I'm calling for backup now."

Her heart raced as she stood up and swayed dizzily. That happened sometimes when she was tired—low blood-pressure or something, that's what Beka used to tell her. She hung her head between her knees for a second and then looked at the TV. Something had happened that she wanted to see, but she had to go. Aileen might be in danger. She had to go.

Then she heard the sound of car wheels crunching up the gravel drive. "Aileen?" Devon yelled. "I got so worried! They haven't picked up Katiti yet."

There was no reply.

"Aileen?" Her heart pounded heavily against her chest. Devon started to reach for her belt holster and hesitantly called out.

"Katiti?"

The doorknob began to twist. It opened slowly.

Devon reached for the gun secured to her back.

A gust of black and white energy swept through the door, as Boo raced into the kitchen and toward his mistress.

"She wasn't there." Aileen shut the door behind her.

"Shit. You scared me." Devon leaned back and sighed.

"Now that's hard to do."

"Was Katiti there? Loch said they're arresting her."

"Everything's fine."

Devon settled back on the couch, pressed search-rewind again, and watched as Beka walked backwards across the dance floor into the loft hallway. She must have danced all night long, but that was the point of a party to Beka—an excuse to do what she did all day long, with more abandon. Devon felt sadness creeping over her again as she watched her friend dance—so young and full of spirit.

Boo licked her face. "Sit down, Boo! I can't see." He sat down but stared at her like the RCA dog. She bopped his head with a resounding pat.

Onscreen, Gabe was talking to Todd and holding his hands up to the sparkling lights dripping down from the parachuted ceiling. Was he making a pass? She tried to imagine what he might say . . . *Come on, Todd. Let's slip down to my studio and I'll make a cast of your hands for Beka. She loves to have mementos of her lovers—she's a serial slut.*

It looked as if Todd nodded his head, but then Alex moved the camera and focused on Godwyn flirting with some girl with bushy brown hair—Katiti.

The camera kept panning back and forth across the room in the most aggravating motions—too experimental for a surveillance tape—but Alex had been an experimental filmmaker back then. She had no idea that fifteen years later the video might provide a clue in an unsolved mystery. Todd was talking with someone else in the corner—Alex spun the camera back across the room and focused on Godwyn—then it was a close-up of Josh and Sam—then back to Todd. Devon pressed pause and stared hard at the frame. He was standing in the way of the camera's point of view and she found herself trying to see around him by repositioning herself on the couch. Obviously, it did not work.

She pressed zoom on the remote control, but it only zoomed in on Todd's back. She zoomed it back out so the picture would include the entire room. There had to have been three hundred people at that party and fifty of them seemed to be onscreen. She pressed the button for the video to move frame by frame. She picked up a pencil to make a note of the meter setting, then dropped the pencil. Her wrist felt funny. She shook it in the air, picked up the pencil again, and wrote down the numbers in order to return to the frame later. Then she picked up the remote to press play, and dropped it to the floor. She reached to the floor and found herself reeling with dizziness from the sudden movement. "I'm whacked," she complained.

"You want some more tea?" Aileen picked up the pot, waving it back and forth in the air

"I drank it all, sorry."

Aileen put the empty pot back down on the table.

"Can you tell who Todd is talking to?"

"It's too grainy. How can you make out anybody on it?"

"We can always digitize the images later. I should have watched it on Alex's big-screen TV, but she was so upset by the memorial service and Godwyn that she headed back to the city for an emergency session with her therapist."

"Like therapy could ever help Alex." Aileen smirked.

"There. He's moved. I think I need glasses." She squinted. Her vision was definitely not what it used to be. "Who is that?"

The phone rang. Aileen picked up the portable next to Devon but did not bother to answer. "Devon?" It was Loch. "Leenie isn't there and Katiti's unconscious. They're rushing her to the ER . . ."

"Oh my god! Leenie, what happened?" Devon tried to sit up. "Are you alright?"

Aileen turned down the answering machine. "Fine. I'm fine. Everything went fine." She was studying the picture of Todd still hovering on the TV. "It looks like Gabe with Todd."

Devon looked back at the television. "But who's next to him?" The picture was still advancing frame by frame.

Aileen squinted her eyes. "I think it's me." She leaned toward the person in question. "Yes, it's definitely me." She smiled down at Devon. "You remember me, don't you? The one who everyone hires to watch their dogs but forgets to ask to the reunion and dim sum."

"You wanted to go? You hate them." Devon blinked hard at her friend, then at the TV.

"You have no idea how much."

Devon was beginning to have one. She was aware that the numb feeling in her wrist had gradually moved up her arms and legs, and they were more anesthetized than after sitting an hour at the zendo. She began to wiggle her extremities, fingers first, then toes, slowly, so Aileen wouldn't notice.

"I was never as important to you as they were. I was your best friend before Beka." Devon looked sadly at her friend—they had known each other since they were in kindergarten. How could she have missed this?

Aileen cackled at her. "You should see your face! This is rich. I'm so glad I waited for this." She leaned down and looked Devon squarely in the eye. "You don't have the vaguest idea who I am anymore. You just think I'm Gabe's sidekick, don't you? Well, I was the mastermind! Me!" Aileen's eyes gleamed at her.

"What are you talking about?" Devon decided to play dumb.

"We were a team, in the most avant-garde sense of the word."

"I thought Beka and Gabe were the team."

"Beka was his biggest mistake. Gabe and me understood each other, but he thought Beka would make him look good. What'd he think I'd do, keep pet-sitting for the rest of my goddamn life? I'm not trophy-wife enough? I hate the Hamptons!" Her voice became more irate.

"You and Gabe?" Devon slumped into the couch. She was stunned.

"Don't play dumb blonde with me. I know all of your tricks, Devon Halsey, but you know none of mine."

"You've been five steps ahead of us all along," Devon agreed.

"And don't you forget it."

"You've committed the perfect crime."

"*Crimes*." She enunciated the "s" with a hiss.

"How many?"

"More than you can count. It wasn't just a New Year's gig, you know. We had work to do. Of course, Gabe was looking for more. He got tired of getting away with it. He had to dump a few in the river just to see if anyone would notice. You cops are all so busy. You'd be amazed what someone can get away with if they're patient and own a lot of land." She had moved into the kitchen as if getting too near Devon were dangerous. "Gabe always liked being the center of attention, and now he is. He wanted people to know. I mean, how many body parts can one artist cast and exhibit before they want everyone to know how they got their models?" She laughed.

"You cast Todd's hands?" Devon asked.

"We did more than that." Aileen seemed to be smiling fondly over some memory. "Gabe was not a wannabe artist. He was a real one. No one really knows how dedicated he was, except me. He wanted to capture the true essence of life, and it was my technique that helped him achieve that. And Todd was our first. It was supposed to end up differently. It was my fault, really, but you know, I just couldn't help myself. I mean, there they were, those two little breathing holes, and I just wondered what would happen if I plugged them. Nothing happened. I mean, he had passed out anyway. He didn't even know he was dying. We cast him until rigor set, then dumped him. It was our little secret, and the rest of you were so distraught. Looking for Todd. Hoping he'd return. Gabe loved it—he hung out with them just to watch the demise of their little clique, and kept Beka around like a souvenir. The next year we found someone just like poor Todd, drunk and confused. It was so easy. We put them out of their misery and he had his models. Gabe liked having willing models."

There was nothing more willing than a corpse, Devon thought to herself. Her arms felt heavy and detached from her body. Norflex. She did not know how to fight the drug, but she knew how to fight the maniac in front of her. If only she could keep her body from betraying her.

"No one even missed the 1985 kid. Poor Freesia—we could add a few more to her measly little list. It's much longer. Much!"

"Where's Todd?"

"You can die with the same question you've always had. He disappeared. That's what happened to him!"

A knife appeared in Aileen's hand; Devon wasn't sure where it had come from because she had blinked and the reflexes of her eyelids were taking longer than a split second. They were as heavy as one of Gabe's sculptures—heavy as *Having Hand*. Her heart flip-flopped. All those people in the sculpture were dead? She had to work hard to force her eyelids open. She did not stare at the knife. She simply knew it was there and meant for her, and she found herself wondering what koan Aileen planned to carve on her body.

"I told her not to marry Gabe. She wanted to marry an artist, though—to be a famous couple. She had no idea what we were up to after hours."

Devon could almost hear Hans telling her to be mindful—stay in the moment. She began to count her breaths and focus on her lungs expanding as she inhaled and collapsing as she exhaled. The deeper she breathed the quicker it would appear she was going under from the Norflex, and the less defensive Aileen would become.

"It was all about art for Gabe. Everything was art. Getting away with it, having you around—and Loch—that was part of the art form." Her eyes narrowed. "And he leaves me out of his will!"

"You saw his will?"

"What am I, chopped liver in the chicken section?"

"How'd you get the will?"

"I walk Goldstein's dog. Did you forget that, too? He was going to sell the land! He was going to dump me!" Aileen's voice went up a notch. "I hate the Halseys! Osbornes! Daytons! Every stuck-up Puritan that ever settled this land! Not a Bonacker, not a whaler in the bunch! How do you think your perfect family is going to like losing both you and Beka? I just wish I could've gotten all of them. All of you 'I used to be an artist but now I play the stock market' types. You all deserve to die! Look at it out here! There's no place to even live anymore!" She was talking so fast that spit sprayed from her mouth and her eyes bulged with hatred. "I can't even afford a one-room apartment in my own hometown!"

"I gave you a place—"

"We used to be sisters!" Aileen snarled back at her. "Then you got that fancy-schmancy private-school roommate—hot twat, Beka. 'This is my best friend, Beka!'" She imitated Devon's voice.

Devon felt sadness creeping into her heart. She had tried to include Aileen in her city life, but she was young and people change. Her girlhood pals were different than her young adult friends; even she and Beka had begun to outgrow each other as they matured— that's what happened. That was life. Wasn't it?

"You think you're so nice to let me live with you and care for your stupid dog? You don't know how to be a friend, Devon, anymore than you would know how to be a wife. Beka told me what you two argued about. She called and talked to me, just like your mother called me, and Godwyn stopped by to chat . . . Everyone talks to Aileen."

"Godwyn?"

"All he did was talk about *Beka this, Beka that*, and how he was under contract to shoot for *Hamptons Magazine* now. Mr. Big Society Photographer. He was going to be one of them! So I saved him from selling out. I just told him you needed him to stake out the back of the zendo and I'd bring him some tea. God, the English love their damn tea."

Boo nudged Devon's hand impatiently with his nose; she couldn't pat him, though. Her motor skills were failing just as Beka's had failed in that last attempt to escape across the lawn of their estate. He licked her fingers and flipped her hand again so it landed on his head. She could feel the blood begin to flow into her fingers; he lowered his head to the couch and gazed up at her adoringly while supporting her hand completely by his head. Now, if she could just get her fingers to move. She began to wiggle them back and forth underneath her back toward her gun. Aileen knew she kept a gun on her at all times. Would she notice?

"It was so easy to frame Beka. Freesia didn't even come down to the lobby to meet her." She waved the knife at Devon as if she were carving up the air. "And Edilio, why would Beka meet him in the city? Men are such idiots. Look at Gabe! He thought I'd just let him leave town. Everything else was perfect; except for the Tyvek suit, but stupid you told me years ago why you have to change them for every scene." That wasn't quite what Devon had told her, but she didn't correct her. "You told me how to get away with it! Who knows better than a Crime Scene detective how to cover it up?"

Devon felt like a fool. She knew better than to berate herself, though, what she needed to do was focus on the present. She breathed deeply, seeking the right words to stop the nightmare she was in. "What's my koan, Aileen?"

"I pet-sit for Barney, too. There you are trying to figure out who Barney barks at and it doesn't even occur to you that he lets me pass him by without so much as a sniff."

"My koan?" Devon's voice was falsely deep and steady.

"I thought you'd ask about the hair. I wanted you to ask about the hair."

"You used a plastic bag."

"How'd you know that?"

"I just figured it out."

"That was good, wasn't it? Put a bag around her hair and chop-chop. Spread the extra around the altar—you told me about that, too. If you fake a scene you have to fake the trace. I'm good, aren't I?"

"You're very smart," Devon agreed with her.

"You liked the koans, huh? Those were for you. I knew you wouldn't be able to figure them out right away. But Gabe hoped that Heron kid would get you involved—too bad he didn't get to see it." She snickered to herself. "That's the problem working in an uncontrolled environment like the East River—here we control everything."

"Beka gave me the answer to her koan."

"How could she?" Aileen was stunned.

Devon could see how it had happened now, and let the camera in her mind play through the events that had led up to Beka's death. Aileen had shown up dressed in Crime Scene gear and told her Devon was working, then playfully, in all her enormous friendliness, handed them the bottle of bourbon. "To Todd," she had toasted, thereby drugging Beka and Gabe. They had hung out, drinking bourbon. Maybe Aileen had told Beka she had information from Detective Freesia about Todd. Maybe something in her manner had made Gabe suspicious, so he took her aside to find out the game plan. That was when Beka called Devon and left her message. What had happened then? How much did she know before she died? Had she walked in on Gabe and Aileen arguing? Somehow she had found out about the boys in the pond after her call to Devon and before she died.

As Beka felt the effects of the drug, Gabe must have become aware that Aileen had also drugged him. That would explain why he was attacked. And while Aileen was killing him, Beka had struggled to get outside, hoping to escape or at least signal some passing car on the road. But it was winter in the Hamptons and no one was driving past the estate, and the drug had weakened her heart—the exertion was too much. She collapsed in the mud, probably slipping into a coma as Aileen slit her wrists, informing her that it was going to look like she was responsible for not only Todd's disappearance, but for Gabe and Edilio's murders as well.

Beka had died knowing that Devon would find her and that it would appear that she were the murderer. But Beka had been heading up the hill toward the barn . . . toward the pond, when she was stopped. Her last efforts had not been to save her life, but to aim herself in the direction of much greater crimes. Only Beka Imamura would have had the ability to control her body despite the spasms of death. Her last dance had been her arms clasped over her head like Shiva pointing the way—if only Devon had recognized it sooner.

She inhaled again, considering her questions carefully. The dumber and more drugged she acted, the more chance she had of surviving. "Leenie," she used Aileen's nickname to keep a sense of familiarity between them, "why would you kill Beka because of Todd?"

"The Daniels started it all with their damn golf course!" Devon didn't answer. "Gabe was going to leave me and the boys behind! And all of that land was going to go for more people, more developers, more golfers! They were talking about leveling the woods all the way down to Trout Pond. The run-off from chemical fertilizers alone would poison the underwater springs. That used to be our swimming hole! Remember how we used to go there every day, all summer long? Do you want another damn golf course poisoning our swimming hole?"

"Of course not, but I don't want to be dead either."

"That can't be helped." Aileen had chewed at her lip until it was red and raw. "With all of you dead, the estate becomes a wildlife refuge and no one ever finds out what's in it. There're too many people in the world, and they're out here every summer!"

Devon had to agree, but said nothing; Aileen sounded a little too much like Ted Bundy for her own comfort.

Aileen had stopped thinking in an organized manner and like all compulsive killers had let her appetites get away from her. "It's the only way to make it work. Beka told me she'd rather die than see it developed. And she would have killed him if she'd found out what he was really doing for art. I just helped matters along. I understood what he was after—you have to make sacrifices for art. Murder isn't so hard once you get the hang of it—no different than gutting fish, really. Remember how we used to gut fish? And Gabe and I had a real partnership—better than any marriage." She was nodding her head convincingly.

"But he betrayed you."

"No," Aileen disagreed, "I betrayed him."

Devon was finding it hard to breathe. Her eyes became parched as the impulse to blink slowed. She was not going to die here. She felt Boo licking her hand, her fingers, her wrist.

"Come on, Boo! Want to go for a ride in the car?"

He looked at Aileen but did not budge. He nosed Devon's hand.

"I would have proved Beka was innocent with or without your help, Aileen. But now you've made it easy. Katiti's not dead."

"That bitch. She should have paid me on time!" She edged nearer to Devon.

"And you've confessed."

"I'm going to disappear. I've been making others disappear for years, don't you think I know how?"

Keep her focused on reality, carving up a one-time friend is more difficult than an acquaintance, Devon reminded herself. But in case that didn't work, Devon thought she should continue trying to short out the circuits in Aileen's brain. "What's my koan, Aileen?"

"In honor of Boo, I was thinking about *Chao Chou's Mu.*" Aileen stepped toward her threateningly. "Come on, Boo, let's go for a walk."

Boo did not fall for that old trick, though, Aileen could have said *cookie* and he would not have left his mistress' side. He pressed his cold nose deeper into Devon's forearm, nudging her arm with his nose as if he were trying to help her hand reach the gun snug in her belt holster. She knew that any quick action might send her into cardiac shock, and yet she had to do something, and the more Boo moved her arm the better the circulation became.

The moment was crystalline—synchronistic with Boo's cold nose on her flesh and the cold butt of her gun touching her hand. It came clearly, like the monk getting out of the tree to show her which way to go—like Beka dying, while making sure that Devon got the message, running outside to show Devon the way. In the end, Beka must have finally known that the answer to Todd's disappearance was in the pond—Daniels' Hole.

Hans always said that when enlightenment came it was so heightened and pure that it carried one above the situation at hand and beyond the realm of the body. She was instantly aware of her connection to all things animate and inanimate, sane and insane, and saw how each was distinctly a part of her being, just as she was a part of all beings. Some conscious part of her knew what Aileen would do next, and in response Devon lengthened her arm down the side of her body.

"*Chao Chou's Mu* asks if a dog has Buddha nature," she reminded Aileen, "and I already know the answer."

Aileen hesitated, looking confused and bewildered, as if the koan baffled her rather than Devon. "You can't."

"I can. Boo told me." Devon's hand pulled her gun out of its holster in one deft movement. Aileen's arm swept upward as she lunged forward. The gun fired, but only lobbed Aileen's shoulder. Under normal circumstances, Devon would have hit her square in the chest, but her reflexes were off.

"How could you? You were my friend!" Aileen grabbed her arm in dismay.

"*Were* being the operative word . . ." Devon's heart throbbed against her chest until all she could hear was its booming between her ears. Aileen rushed at her again, the knife plunging in a downward arc through the air. Devon adjusted the sightline for her discrepancy of vision and pulled the trigger once more.

She fell into darkness, reaching for the phone that had fallen out of Aileen's hand, or was it the remote? Pressing numbers that looked like 911, she prayed she hadn't just changed the channel on the TV. She was not even sure if it was her voice yelling, "*Officer down! Officer down!*"

* * *

"Don't move." Lochwood's voice was soft and reassuring.

Devon blinked and tried to focus her eyes, but his face was still blurry.

"You had a minor heart attack."

She was disoriented and her throat was sore from where they must have placed oxygen tubes while she was unconscious. She must have been unconscious. She tried to sit up but Loch gently forced her back down.

"You're in Southampton Hospital. Detective Freesia heard shots as she came up the driveway and found you clinging to the phone. The 911 operator thought your call was a hoax and hung up on you. Freesia administered CPR until the ambulance arrived. They had a little trouble subduing Boo. He liked Freesia but wouldn't let EMT get near you."

Devon tried to look for her dog. Lochwood pointed to the corner of the room, where she could just make out the blur of spotted light that was Boo fast asleep on the floor. "He's just a little tired."

"He saved my life." There was a darker shape behind him. "Hans?"

"Yes."

She tried to smile but wasn't sure if her facial muscles were smiling or grimacing. "I got my koan."

"When you least expected it."

"I think I'm figuring out this koan thing, myself." Loch's face was starting to smooth around the edges so she could see the worry and puzzlement in his eyes.

"Murder is a koan." Hans folded his hands and bowed toward Devon.

Loch nodded. "I was on my way to your house when I heard the police band for shots fired in Sag Harbor."

"Enlightenment comes in a flash." Hans's voice was soft.

"Of gunpowder," Loch added. "Josh said that Godwyn told him he had planned to meet you in the back of Hans's house. So I looked at his statement a little more carefully, despite the evidence, because quite frankly, Josh does not seem like the murdering type. Then you called about Aileen going to Katiti's. I was sure it was Katiti."

"Is she alright?"

"Just barely, but she will live to bitch again. We went over our timeline and figured that either Maddie or Aileen could have put on Josh's shoes and gone out back to Godwyn. I started thinking about your cellphone batteries, and how they ran out. And your beeper disappearing." She nodded. "And Aileen's the only one who knew you were going to Gabe's studio that night, because I told her."

"She was withholding my messages, too. I think Beka tried to call me and I never knew."

"Beka wanted to make up," Hans assured Devon.

Her heart ached. "She got out of the tree to show us the way, Hans. That was her answer to the koan."

"*Mu,*" the monk sighed heavily, the sound reverberating out of his chest and into the room. "There is the Weeping Buddha, but also there is the Laughing Buddha. Do not spend all your life being crushed by fate." Hans bowed to her and smiled. "I'll go get your parents now." He shuffled out of the room, leaving them alone.

Loch squeezed her hand, pressing his face against her knuckles.

"Have you found him yet?"

"Not yet, but we will. We're dredging the pond now. They've found some bones, and two skulls—we're running dentals."

"I'm missing the fun part." She tried to smile again but failed. "Poor Leenie. She was really good with dogs."

"She just didn't like people a whole lot." He had almost gotten her to crack a real smile, but laughing was too painful. "You're going to need to find a new pet-sitter, but I think I found someone with the right kind of credentials," he said softly.

"Already? Who?"

He took her hand in his, turned it upwards, and kissed the heart of her palm. "Me."

* * *

Also from AKASHIC BOOKS

Adios Muchachos by Daniel Chavarría
2001 Edgar Award Winner
245 pages, paperback
ISBN: 1-888451-16-5
AKB12 - $13.95

A selection in the Akashic Cuban Noir series. ". . . [A] zesty Cuban paella of a novel that's impossible to put down. This is a great read . . ." –*Library Journal*

The Eye by Daniel Chavarría
463 pages, hardcover
ISBN: 1-888451-25-4
AKB23 - $27.00

Akashic's second release by celebrated Uruguayan mystery novelist Daniel Chavarría is equal parts historical epic, whodunnit-style thriller, highbrow erotica and philosophical discourse. Set in late fifth-century B.C.–during the reign of Pericles–the novel fictionally recreates the behind-the-scenes scandals and political intrigues that occupied the Athenian home front at the height of the Peloponessian War.

Hell's Kitchen by Chris Niles
279 pages, trade paperback
ISBN: 1-888451-21-1
AKB19 - $15.95

"If the Olympics come to New York, apartment-hunting should be one of the events . . . Niles's fast-paced *Hell's Kitchen* plays with the city's famed high rents and low vacancy rate to put a new spin on the serial-killer novel. Taking aim at contemporary romance, the media, the idle rich, and would-be writers, Niles has written a thriller that's hilarious social satire." –*Detroit Free Press*

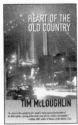

Heart of the Old Country by Tim McLoughlin
Selected for the Barnes & Noble Discover Great New Writers Program
216 pages, trade paperback
ISBN: 1-888451-15-7
AKB11 - $14.95

"Tim McLoughlin writes about South Brooklyn with a fidelity to people and place reminiscent of James T. Farrell's *Studs Lonigan* and George Orwell's *Down and Out in Paris and London* . . . No voice in this symphony of a novel is more impressive than that of Mr. McLoughlin, a young writer with a rare gift for realism and empathy."
—Sidney Offit, author of *Memoir of the Bookie's Son*

Kamikaze Lust by Lauren Sanders
2000 Lambda Literary Award Winner
287 pages, trade paperback
ISBN: 1-888451-08-4
AKB05 - $14.95

"*Kamikaze Lust* puts a snappy spin on a traditional theme—young woman in search of herself—and stands it on its head. In a crackling, rapid-fire voice studded with deadpan one-liners and evocative descriptions, Rachel Silver takes us to such far-flung places as a pompous charity benefit, the set of an 'art porn' movie, her best friend's body, Las Vegas casinos, and the psyche of her own porn-star alter ego, Silver Ray, all knit together by the unspoken question: Who am I, anyway? And as Rachel tells it, asking the question is more fun than knowing for sure could ever be." —Kate Christensen, author of *In the Drink*

These books are available at local bookstores.
They can also be purchased with a credit card online through www.akashicbooks.com.

To order by mail, send a check or money order to:
Akashic Books
PO Box 1456
New York, NY 10009

Prices include shipping. Outside the U.S., add $3 to each book ordered.